Broken PROTOCOLS

Broken Protocols collection

Dale Mayer

BROKEN PROTOCOLS 1–4
Beverly Dale Mayer
Valley Publishing Ltd.

This is a work of fiction. Names, characters, places, brands, media, and incidents are either the product of the author's imagination or are used fictitiously. Any resemblance to actual events, locales, or persons, living or dead, is entirely coincidental.

ISBN-13: 978-1-773361-01-7
Print Edition

About This Box Set

Cat's Meow

After a year of hell, Lani Summerland's life is just getting better when she's tossed unceremoniously a few hundred years into the future with her orange Persian cat, Charming Marvin, in her arms. With no way to fight it, no way to go back, things are only looking to get worse fast.

Breaking protocol is cause for severe consequences in the time and world Liev Blackburn lives. But, after a year of government regulation, the crackdown is easing up and he begins to relax. Everything he's worked for is hinged on keeping his reckless brother in check. But, while he's been protecting Milo from falling under the government's ever-vigilant radar, his brother has been working on a surprise present for him, one that's the cat's meow... Lani is that gift—a woman from the past that Liev has been fixated on.

Milo never anticipated having his brother's dream girl come to their time with a snarky cat that can not only talk but doesn't have a clue how or when to shut up!

Cat's Pajamas

The future—where protocols must never be broken—is a very dangerous place indeed...

To save herself and her new lover, Lani Summerland agrees to marry Liev Blackburn. If not for the fact that the two of them are pawns in a game with no rule book, this might be a good thing for both of them.

Liev can't believe how lucky he is. But someone is after Lani, and, until he finds out who that is, there can be no honeymoon bliss.

Lani is targeted with not a clue what the stalker wants. The bodies begin piling up behind them. Luckily, they're not alone in their fight for survival. Lani's talking, super-intelligent cat, Charming Marvin, intends to save the day and his mistress so he can get back to his own chosen bliss— a much-needed cat nap.

Cat's Cradle

Lani and Liev Blackburn have slid from the frying pan directly into the fires of Hell. When they uncover insinuations of a dangerous conspiracy that can be traced directly back to the foundations of society and permeates every part of life as the world knows it, they realize that to expose this evil is to shake the Earth to its core.

One by one, people begin disappearing. If not for Liev's twisted, genius brother Milo and Lani's talking cat Charming Marvin, the two of them would also be missing—or dead. But someone is still playing games, stalking Lani and everyone connected to her, and the cat's cradle web they're weaving is becoming impossible to escape. Unless they can find a way to expose this massive cover-up and who's behind it all, they'll become the next vanished.

Cat's Claus

Charming Marvin is always thinking, always talking, always learning, always looking for interesting new distractions.

After the talking, mega-intelligence enhanced feline inquires when Christmas Day would be in their new timeframe, it sets in motion events that might not make everyone so holly or jolly.

Charming's mistress, Lani Blackburn, realizes that although she's gained so much, she's also lost some things she loved in being brought forward two hundred years in the future by her husband Liev's slightly abnormal, genius brother Milo.

All holidays were banned from society by the government long ago. Though he hates to deny his beloved anything, Liev has no idea what Christmas is until he does a little research that makes him wonder if they can find a way to return the festive miracle to their small family, if nowhere else.

The best of intentions for a wondrous celebration of peace on Earth and goodwill toward mankind quickly becomes very complicated in world that doesn't always know the sentiment, let alone the Christmas spirit…

Sign up to be notified of all Dale's releases here!
https://geni.us/DaleNews

Cat's Meow

Broken Protocols 1

by
Dale Mayer

Protocol 1:3:1. You will in no way use technology to damage the life of another—particularly if those actions are to selfishly enhance your own.

CHAPTER 1

LANI SUMMERLAND WAS on top of the world. It had taken several years, but she'd finally put her past behind her. A new day had begun. A new job, her first date in a long ... okay, in a very long ... time, and, for once, her future looked bright.

It had been the years of hell, especially this last one.

She glanced at her plain black watch and realized, after working later, she was running a little behind. She wanted time to prepare for her date. She'd actually hoped to have a lot of time to prepare, but her boss hadn't been easy to deal with today and insisted she complete some work before leaving. Normally it wasn't a problem, but today was special. Only she was new to her job and didn't dare do anything but what was asked of her with a bright smile.

As soon as she completed the job, she'd logged off and bolted out of the building. She walked faster on the busy street, her head bent against the wind and the rain that threatened. Rush hour had peaked, but plenty of people still raced to get home. Equally focused on their destination as she was. Her apartment was just a few blocks around the corner.

For the umpteenth time, she pulled the faded, crumpled photo of her and Lawrence from her pocket. He'd been everything to her. Now, one year after her very public humiliation, she could finally say she'd recovered. She was at a crossroads in her life. A good one. A place she'd worked to reach for the year. But she'd made it. Now it was time to get rid of the picture. She'd hung on to it as a reminder. Of a painful lesson learned, to never be forgotten. Some rules were never meant to be broken—and ignorance was not an excuse. She'd had some inkling that things with Lawrence weren't as they'd seemed, but young love and all the rest of those glorious emotions, guaranteed to get her into hot water, had overruled her better judgment.

So she'd ignored those little nudges. Until she had found him at a company event, as the host, in fact—with his beautiful young wife at his side.

That had been the most disastrous evening of Lani's life. The wife's mocking look and laughing comment to Lani later in the ladies' room about being her husband's latest side piece hadn't helped. That the woman knew had been bad enough but from her words, it was obvious she and her husband had laughed about her. Just the knife twisting in the wound. The pink slip from his legal firm the next day was just another insult and another piece of her education.

Never have an affair with the boss—especially when it turns out he's married.

She'd been such a fool. She hated that the other staff had known—and no one had said anything to her. That they all believed she was the kind to have affairs with married men. Now she got those snide comments she hadn't understood at first. The mocking and disgusted looks she hadn't connected to the truth. Too bad someone hadn't blurted out something to clarify the situation. It might have been painful and humiliating at the time, but she'd have put a stop to the affair immediately.

Nothing like learning about men, life, and consequences the hard way.

A garbage can was up ahead. She stopped, carefully ripped up the picture—one that she'd once loved and held dear—into tiny pieces and fed them slowly into the can. She smiled, feeling a wonderful sense of freedom as each piece disappeared from sight.

Then she turned, pulled up her coat collar, and raced the last few blocks home.

Time to let go and to create a better future. And, as of today, it looked damn bright.

"WHAT THE HELL?" Liev studied the massive wall of monitors in front of him. The computers should all be locked behind the security field at this point. He glanced around the large empty office to see if anyone had slipped in behind him, but he was alone in the encroaching darkness. Then again, he should be. It was damn late, and it was his brother's office. No one was allowed in but the two of them. Not in this age of computer espionage. His world lived on computers, and his brother was a genius when it came to programming. There was nothing he couldn't create.

Hence the large company that they started together, with a few family backers, and the heavy security measures they used to keep their inventions secure until their official release. Some were not meant to be released. Ever. If it weren't for Milo's recent odd behavior, that little-kid look of having a secret he desperately wanted to share, Liev wouldn't be here now. Genius Milo—chocolate-munching, green-mohawked, geeky Milo—had been acting suspicious for days.

That would give anyone nightmares.

As Milo's business partner and older brother, and company CEO, Liev didn't dare let Milo go off half-cocked again. Genius he might be, but he lacked a certain level of common sense, as proven by the slap from the Commonwealth Council Protocols Association (CCPA) special Regulatory Commission Group last year. And their intensified monitoring of Milo thereafter. No one doubted Milo's intentions—just that they weren't clearly thought out. At the end of the nerve-racking CCPA review, the board had determined that the brothers would be allowed to continue their IT company, but the genius needed to be carefully watched.

A year later, the regulatory overseeing eye had eased—slightly. But the scrutiny had chafed for both Milo and Liev. For Milo more so.

And, as Liev stared at the complex coding on the screens mounted in the center of the wall, he realized that Milo was in deeper than before. But what was he creating? And how much trouble was it going to bring them all? Liev's heart sank. This last year had done nothing to smarten Milo up. This program looked to be almost complete, if not ready for testing. But Liev knew nothing about it. And why was that?

"I wondered how long it would take you to check up on me." Milo's quiet voice spoke from behind Liev.

Liev dropped his head into his hands, wanting to pull his hair out. Instead, he said in a low worried voice, "What have you done?"

"It's nothing bad. In fact"—Milo's voice picked up enthusiastically—"it's kind of awesome."

"Kind of awesome?" Liev spun around to glare at his kid brother who didn't know when to quit. "This could mean jail time. You know that." He towered over his younger brother. "This could mean losing the company. Years of our time and effort. Years where the family helped us, backed us, protected us. Did you even think of that? Did you once think about the consequences? About what will happen to me? Or does any of that matter?"

"No. No, it doesn't." Milo rushed over, wringing his hands. At least the childish delight of the last few days had dimmed. Milo just didn't get that rules and regulations were there for a reason. Liev did. He lived by them. His brother didn't even acknowledge them. And Liev had been bailing Milo out since he was a little boy—he wouldn't change now.

Milo loved history. And, when he added in his crazy geek skills and a complete lack of comprehension of the limits to what he could do, all manner of hell could happen. Had happened. Was possibly about to happen again.

"You don't understand." Milo beamed with excitement. "See? It works this time."

Liev shook his head, not mistaking his brother's meaning. He was talking about the same damn project that had gotten them into trouble last time. "No. It doesn't."

"Yes." Milo hopped from one foot to the other. Passion and joy were on his face and in his voice. "It does. It docs. Honest."

"There is no way. You can't just go back in time and yank a person forward a couple centuries into our world. Look at what kind of trouble that got you in last time." Got us, but he kept that bit quiet. Milo's enthusiasm got him— them—in trouble every time. But, every once in a while, Milo came up with something so earth-shattering that most people had no trouble overlooking the problems that came with Milo. Then again, they weren't the ones having to clean up after him.

Milo walked over to the keyboard, his fingers dancing so fast that Liev could barely follow what he did on the screen. Colors and figures flashed at alarming speeds on the massive wall of monitors in front of them.

Liev might not be the creative genius that Milo was, but he still knew more than most about coding. "Hey, stop. You can't test this right now."

"Sure I can. It works. I actually planned to test it tonight anyway. I just didn't expect to have you here. Having you here though … it's perfect."

Raising both hands in frustration, Liev gave an exasperated snort. "You were hoping that I wouldn't be here. Right?"

Milo shot him a resentful look. "You never let me have any fun."

"Fun?" Liev said ominously. "Going back in time, snagging up any female you want, and dropping them into our time is fun? You do remember what happened last time, right?" His glare deepened. "The massive power outage you caused?"

"I figured out how to stop the massive power surge. Besides, I only wanted to brainstorm with Marie Curie," he said resentfully. "She was an intelligent woman. We'd have had a great time."

"If you didn't kill her in the process," Liev snapped.

Milo spun around to face him, his grin once again splitting his face. "No, I fixed that. It's safe now."

"Says you." Liev eyed his brother suspiciously. He didn't know how to get this into his brother's head. This was too important. "This is big. Like *seriously* big stuff. And the chances of you doing this successfully … You know the protocols are very specifi—"

"Ah, but the protocols are poorly written." His elfish grin flashed, and he added, "Besides, they are more like guidelines."

Milo nudged his brother to the side. "You might want to get out of the way."

"What? What for?" Liev spun around and caught sight of Milo reaching for a button on the side. "No. Stop." And he knocked his hand away. Milo stumbled backward, tripped, and fell against his keyboard. The screen went nuts as Milo's elbow smacked the button anyway.

Immediately a high-pitched whine filled the room. Liev slapped his hands over his ears, even as his eyes stared in panic at the monitors dancing with flashing computer code.

"What's happening?"

"Everything!" Milo danced, laughing like a loon. "But it's nothing to worry about. It's supposed to be like this."

A flash of light exploded in the center of the room, blinding them both.

CHAPTER 2

L ANI GLANCED AT the clock, realizing she had just
 enough time for a cup of tea and a snack before getting
dressed. She filled her teakettle and placed it on the stove.
Her trip home in the brisk weather had left her chilled
inside. The tea would help. The snack would take the edge
off her hunger until she was served dinner. She smiled,
wondering what restaurant her new beau was taking her to.

She danced a quick jig across the living room. Perfect
day, perfect date, and a perfect evening to come. If she had
any misgivings that her bubble was about to burst, it had to
be residual negativity left over from the years from hell. And
maybe a twinge of a reminder that Murphy's Law had been
formulated specifically with her in mind.

But that was over. She was all about new beginnings.
And that meant she could open the bottle of wine she'd been
saving for a special occasion. Screw tea. Wine would warm
her up too. She reached into the back of the fridge and
pulled it out. Twisting the top off, she poured herself a glass
and held it up to sniff it.

Charming Marvin, her overgrown orange Persian cat,
jumped lightly onto the counter. She bumped the wineglass
gently against his nose.

"Cheers!"

Meow!

Lani flipped her long blond braid behind her back and laughed. "Right back at you, big guy. Here's to us." Eyes closed, she took a large gulp of her wine. Still too buoyed to relax, she put her glass down and snagged Charming up. Humming a tune in her head, she twirled him around.

"We're gonna be just fine."

Meow!

She laughed and twirled him again. She wanted to enjoy this moment. It had been a long time coming, but it was all good. She felt fine. In fact, she felt better than fine. She felt great!

Her life was back on track. It had been a long, painful struggle, but she'd made it.

Tonight would be good too. Danny was a cute single guy who had transferred into the company last month. Life was good again. Joy filled her heart. It had been a long time since she'd felt this way. She glanced down at her cat, and said, "You know what I've been through, don't you?"

Meow!

"I wish you could talk, Charming. Just think how great that would be." She did a quick pirouette with him. Just as she slowed down, a white light exploded in her living room.

Invisible waves blasted her, picking her up and throwing her against the couch, Charming clutched fiercely in her arms, his claws digging deep into her skin, a strange howl ripping from his throat. Mist swam through her brain, and her eyes burned. Her chest squeezed tight. She couldn't breathe. Her ears rang, and her lunch was crawling up the inside of her throat. She tried to cry out but no words came out.

What the hell had just happened? She could only hope the property damage would be minimal. Otherwise her landlord would freak.

She had to get out of here. If that had been an earth-quake it could happen again. If it had been some kind of accident then fire could be next. She didn't dare stay inside. Besides, her lungs were screaming for fresh air.

She sat forward, clutching Charming tightly, afraid he'd take off, and that she wouldn't be able to find him again. Moving slowly, her muscles heavy and unwieldy, her body in major shock, she struggled to her feet and headed for the doorway. Smoke filled her living room. She stifled a cough and covered her mouth with her sleeve to avoid breathing the reeking aroma.

She crouched low, gasping for air.

Had there been a gas leak? A bombing?

Then she heard voices. Oh, thank God. She struggled toward them.

A strange voice cried out, "Damn it, Milo. What did you do?"

"Wowza." A cackle filled the air. "Look. It worked!"

Through the mist, she spied two men, … or, at least, she thought they were men. The one in a purple and turquoise skintight suit with a green mohawk bounced in front of her, a maniacal laugh coming from his mouth. Then her shocked gaze landed on the second man.

Lawrence?

And that couldn't be.

Her heart slammed against her ribs, and then she really couldn't breathe. She gulped for air as she stared at the one man she'd loved and hated—and had spent the last year trying to forget—who now stood in front of her. Staring at her—was it possible—equally shocked?

Unbelievably, after all this time, her anger rose in a red

haze. She stepped into his personal space and smacked him—hard.

His head flipped to the side, then came back around slowly, a red mark quickly rising on his cheek. Shock lit the deep dark depths of his eyes.

Uh-oh.

She took a step back, her ribs frozen and locked.

He took a step forward.

Finally her lungs expanded. She took a deep breath, spun around, and ran.

She raced out the door and headed toward the elevator. And somehow got turned around. There were no walls of elevators. Nothing looked right. … Nothing looked normal. What the hell … Blindly she ran from door to door, until she found one leading outside and bolted through.

And came to a skittering stop. Her mind couldn't process what her eyes saw. She was on a balcony—a very high up balcony. And that couldn't be either. Her apartment was on the third floor, whereas, from the scenic panorama laid out before her, she had to be at least sixty floors up—if that was even possible. There were no buildings in her town even a third that tall.

The view in front of her was like nothing she'd ever seen before. It appeared to be a city. Or rather a metropolis on steroids. Buildings rose in weird space-agey-looking domes, and railcars raced along big circular runs. And—God help her—vehicles flew high above her head.

It looked nothing like Vancouver, BC, where she lived. In fact, as she shuddered and leaned against the closed door behind her, this didn't even look like her planet.

"WHERE DID SHE go?" Milo cried out. He spun around and said, "She's gone."

And damned if he didn't look like he would cry. Liev dropped his hand from his cheek only to raise his hands in irritation and snapped, "What did you expect? You snatched her from her world and dumped her here. She panicked and ran. Of course, she did. We have to find her."

"Find her? Where else can she go?" Milo dashed up beside Liev. "She can't go anywhere. That's the beauty of this."

Liev spun on his heels to stare at him in shock. "Really? I think you forgot to tell her that." Exasperated, Liev raced out of his brother's design room and into the short hallway. There weren't many places for the woman—and whatever she clutched in her arm—to go. This was an office building, thankfully at nighttime. The security system was on and most of the offices would be locked up tight. Several more doors were ahead, and he could only hope she'd gone in a straight line. Actually, he could hope that this disaster was just a bad dream, but knowing his brother …

"We have to stop her before she finds a way outside." To lose her in that jungle would be a tragedy. And he had had enough of those on his hands with this damn technology as it was. If the government got wind of Milo's latest experiment, Milo and Liev could both be thrown in jail and their technology confiscated, never to see the light of day—unless those in power wanted to use it for themselves.

And that would be disastrous.

The ruling governmental Council had too much power now. Dealing with them was worse than dealing with the CCPA. Much worse. Who knew what the Council would do with something like this technology? Knowing how corrupt the Council was—it would be nothing good.

Liev couldn't believe Milo had finally succeeded with his time-travel project. His kid brother was a genius like none other, sure, ... but to do something like this? ... Liev kept moving forward and opened every door he came to and still found nothing. He raced for the front door, his heart sinking. Please don't be outside. Please ...

"Wait—"

Too late. Liev had already barreled ahead and made it outside before his brother's words infiltrated his frustration. "Okay, this is bad," Liev said. As he watched, the line of buildings in front of him slowly went dark, one after the other. Just like last time. "So very bad."

"I didn't do that," Milo said when he caught up to his brother. He held up his new SXC4500 fingerboard computer and shouted. "I have her on the camera."

Liev spun around. "Where is she?"

"She came back inside." Milo flipped the comp around so Liev could see.

"Really?" That stopped Liev in his tracks. He peered at the screen. "That was actually a really smart move."

Milo grinned. "Yeah. See? I didn't choose a bimbo. We need someone with enough brains to handle this type of switch in her life."

"That's not measured by brains. So much more is involved here."

"Oops," Milo said, looking back at the screen. "She's on the move."

Milo's new rocker boots clicked as he raced behind Liev back into the facility. Liev shook his head. Milo needed a keeper himself. How could he possibly determine the type of woman who would not go crazy from his damn experiment? Anyone would be completely freaked out by such a trip. And what about her physical state? That she was on her feet and moving was incredible. That she appeared to be cognizant enough to be searching for a way out was … well, that was beyond belief. And fit right into the scope of Milo's unbelievable success. Regardless of the poor woman's health and emotional or cognitive state, Milo had pulled this female from wherever she'd been living happily, and he'd somehow dumped her in his office.

Still blown away, the two brothers retraced their steps as they tracked her through the building. Minutes later they ended up back in Milo's office with still no sign of her.

"She's in here somewhere," Milo muttered while clicking away on the tracker. "The tracker is operating erratically. I'm struggling to lock onto her position."

Liev searched behind the chairs and under the desks. "Please tell me that you can send her back." Liev turned to his brother. "That you can reverse this process."

"I don't think so." Milo threw him a sideways grin. "Besides, we don't want to send her back."

"I do," Liev snapped. "And I'm sure she wants to go back too. She has a life. Remember?"

"*Hmmm.* According to my research, Lani Summerland doesn't have much of one." He clicked through his finger board computer and read off the list. "No partner. No career to speak of. Failed business after one year. Managed to stay gainfully employed. No marriage. No children. No long-term friends on record."

CHAPTER 3

T HEY KNEW HER name. Lani sank lower in the empty
closet she'd hidden in as the painful litany of her failed
life washed over her. She buried her face against Charming's
fur, her arms tightening until he protested. Only his voice
was hoarse and weak. Then she wasn't feeling all that great
either. That kid's words weren't helping. What a horrible
dissection of her years to date. Surely it hadn't been that bad?
Besides, it's not as if her life was over. She could achieve
greatness yet. Couldn't she?

"It's not that simple, Milo."

Lani heard the discussion despite the noise of doors being opened and closed. The kid's name was Milo? And what
was his relationship to Lawrence? Her mind spun on endless
questions as she struggled to sort out where she was and how
she got here.

The deeper of the two voices spoke again. "She has reasons for what happened in her life. Sure, she *might* be up for
a move a couple centuries into the future. She *might* consider
it an adventure. She *might* consider it an improvement on
her old world. But you didn't ask her. You didn't give her a
choice, and that makes all the difference. You just yanked her
out of her old life. For all you know, she might have a major
plan about to come to fruition, and you stole that from her."

"I did not," Milo protested. "I did my research, Liev. I'm

not an idiot. She had nothing. She was nothing. She would have become nothing. Now she is something—special."

Her heart squeezing tight, Lani listened to Liev—not Lawrence—and Milo discuss her life. As if they knew her. As if they knew everything about her. And she meant *everything*. How was that possible? And then came the big question of why? Why her?

"And where in her psych profile, Milo, did it say she'd be up for a complete shock like this?"

"Ahh …" Milo stuttered.

Liev's voice dropped to an ominous level. "You didn't get a psych profile, did you?"

"Well, it's not so easy. They didn't do them regularly back then. They were quite primitive people. Remember? Those types of analysis only happened with people that were unstable."

Liev snorted.

Lani's chest locked tight. A couple centuries into the future? They were kidding—right? But, from what she'd seen outside, before instinct had her spinning around and returning to the one space she knew—this room—she was not in Vancouver, British Columbia. At least not Vancouver as she'd known it. And she'd lived there all her life. Her city was gone. Her apartment building was gone. Her living room was gone. She was alive but her life as she'd known it was … gone.

She squeezed Charming tighter against her chest and buried her face against his thick orange fur. Thank heavens he was safe with her. The two of them could have gotten blown up in the blast. "You're all I have left," she whispered. And got the next biggest shock of her life.

"Hey. What do you mean *all?*" Charming said, twisting

in her arms, his paw reaching out to bat her chin. "You make it sound like I'm nothing. And I'm a whole lot more than nothing."

Lani reared back and stared into her beloved cat's glowering eyes. She shuddered and closed her eyes briefly. Maybe she had a head wound? A concussion, she thought hopefully. That would explain the crazy phenomena. Immediately, she felt better. Until her gaze landed on her cat.

"Charming?" she asked cautiously. "Is that you talking?"

No, it can't be. How stupid. She shouldn't even have asked that question. It had slipped out instinctively. No way her cat could talk. Then again, no way could she have been yanked two centuries into the future either. She dropped her head back. She was losing it. Tears gathered in her eyes. Why her? All she'd ever wanted was to be happy. Was that so much to ask for?

Questions rippled through her mind. Terrifying her. Making her heart stall, then race like she was being chased. She squeezed her eyes shut again. One tear rolled down her cheek. She turned her head to wipe her face on her sleeve. She needed some normality here. Something real she could grab and hang on to. She took a deep breath and whispered, "Please, Charming, don't tell me you can talk."

And, oh, God, ... he actually answered her.

In a deep voice, unlike anything she'd ever heard before, Charming said, "I could always talk. Since when did you learn?"

She swallowed, opened her eyes, and stared at her best friend. And found him staring at her, his face only inches from hers, with a puzzled look in his eyes. Such a human look in that gaze. Such a human-sounding voice. And words ... English words. Strung into normal sentences.

Except the claws in her flesh were all feline.

Her mouth dropped open, and she shook her head in denial. "Not possible. It's not possible. It's. Not. Possible."

"Well, it's possible but it's not *probable*. I figured you were too primitive, too underdeveloped to learn such a skill." He brightened, that wide mouth twisting up into a grin. "But you surprised me. You actually learned to talk."

At last she understood.

She was crazy.

She'd finally turned some invisible corner into a complete fantasy world in her mind. She'd always wanted to talk to animals. It had been a secret dream ever since she had been a little girl. Obviously reality had become too much, and she'd retreated to her childhood state. It was almost a relief in a way. To have an explanation for this insanity.

It was either that or she was having a crazy dream. And that was all too possible. Not to mention being a better option.

She beamed at her cat. "I'll wake up soon, and this will be just a happy memory."

"I wish I was dreaming." Charming snorted. "This little room is nice and cozy and all, but where is the couch? Or your bed? A big fluffy pillow? I need my nap."

"Sleep? You need to sleep?" She shook her head, staring around the tiny closet. "I was getting ready for a date."

"Yeah, great." Charming gave a jaw-splitting yawn before tucking into her shoulder. "Who needs a date? Well, okay, you do, but really I need my beauty sleep." And he closed his eyes.

She stared at her cat and whispered, "Please let this be a bad dream. And please let me wake up soon and find everything back to normal."

"I hope so," Charming muttered, "because you forgot to feed me dinner before we time-traveled."

At the words *time-traveled*, she forgot to breathe again. When she finally got oxygen back into her lungs, she cried out, "Don't say that."

Suddenly the closet door opened. The same two men peered in, but the green mohawk, so large and long, was all she could focus on.

A scream caught in the back of her throat. But no sound came out.

"Aha. There you are," said the owner of the mohawk, Milo, if she'd gotten the names right. "And who were you talking to?"

She wanted to fight. Wanted to kick them both in the teeth so hard they'd never eat again. The older one, Liev—or at least more staid and adult looking male of the two according to what she'd seen and heard, even though he was the spitting image of her nemesis—peered around the green hair. This close, she could see he looked very similar to Lawrence, but something was younger, cleaner about his features. And maybe nicer. Lawrence had gained a seedy look to his cheeks and a perpetual smirk to his eyes.

As if he was always one up on you.

Which, in her case, he had been. And, if Liev wasn't Lawrence, she had just smacked a complete stranger for no good reason.

Damn.

She risked a look at Charming, saw the feline smirk as if to say, *Uh-oh, now you're in trouble*, and she shuddered. In a low voice, she said to Charming, "You can bite them in the balls while I run."

"Not happening." And damn if her cat's voice didn't

drop low to match hers.

Liev reached down, grabbed her elbow, and yanked her to her feet. She tugged her arm back, climbing out of her hiding spot on her own, holding Charming protectively away from him. She shot him a dark look. "You don't have to hurt me."

He retreated instantly, his hands out in front of him apologetically. "Look. I'm sorry. We won't hurt you. Please. Let's sit down, and we'll explain everything."

She raised one eyebrow and proceeded to repeat everything she'd heard them say. Their eyebrows shot up. She added, "As you can tell, I can hear just fine. Now I want you to tell me how the hell you'll fix this." She glared at Milo. "I want to go home."

Milo jumped forward, his face earnest and proud at the same time. His eyes glowed with excitement. "See? That's the thing. We can't. That's the beauty of this technology. It can't be reversed."

"And that's beautiful?" she asked ominously, her heart and mind screaming their protests in sync. "How do you figure?"

While she waited for that explanation, she realized the men were guiding her into a glass cube she hadn't noticed in the dark room. She could barely see her surroundings, but the room looked like a futuristic office with huge wall screens she'd never seen before. And some kind of center console. The wall screens looked see-through and had all those weird colors. She couldn't tell what was outside that wall from her current position inside the cube. With *them* joining her.

Once inside, she sank into the deepest corner to avoid their touch, holding Charming tight. He was her one link to normalcy. He stared up at her and opened his mouth.

She slapped a hand over it and glared at him. And realized that, if Charming could talk—there was nothing *normal* left.

Trying to process the situation faster, she studied the men with her and Charming, waiting for something to happen. Liev pushed something on his wrist, and the cube took off. She shrieked, reaching out a hand instinctively to steady herself, only to find the ride smooth and quiet.

She couldn't help but be reminded of the old *Charlie and the Chocolate Factory* story with the glass elevator that seemed to travel outside of buildings. Except this wasn't likely to have as happy an ending as that story did. As the glass cube swept around corners, she noted it wasn't on rails. In fact, it didn't appear to be attached to anything. She gasped and squeezed her eyes closed. "Where did the ground go?" she whispered.

"It's there. Below us."

She peeked through her eyelashes to see the bottom of the glass cube and nothing else. Just a swirling whiteness—as if they were in the middle of a cloud. Her arms clutched Charming reflexively. Her mind spun, grasping for any reasonable explanation—and came up empty. She fell against the glass cube, hyperventilating. "Oh, this is not good. This is so not good."

Milo explained, "It's just a modern elevator."

That didn't deserve a response. There was no *just* about it. His idea of a modern elevator and hers were miles apart. She shifted Charming in her grasp but dared not loosen her hold. Not that she had any chance of dropping him with his claws dug into her arms. She wouldn't be surprised if he'd drawn blood. If so, she'd be dripping blood onto their glass floor.

The elevator changed directions again, sending her lurching sideways. Oh, shit. Oh, shit. *Oh, shit.* She felt the beads of sweat rise on her forehead.

"It'll be fine," Milo said with a wide grin. "We're perfectly safe."

At the end of his words, the glass box came to a complete stop. And it dissolved around them. As in, here one minute and gone the next. She slowly straightened wondering how it was she hadn't fallen backwards. But there'd been support right up to the end.

The men exited—if there was a cube to exit. They'd barely traveled. It almost looked like the same building—or maybe the same set of buildings? There'd been no sign of the outside world at all.

She straightened, took one step in their direction, and, without warning, her stomach heaved and the effort landed her on her butt.

"OH, YUCKY. THAT'S so … yucky." Milo danced away from her, his face a picture of morbid fascination. "I'm calling someone to clean that up."

"Fine, but let's not be here when they arrive." Liev knelt by the woman's side, trying to ignore the reek from the mess at his feet. Sweat had beaded on Lani's forehead—at least that's the name he thought Milo had called her—and her color had gone a pasty gray. Her breathing had turned shallow and irregular. Probably a delayed reaction. Rushing forward a couple hundred years had to be tough on the stomach, if not the rest of her. That she could even walk and talk and … look half as sexy as she did was amazing. And he shouldn't be noticing. Now she'd curled into a small ball, her slim frame rocking back and forth. The massive furry critter in her arms made a horrific howling sound that set Liev's nerves on edge. He might have sympathy for her, but that animal …

Through the noise, he heard her whispering into the animal's fur, "It's okay, Charming. It'll be okay, baby."

"I know it's hard to believe, but you are right. It will be okay," Liev said, hoping he wasn't lying to the poor woman, "but there is no way I can agree with you calling that … that thing *baby*."

And damn if that furry thing didn't rear back and glare at him. As if it heard and understood.

Lani froze, lifted her head to stare at Liev, and then she did something that completely disarmed him.

She started to giggle.

CHAPTER 4

L ANI COULDN'T STOP giggling. She tried, but her laughter came in never-ending waves. It was more stress relief than hilarity. She had to stop. If she didn't, her out of control glee would turn into tears soon. And that would be bad news. For everyone.

"Oh, brother. What an ass," said Charming in that low guttural whisper. "You can pass on this Lawrence too."

Her laughter rolled out freely. She caught sight of the two men and the combined shocked looks on their faces. They might have managed to toss her forward a couple hundred years, but she'd managed to shock them. And she planned on keeping them off-balance.

She had to find a way home, and she needed their help. But she'd be damned if she'd let them walk all over her. Knowing what was outside the building scared her shitless, and, for all she'd been trying to shake off her old life, she hadn't meant to shake it off this far.

And who was this Liev? With each glance to confirm that Liev looked so similar to Lawrence, she had to consider he'd come forward in time as well. But she had discerned just enough visual differences too. Then again, she hadn't seen Lawrence in over a year. That could account for some of the differences in his appearance. She stole another look in his direction. No, Liev was younger. Much younger. Besides, how likely was it that the two of them were dragged forward in time? And, if they had, were others like her here? She perked up at that idea. If there was a group them, maybe they had a way to go home too.

"It's not the same guy," Charming muttered.

She wiped the tears from her eyes as her laughing spell ended and holding Charming so the men couldn't see her talking to him, whispered, "Why do you say that?"

"Because you're in the future. That means he's not the same man." He shot her a look of disgust, adding, "Duh!"

She pursed her lips at the sarcasm, not even close to being able to digest Charming's new communication abilities or indeed the sarcastic responses that seemed to roll off his tongue and, stared up at Liev. He had the same tall, lean build, the same jet-black hair as Lawrence. The same quirky smile. But the whole package was fresher, softer, like a younger brother. Not so jaded, or cynical. Still, she had to know. She asked him point-blank. "So did you come from my century as well?"

Liev shook his head in a slow movement that made his slightly long hair curl on his shirt collar. If they were two hundred years in the future, the men still wore shirts and pants. Although outside of the fact that material covered both his legs and chest, the clothing was unlike any she'd seen before. His weird-looking friend with the green mohawk could have been from any number of places in her time, so he looked odd but not that odd. Outside of the technology, like the elevator—and, God, how creepy had that been—the rooms she'd seen so far looked almost normal. High tech and definitely futuristic and with almost a movie scene look to the space with the massive wall of monitors and a wall length console instead of keyboards and individual desks. It's what had been outside that had shocked her. Flying cars? Rooftop rail systems from building to building while something else snaked around the building going up? And the weird bright reflective silverishness to the buildings? Maybe the city was even domed. She didn't look out the windows around her. In fact, she deliberately avoided looking around. Her gaze locked on Liev.

"I'm sorry. I don't know you." He tried for a friendly smile and added, "Yet."

She rolled her eyes. "You would say that."

He gave her a hand to help move her away from the mess. "You must be mistaking me for someone from your time."

"Yeah, right. Like you aren't the spitting image of Lawrence Blackburn."

Liev stiffened. "That *is* my last name. And Lawrence was a blackhearted ancestor of ours. I'm sorry if you were harmed by him. I can only assure you that I am not him in any way."

She stared at him. "Doesn't that figure? Well, at least tell me that he's dead. That would almost make this worth it."

"That I can do." He smiled and held out his hand as if to shake hers. "I'm Liev Blackburn, and Lawrence is definitely dust by now."

The younger guy bobbed his head up and down. The long skinny body bobbed in a matching tune. She wondered if he had an iPod or something in his ear because he seemed to move to some inner beat. He gave her a huge grin and said, "I'm Milo. Liev is my older brother."

Her gaze widened. "That is so wrong."

The smaller guy narrowed his gaze, confusion clouding his eyes. Liev said, "Wrong or not, it's true. Milo is also a genius."

She snorted at that. "Oh, right. That whole genius thing about creating some kind of time machine that snatched me out of my own life without my permission. Well, thanks for nothing. So, before we go too far down this road, how about you reverse the results and let me return to the time where I belong."

A long strange silence filled the room. She narrowed her gaze suspiciously. "Why did you say that's the beauty of this—that this isn't reversible?"

And Charming gave voice to her thoughts. Thankfully it came out in a garbled whisper. "Uh-oh."

Milo looked at his feet and shuffled from left to right and back again. Yeah, he was guilty as hell. She switched to Liev. And he was staring at Milo.

"You didn't figure that you needed a way to reverse the process?" She motioned to the nonexistent elevator that had dumped her in this futuristic office around her and said in an ominous voice, "You figured anyone—any *female*—would be delighted to find herself yanked away from everyone and anything she holds dear into a foreign world where she has no way to support herself?" Her voice rose at the end to shrill tones. "Dependent on you two for my living?"

Both men winced in sync.

She lowered her voice and continued in an angry whisper, "And while I'm running up a list of questions, here is a biggie." She paused. "Why me?"

LIEV WAS NONPLUSSED. He didn't know what to do or say to this poor woman. Even shocked and overwhelmed, she was glaring at him and his brother, her back stiff, but holding it together. He admired that. She had grit. That was amazing given the era she was from. She knew his ancestor, a man who'd left a horrible legacy of infidelity and distrust. He had been a wily liar, cheat and eventually, he had sunk under multiple embezzlement charges before being stabbed later in life within the prison system. That she mistook him for that man was a huge insult. He tried to remind himself that he didn't know her and that she didn't know him, but she'd jumped to one hell of an assumption. And she was pissed. The tears, the loud voice, and the death grip she had on her pet also said she was terrified.

And that he could understand. His heart melted at her plight. This was not her fault. That was all on his brother, Milo.

It struck him then that … she also looked familiar. Like very familiar. At least her facial features. That tiny delicate body and luminescent skin, no. But he hoped she'd become more familiar to him. Then it hit him. He reared back to study her closer. Was she the girl in his favorite photo? There were differences, but she was close, … oh, so close. He wanted to pull it out of his pocket and compare it to her but didn't dare. He turned to glare at his brother, wanting to question him on the spot. But it wasn't the time. Still, it left him wondering, … was it her?

She looked ready to cry, and a woman's tears broke him every time. He leaned forward and softened his voice. "Please. Let's go to our place. We can explain the facts and come up with a plan of how to fix it."

His words appeared to drain all the stuffing and the ire from her body. She curled in on herself hugging her pet tightly as she buried her face in the animal's fur. He reached out gently and touched her shoulder then nudged her forward. "It will be okay. Come with us and we'll sort this out."

She moved as he directed. Silent but passive. That state worried him more than any he'd seen of her so far. Home was right around the corner. Thankfully it was in the same block as his office, with aboveground and underground access between the two. He liked to live close to his place of business.

He walked her forward a few more steps. "That's good. Just a little way to go. Please. Let me just get you in a place where we can talk privately."

At his wording, her compliance stalled and so did her footsteps.

He wanted to pick her up and carry her, but that damn pet of hers glared at him. He'd claw Liev's eyes out if he gave him a chance. With another firm nudge, he added, "Come on. You're safe with me."

And then they were there.

Milo entered first; then the young lady followed. Liev brought up the rear and reengaged the alarms, locking them in.

"Privacy on."

The buzzes and clicks told him that the security system had scanned the space and found it clean.

Feeling a tad better, he strode forward and poured himself a large shot of whiskey. And downed it.

He spun to glare at his brother. "Jesus, Milo. What will we do now?"

Milo collapsed onto the couch. The air couch lifted and fell as he settled into his preferred space somewhere in-between fully inflated and fully deflated then rose to float somewhere between floor and ceiling.

The young woman stood immobile in the center of the room. Ash-blond hair, fine-boned, but she moved well.

Maybe she was a dancer? There'd been ire in her voice, and fire had spit from her eyes. So a lively and brave spirit was in there. In spite of the circumstances, Liev admitted he was intrigued.

"Welcome to our home," he said gently. "Now, I introduced the two of us, Milo and I'm Liev. Please, won't you tell us—what's your name?"

She spun slowly. "Lani Summerland, of course."

Silence.

It took her a moment, then she got it. "You brought me into your world, and you don't even know who I am?" The shocked horror in her voice hit him hard. Then he saw the hurt in her eyes. Contrarily he wanted to enfold her in his arms and hold her close. To tell her that it was all okay. To let her know he wouldn't desert her. That it would work out fine.

But he'd never been a liar before, and he wasn't about to start now.

"I didn't choose you. Milo did." He motioned to his wacky brother, floating suspended in the middle of the room, his mohawk hanging over the edge of the now-deep-purple airbed. His eyes were closed, as if he'd dropped off to sleep.

"Milo did? And what the hell is he laying on? Whatever it is, I want one too." Her body swayed in protest to being vertical. "It wasn't purple, and it wasn't floating when we walked in."

"No, it wasn't." Liev sighed. Life had changed a lot since her era. "That's only one of the many things you'll have to get used to now."

She shook her head and said in a forlorn voice, "That's just it. I don't think I can."

CHAPTER 5

"NEVER MIND. LET'S just shelve this for the moment." Lani tried to straighten up, but her legs had taken on a rubbery sensation and refused to hold her properly. She clutched Charming even tighter. That he didn't complain worried her, but she was too overwhelmed to process what to do to help him. "I don't know if this is a delayed reaction, different oxygen in the air, or ..." Then her brain shut down. "I don't know," she whispered. "I don't feel so good."

The room swayed and circled around her.

"Easy." Liev grabbed her and led her toward the side of the room. Charming sagged against her, his weight increasing by the second. "You can stay in here. You need to rest. I don't think traveling through time was easy on your system."

"You think?" She laughed brokenly, but even her voice sounded odd. "Did your genius brother consider the damage to my DNA? That the reconstituted cells of my body didn't pull together the same way that it was when taken apart?"

"Nothing like that was supposed to happen." He motioned to the doorway in front of them. At least that's what the rectangle looked like. "The bedroom is through there. And chances are your body is fine. It just needs time to adjust."

She didn't have the energy to argue. And, with every step, her body got heavier. The effort to lift one foot after another was almost beyond her. Before she understood what was happening, Liev was helping her to a long white surface. She desperately wanted a bed to sleep in, but being horizontal on any surface would do. The sleep would follow regardless. She shifted the limp Charming in her arms, struggling to hold him now. Her arms were rubbery and her fingers were losing their grip.

"I think I need a doctor," she whispered. "I think there is something seriously wrong with me."

"We don't have doctors anymore," Liev said. "At least not like you mean. Our health care is very different today."

"Great. In the future, there are no doctors. Now really make my day and tell me there are no lawyers either." After all, Lawrence had been a lawyer.

Suddenly they'd reached the white object, and damn if he didn't push her on top of it.

"A hero you're not."

She felt more than saw his surprised look; then her own shock took over as the white surface softened and stretched, supporting the contours of her body like she'd never felt before. "What is this thing?" she whispered.

"A bed."

How that could be, she didn't know, and she no longer cared as the bed cradled her aching body just in time. Charming crashed spread-eagle on her chest, her arms fell to the side and with a soft groan, her eyes drifted closed, and she let go.

Into a deep sleep.

LIEV STARED DOWN at the impossible woman, proof of this impossible situation, brought on by his impossible little brother. Lani didn't look well. Her skin had a gray pasty look to it, and there were large dark circles under her eyes. There was a frailness to her he hadn't noticed initially. And that animal in her arms ... it collapsed sprawled out on her chest ... dead. He reached over hesitantly to check if it was still alive. Just as his fingers went to brush the thick fur, the animal shifted stretching out a paw as far as it would go as a tummy deep sigh escaped.

He didn't have an exclusive medical unit here. If he had, she'd be lying in it right now. There was one in the building. His friend Johan Strand owned it. If he was away, Liev would have taken her there instead of here. But Johan was home, and he'd be entertaining—like he always did.

Walking to the door, he cast a last look at the sleeping beauty. Compared to today's enhanced and cosmetically perfect women, she had character. She wasn't stunning. But she was pretty. Huge eyes that showed every emotion, a nose that turned up at the end ever-so-slightly, and a mobile mouth that caught his attention and held it whenever he was with her.

What would he do with her? Liev left her to talk to his brother. "Damn it, Milo. What are we going to do?"

No answer. He walked over to find his brother either deep in contemplation or ... asleep.

"Milo?"

No answer. He walked closer to find that his brother had his headset strapped on to his virtual-reality goggles. Damn. He was in the zone. Now was it the game zone or the creative zone? Except, with Milo, there was often no difference. Only this was no time to duck out. He reached across his brother's body and pulled off the goggles.

"Hey." Milo tried to snag them from Liev.

But Liev held them out of reach. On a hunch, he put them against his eyes and gazed through them. Two young, lithe females cavorted in front of him with come-on gestures, enticing him to join them.

"Hell, Milo." He tossed the VR set on his brother's chest. "This is hardly the time for a sex romp."

"Hey. It's always time, bro." Milo went to put them back on his face when Liev grabbed them again and tossed them across the room.

Milo roared.

"Damn. Get serious." Liev planted his hands on his hips and glared at his outraged brother. "We have a problem here. A big one. You know she's sick, right? Like seriously sick. Like she could be dead by morning?"

"Nah. She's fine." Milo stood and stretched and sidled to where his goggles were. "I'll head to bed now."

"Touch those goggles and I'll lose them permanently the next time you are out of the room."

Milo froze. "Hey, that's not fair. I do some of my best thinking when I'm sex … in a playful mood."

With a snort, Liev shook his head. "Like hell. You say you do your best thinking as an excuse to do whatever the hell you want." He reached his brother in seconds, grabbed him by the shoulder, and gave him a shake. "Stop kidding around. We have to solve this problem."

Milo cringed and stepped back, out of his brother's reach. "We don't have a problem. I brought her here for you. Therefore, you have a problem." With that, Milo snagged his goggles and walked from the room.

For him? Liev stared after his brother in shock. And once again brought up the question of Lani's identity in relationship to the photo.

But his brother was gone. Walking away from something he didn't like. Didn't want to deal with. Dumping the problem on someone else's shoulders. Again. In this case—Liev's shoulders. Again.

Being sixteen forever was getting old. At least for those who had to live with Milo.

Liev tilted his head back and closed his eyes, waiting for the anger to drain and some reasonable next step to rise up from the depths of his own impressive brain.

Bottom line, she was hurting. And he was indirectly responsible. How could he help her? There really was only one way. She needed a medical pod. And fast.

That meant Johan. His longtime friend walked a fine line between legal and illegal business activities. So far he was doing well with it. They both had a hatred for the Council and the multitude of government regulations being stuffed down their throats.

He glanced at the time. Maybe, just maybe, Johan hadn't started partying yet.

It was worth a try. In person or by comp? Comp would be faster.

He punched in Johan's name. And closed his eyes briefly when Johan's face filled the screen. "Hey. Glad I caught you."

"What's up, Liev?" Johan's bright, inquisitive grin popped out. "Looking to hook up tonight? I've got some prime flesh coming by soon."

"No. No. I've got some of my own here, but she's sick. I was hoping to use your unit." He waited a moment and then, in a quiet voice, added, "Please."

"Sure. No problem." Johan nodded agreeably. "You know the code. Go for it. With any luck, I won't need it tonight."

Liev wiped a shaky hand across his forehead. "Thanks, Johan. I won't forget this."

"No biggie. If she doesn't pick up, and you're still looking for some action, there will be plenty here all night long."

"As usual." In an effort to appease his friend, he added, "We'll see. I might pop by later on."

"Pod is empty now, so go for it." Johan's face blinked out.

As he closed his comm, Liev wondered about the sensibility of waiting until later. But how would he get her up there when she was out cold? Liev returned to where Lani slept. He frowned at the critter guarding her. How could he get her to the healing pod without that?

Then the critter dropped its head on Lani's chest, like the weight of his head was too heavy to hold. And Liev realized that the critter had endured just as harsh a trip as Lani. It probably needed the healing pod too.

That could really be tricky. He could use the elevator to get them all up there, and the healing pod had a room all to itself, but would the critter cooperate? Would Lani stay asleep for this?

It would be best if she did.

He really was out of options. And out of time. He opened a cupboard and pulled out a blanket. With some difficulty, he managed to wrap up the two newcomers. He lifted them both into his arms, more disturbed than he realized when neither moved. Maybe they were badly injured internally. His gut twisted. He should've done this earlier.

He raced outside his apartment. "Stealth mode on." The elevator swooped down, encompassing them all. "Johan's healing pod."

The cube took off silently.

They'd made it this far. He hoped the rest would be so easy. The elevator delivered him outside Johan's pod room. He stepped in, relieved to find the room empty and the pod open. He laid his lightweight burden down gently, realizing as he did so how delicate her frame was. Even the critter was deceptive looking, in that he appeared big and bulky. He carried so much fur on his body, and the face appeared to have been flattened in the birthing process, but, as far as actual poundage went, her pet weighed almost nothing.

And maybe muscle and bone-density loss was a side effect of the time-travel. He didn't know if the pod could heal that. It was a little out of the generic pod's scope.

He walked over to the door, closing and locking it behind him. Then he turned his attention to the two comatose patients on the table. He closed the lid of the pod on them, blanket and all, and walked to the diagnostic table. "Start scanning," he instructed the computer.

The machine made a weird beeping sound, then said, "The blanket and outer clothing of the patients must be removed."

"Scan patients in the condition they are in," he said.

"We cannot," chimed the robotic voice. "Something is stopping the scan from initializing. Please remove the blankets and outer clothing."

"Damn." He returned to the pod, opened the lid, and, with difficulty, he tugged the blanket free. Lani wore pants of some stretchy material and a short-sleeve shirt. He didn't want to remove it if he didn't have to. "Start scan."

The beeps picked up, and a blue laser light started at Lani's head and swept down to her feet. Liev breathed a sigh of relief. Good, it worked with her dressed. "Scan results?"

"Patients are experiencing an extreme reaction to the atmosphere. Muscle weakness, rapid heart rate, and irregular breathing indicate a reaction to high stress."

"Tell me something I don't know," he muttered. "Will she be all right?"

"Patient is exhausted. We are giving her high doses of vitamins and lowering her vital signs. Sleep is paramount. Her body has undergone a great shock. We are adding her condition to our database."

"No," he snapped. "Cancel that. Do not add her condition to the database."

"It is protocol," stated the computer. "This is a condition we have not encountered. It must be added."

"Shit. Shit. No!" he said urgently. "Do not add at this time. Should the patient not recover quickly, then it can be added. Everyone reacts to stress differently. This is hers."

"This is most unusual."

"Yeah, that's me." Liev walked over to Lani. "What about the critter? What is its condition?"

"He appears to be suffering the same muscle weakness as the woman. Also the same increased heart rate." The computer stopped, then added, "Interesting."

"Do not add this to the database," he snapped.

The robotic voice spoke again. "We must. It is protocol."

Frustration rolled through him. "And yet, like the woman, the critter will likely be fine."

"If that is true, why did you bring them here?"

And what was he doing, arguing with a healing pod? Computers had taken over his world. They now argued and chastised and nagged like an old fish wife.

"I wanted to make sure that there was no internal damage," he muttered.

"We did not scan for that."

He stopped and turned to look at the console. "Why not?"

"You did not remove her clothing. We could not go through all the material."

"That's crap. Of course you can."

"We do not know this particular blend of materials. We must add it to the database."

He was going to pull his hair out. "Do not add it to your database."

"We must. It is—"

"Protocol, yeah, I know." He walked over to the pod. "If you are done with the booster shot, I'll take off her shirt and pants. Then you can do a deeper scan."

"Acknowledged."

At least *that* wasn't breaking protocol. He opened the pod and tugged her boots off her feet. Then he opened the closures on her pants and tugged them off. He swallowed at the sight of the purple underclothes. Yeah, lingerie hadn't changed much in the last couple of centuries. It was as sexy back then as it is now. Walking to the side of the pod, he opened up the buttons that held Lani's shirt closed and spread apart the material. He could feel his own heart rate increase at the sight of her firm breasts rising from the matching purple bra. Crap, he felt like a pervert.

But she was something.

"Can you do a complete scan with her like this?" He rearranged the critter down the long, lean length of her, its head resting against her ribs. If she woke to find the critter dying or missing, then there would likely be hell to pay.

"We can."

"Good. Then please complete the full diagnostics."

He closed the pod lid, and the blue laser light swept slowly down the length of the bed. Then it reversed all the way back up.

"Scan complete," said the computer.

"And the scan results?" Liev asked.

"The patient has no severe internal damage. There have been some recent adaptations to her physical body that we have not seen before."

There was a hum. "We have added that information to our database."

"No," he shouted. "Damn it, do not add it the database."

"It is protocol."

He dropped his forehead against the glass top of the pod, wanting to smash his fist against the smooth unyielding surface. "And what of the critter?"

"The same odd changes have also recently been done to its body. We have added this information to the database."

He didn't bother arguing. He'd try to wipe the memory after he was done. "What kind of changes have been made?"

"We do not have a scan from before these changes in order to say." The robotic voice was not being helpful.

"Right. Then how do you know changes have been made?"

"There are signs of new tissue," continued the computer. "Signs of healed muscle and skin. The DNA has been altered."

He swallowed on that last bit. Milo had said that wouldn't happen. Then he'd probably worded it in such a way as to avoid an outright lie and still not tell the truth. "Are these changes dangerous?"

"Not that we can see at this time." A series of monotone clicks repeated, as if the console was shutting down.

"So is she healthy?" Liev asked urgently before it turned off. "Good to leave?"

The clicks paused. "She is exhausted. She must rest for twenty-four hours minimum." The robotic voice stopped, as if considering its next words. Then added, "Maybe longer."

He didn't want to consider how this console's actions imitated human thinking. "And can you help her do that?"

"It is done."

With a sigh of relief, Liev opened the pod, gathered up her clothing, and wrapped both Lani and the critter in the blanket, along with her clothes. And stepped out into the hallway.

Just as she woke up.

CHAPTER 6

THE BOUNCING AROUND woke her up. Lani forced her eyes open. Heavy and unwieldy, they didn't want to obey her orders. But it felt like she was being carried. Only to find she was tucked up against a man's chest, carried like she was a precious child.

She'd been sleeping so soundly; then the nightmares had kicked in, and she'd surfaced, feeling like she'd been through the worst night of her life.

As the memories drifted in, she wondered if she had.

Except for the male carrying her. *Liev.* His name drifted through her consciousness. He smelled so wonderful. And the strength, the ease with which he carried her, … he wasn't even breathing hard.

His heartbeat pounded under her ear. Slow, steady, and strong.

She sighed happily. She didn't know who he was or where she was, but this part was good. Momentarily she could forgive his role in this nightmare. She sighed happily once again.

Until the pain penetrated her consciousness. Everything ached. Had this person hurt her? Was she in danger? It didn't feel like it. But then …

Her body was jostled again, … and that set parts of her to hurting in the worst way. Bones ached. Joints throbbed.

Muscles burned. She tried to shift away from the pain. She moaned.

"Easy, Lani." Lowering his head slightly, Liev whispered, "Take it easy. We're almost back. Just lie still."

"Where?" she murmured. "Back where?"

"Back to bed. I took you to the healing pod. It should have helped."

"I hurt. Everywhere." She shifted her legs restlessly. She wanted it to stop. "Put me down." Then her voice broke at the pain. "Please."

"*Shh*. It's all right. You'll be fine. We're almost home."

Home sounded good. She felt the urgency in his movements as he walked faster. He was worried, racing somewhere. Then the air changed, calmed. Liev slowed down immediately.

In the background, she heard him call out, "Stealth on."

She was taken into a darker room. Her eyes were open only a slit, enough to see the atmosphere change but not enough to see the details of her surroundings. She opened her eyes wider, happy it appeared to be easier to do now. Her body was jostled again before being laid down on a hard surface. Immediately, she cried out as pain radiated into the corners of her body. "Oh, it's hard. It hurts."

The surface softened, cradled her, eased her pain. She sighed in relief, her body shuddering in reaction.

"It's okay now," he said. "You're back in bed. Just rest."

She tried to shift, her arms struggling with the blanket, until something big and furry was placed in her arms. She whispered happily, "Charming."

He made no reply, but she knew it was him, and his soft, gentle breathing reassured her that he was well. Now if only her body would stop screaming at her. She rolled over, felt something tugged up and placed atop her shoulders, and then soft, gentle music filled the room.

"Sleep. You'll feel better in the morning."

That made sense. She let herself drift away.

Until a few hours later, when she woke up in agony. Pain radiated throughout her body. She'd never done much jogging, but her body felt like she'd done a full marathon. And it complained bitterly. Barely cognizant that she was only in her underwear, she stumbled to a doorway that led to the bathroom, tears running down her cheeks. By the time she was back in bed, she could barely move. With every step, her muscles had seized up a little more. Charming lay in the bed motionless, his huge eyes wells of pain.

"I know how you feel, buddy." She stopped and considered what she just did. "I had to use the bathroom. What about you?"

He had to go sometime. If he hadn't already. She didn't want to check the corners of the room too closely. "What can I do about a litter box for you, Charming?"

She looked around, but nothing resembling a decent container would work for this purpose. She thought about the bathroom. "Charming, can you use the toilet?"

He shuddered and gave her a horrified look. "Water is in the toilets."

She winced. Actually, she wasn't sure water was in this bowl. She'd noticed a blue jelly substance she'd refused to check out any closer. "I know. But we have no sand or litter here. I don't know what to do for you."

Charming stood and jumped off the bed. He landed, then collapsed. She cried out and reached over to pick him up. "Our muscles don't work right here."

"Yeah, I got that," he grumbled. "How about that litter

box thing?"

"How about a water one?" she asked hopefully.

The horrified look in his eyes made her laugh.

"I have to go," he growled. "Let's take a look at it."

She carried him into the bathroom. It had taken her a bit of time to figure out the system. She had no idea how to help him understand. The seat seemed to adapt to the size of the butt sitting down. Kind of like the couch and the bed. She opened the lid so he could see the seat, then perched him on top.

"This is what there is. You go pee in the hole."

He stared at her.

She gave him a winning smile, and said, with bright encouragement, "You can do this."

"So not."

"I'll just leave you so you can have some privacy."

And she escaped.

Oh, Lord. What was she doing here? They both wanted to go home. They didn't belong here. They couldn't even move properly. How the heck were they supposed to survive? They had no papers, no identification, no family or friends. No job and—worse yet—no money. If such a thing still existed. And then there were those two idiots who'd brought her and Charming here. They weren't to be trusted.

On the heels of that thought, she sat on the bed and remembered the strength of those arms, the soothing tone in Liev's voice as he had told her to rest. He'd been gentle. Caring. That was very sexy. A man who looked after you when you were hurt and hurting was something special.

If only he hadn't been part of the plot to bring her here.

He said he'd had nothing to do with it, but …

And, speaking of which, she planned to nail Milo tomorrow and find out how and why she'd been chosen.

She had no great skills. She was no beauty. She had left no legacy—at least at the time of her kidnapping. And that was on top of the dismal overview of her life to date that Milo had read off earlier. How had they even known who she was to swoop down and scoop her up?

A weird scratching sound came from the direction of the bathroom, followed by a heavy *thud*, which hinted that Charming was done with his business. As he strolled out, heavy limbed, his head dipped lower with every step. She winced and then headed toward him. Slowly. "See? It wasn't so bad."

"It so was," he said darkly. "What kind of place is this that they don't have a decent dry litter box?" He walked toward her and twined around her legs. "Do you realize how long it's been since we ate?" He plunked his furry butt down on the weird tiled floor and stared up at her. "Do you think they know what food is? If they haven't heard about litter boxes …"

How typical. His stomach was always a priority. "I'm sure they know what food is. Chances are good we might even recognize some of it."

He shot her a horrified look, jumped up on the bed, and proceeded to turn around in circles before collapsing. "I'm going back to sleep. Maybe when I wake up the next time, this nightmare will be over."

"That's a good idea."

All she could hear was his heavy breathing. She climbed up beside him and curled herself around his pudgy body. She really wanted her life back. To be back in her tiny apartment, getting ready for her date. She'd been so excited …

How could they take that away from her?

And she fell asleep once more.

LIEV GROANED AND rolled over yet again. His mind wouldn't shut off. Although he had done his best to wipe Johan's pod of any evidence of his and Lani's earlier visit, Liev still wondered if the pod's treatment would work. He had no idea how to stop this mess from changing his life as he knew it. His brother had done the unthinkable. At the same time, it was a major scientific achievement—and no one could ever know.

His brilliance had to stay hidden. It was too dangerous to let the world know.

And what was he supposed to do with Lani? This charming young woman hadn't asked for her life to be destroyed at Milo's whim. Liev didn't even know how she'd been chosen. She wasn't Milo's usual choice when it came to women. Lani had no visible piercings, and her hair was all the same color.

Then again, Milo had mentioned that he'd picked Lani for Liev. That brought the old photo to mind again. Was he so pathetic that his kid brother felt he needed to get Liev a girlfriend? Sure, Liev was going through a dry spell, but that was by choice. He didn't like Johan's party scene. It had been fun once or twice, but he preferred to be with a woman because he liked her, not because she had the requisite body parts. And—he twisted his lips in a dour smile—he was a romantic. Old-fashioned. He wanted to love and to be loved. Was that so impossible?

He rolled over again. How could he stop the world from finding out about Milo's accomplishment? He also had to stop Milo from repeating his actions. But he needed to find a way to send Lani home first. Although Liev wouldn't mind if she stayed for a bit—if she wanted to.

Was it wrong of him to want her to stay? Instantly he crushed that thought. She wasn't meant to stay here. He didn't dare get attached to her. She wasn't a pet. He couldn't just keep her.

But a part of him was considering it.

Just as the morning light drifted into his room, and he thought he might finally go to sleep, a pounding came at his front door. Groaning, he pulled on a shirt and pants. When the noise came a second time, he stumbled to the door, calling out, "Hang on. I'm coming."

He pulled open the door, his hand hiding a yawn. And froze.

Two suits with cold flat stares stood there with a crumpled looking Johan sandwiched between them. Liev glanced at Johan, a question in his eyes, but asked the two others in a genial voice, "What's up, gentlemen?"

One man said, "You're wanted for questioning at the Council." His tone was stiff, uncompromising. Just like the look on the first man's face. Liev glanced at the second man's stony expression. Council henchmen. Great. He was in trouble again. He cast his mind back to see where he had messed up. And how to recover …

Liev frowned at his friend. "Johan, what's going on?"

Johan shrugged but wore his customary careless grin. "Damned if I know. I was trying to sleep off my party when they came knocking. I'm being hauled in too."

Not good. Liev straightened, looked at the first man, and said, "Do I need my lawyers, gentlemen?"

"If you feel you need one, you may certainly call in representation, as is your right. However, at this moment, while we are requesting your presence at the Council, it is not an order."

The unspoken "yet" hung in the air.

"Right. Give me a moment. I'll get dressed and meet you there."

The second suit, who'd yet to speak, said, "No. We will wait and escort you there."

So this was serious. Liev nodded and returned to his bedroom. He swallowed a booster, hoping to make up for his lousy night. He walked to his wardrobe, where he pulled out a suit and dressed carefully. Milo did creative. Liev did power and intimidation.

After a quick glance around, he pocketed his comp and walked out. He needed Lani and her critter to stay asleep for this. Hopefully he wouldn't be too long. He could count on Milo not surfacing for a few hours yet.

Johan at his side, the four men traveled to the Council building and were escorted into the inner office immediately.

No waiting. No coffee offered. Immediate reception.

This was very serious.

They were led forward to face four Councilmen, all seated on a raised podium, watching as Liev's group approached.

Liev recognized all four of them. His stomach sank. He didn't exactly have a good relationship with the Council after Milo broke protocol over a year ago. Except for one member, Stephen Cavendish, a junior member who was also an old friend. As a junior member, his presence on the Council was sporadic.

No sound was heard for a long moment as the Councilmen assessed him and Johan. One of the two Councilmen in the middle finally spoke up. "Johan and Liev, thank you both for coming. We understand that a disturbance occurred on the health pod registered to you, Johan."

Ah, shit.

So much for his orders to that damn computer. It hadn't wiped the data and had instead submitted it as per protocol, and his attempts to fix it afterward hadn't effectively amended those either. That had raised flags. He'd expected the power outage to have done that. Although there'd been several of those lately, unrelated to Milo's work. He frowned. Or were they? Had Milo tested his program out earlier?

Johan raised his hands, palms outward. "Anything is possible. It experienced heavy use last night as several of my guests took advantage of my personal unit. In fact, likely a dozen or so could have used my pod. I had a big party, and many people, not having their own pod, come specifically for that purpose. I don't mind. I never have."

"You will have no problem supplying us a list of your guests then?" the speaker asked, who Liev thought was called Carlson, peering over his glasses at Johan.

Liev wondered at the glasses. No one used them for vision anymore. Chances were good the speaker was running all kinds of scans on Johan right now. From financials to health statistics. The speaker settled back with a frown, removing the glasses.

That was interesting. Liev turned slightly to study the man at his side. Did Johan have a way to block the scan? If so ...

"I'll get as many names as I can, but I have an open-door policy with regard to guests." Johan gave them a fat grin. "The more, the merrier." He held his hands up in appeal. "What is this about?"

"Data from the pod proposed a few questions last night. We are obligated to check it out further." Again the man lifted his glasses to study the two men. And again frowned and took them off to lay on the desk in front of him.

Johan's eyebrows shot up. "Interesting." He glanced over at Liev and shrugged.

"And I'm here why?" Liev asked coolly.

"We have information that you asked to use the pod last night."

Not good. Liev tilted his head slightly. "That is correct. And what regulation did you violate to find that information?"

Johan snorted. "That's a damn good question. Are you recording my calls?" he asked in outrage. He pulled out his comp and jotted down notes. "That is something I will be looking into."

"In the case of issues of national security, we are within our rights to record calls."

"National security?" Liev spluttered. Inside, his nerves jangled. "What are you talking about?" He pulled out his comp and sent a nudge to his own lawyer, Hahn Driscoll. With any luck, he could keep this tied up long enough to solve the problem. Liev also checked to make sure his comp was recording this session. That was just a basic precaution he'd used since the last blow up.

"We don't have enough information to complete a full analysis of the problem. The data stream from the pod was corrupted. We must also investigate a massive power outage that occurred earlier on that same date."

"Ha, corrupt data is the norm half the time. And lately there have been more power outages than not. You know that." Johan laughed. "Any one of my many guests could have broken it." He shook his head. "You will also note that I have it repaired on a regular basis."

"We will follow up on the guest list you supply. If you

have no further information to offer, you are dismissed."

And that tone of voice had Liev's back going up. He glared at the four men staring down at him, identical looks on their faces. But this was not the time or place to start an all-out war. He'd warred with these men before. Milo often got into trouble.

And Liev always worked to get him out of it.

He wasn't sure that was possible this time.

Johan tugged his arm. "Come on, buddy. It's time to get a coffee. Let these guys worry about national security." He snickered. "Coffee is on me."

Liev let his friend tug him outside. Besides, it would give Liev a chance to ask Johan if he could block scans and if he would share that technology with Liev. They went through the austere building in complete silence, but, once outside, Johan lost it. "They were monitoring our freaking phone calls? They will not get away with that."

"Sorry if I got you into this."

"Ha, it probably wasn't even you. Dozens of people were in that thing last night." Johan shook his head. "Besides, I'm glad you did. I need those bloodsucking lawyers to earn their retainers. I've been paying them for years, and they do nothing. This"—he held up his comp—"is not allowed."

He glared at Liev. "Do you know how many laws they've broken? Do you have any idea how many secrets of mine they might have uncovered?"

Liev was surprised at the sheer level of fury in his friend's voice. Maybe he had a reason. Maybe he was hiding something. Liev didn't care. He was hiding something himself.

A light rain drizzled on the two men. Liev looked up, surprised to see a storm gathering above the buildings. Flash storms were unusual here when the weather was computer controlled.

Johan motioned to the sky. "It's been going on since late yesterday." His face twisted as he studied it. "Wonder what the hell is going on."

Liev's stomach knotted. *Please let it have nothing to do with Milo's damn experiment. Please.* "No idea," he said lightly.

Johan motioned across the street where the coffee shop was. "I know I mentioned coffee, but, if you don't mind, I'll take a rain check."

I'll ask him about blocking scans later. "Not a problem. I've got to get to work as it is."

Johan slapped him on the shoulder. "It's been a weird morning already. Let's hope it improves." And he walked away. His long legs ate up the distance. Johan had a specific goal, and his temper still rode his emotions.

Liev hoped Johan and his lawyer would raise a little hell. Liev planned to do just that himself.

After he checked up on Milo and Lani.

CHAPTER 7

L ANI WOKE UP slowly, her eyes drifting open, then sliding closed again. Only to come awake to wild green hair framing a looming face. She screamed and bolted upward. Trapped by the wrappings, she fell sideways onto the soft mattress. Expecting to fall and still trying to get away, she crab-walked backward to escape on a bed that seemed to grow in the direction she moved. Criminy.

"Calm down. I was just looking to see if you were awake." Milo danced back as Lani retreated a little more. "Hey, I'm not here to hurt you."

Lani took a deep breath and tried to shake off the panic of waking up to a strange face looming over her. "Why couldn't you just call out to me?"

"I did." He held his hands up in front of him. "Sorry. I should have called out louder."

She shuddered and slowly sat up. "Yeah, okay. I'm awake." She pushed her long hair out of her eyes. "Now why did you wake me up?"

"I didn't want to." He stepped back again. "I was just taking a look."

She stared. "At me? While I was sleeping?" She glanced down and gasped. She only had on her underclothes. And the fallen blanket had left much of her exposed. She snatched the cover and clutched it to her chest before glaring at Milo.

"No. No. I wasn't looking. Honest." He shook his head, a blush climbing up his neck and face. "Liev called. He wanted to know if you were up. So I came to look. That's it."

"Well, I am now." She stared at the weird bed. And caught sight of Charming curled into a still fur ball. "Charming," she cried out and scrambled over to him. Gently she stroked his still form and almost bawled when she realized that he was breathing. "I was so scared that you'd died during the night," she said to him.

"He shouldn't die." Milo interrupted their cuddle to add, "His DNA may have changed a bit, but he will live a long life."

Lani shot him a disgusted look. "You have no idea how he's changed."

"And he won't ever know if you don't tell him," Charming muttered in a strangled yowl. He opened his eyes and glared at her. "I could use some more sleep." He stretched out his front leg and yawned, then tucked up into a tight ball and went back to sleep.

Still smiling, she turned to stare up at Milo. Only his gaze whipped from the cat to her and back to the cat. Oh, shit. He'd heard.

"You can hear the cat talk," he whispered in awe. "And, like, wow. It talks back."

"Right. Charming is special." That he'd heard Charming speaking wasn't perfect timing, but it's not like there would ever be a good time to bring up this. And Milo would have found out sometime. She snorted and shoved the bedding back to free her legs. "Now, if you don't mind, I have to go to the bathroom."

Flushing wildly, Milo backed up. "Sure. No problem."

He gave one last fascinated stare at Charming and bolted toward the door. At the doorway, he paused. "Do you need anything?"

"You mean, like all my clothes from home? The shampoo and soap I love so I could enjoy a shower? Oh, and how about some food for me and Charming? And if you guys know what coffee is …"

Milo's eyes lit up. "I can do the coffee part. We have awesome coffee here."

"Well, that's good. At least you have something decent," she muttered as she pulled herself to the edge of the bed.

With that, Milo escaped for the kitchen. She hoped.

Her legs were slow and shaky, but at least they held when she stood up. Only the bathroom looked damn far away.

When she was done, she all but collapsed on the bed. She couldn't help but be grateful a toilet was still a toilet. Then they hadn't changed much from the centuries before her time either.

She'd barely covered up again, the bed softening and curling around her, when Milo returned, carrying a tray with both hands. She eyed him suspiciously. Was he trying to make her feel better, or was this normal behavior in his time? If so, then obviously she knew of a few good things about living here. Still, she figured he was working on that whole *keep her happy theme* so she didn't explode on him. She could work with that.

"Here is coffee and a snack. Liev is on his way home. We'll eat then."

She stared at the pretty setting and the tiny cup on her tray. If she didn't know better, she'd have thought she was in Europe, having a cup of espresso. She picked it up and took an experimental sniff. It smelled like coffee.

"It's safe," Milo said. He bounced from side to side. "Go ahead. Try it."

She eyed him over the rim of her tiny cup. Why was he so excited? She studied the rich liquid suspiciously. Then took a tiny sip. And sighed. Oh, joy. They actually had real coffee. She almost melted with her second sip, and, by the time she'd reached the bottom of the minuscule cup, she was looking for more.

Milo disappeared and returned immediately with a small silver pot. He refilled her cup and took a step back. She glared at him. Then at the pot. Still in his grip. And back at him.

He swallowed. "Sure. I'll just leave the pot here. You can have as much as you want." He gingerly added it to her tray.

"Thank you, that's very generous of you," she murmured, keeping a close eye on him. "And you're right. It is good coffee."

He beamed. "Thank you."

"Did you make it?"

Confusion made his smile go away. "Umm, I guess."

Okay, smaller steps. "Did you grind the beans and pour water into a pot, measure the coffee, and start it dripping?" At least that's how coffee used to be made at her apartment and at most of her jobs.

He shook his head so fast the bright green Mohawk waved in the wind like a hand. "No. No. I just pushed a button."

Interesting. Then again she should expect that everything here would be computerized, technological advancement being what it was. She should probably be grateful she hadn't been dragged into the Flintstones' era.

Coffee like this with a push of a button definitely had something going for it.

"Hello? Lani?" Liev called out. "Are you here?"

Really? Where else would she be? That was one huge world out there, and she had no money and no ID. It would take a braver person than her to venture out there alone.

Milo bubbled out with, "We're in her bedroom."

Yeah, like she always entertained men in her bedroom.

Just then Charming sat up and stretched out a paw. She watched as he hooked the treat Milo had added to her tray. It appeared to be a sweet bun of some kind, but she'd yet to try it. She wasn't sure her stomach could handle anything solid right now. But she wanted to. Her last meal had been a long time ago.

Liev filled the doorway.

"Isn't this awfully cozy looking," he said coolly, his deep purple eyes taking in everything, assessing it all.

She lifted her chin. "Milo offered me coffee, and I took him up on it."

"Liev, what happened this morning?" Milo asked worriedly. "I heard the door, and, just like that, you were gone."

Lani studied Liev's face. He looked everywhere but at her.

"It was about me—wasn't it?" And she knew. Somehow, someone had found out. "What did you tell them?"

He looked straight at her, then walked forward several steps. "Nothing."

Milo stepped between the two of them. His gaze darted from one to the other. He asked his brother, "What did you say?"

"Nothing." He ran his hand through his dark curls. "They asked a few questions, and I answered. They didn't ask about you specifically, so I didn't have to lie."

Milo bounced forward. "What did they ask about?"

Looking very uncomfortable, Liev said, "They asked about the pod."

"What pod?" Milo stepped forward to look into his brother's face. "Liev, what pod?"

"Johan's healing pod. I took Lani up there last night. She was hurting. I figured, if she had sustained internal damage due to the time-travel, the pod could heal her."

"Oh, no. Oh, no." Milo danced backward in horror. "No, you didn't. Please say you didn't."

"Considering you refuse to have a pod of our own, I didn't have much choice. Also, considering you dragged her through a wormhole and dumped her here, her body is suffering. Did you even consider the impact on her physical body?"

Lani watched the brothers. Liev, the older and more responsible. Milo, the younger incorrigible genius with little sense of reality. He'd been protected so much that he wasn't held accountable for all his actions. Like what he'd done to her.

And Liev was doing his best. She spoke up. "I'm sorry for your troubles, taking me to this pod, but thank you for thinking of me and my health."

Both brothers turned to stare at her. She gave a little finger wave. "Yeah, I'm here too. Remember?"

"So, if we'd had a pod," Milo said slowly, "this wouldn't ever have happened?"

Liev snorted. "No. *And*, if you'd listened to me in the first place, *this* wouldn't have happened."

Milo's face twisted in thought. Moodily Liev kicked the door. "Besides, a pod is being delivered today."

"No, no. I hate them." Milo backed up, shaking his hands wildly in front of him. "They are dangerous. We can't have one."

"Well, too bad," Liev snapped. "You should have thought of that before you hurt Lani."

Milo spun around to look at Lani. "I didn't hurt her."

"Yes, you did. And she's still suffering. For all we know, she could have long-term health issues. She needs our help now."

"But a pod will be connected to *them* ..." Milo hissed.

"No." Liev smiled. "This one is unregistered."

Milo gasped, hot color flooding his face. "But that's ... illegal!"

It was Liev's turn to stare at his brother. "A little too late to worry about that now," he said.

Lani laughed at Liev's glare. "You two are obviously brothers."

Both turned to glare at her.

She shrugged and took another sip of coffee. "So, when is this healing pod arriving? Because you're right. I could sure use it. Not to mention some food."

"You just had a snack and coffee," Milo protested.

"How about real food now?" Lani stared at the crumbs Charming had left her and sighed. "Like eggs, bacon, some hash browns?" At Milo's disgusted look, she smiled hopefully and added, "Even toast sounds wonderful."

"We don't eat garbage like that anymore. We care about our bodies here. We drink synthetic and highly nutritious shakes now."

"Only shakes?" she asked in horror. "What about real food? Like fruit, veggies, fried chicken, cheesecake, ... and other essential foods."

Milo shuddered in revulsion. "I'm a vegetarian. As we all should be."

"See? That just won't work for me." She sat up in bed. Charming rolled over and stretched his paws. "I like food," Lani said. "Real food."

"And we have food," Liev said. "Real food. My brother has been this way since infancy. I, however, still eat real food."

She brightened. "Awesome. Any chance of some?" Her stomach took that moment to grumble and growl very loudly. She smiled hopefully. "And soon?"

Liev stared at her. His eyebrows shot up, and a big smile overtook his face. He said, "I can do that. I'll be a few minutes." He turned and left. The room seemed lonely, empty.

"Oh, that's great." Milo grinned. "He loves cooking. Now he has you to look after food-wise too."

Lani stared at him, then broke out laughing. "You mean, you guys are so advanced but you still have to cook?" For some reason, that struck her as funny. She laughed and laughed. "If I were home, I'd have picked up the phone and just ordered in."

"We have takeout too." Milo bounded closer. "High-end food."

"Yeah, sure," she scoffed, smoothing the pleats in her incredibly soft bedding. Now that she was awake she was taking note of the differences around her. Like the custom fitting bed, the butter soft bedding. The light colored walls that had a luminous glow. Was that the paint or the sunrise behind it? Not wanting to think about what was outside, she added, "Like the rest of your supposed advanced lifestyle."

"We do! Healing pods. Awesome elevators." He motioned to the tray with the coffee. "The best coffee ever. A technologically advanced society you couldn't even imagine. Climate controlled green lifestyle that was way past what you could have envisioned back in your time. And that's just for starters."

"I'll give you that on the coffee, but your lifestyle seriously sucks. Look at this tiny-ass apartment, the monster cities ..."

"Ha! Look what I did with you." Milo did a fast two-step. "See? Gotcha there."

Immediately the air cooled, and her smile fell away. She dropped her gaze. "Yeah, that's a big gotcha."

"*Uhmmm*, yeah. I'll go make more coffee." He scooted backward from the bedroom. Escaping ...

She let him go.

If Lani could get up and walk into the kitchen, she would help cook, but any movement seemed to steal all her energy. She sank back against the pillows. She felt like a fat slug whose body had grown so big, so heavy, it couldn't carry its own weight. Considering the look on her baby's face, she had to wonder if Charming didn't feel the same. She bent to scratch the back of his head. He rolled over slightly and stared at her, but the look in his eyes made her shift and tug him, blankets and all, into her arms.

His head fell back.

"Don't feel so good, do you? Do we?" she corrected. She nuzzled his neck, reassured when his engine kicked in and his heavy purr filled the room. "At least that much of you is working."

"Yes, but I'm tired." He closed his eyes and laid his head back down.

"Me too." She wondered what the pod had done for her

last night when she still felt so rough today. Then again, maybe she wouldn't have woken up today without it. Apparently they had an unregistered pod being delivered today. What kind of a government system had pods register the medical knowledge and defects of its contents without the people knowing? There was such a thing as too much government intervention.

And would having an unregistered unit get the brothers into more trouble?

Then again, if they were found with a nonregistered person, … she couldn't imagine having to explain her presence. Hell, she had no answers. She'd have to tell the truth about what she did know. And would likely end up in a psych ward.

Who'd believe her?

Who could?

At least the brothers could have brought her clothes with her. Then again, as she stared down at Charming, they had brought the most important part of her life. Presumably because she'd been holding on to him at the time. And, as she thought about it, when she was whooshed away from her apartment, she'd been wishing he could talk. Coincidence?

What had happened to her old life? Had anyone reported her missing? Did she just disappear forever? Was she a missing person in the history books? Or did the apartment blow up, and Milo's little time-travel trick caused the deaths of a couple hundred people? Could she find out? Would she do a search on the internet and find herself? Did they even have internet here?

And, if they did, would her search be reported to someone that she was researching this person in history? Did the government keep that close an eye on its citizens?

If they kept that close an eye on everyone's health—maybe.

She had a lot of questions and no answers. The biggest one was still unanswered—was this really a one-way trip?

LIEV WORKED IN the kitchen, quietly and competently at the counter. She needed food. It would be these mundane details that would keep him focused. Maybe while doing the mundane, he'd come up with a solution for everything else. He glanced up at the screen on the wall. Still a half hour until the pod was delivered.

He didn't want anyone else to see it. He'd asked for a call when the delivery left the warehouse, so he could put on the special effects. Special effects he'd set up after Milo's genius started to show. And the lines Milo had started to cross.

Innocently of course. Yeah, right.

Just as he took the scrambled eggs off the heat, his comp buzzed.

He checked the message. The pod was en route. Good. "Milo, engage the privacy mode setting out front."

"Woohoo." Milo jumped up from the table and raced over to the control unit. "I never get to do this."

"Well, this time, it's necessary." He checked the digital readout on the screen. "Good, it's all working." He set the plate on a tray. "Take this to Lani. I have to accept the delivery."

Milo looked at him. "Are you sure about this?"

Liev stopped, handing Milo the tray. "It's a little late to be asking, isn't it?"

Milo's lively features twisted in regret. "I'm just realizing that this is all my fault."

Liev stared at him. "Really, just now?" He leaned on the counter to stare at him. "You really don't get it, do you? This isn't some game. This isn't a rush to beat the technology. This isn't something you can just do, then forget about." His temper fired as he thought about all he had to deal with. "You have damaged lives—in ways we can't begin to know about. And you have ruined Lani's."

"I haven't ruined Lani's at all. Don't you see this is beautiful? She has a great life waiting for her here. We'll make it great."

"But you didn't give her any choice. You did this *to* her not *for* her. You made her a victim of your machinations. And that's just wrong. She should never have been brought into our world. You didn't ask her if she wanted this. You didn't care."

Liev stopped and stared, wondering what it would take to get through his brother's head. "What you did was wrong. On so many levels. And you've left me to deal with your mess again."

"She's not a mess. She's a miracle." Milo stepped in front of Liev. "Look. I'm sorry for the problems right now. I'm sorry for any that might still come, but, damn it, Liev, I did something that no one else has done." His eyes glittered with excitement. "Can't you see the greatness here?"

Liev choked. "And that's all this means to you, isn't it?" Would Milo ever see what he'd done? "And what about Lani? Do you think she'll consider this greatness?"

A buzzer sounded.

"Damn it. They're early. I hadn't expected them so fast." Liev raced to the door, leaving the food tray behind with Milo. Liev opened the door to see his delivery.

"Bring it in here." He stood by as the pod floated toward him. He led the way to where it would stay. He'd planned on getting one a year ago but had had a hard time with the registration requirements. "Thanks."

"No problem. You'll pay through the nose for this, but, hey, it's worthwhile."

"I hope so," he muttered. He took the paperwork, glanced at the bottom line, and said, "So we're good?"

"We are. As long as I get that software, we're done."

"It's already in progress." And it was. He smiled at the man who would prefer to not be named. Liev knew him vaguely. Liev had had to go to a friend of a friend to make this happen as it was. So he had taken his first step on the wild side. Then again, Milo had pushed them all over there already.

But Lani needed healing. Liev couldn't leave her like she was.

Speaking of which, he went through the simple process to open the pod and to check it over. "Lani," he called out loudly, "do you think you can walk over to me?"

He didn't hear an answer. He walked to her room to see her struggling to get out of bed. Just that much effort had her sweating. Damn Milo.

And she still wasn't fully dressed. He cursed himself for looking. As she struggled to tug the blanket around her shoulders, he cursed himself again for not taking a better look while he could.

He raced over. "Here. Let me help."

She gasped from the effort. "I thought I'd be fine. I got up on my own this morning." Her face flushed, then paled.

He frowned, hating that she was hurting. "And you will be fine again. Let's get you into the pod. That will help."

He half carried her to where the machine waited, then helped her lie down inside. The pod, once fired up, would read her statistics. That stage could take a while. Before shutting the lid, he glanced down at her, wondering what he'd forgotten. Mentally he went through the process from the previous night and brightened. "Right. The critter."

He ran back to her bedroom and winced. The cat didn't look very good at all. It only opened its eyes and stared at him, its huge golden eyes wells of deep dark pain. "I'm so sorry," he whispered. He scooped him up and carried him to Lani. She lay with her eyes closed, never moving as he approached.

Carefully he lay the critter on her stomach. On the shelf below the pod were several blankets. He picked one up, opened it and tucked it along her side. If she wanted it, she could easily pull it over her.

Her eyes flew open, saw her pet, then her gaze shot up to stare at him in surprise.

He shrugged sheepishly. "He looked to be suffering too."

"He is," she whispered, her gaze gentling. She studied Liev's face and then smiled.

A real smile. No sarcasm, no anger, just a slow blossoming movement that he couldn't tear his gaze away from. And then the smile hit her eyes.

He was enthralled.

She might be mad sometimes, and she might be sarcastic, but now that she was smiling at him, he realized how honest she was. There was no artifice with her. Stretched out on a soft blanket in his new pod, she was a beautiful innocent to his world.

She was who she was, and to hell with what anyone thought of that.

He realized how unique she was. And how much he was falling for her—damn it. Milo had been right. He was interested.

CHAPTER 8

L ANI SOAKED UP the warm healing rays. It was like lying
in warm sunshine in a babbling creek as waves ... or
something similar rippled over and under and maybe even
through her. Whatever it was doing, she didn't ever want to
leave because it felt that good. This pod was amazing. She
needed one of her own. She'd skip the bed and sleep in this
every night. She wanted to sleep now, but, at the same time,
she didn't want to be unconscious and miss this experience.
The only unsettling comparison was its coffin-like appearance. Yet there wasn't any sensation of being confined in any
way. There was such a peaceful sensation to being in here, it
soothed her emotions and thoughts.

Charming snoozed beside her. She wondered if he was
worse off with this time-travel thing than she was.

At least she could talk and walk. Charming was more or
less flat-out. She reached down and scratched the back of his
head. He was definitely more laid-back right now. No
nagging for attention. No nagging for food. And speaking of
food—the pod had arrived before they could eat. Her
stomach growled then silenced almost instantly. Was that the
pod telling it to be quiet? Or was her body happy to accept
this healing time right now knowing that food was coming?

She was more worried about Charming than she was
about her own situation at the moment. Her heartstrings

tugged at the thought of losing her best friend. She had nothing left of her old life but him. He'd been with her for four years and was a major part of her life. To see him hurting like this …

Charming raised his head and gave her a pitiful look. "Food?"

She smiled in relief. "There will be food soon."

He groaned. A long, slow, guttural sigh that made her laugh.

"I'm glad to hear you are feeling better."

"Feel awful," he whispered in a low throaty voice.

"I love how you can talk now." She tilted her head in thought and added, "It must be a side effect of the time-travel."

"I love how you can talk now, too," Charming mimicked. "It must be a side effect of the time-travel."

She gasped, then laughed and laughed. And maybe he was right. Maybe she'd been the one to learn to talk cat and not the other way around. But if that was the case Milo wouldn't have heard him either. And she needed Milo to have heard him so she didn't think she was crazy.

She relaxed, her hand resting on his ruff, letting the hum of the pod do its thing. Whatever that was. The lights were a soothing blue, and no computer voice disturbed her peace and quiet. Food and more coffee would be good, but, barring that miracle, for the moment, she was doing just fine.

She closed her eyes and fell asleep.

LIEV WALKED INTO the newly designated pod room and smiled. Both guests were sound asleep. The pod would work better, faster, if they stayed that way. At least until it did its job. Getting her healthy was just the first stage of this process. Time to work on the second.

He opened his comp and dialed a number that was likely to be a popular one for him over the next few days.

When a computerized voice answered, he read off a series of numbers he'd memorized. When a voice came on the other end, he stated, "I need an ID for one young female."

Silence.

Liev held his breath. There was no guarantee that he'd get his request fulfilled, but he didn't know where else to go. Lani needed a solid ID to go anywhere. And she needed to be tagged. Thankfully he and Milo made a lot of money because taking care of Lani would become a major expense.

"Anything else?"

"Yes." He winced. It was from here that things could get dicey. "I need a tagging completed."

The person on the other end sucked in his breath. But, when he spoke, his voice was calm. "That is an expensive process."

"I know."

"You have the funds?"

"I have the funds." There was no point in elaborating. They either believed him or they didn't. And he'd pay the price, regardless. He had no choice.

Silence.

He waited. If this person refused, it would be one person more who would know his secret. And such a secret would be dangerous, especially for Lani.

"When?"

"As fast as possible." Then he reconsidered. Maybe not so fast. Lani was still healing. He didn't want these people to know why she had no ID or tags. And they might if they saw her now. If it could be in a few days, that would give her longer to heal. He had no idea how long it would take, but she needed every day. He'd have to take her out of his place soon. But she needed to be strong enough to handle everything that was coming.

His world was not for the faint of heart.

"Tomorrow morning. No food or water for twelve hours prior."

And the voice rang off.

Liev stared at the comp in his hand. "That went well." Maybe. They didn't give him a price. They didn't ask for his address. They didn't ask for any medical details about who was being tagged. Would they contact him again or just show up on his doorstep?

He immediately removed all trace of the call, then just to be sure, destroyed the comp in his hand. He'd get another one from his home office later. Secrecy was paramount.

He walked to where Lani slept in the pod. The top was glass so he could see her inside. The critter stretched across her belly. She'd taken to the pod as if it were the answer to her prayers, and, given the fact that it was easing her pain, it probably was. Stunningly beautiful in sleep, Lani was both a problem and a gift. He stood, enjoying the sleeping beauty, when he realized he really didn't want to leave her. That, more than anything, sent him bolting from the room.

Back in the kitchen, he came face-to-face with Milo.

Milo, dark overtones in his young voice, asked, "Did I just hear you correctly?"

Liev's stomach sank. Milo would need to know eventually, but Liev didn't feel up to a fight now. "What did you hear?"

Milo looked around furtively. Liev rolled his eyes. "We're in our home. Stealth is on. No one can hear us."

"You can't be sure of that," Milo cried out. "What if someone has this place bugged?" He reached up to grab his colorful green mohawk with both hands.

Liev stared at his brother in disgust. "You care now?"

Round glazed eyes stared back at him. "You don't understand. I can't have people knowing about her."

Liev narrowed his gaze. "Why?" he asked, his tone ominous.

Milo shifted uneasily. Not quite bouncing but neither did he stand steady. And that wasn't good.

"Milo, what are you talking about?"

He leaned forward. "It's my technology. My design. My invention."

"And?"

"And, if people find out, they will steal it." He wrung his hands.

"Damn it, Milo. This isn't about keeping your code secret. This is about a young woman whose life you destroyed. You do realize she could die, don't you?"

Milo stared in the direction of the healing pod. That he seemed to be considering the pros and cons of Lani's death pissed Liev off. His brother was naive and simpleminded over some things, other people's things, but he was also incredibly focused on his stuff.

"No," Liev snapped. "That is not a good outcome."

Milo slid him a sidelong glance. "I wasn't going to suggest we kill her, for God's sake, but if she should happen to die …"

"Which I'm trying my hardest to avoid happening, if you hadn't noticed." Liev strode to the liquor cabinet sunk into the wall. He couldn't believe the bizarre turn of their conversation. He poured himself a hefty whiskey and threw it back. He shuddered as the firewater coated his throat and prepared to do battle in his stomach. He had been doing this a lot lately.

"You really shouldn't drink that stuff. It's bad for you."

Liev choked. "You're worried about my health while you talk hopefully about Lani's death?"

Raising his hands in surrender, Milo snapped, "I'm just saying that, now that I know it works, she's the proof. If she dies, I'll still know that it works, but we won't have to deal with the evidence." He shrugged. "No biggie."

Liev poured a second shot and took a sip while he stared at his brother. Forced to question his kid brother's ethics, ... his morals. His conscience. And that was an alarming step. He swirled the golden liquid in his glass. While Liev had been bending over backward to keep Lani safe and to make her as comfortable as possible, his brother had been contemplating the advantage of his experiment dying.

How did that work? In his world, not very well.

"Milo," he said in a deep hard voice, "I don't ever want this discussion to come up again."

His brother pouted.

That was the only description Liev could come up with. His brother was actually pouting. Again reminding him that, for all his genius, Milo essentially had the mind of a sixteen-year-old male trapped in a twenty-two-year-old body. Maybe one day the two would match up, but Liev hadn't seen any sign of the gap closing in years. Milo had hit sixteen with such enthusiasm; it was as if he'd found a way to not age again.

That concept startled him. If Milo had found a way to

haul in some poor woman from a couple centuries ago, had he also found a way to slow or stop the aging process?

If so, if anyone found out, neither of them would ever be safe again.

CHAPTER 9

WHISPERED CONVERSATION SLIPPED under the edge of the pod's hum, disturbing her rest. Something about her dying? Really? Worriedly, her hand automatically searched for Charming, reassured to find his warm body snuggled up against her. He was still alive. She waited for his chest to rise with his next breath, then relaxed. Was she close to death? Or was that a hypothetical statement if the pod didn't do its job?

Dry-eyed, she studied the running green light shifting along the edge of the pod. Was she so badly damaged by Milo's experiment that she wouldn't survive? Assessing her own situation, she realized that, outside of a deep permeating fatigue, she didn't feel bad. Walking was a problem though. As if every step required too much effort, like she weighed hundreds of pounds more than she had before her time-travel trip.

That had to be due to the change in atmosphere or maybe gravity—as if she were living on Jupiter.

Only she wasn't. But time had obviously changed the atmosphere in the future. Or her body felt it had. Or maybe it was the oxygen levels? Were they different here? Was she at a much higher altitude than she thought? And maybe the why didn't matter. If she couldn't go back, she had no choice but to go forward. If she could ever get up.

She shifted her legs tentatively. They didn't ache the same as they had. So maybe the pod was doing its job. Her arms worked fine; her mind was clearer. She didn't know if she was supposed to live in here until she was fully healed—if such a thing was possible—or if there was a day-to-day booster thing going on.

She wasn't opposed to coming in here daily. She did feel better in the pod. Maybe it was a weaning-off thing. As she strengthened, she'd need it less. She was truly grateful they had such technology. Too bad she couldn't take a unit back home. The people there could use this.

And this time period needed better food. Her stomach growled again. It had been getting worse since she first woke up. She'd lost track of time and didn't know if it was day or night, and her stomach didn't care. It needed sustenance.

She pushed against the lid. Instantly it opened so she could see out but it kept working on her and Charming.

She glanced at the partially closed door where the voices drifted toward her. Were they still talking about her impending death? More likely she'd die from starvation at this rate. Should she search for food herself? And would she recognize it if she saw it? Or did the cupboards hold mostly shakes and boosters, like Milo had threatened?

That sent her stomach careening to almost heaving. Immediately the racing lights warmed and slowed. Probably in response to her discomfort. She closed her eyes. In truth, she didn't want to leave the pod. She was warm and comfortable and pain free. But very hungry.

"Liev?"

No answer. She called out louder. "Liev?"

Still no answer. Damn it.

She tried to push the top of the pod higher and found it

wouldn't budge. Shit. Was she locked in here? It's as if it had opened enough for someone to check on her, talk to her but not enough to release her.

And, if so, how would she get out?

"It won't open unless it is done with its work." Liev stopped at the doorway. "Or, if you need to go to the bathroom or have another physical discomfort, it's set to automatically shut off when the patient has other needs that supersede the healing." He frowned. "But I can adjust the settings so you can open the lid just by pushing on it."

She stared at him. "The only body function that is paramount at the moment is my appetite. I'm incredibly hungry."

He approached the pod and pressed some buttons on the console. After a moment, he glanced down at her and said, "I raised the height of the lid so you can lie sideways easier." He stared at her. "I guess you didn't get anything to eat yet?"

"No." She gave him a tentative smile. "And, if possible, I'd really like to change that."

For the first time all day, a real smile lit his face. "I can do that." He winked at her in a surprise move that left her doubting what she'd seen.

She watched him leave, feeling happier than she remembered in a while. The resemblance was only a passing glimpse now to Lawrence. Liev was a different person. She no longer felt any animosity toward him. He wasn't responsible for this. She understood he was trying to help.

He was his own person, and she really wanted to know him better. He'd been nothing but kind to her and patient with his brother. There was something so very attractive about that kind of caring.

Being pampered like this was addictive.

But Milo? … Now him, she wasn't so sure about.

As she came to terms with her new reality, she felt better emotionally. Sure, she'd lost so much, but maybe, just maybe, she'd also gained something.

According to Milo, her life as she'd known it hadn't ended up too special. As in, she'd never married, never had children, and she'd never had a major career that he could find.

That was quite depressing. She'd just been approved for a special Internet Security program at the company she'd worked for. She'd worked hard and had kept her head down at that company, making sure she did nothing to get into trouble. It had been gratifying to have them recognize her value – until she lost that opportunity, compliments of Milo. She couldn't even imagine what happened to all she'd left behind. Had her date shown up to think she was avoiding him? Would anyone call the police to say she was missing? Would her boss call her cellphone more than a few days before deciding she'd just quit?

Her furniture?

Her bank accounts?

Her car?

Would she end up forgotten, as a dusty missing person's file in the back of a rusty file cabinet? Or worse on the side of some old milk carton emblazoned with her face. Although she was pretty sure only missing children were put on milk cartons.

Bottom line, as far as anyone in her old life was concerned, she'd just upped and disappeared one day. And she had no way of changing that.

Thank heavens she had Charming with her when Milo decided to pull the trigger … she couldn't imagine her poor pet behind left behind to fend for himself in a locked up apartment. It just brought back how completely selfish and inconsiderate Milo had been... in more ways than one.

If she could return to her own time, she'd try harder to make something of her life there. She'd like to think an event like this would be a wake up call to enjoy the time she had. But, if returning was no longer a possibility, she wanted to make the best of whatever life she had here.

Maybe she could make a success of it.

She didn't know how society worked here, but, with Milo and Liev around to help, maybe she could make a difference.

She'd overheard Liev say something about tagging. She didn't know what that meant, but—if it allowed her to be one of them with a proper ID—she was all for it.

She was so busy making plans that Charming had to forcefully let her know something was different.

He pushed himself up on his front paws, yelling, "Food!"

Lani struggled to get out of the pod. It seemed to resist her efforts at first; then, all of a sudden, the lock released, and it opened. She really didn't want the two men rushing in here to find Charming screaming like he was. But the poor thing did need a square meal. So did she.

When she stood on her feet, a chill settled in. Already? How did that work? She cast another glance at the pod. Charming had collapsed on the top of the blanket, and the most godawful sound came from his mouth.

"Food. *Foooooooood,*" he moaned and rolled over sideways in a dramatic movement. He was proving to be a major prima donna.

"I'll see what I can find." She tugged the blanket from

the pod and wrapped it around her shoulders before she stumbled forward, her gait unsteady. She leaned against the wall and made her way to the unusual doorway. Tall, almost to the ceiling, the doorways were narrower than she was used to. The floor smoother as if made of glass. Maybe the people were skinnier today than in her time. Lord knows that would be an improvement.

She staggered into the next room, trying to sort out the layout. How had she gotten into this place? And where the heck was the kitchen? Her stomach growled loud enough that, if anyone was in the apartment, they'd hear her coming.

Good. She slipped her hand over the wall, but there was no light switch. "Of course. That would be too easy."

With one hand on the wall, she kept moving forward. The hallway opened up into a large spacious room. Something along the lines of a living room. There were several open sitting areas clustered together in little cozy conversation corners. Massive artwork was on the wall ... one appeared to stare at her. She quickly glanced at the rest of the living room.

"The big-ass living room," she muttered, staring around her in surprise. For some reason, she'd thought this apartment was tiny. She hadn't seen much of the apartment since she'd been here, but where was the damn bathroom again? Then she needed food. And so did Charming.

Slipping around the corner, she stopped. There was another bathroom. A monster-size room and different from the last one she'd used. She used it, then, after washing her hands, she stared into the mirror and shuddered. God, she looked pathetic. Even seeing that, she straightened her spine and tried to put a smile on her face. That looked better. She took a couple deep breaths and smacked her cheeks lightly to put some color on them. Having done what little she could, she opened the door and shrieked.

"Whoa. Take it easy." Liev reached out to stabilize her. "Come on. Let's get you back to the pod."

"I need clothes and food. And Charming needs his kind of food," she whispered. "I'm so hungry. He's going to be just as hungry if not more so. I normally feed him twice a day. And he gets dry food all day long in case he gets hungry."

"I'm preparing food. Wait a second." He disappeared, only to reappear with a long flowing robe. He quickly dropped it over her head flickering the blanket she wore away. Immediately her body warmed.

"Now, hold onto my arm, and I'll take you to the kitchen. After you eat, it's back into the pod."

"I do feel better and warmer. Thanks for the robe, it's lovely and cozy." She gave him a small apologetic smile. "I just feel much better."

"The pod will do its job, but it'll take some time. The robe will adjust to your body temperature and warm or cool you as needed. Give both time to work."

"Seriously? The robe is magic like the pod." She stumbled forward, every step a triumph. "At least I'm walking. Although very awkwardly. Like a day-old fawn…"

He laughed. "You're not that bad."

"I hope not but I doubt I'm much better." She managed a tiny chuckle. "Thanks for helping."

"Not an issue. I'm just sorry that you're hurting."

By the time he'd finished talking, he was helping her into a chair at a table. She stared around and realized the kitchen was more or less normal-looking. After Milo's talk about shakes and nutrients, she was scared to imagine what food Liev had come up with. "I'm just so hungry. I wonder if it's a side effect of the time-travel," she said.

"Maybe. You need food for healing." He opened a section of the wall before she had a chance to see what he'd done. "Is that a refrigerator?"

He turned to look at her. "It's a cooler. I'm not sure what a refrigerator is." He placed a clear plastic jug with eggs and something resembling cheese on the counter. Her mouth started watering. "Could I have a piece of cheese?" she asked, her voice faint with hunger.

He brought a thick slice over for her. As if he knew she had food, Charming meowed steadily from the back room. She winced, feeling guilty over her cheese. "Is there any chance you have something for him?"

He grimaced. "I don't have anything resembling cat food, but there is some ground chicken in here."

"Ha," she said. "He'd love that."

And he did.

Instead of taking the food to the pod, Liev brought Charming to the kitchen table. Charming howled pitifully the whole time. Once at the table, Lani wrapped her arms around him, trying to keep him calm until some food arrived. But he wouldn't be calmed. He definitely wasn't living up to his name.

Finally Liev brought a bowl of minced chicken over. "Will he eat it raw?"

"I think he'll eat your hand as well if you don't give that bowl to him."

Liev lowered the bowl, and Charming damn-near jumped into it. Lani was actually embarrassed. "Sorry, he's usually better mannered."

Charming stopped eating and turned to look at her.

"Get over it. I'm hungry."

Her gaze whipped to Liev to see what he thought of her cat's speaking abilities. He took a step back. Then a second step and a third, until he'd come up against the counter. His gaze went from Charming to her and back again. His face flushed red then turned pasty white with shock. He swallowed loudly several times as he stared at Charming. "Did he just talk?"

"Oh, I'm so glad you and Milo can hear him too." She grinned happily. "I was afraid I was going nuts."

Liev stared at her in shock. "Are you serious?"

"Oh, I'm serious with being happy I'm not the only one who can hear him." She leaned forward and said in a conspiratorial whisper, "He's only been able to do this since Milo's little trip. This cat could never talk before."

Charming snorted and shook his head, spraying flecks of raw chicken across the table. "Yes, I could. You couldn't hear me."

She raised one eyebrow and stared at Liev. "Is that possible?"

"What? That the cat talks? Hell no." Liev shook his head rapidly back and forth all the while staring at Charming in fascination.

Little did he know. Lani grinned, enjoying herself. "No—that I'm the one who is different? And you two are more advanced? Maybe that's why you can hear him? Or did the trip through time make him able to speak?"

"Or both. If one of you has changed in such a major way, then it's quite likely that both have." He ran his hand through his hair, leaving it looking wonderfully tousled. And, damn, she wanted to run her hands through it too. Her stomach growled again.

And didn't Charming inhale his food faster, as if he thought she would get close and eat his food?

She leaned closer on purpose. "Hey. Don't worry. I won't be eating your chicken."

"Oh, crap." Liev straightened, staring at the eggs. "I forgot about your food." He exhaled sharply. "I'll make a cheese omelet." He grabbed a bowl and cracked two eggs. His movements smooth and practiced. She liked that about him. What he did he did well – at least the little she'd seen of him.

She coughed. "Uhm, I don't suppose you could make that a big omelet, could you?"

He raised his gaze to stare at her, as if asking if she was serious. At her hopeful look, he cracked two more eggs. "I think your eyes are bigger than your stomach."

"Not a problem. I'll help her." Charming sat on the table cleaning his paws. At the odd silence in the room, he looked up to find them both staring at him. "What? I'm still hungry."

While Liev whipped up an omelet—and she was amazed to know that they were still making omelets this far in the future—she found a cloth and wiped up her cat's mess. He'd been so hungry he'd inhaled the food with the end result he'd spread it everywhere.

At least it was real food she'd be eating. She had been afraid they'd replaced food with pills. And, to a certain extent, they might have. If she could take a pill and make her stomach feel like she'd eaten a roast chicken with all the trimmings, she'd swallow a half dozen of those pills and maybe feel like she was back to normal. Right now, her toes were so empty that she was pretty damn sure she wouldn't make the walk back to the pod. Charming was obviously no better as he eyed every move Liev made with in an intensity that almost laughable. And if she had any energy to laugh, she would.

Just when she thought she'd cry from hunger, a plate was placed in front of her. The aroma hit her nose making her moan in joy. It was rich, warm, and soooo fragrant. Melted cheese filled the inside of a golden omelet. She could taste it already. Cutting up a section into small bits to cool, she forked up the first bite and closed her eyes and moaned. "Oh, that's good."

She opened her eyes to find Charming whacking at the piece closest to him. He caught it in his paws and dragged his prize toward him.

"You get that piece because you got it covered in raw chicken, but that's it. No more."

Charming ignored her as he tried to eat it, but the piece was too hot. He meowed and batted the piece a couple times, then tried to bite it. Whining, he gobbled it down anyway.

"Geez. Aren't you full yet?"

Charming stared, his gaze never lifting from her plate. "I'm hungry."

"Oh, man." She cut him another piece and slid it toward him. "That's it. The rest is mine."

She wrapped her arm around the plate protectively. She glared Charming into backing up.

Liev laughed, a refreshing, open laugh.

Lani ignored him until she'd finished every piece of omelet on her plate. Unfortunately she was still hungry. She turned woeful eyes to Liev. He stared, switched his gaze to her empty plate, then back to her face. "Really?"

She nodded. At her side Charming meowed in agreement.

"Both of us are still hungry."

Blowing out his breath, he turned to his kitchen cabinets and brought out a loaf of thick crusty bread. Her eyes lit up at the sight of it. "Now that would be great. I love bread. Not sure how Charming feels about it."

"I've got cheese to go on this." He cut two thick slabs and brought it over for her, then went back for cheese and butter. She munched happily as Charming worked through a chunk of cheese. "That feels so much better," she said when she was done.

An odd sound rang through the apartment. She stiffened. It sounded like an alarm. "Is that a fire alarm or something?"

"I don't know what it is." With a sharp look in her direction, Liev said, "Stay here. I'll be right back."

He disappeared. Lani looked at Charming, but he'd taken off. She didn't blame him. Feeling scared and hating being alone in a place she knew nothing about, she retraced her steps to the healing pod as fast as she could. And, sure enough, she found Charming hiding between the folds of a blanket inside.

"Good idea. Maybe we can hide away in here until this calms down." The noise was horrific enough to hurt her ears while in the kitchen, but, as soon as she crawled inside the pod and closed the lid, the noise disappeared. "Oh, thank heavens," she murmured as the assault on her ears stopped. Just as she started to relax, the lid lifted. Milo, his face twisted with urgency, said, "Come. You have to leave. Now."

She was dragged out of the pod. At the last moment, she snatched up Charming before she was shoved ahead of Milo. "Where are we going?" she whispered. "I have no place to go."

"Liev has a place for you. Hurry."

Within minutes, she was hustled into a room she'd never seen before in one of those weird cubes she hated and spinning at a speed her body couldn't stand—upward.

"Where's Liev?" she asked angrily.

"He's coming." Milo chewed on his fingernail and shifted on his feet anxiously.

"Not good enough. If you think to dump me somewhere and hope I'll take care of myself, you're sad—"

"Lani. I'm here." Liev appeared on the other side of the glass. Then, while she watched, the glass between them disappeared. Damn, she wished she knew how that worked. "What is going on, Liev?"

"It's a security inspection. My system warns me when trouble is coming." He pushed her ahead of him. "Milo, go back and let them in. Be natural. I'll engage stealth on the pod and the apartment."

"Got it." Milo took off.

"I don't think I like your world," she said.

Liev tugged her forward, making her hurt as she tried to move faster than she could. "Stop pulling on me."

Spinning to face her, he stopped at the look on her face. "Please hurry."

Looking at the worry in his face, she realized this was big. Dangerously big. If anything happened to separate her from Liev, she'd be lost. And with Charming having his unique ability to speak, ... he'd be taken away from her too.

Ignoring the pain, she started to run.

THANKFUL THAT LANI finally seemed to understand the urgency of the matter, Liev followed just slightly behind. He didn't want her to collapse when she ran out of energy. And, if she did, he wanted to be there to catch her.

The pod appeared to have been working as she held the pace steadily. He slipped past her to open a door. Inside was the rooftop elevator. With the three of them inside, he sent it to the top beside Johan's place. Liev kept a worried eye on Lani. She was breathing hard, and her color was pale, but she still stood.

Charming looked up at him. Liev glanced away, still not able to reconcile what he'd seen and heard. A talking cat. Holy crap. He couldn't even begin to think about the ramifications of that. If the cat talked as a result of the time-travel, Liev could just imagine what the scientists would say. And what they'd want to do to Lani's pet.

It would be disastrous for society at large.

And this feline gave him the creeps. Those huge golden eyes seemed to see into his soul. And who was to say the cat didn't? If it could talk, what else could it do? Liev shuddered inwardly. He really didn't want to know.

At the rooftop, he could hear loud music at Johan's. Should they blend into one of his constant parties or try for the private rooftop garden that, in theory, the others didn't know about? The only problem was that the garden was damn small. It was a space he used when he needed a few moments away from everything. It would be a tight squeeze for the two of them. And he was almost looking forward to that.

His gaze caught sight of Charming.

Okay, the three of them.

But, given the sudden raised voices at Johan's and the now silent music, Liev would take a squeeze over trouble. Lani couldn't be seen yet. He led the way quietly around the rooftop garden to the back maintenance section. Slipping around several large vents, he stepped out onto his tiny private deck.

Lani gasped and spun around. "Oh my! You can see the whole city from here."

He smiled. "Not quite. I do like to come up here though. It's pretty spectacular." Liev stood by Lani's side. "I guess this doesn't look like what you are used to?"

She stood, shocked, and stared out at the city. It was a replay of what she'd first seen after escaping the office. And more—so much more. Oddly shaped dome buildings that stretched out as far as she could see. Gemstone colors glowed off the sides of some walls with multiple green spots dotting the area ... And the air traffic? ... She shuddered at what appeared to be loads of air traffic. Her gaze flitted from one thing to another. "It's beautiful," she said, "but it's so, ... so ... foreign-looking."

"In what way?" Liev asked, looking at her.

"It's surreal, like a science fiction movie set. Foreign. Alien." She shifted Charming in her arms. "It's nothing like what I'd expected. Huge buildings in weird shapes and colors and lights. The way vehicles move. In my time we still drove on paved roads that were on the ground ..." She shrugged. "It's just so bizarre to think that I'm actually here."

Liev grinned. "It is. Don't tell Milo, but it's also great."

She stared at him. "We'll see. That he managed to do what he did is pretty amazing. I'm not sure I appreciate it still, but I do understand the genius required to make this happen."

Liev stood in front of Lani. "You aren't afraid of heights, are you?"

She shook her head. "I'm fine," she murmured. "It is

pretty spectacular. Scary but beautiful."

"It is." He glanced around. "It's also private."

"I presume we're hiding here until it's safe to go home again?" At his nod, she rubbed her temple. "It's because of me, isn't it?"

"In a way. You don't have ID or tags. If anyone were to find out about you at this stage …"

Liev hated to admit that the government was corrupt and getting worse every day. He'd love to reassure Lani that this world wasn't worse than the one she'd left. But it would be hard to find proof of that.

Still, her world wasn't perfect either. And, as long as one kept a low profile in his world, everything would be fine. Most people never had any run-ins with the authorities, and life continued in an easy way.

If Liev didn't have Milo to contend with, Liev's life probably would have been easy too.

"How long do you think it will take? I'm getting tired," she asked. And, for the first time since they arrived, he took a good look at her. She'd slumped against the wall, and her color had all but disappeared. She appeared to be doing a long slow slide to the ground. She pressed her lips together and shifted the huge cat in her arms again.

"Do you want to sit down?"

She looked around. "There isn't a place to, is there?"

"On the floor."

His comp emitted a *beep*. He pulled it out and smiled. "That's Milo. All clear. The suits came. They visited with him, asked a few questions, got a few answers, and now they've left." He smiled. "Hopefully satisfied enough that they won't be back."

Lani smiled. "Good. Let's go."

"Not so fast." Liev clicked through his comp, searching his security readouts to make sure his place was empty. It appeared to be. He did a search throughout the building. Checking for an anomaly, something else that was illegal. A few people were in the building, and, like Johan, most had secrets. Authorities were not welcome here. Liev checked his wrist unit. "This building is supposed to be exempt from those raids. Lord knows we pay enough for that, but we still seem to have one or two a year." He looked up. "Okay, it looks good."

"Going back the same way?" Lani asked, heading toward the corner.

"Yes, but slowly. Just in case."

They made their way back to the rooftop elevator. Loud music was once again blasting from Johan's place. If it weren't for Lani, Liev would suggest they blend into the festivities. But, with the cat and her current level of exhaustion, she'd stand out as new and different. It also wasn't safe to bring her into a social situation yet. She needed to learn more about this world.

Within seconds, they were in the elevator and scooting back to his floor. He led the way home, and, as soon as they were inside, he set up stealth mode again. As far as anyone outside this place would know, the place was empty. There would be no power readings, water usage, lights, or heat showing up on scans. It was about all he could do. And, considering Milo, it wasn't enough. But it was more than most had. Liev walked into the kitchen and set up the coffee. When he turned, two sets of eyes stared at him. Fatigue in both but also hope. He was stumped. He tilted his head and asked, "What do you want?"

Lani grimaced. Charming had no such problem stating his need. "*Foood.*"

CHAPTER 10

LANI WATCHED THE shock settle on Liev's face. "Sorry, but I'm hungry again too. All I want to do is eat and sleep."

He shook his head and motioned to the bread still on the table. "I have some cooked meat in here somewhere." He turned to rummage in the cooler.

After placing Charming on the kitchen table, back where he'd been sitting earlier, Lani picked up the knife and started cutting the bread. Milo walked into the kitchen and stared at her.

"See? I told you shakes would be better," Milo said. "Her body needs nutrients. She'll need a lot of food to make up for what she could get in a vitamin drink."

"If that's the case," Lani said, "a shake and food would work. Just a shake, no way."

Behind her, Liev said, "That's actually a good idea, Milo. Make them a booster. Get the data from the pod, and fix one for each."

Charming, staring at the bread in her hand as she buttered it, asked, "What's a booster?"

"A shot of vitamins in this case, to help your bodies adapt," Milo said.

"Ah. So food." Satisfied, he sat back and watched every move she made.

"If possible, Milo," Lani said, "could you make Charming a very small booster portion with cream as a base? He's not likely to drink anything else."

Charming nodded. "Cream. Cream is good."

"Cream is not good for you. It's fat. And not a good fat." Milo made a disgusted sound. "It's awful, and it will kill you." He stalked off in the direction of the pod.

Lani turned to look at Liev, who appeared to be slicing a hunk of meat. She just didn't know what kind it was. And she hated to ask. She was so hungry that, if it was cloned, she probably wouldn't care. Tomorrow was a different story. "Milo has strong views, doesn't he?"

Liev looked up with a smile. "Always has. Not to worry. He has a big weakness for chocolate." At her surprised look, Liev's grin widened. "Makes him seem more human, doesn't it?"

"What about your parents? Are they alive? Live close by?"

He stacked the meat up on a plate and brought it to the table. "They died when Milo was little. I've been looking after him for a long time."

"That must have been tough." She couldn't imagine. She'd had a hard enough time looking after herself. She'd had parents, though they'd never been close. And now ... she stared down at her bread. She hadn't spoken to them in over five years. Would they even know she'd disappeared?

She asked, "Is there a way to research the people who lived in my time?"

"There is. The record-keeping of today is something quite different than in your time. So you'd need training, but we can certainly do that. You'll need to learn our way of life. In fact, I had considered taking you to Johan's while we were up top, but I figured you'd need to familiarize yourself a little more with our ways before socializing."

She stared at him. Took a bite of bread and meat and chewed. Her mind reeled with the implications of all she'd have to learn. The pitfalls waiting for her. She swallowed.

"I can't imagine." A shudder slipped down her spine. "It's hardly like visiting a foreign place."

"That's exactly what it is." He dropped a piece of meat in front of Charming to go with the other pieces already lined up. Charming showed no sign of slowing down or being distracted from his food. "You'll be fine. There are a lot of things to learn, but it could be worse."

She stopped and stared. "In what way?"

"We all speak English."

He had a point.

Milo returned with a large glass of something fuchsia pink and a small bowl of something much less bright. He placed the glass in front of her and set the cream in front of Charming.

Charming asked, "What is it?"

"Cream," Lani said helpfully. "Their version here. Try it. So far you've eaten everything else."

He sighed, leaned in, and sniffed. "Doesn't smell like cream."

Feeling like she was enticing a two-year-old to eat his spinach, she said, "It will be good. Besides, it's to make us feel better. To help us heal."

He looked over at her, his huge golden eyes staring at her, unblinking. "Then you try it."

She should have seen that one coming. Shooting Charming a disgusted look, she picked up her glass of pink drink, took a deep breath, and swallowed a big gulp. And felt her throat close and her eyes water. She gasped for a breath, desperate to keep her reaction minimal as Charming watched her with a smug look.

"It's different. Hot almost. Definitely different." She gave Charming an encouraging smile. "Try it."

"Yours is much stronger than his, as you are bigger, and the damage to your system is a little more extensive." Milo slumped at the far side of the table, a glass of something rich and creamy with a light green tinge to it in his hand. He held up his drink. "Mine is an everyday dose, whereas yours is intensive."

"I'll say," she muttered. With a grimace, she picked it up again. Resisting the urge to plug her nose so she couldn't taste the drink, she downed it in one gulp. It was the only way she would get it down. She just hoped it would stay there.

She placed the empty glass on the counter and gave Charming a fat grin. "Your turn."

He glared at her, then at her glass, before slowly approaching his bowl, nose first. He sniffed several times, then reached out and licked several times. And missed the cream each time.

"Oh, no, you don't. You drink it all up, just like I had to." And she hoped she'd never have to again. She leaned in closer and watched as Charming tried again. This time he got some of the pink stuff and froze. He licked his lips several times and said in surprise, "Hey, it's good." He lowered his head and lapped at the cream.

"Damn. How come his tastes decent, and mine is so strong I feel like puking?"

"Yours had to be stronger." Liev stood, walked to a cupboard, and pulled out a glass. He held it to a wall, and it filled automatically. She hadn't even noticed a spout. He brought it back to her. "Plain water."

She reached for it and drank the whole thing, then held it out, asking for more.

"Wow, she drinks like she eats. Told you she'd be perfect for you." Milo grinned up at his brother.

Liev quietly brought a second glass of water back to her. Then carried on out of the room.

She accepted it and turned to Milo. "Did I hear you right?" Lani asked, a new hardness, coldness in her voice.

Charming sat back and stared at Milo. "Ha. You are so going to get it now."

Milo took another sip of his drink. He shrugged his shoulders nonchalantly. "What's the problem? I said he'd like you. So what's the big deal?"

She stood. "Did you actually go back in time … to snag me … for your brother?"

LIEV WAS ABOUT to join them again when he heard Lani's question. And he really wanted to hear his brother answer that. He stepped up to the doorway and listened.

Milo's face twisted at Lani's words, like he'd sucked on a grapefruit. Lani eyed him suspiciously. "You did, didn't you?"

He shrugged and stared at his drink.

"Why me?" It seemed that was the burning question in her mind. Like, how had he come to choose her? Then it was a good question. Liev wanted to know the answer too. His brother had gone to a lot of trouble but why her?

"I had to find a target, … er, … a person to use for the experiment. Liev has horrible taste in women." He gave an exaggerated shudder and a quick sidelong glance at his brother. "So I figured I could do two things at once. Find a lovely woman for him, add a few enhancements, and try out my experiment at the same time."

Liev winced. Is that what Milo thought of his girl-friends? While he mulled over the pathetic state of affairs, Lani spoke up.

"Enhancements?" she asked in a low dark tone of voice.

Milo shrugged. "That part didn't work out the way I expected it to."

"In what way?" Liev spoke from the doorway. It was the first he'd heard anything about enhancements. "What did you do? You never mentioned enhancements before. What kind of enhancements?"

"Hey." Milo held out his hands defensively. "I was just enhancing her communication abilities."

Liev stared at him in shock. "Why?"

"Because you're deep, man. You like to talk. You like to communicate. I figured, if she wasn't much of a communicator, that could be easily enhanced."

Somewhere in the background, as Liev tried to work his way through the maze of thoughts crowding his brain, he heard laughter. As in maniacal, off-the-wall laughter. He stared at Lani.

She was bent over, and damned if tears weren't rolling down her cheeks.

Liev waited. Charming reached out and smacked her with a paw. She appeared to slow down after that. Finally she choked back the last of her giggles.

"Care to explain?" Liev asked.

She took a deep sobering breath, wiped her eyes, and pointed at Charming. "Milo's enhancement did work. It worked on Charming. He's the one who got the gift of communication. He can talk now..." She giggled again. "Thank God, Milo didn't add bigger boobs or something just as ridiculous. Imagine how Charming would look then."

"Really?" Charming sniffed the air. "That would be preposterous."

The two men stared at her, then at Charming.

"You were supposed to come alone," Milo said slowly, staring in fascination at the cat. He opened his mouth, as if to add something, then closed it, and just shook his head. "And I thought that enhancement was minor for your body size, but if they, … it …" he corrected quickly, catching Liev's attention for a moment, adding, "went to him, … considering *his* size, … it would almost make sense." He slumped down on the closest chair. "Wow. Just like, … wow."

There was a long silence while everyone stared at Charming.

He preened.

Lani couldn't believe it.

"Those must be some enhancements," she murmured.

He wondered briefly what the enhancements would have done for her. Then again there was no going back to find out. He then returned his attention to Milo. "There are a couple other problems with your logic."

Milo raised an eyebrow.

"Of course there are." Lani shook her head, her face twisting in disbelief, as if overwhelmed at the casualness of his actions. "First off, what if you did choose the perfect partner for Liev and destroyed her in the process?"

Milo blinked.

She snorted.

Such a thought hadn't even occurred to Liev. And he didn't want to consider it now. "Did you even think about failure?"

Milo laughed. "No. Nothing is a failure in life. There are just times where I've learned something didn't work. And, if this didn't work, no one would know. You'd have just been vaporized or something."

"And what if only half of me made it?" She felt sick inside. "What if, only from the belly up, I lay in a gory pool of blood on your floor?" she asked in an ominous voice.

Milo's skin took on a greenish tinge. Then his lips twitched. "Nah. It was either all of you or none of you."

"And how could you know I wasn't some serial killer you were bringing for your brother?"

He grinned. "We have all kinds of DNA markers for that sort of thing. Serial killer material you're not. You actually pick up spiders and put them outside so they don't die."

She frowned, a little weirded out that he knew that about her. "But I won't touch them with my hands."

He laughed at that. "See? That's perfect. Caring but careful."

"And a personality profile?" she asked. "No way you could have done one of those on me. Not when I lived hundreds of years ago."

"We have advanced profile markers for many traits today. Sure, it was a gamble, but you had the same general look that Liev loved, and you fit the other parameters I needed, so it was a good gamble." He straightened. "And you're here all in one piece, so it's time to move on."

Move on? What did that mean? She tilted her head. "Move on?"

"Time to adjust. Time to adapt. Time to deal." Milo leveled a look her way. "This is your life now."

He turned and sauntered in that casual no responsibility, no regret manner of his.

Liev moved closer noting the pale color of her skin, the slight stoop to her shoulders. "Time to go back into the pod. Tomorrow could be stressful."

"More than my life already is?" She made a choked sound half laughter and half protest. But her gaze stared up at him hoping he'd brush it off as a minor visit.

He couldn't lie to her. Tomorrow was important and likely to be difficult. "Unfortunately"—his face turned grim—"yes."

CHAPTER 11

B ACK IN THE pod, the lid closed encasing the two of them in warm healing waves, Lani and Charming slept, woke, and slept some more. When Liev walked in the next morning, she felt much better. Until he said her specialist was here. He dropped a stack of clothes on the bed and walked out.

Like, what the hell was a specialist here? It's not like he said what kind of specialist. And why was he *hers*?

She frowned at Liev's retreating back but struggled upright, gasping at the lingering aches and pains. She hated to leave the warm coziness of the pod but it's not as if Liev had given her a choice. She was sure if she didn't get out, he'd return and help her out himself.

"I'll be there in a minute," she called out as she stumbled to the bathroom. She took a few precious moments to wash up and try to run her fingers through her hair. Once back into her room, she dressed in the unusual but cool clothing. That they fit like a glove was a little disconcerting. How had Liev known her size? Still, they looked good on her. She smoothed her fingers over the silky black material of the cropped top, loving the exotic feel. It met the half skirt along the back of the shorts and it was like nothing she'd ever seen before. Then neither were the interesting gemlike diamonds decorating the top. The shorts were knee length and were closer to capri leggings if she wanted something to compare them too. The skirt went down her legs but only along the back and sides. And the material ... she'd never felt anything like it before.

Liev had left two small pieces of material that looked like ballet slippers but again so soft she didn't know if they were meant to wear outside or were meant as slippers only. She slipped her foot into the first one and moaned as it wrapped about her foot in a warm soft yet perfect fitting slipper. Smiling in delight she slipped the other midnight blue slipper on, realizing they matched her clothing. Did everything here match naturally? Could the colors of the clothing change? 'Cause now that would be beyond cool.

She made her way down the hallway, doing a quick twirl to watch the skirt flare out. Nice. She grinned. Not only that, she was grateful that, although hungry, she didn't feel like she would die anytime soon. Staying in the pod appeared to be the best answer. Besides it had become a warm nest she felt safe in. Too bad she had to leave it now.

She walked into the kitchen. As she caught sight of the stranger, her breath lodged at the back of her throat, her steps slowing. Two hundred years into the future made no difference here. There was a specific look to those who walked the shady side of life. A thinness to his lips and thickness to his brow, but it was that flat gaze that clinched it.

Not saying anything, he motioned at her to sit down. She glanced at Liev, uncertain. Immediately he stepped closer and motioned to the chair, a gentle smile on his face. "Sit, Lani. It will be over in a moment."

Uncertain but willing, she took her place. And waited. Behind her, the specialist unpacked a bag and lay items out on the counter.

She looked at Liev and whispered, "Will it hurt?"

He shrugged, his gaze on the man behind her. "Maybe a little. You can go back into the pod afterward."

Lani twisted around, but the specialist showed no signs of hearing their conversation. Considering he hadn't said a word yet, he might be a deaf mute. She turned back and waited.

She shifted restlessly when nothing happened after several moments. She twisted around again to see what the stranger was doing, but this time Liev stepped in her line of sight. She glared at him. Just then the specialist stepped forward and grabbed her arm. He searched the soft tissue above her wrist, the rough skin of his fingers almost scratching hers. After a moment, he dropped her hand and checked the other one.

She frowned. "Anything wrong?"

He never said a word and just returned behind her. She opened her mouth to speak again when Liev picked up her hand and pressed her fingers into the same place on his wrist. And she felt some hard material inside.

Her gaze widened in fear as she understood. This specialist now knew she didn't have one. Her mouth fell open, and she leaned in close. "But now he knows."

Liev nodded, bent lower, and, with his lips against her ears, murmured, "He's here to give you one."

"But isn't that dangerous? For you?"

"More for you. Don't say anything more to him. Cry if you need to. The pod will fix any damage afterward."

"Oh, God, it'll hurt, won't it?" And her heart started to race. She clenched her fists. She was such a baby with pain. Tears burned in the back of her eyes. She couldn't do this.

As if understanding, Liev crouched down beside her, wrapped an arm around her shoulders and squeezed gently. "Easy."

She swallowed hard. She had no choice. She had to have whatever that thing was that Liev had. She couldn't even ask for details without letting the specialist know the extent of her ignorance. And that would only bring more questions. And more problems. She hated the subterfuge, the necessary lies. She'd never been at any good at those. She'd be sure to mess up one time.

Not to mention the way words tended to blurt from her mouth without warning.

Liev massaged her shoulders, making her realize she'd frozen in place, her muscles locking down.

Just when the wait seemed interminable, the specialist walked over again—holding a gun of some kind in his hands. She gasped in shock, and Liev gripped her shoulders—not quite forcing her to stay in place but letting her know he could if needed.

She didn't want to watch what happened so she kept her gaze forward. The stranger snagged her arm and turned her hand palm up.

Something cold was placed against her skin.

She closed her eyes and held her breath.

There was a hard pinch, then nothing. She frowned. Was that it? All that worry over nothing. Just as the thought filtered through her brain, her head lolled to one side, and she blacked out.

LIEV LET HIS breath escape slowly when Lani's head drooped to the side.

"Hold her still," the stranger snapped.

Liev grabbed her shoulders to stop her from slumping in the chair, then slid his arm under her head, his other arm wrapping around her ribs to hold her still. "I've got her. Go ahead."

The specialist nodded and proceeded to do the quick laser surgery to open her wrist. Liev knew he was taking a chance doing this. At birth, newborns were tagged within the first hour of life. When they hit sixteen, the tags were switched to the ones they'd have for the rest of their lives.

At birth, it was easier as the bones and tissues were soft, pliant. The initial tags were easily replaced as the body was already well accustomed to their presence. Lani had never had a foreign object implanted under her skin, as her computer scan had confirmed at Johan's place. Her nerves were fully grown. Any damage at this stage and she could lose the use of her hand. Scar tissue was yet another problem. He could only hope to get this over with and to get her back into the pod quickly. It should mitigate the damage to this morning's surgery—if nothing went majorly wrong.

He watched the man work fast and efficiently. When Lani's wrist was opened, Liev had to look away. There was little blood with the high-intensity laser but holy crap ... He gritted his teeth, and, unable to help himself, he dropped a kiss on her head. After another long moment, he risked a second look at the surgery, relieved to see the tag lying nestled in her muscles. The blood loss was minimal so hopefully the after effects would be too. He could only wonder how her body would adapt to such a thing at her age. His society had been using ID implants for a long time. They appeared to be the answer. They couldn't be lost, transferred, or stolen. When surgically removed from the body, an alert was automatically sent to the Registrar.

"Will this work?" Liev asked. At least the specialist appeared to be competent.

He nodded. "Should."

"It's registered?" He couldn't help asking questions. If this didn't work, Lani's life was in danger. And that was unacceptable.

The specialist nodded again. "It is. When I get this closed up, I'll start the programming."

Ah. Right. The whole computer world that his society ran off of. Lani had to be included, or else she'd always be an outsider. A fugitive. And that would be very difficult. Fringe groups were in his world, as have been in every century. They lived free of the government restrictions and regulations but barely eked out a living, always on the run from the military. He sighed, staring at the gentle soul in his arms. She didn't deserve that. She didn't deserve any of this. She'd been the innocent victim in all of this, and honestly she'd taken what had happened with a grace that continually surprised him. He didn't think he'd be as half as accepting if he'd gone through what she had.

"Done."

Liev looked up, relief flooding through him. "Are you?" He studied Lani's wrist. The laser had closed the wound. It was red and puffy but surprisingly healthy looking. The man waved a healing wand over it, and that improved the look of the skin again. Liev exhaled. "Will she be in pain when she wakes up?"

The specialist shrugged. "It's possible. The body needs time to adapt. Her wrist will ache. The fingers could go numb off and on and could potentially swell."

All things the pod could help her with, so it was minor

in the scheme of things that could go wrong. The specialist stood and collected his instruments. He repacked his bag, then opened a side pouch, and removed a comp unlike anything Liev had seen before. The man pulled a chair forward and sat down. Using an odd-looking antenna, he angled the comp so it faced Lani's wrist. He clicked a few buttons, and a series of lights under her skin lit up. Liev's eyebrows shot up. He hadn't realized how much programming went into this.

But the stranger seemed to relax into his chair now that he realized the system was active. He bent his head and worked his thumbs on the keyboard. The lights on Lani's wrist continued to beep and flash, then settled down to a steady pulse.

Liev looked at his own wrist. There were no lights. No beeps. Not now. But, if he bought anything, a series of lights appeared at his wrist as the exchange system went through its security checks. He wondered how long this would take and how much information he'd need to give to make Lani a history. She had to have a full background for the databases to be happy.

He waited quietly for the stranger to work.

The man looked up. "Her name?"

"Lani Summerland."

The stranger keyed it in. Without looking up, he asked for her birth date.

Doing the math quickly from the little he knew, Liev picked July first, twenty-four years earlier.

There were several other questions, like gender, which he could easily answer. Then came the harder ones. Family history. He stalled. He could give Lani's real parents' names. He'd seen their names in Milo's file, but he had no dates for them. He gave up their names willingly enough and waited, hoping more wasn't required.

"We'll put down that the records were destroyed in the Felonia Crash, shall we?"

Relief washed through Liev. So much information had been lost in that disaster. It was the perfect answer. And he realized that excuse had likely saved a lot of people. No records meant create your own and that was exactly what he needed to do right now. "That works."

The specialist switched to a series of questions about her medical history. He, of course, had no idea, but the pods hadn't found anything major, so he presumed she had none. At least as far as the database was concerned, she was incredibly healthy.

He had no idea what other information was being placed in Lani's fake background. And he didn't care as long as it was neutral and wouldn't raise any flags if checked. She needed to have flaws, just not big ones.

A few more questions followed about her education and schools. Not knowing many, he used the same schools that he'd gone to and gave her a degree in IT systems. At least he could train her for that. And, since so many people had a similar education, it was a common course for her to have completed.

Then finally it was done. Lani was a single orphaned female, twenty-four, educated, healthy.

The specialist said, "Last section. We have to connect to her financial information."

Liev nodded, ready for this. Last night, when he realized what this process would mean, he'd opened some accounts under Lani's name. He punched in his access code on his comp, then brought up the account. With a few swift clicks,

Lani was connected to the credit system of his times to her implant. He'd transferred a moderate chunk of money to help her get established but not enough to raise any alarms. He had no idea what she would need over the next year, and he knew he'd use what money he had to make her life as good as he could make it.

That was the least he could do.

But she'd need so much more. He couldn't even think of how much she had to learn. She was going to need special training to understand their technological world. She'd need history lessons so she could even hold a conversation with others and not give herself away. And that was just the tip of the iceberg. She had a million minefields yawning under her – their – feet.

The specialist packed up the comp and closed his bag. He turned to Liev and held out a porter. Liev stilled. This would be the first time he would see the price for Lani's tagging. He reached for it, took a look, schooled his features to not react, then held the unit to his own wrist and pushed the buttons, allowing the payment from his account. He wanted to laugh at the mockery of the company name on the specialist's bill. Liev had just paid for cosmetic upgrades for Lani. How true. It would be hard to consider any other body modification that would match this expense.

When it was completed, he handed the unit back to the specialist, who nodded, put it in his pocket, and proceeded to walk out of the apartment.

Feeling odd, yet relieved about the whole thing, Liev reengaged stealth mode on the apartment. A part of him wondered if he wouldn't be better off relocating so as not to be found again.

He'd paid the bill. But he'd also opened himself to potential blackmail in the future. And Lani, now safe from the government, was in danger from the very men who'd helped save her. There was one other thing he could do to protect her—but it was a last resort. And it would involve his family. He wasn't quite ready for that step yet.

His mind raced for ways to protect them both. She moaned just then, and he realized she needed the pod. He could work out the rest of the details later. Surely Milo could find something on these men to help balance the scales.

When both sides had secrets to hide, the playing field was leveled.

And that would be best.

But first he had to see to Lani's care.

CHAPTER 12

L ANI WOKE TO tears rolling down her cheeks. She tried to swipe them away and cried out, instinctively cradling her sore hand to her chest. It took her moment to settle the pain and realize she was being carried in strong arms again. A protective and caring set of arms. Liev.

"Easy, Lani. It's over." Liev's comforting voice washed over her.

She tried to understand what was going on. Liev was speaking, but she didn't understand what he was saying.

"I'm taking you back to the pod. After an hour in there, you'll feel much better."

The pod. Healing. Her sore wrist.

Then her memories came rushing back. That stranger— her specialist—and him picking up her wrist. She didn't know what he did to her but whatever it was had knocked her out. Or ... she'd passed out. That would be a bit much as she'd never fainted in her life. Considering the pain she was currently in, major fainting had been the easy answer.

For some reason, this injury, this injustice was done in an attempt to make everything right ... had become the last straw.

Maybe because she was tired, maybe because she hurt so, and maybe it was just because it had all become too much, but, once she started crying, she couldn't stop the tears.

"It'll be all right, Lani," Liev's worried voice whispered in her ear. "I'm so sorry we had to do this."

"It's all right," she sobbed as the tears poured out. "It's not your fault."

"And yet it is." He sighed as they entered the pod room. "Milo is my brother, and he brought you here for me. I certainly didn't ask him to do this, but, because of his actions, your life has been ruined."

They entered the small room and he shifted her in his arms. He laid her down in the pod. She moaned as her wrist was jostled.

"I'm so sorry," Liev said. The pain in his voice was so evident that she wanted to reassure him it was fine—only it wasn't fine. Her wrist throbbed with pain such as she had never felt before. Charming meowed and shifted to lie at her feet. She wiggled her toes against his thick fur, loving that he was here with her.

"I am too," she whispered, lying back and shuddering. "I had no idea it would hurt this much."

"It shouldn't," Liev said quietly. "He gave you some-thing for the pain, but I'm not sure your body can handle the drugs of today."

Not a nice thought. She wasn't sure she could handle much of his world that she'd seen so far. "The pod might help." She curled into a ball, her injured arm lying on her side so that the pod's rays could gain clear access. She closed her eyes, tears still leaking through and took several calming breaths.

"I'll go mix a pain cocktail." He lowered the pod lid. "I'll be back in a moment."

She could hear his footsteps retreating. Thank God. She was set to have a royal bawl but hadn't wanted to while in his arms. She'd been holding back, but, now that she was alone, the sobs rolled free. Everything hurt, and it seemed like her life was the absolute worst it could be. She cried and cried, letting the tears and the stress and the pain drain from her overwhelmed system.

She'd always been proud of her ability to adapt. Her ability to stand up tall and weather the storms around her with grace and acceptance. She wasn't sure she could in this situation. She would try hard, but, damn, this was a mind-bender to set anyone off-balance. Oddly enough, by the time she stopped bawling, she felt better. Just to let go like that had helped her ease back the stress levels.

Sure, her wrist still hurt, but the coiled sense of being too full, too hurt, too … whatever, was gone. She let the last of the sobs hiccup out before she took several deep breaths.

"Are you okay now?"

Liev's worried voice came from the open doorway.

Damn. She sniffled back the last bit of the tears. "Sorry," she whispered, her voice thick and ragged, still clogged with tears. She knew her face would be red and puffy. She could only hope he didn't open the pod. She didn't want him to see her this way.

At the reminder of the pod, she brightened. Maybe it could heal her puffiness at the same time as it worked to heal the time-travel damage. She turned slightly so her face was directly under the pod's flashing lights. She didn't know if it made a difference, but her skin immediately started to lose the tight hot sensation.

"Don't be." Liev stood there beside her and lifted the pod's lid. "You've been through a lot."

She rolled her face into the blanket. It was an instinctive, yet childish reaction.

"Hey, don't do that," he whispered softly. "You don't ever need to hide from me."

That surprised a laugh out of her. "Sorry, I just know what I look like after I've been crying."

"Crying is a great way to release all that pent-up emotion. If anyone has the right to feel overwhelmed, it's you." He smiled down at her. "Give yourself a break. I think you've done wonderfully well."

In a surprising move, he lay down beside her in the pod and tugged her into his arms. Was he for real? Could any guy be this good? Or was it the men of this century? Because, if so, then wow!

And inexplicably, his acceptance brought on more waterworks.

Through her gentle sobs, Lani heard Liev's distressed voice. "Please don't cry, Lani. We'll make it work out. I'm so sorry Milo did this, but I promise, ... I'll do what I can to make it as good as I can. This really is a wondrous time to be alive. There are so many marvelous things I want to show you."

He kept talking and murmuring gently as if the sheer mass of words would help calm her down.

It was working. She wiped her eyes, surprised to find the pod had adapted its size to accommodate the two of them. Truly many innovative things were here. And somehow Charming had taken the opportunity to leave. And maybe it was time she stopped being such a wet dishrag and realized what an opportunity she had.

"I'm sorry," she whispered, though he'd told her not to be sorry. "I don't normally cry like this."

"It's like the physical effect on your body. There has to be some kind of emotional reaction too. Tears only make sense." He smiled at her. And damn if she wasn't starting to like that smile. A little too much. He had wormed his way into her heart. She really wanted him in her life.

She snuggled in closer and sighed happily. Maybe life wasn't so rotten after all.

He dropped a kiss on the top of her head. She smiled. He really was a protector. Another kiss landed on her side of her head. She shifted slightly at the same time he slid down a little, and she found herself staring into his eyes. Huge, deeply magnetic purple eyes. Like, how could that be? She so wanted eyes like that. Just gazing into them made her insides melt.

A tiny sigh escaped. He was so damn beautiful.

His eyes darkened.

She caught her breath.

Then he lowered his head ... and kissed her.

THE SWEETNESS OF her lips disarmed him and made the next kiss inevitable. His lips moved gently on hers. Tasting, exploring, feeling a response that set his pulse pounding. He deepened the kiss, needing more. Needing to know she wanted more.

That she wanted him.

Like he wanted her. He couldn't believe how much. He hadn't even known of her existence a few days ago, and it galled him to think his brother had found her and had retrieved her for him. Even worse to know that Milo had been right—she did look perfect for him—at least at first glance.

She twisted beneath him, her feet sliding up his calf, hooking under his pant leg and stroking his skin. He shuddered, sliding his hand around her back and down across her bare midriff. He'd chosen the clothes without realizing how sexy they'd look on her. Small and delicate, the clothing looked like they'd been created with her in mind. Add her almost ash-blond hair, and she looked like a slave girl from centuries ago.

He paused. She *was* from centuries ago.

She moved, twisting her body until his hand rested just below her chest. His breath caught in the back of his throat. As if his hand had a life of its own, his long fingers smoothed upward to cover her small rounded breast.

She gasped and arched into his hand.

He bent his head and lapped at the pouting nipple through the soft-as-silk material.

Her moan turned to a groan, and she shuddered.

God, he shouldn't be doing this.

It wasn't fair.

She needed to heal.

She didn't know what she was doing.

She couldn't know what she was doing.

She was dependent on him.

It was too fast.

She needed more time.

Argh. He pulled back, panting. "No," he groaned in a harsh whisper. "You're hurt."

"I'm hurting," she corrected. "And it'll hurt more if you don't kiss me again."

He raised himself higher so he could look into her blue eyes. "Are you sure?"

Her gaze widened. "I get that you're thinking of me. Giving me a chance to change my mind. But ..." She arched her back, brushing her breasts sinuously against his chest.

"Unless you've done away with sex in your time …"

"Lord, no." His voice was filled with desire, and he lowered his head again. This time, he held nothing back. He wanted her, and he wanted her to know how much. All the reasons why this wasn't a good idea no longer mattered.

He wanted to show her how much he cared. To show her how good this could be between them. Instead it seemed like his fingers were all thumbs, and his normal suave skill had taken a hike. He was considered a skilled lover. But today, with her, it mattered too much, and he couldn't seem to get it right. And she didn't appear to notice.

He was all heat. Animal passion. And raw need.

He couldn't get enough of her.

CHAPTER 13

LANI COULDN'T THINK. She didn't want to try. Sensations rolled through her, lighting nerve endings, sparking a hunger she hadn't expected. Her body shifted restlessly, rolling from side to side, following his touch. Needing his touch, needing his kisses, needing ... everything.

"Lani? Are you sure?"

She stilled. Her eyelids drifted open, the haze of desire parting just enough for a little comprehension to slip in. She stared up into his deep purple eyes. She wanted him. Did it matter that she barely knew him? Not right now. Did it matter the circumstances of how they came together? Not when she already knew him better than she'd known his ancestor.

Liev had shown heart in a tough situation. He came from a position of caring. He'd shelled out a lot of money to help her, and he'd been looking after his incorrigible brother since forever.

She'd enjoy getting to know him better, but she already knew everything that counted.

She felt him pull back, withdrawing. Shit, she'd taken too long.

"Yes," she whispered, her gaze deepening. "I'm sure."

He stilled, then shifted, searching her eyes. Whatever he

saw made his own warm, deepen. He smiled tenderly. "Good."

And he lowered his head. This time nothing was hesitant about his touch. He stroked her breasts, cupping them to explore their weight, brushing the hard pebbles with his thumb. As she shivered uncontrollably beneath him, he learned her body with sure strokes, stopping when something fascinated him before carrying on to the next spot. She cried out, wanting the same freedom to touch him, but every time she reached for him, he shifted back or did something else to drive her crazy.

"Just lie back. Relax," he whispered.

"Only if I get my turn later," she murmured.

Deep dark laughter filled the pod as he said, "My pleasure."

She smiled and stretched out beneath him, her arms above her head, letting him do as he will.

And he took full advantage. He slipped her top over her head to toss on the floor beside them. His breath caught in the back of his throat as he stared down at her breasts.

She gave a catlike smile and arched upward.

He bent to take one pouting nipple into his mouth and suckled.

A deep, pulling sensation started in her lower belly.

Liev stroked down her ribs to rest at her tiny waist, his fingers flaring out to wrap around the swell of her hips.

She felt a shudder run through him. Lifting one foot, she stroked up and down his leg. "Aren't you wearing a few too many clothes for this activity?"

A wicked grin crossed his features. He slipped out from under the pod lid and stripped efficiently. She watched as his shirt went flying to the left, and his pants and boxers dropped—oh, nice—where he stood. If he had socks on, she didn't know or care. She was fascinated as he stood proudly in front of her, fully erect.

She pushed the lid of the pod up higher and patted the bed beside her. Instead he leaned over, slipped his fingers under the waistband of her half-shorts, half-skirt ensemble, and slowly removed everything, even her panties.

She lay under the glowing pod's healing rays and stretched under his heated gaze. While he stared, she whispered, "Are you planning on just looking?" Her voice husky and deep. "Or will you join me again?"

He walked to the end of the bed, grabbed her ankles, and gave a tug. She slid, legs open, all the way down until the heart of her was pressed up against him, with her legs wrapped around his hips.

She laughed. "Nice."

He grinned and tugged her upright until she was seated. She wrapped her arms around his neck and kissed him. His lips opened, his tongue wrangling softly with hers.

Swiftly he built up the heat between them, his hands restlessly stroking her body while his tongue drove her crazy. He slipped his hands down to her hips and held her firm.

And plunged deep into her center.

She gasped and arched. Shifting to ease the unexpected fullness, she wrapped her legs around his waist and tightened her inner muscles.

It was his turn to groan. Slowly he withdrew, paused, only to plunge back in deeper. He ground his hips tightly against her for a long moment, then started to move. His rhythm took over her thoughts and mind as he drove her quickly to the edge.

She cried out, "Liev!"

"I'm here. Fly with me." He grabbed her hands and stretched them above her head again. He kissed her hard and plunged inside once more.

His guttural groan sounded above her. Then a kaleidoscope of sensations exploded inside her, overwhelming and filling her, but still, something wouldn't let her fly free. An edgy nervousness rippled through her.

Liev's hand slid across her palm to entwine with her fingers.

She was no longer alone.

And they flew off the edge together.

LIEV PULLED LANI close to his heart. He could only hope this had been the right thing to do. He didn't want her to regret this step in their relationship. In fact, he wanted to love her all over again. And wasn't that a word to scare any single male?

Lani nuzzled against him and gave a happy sigh.

He cuddled her closer. "Are you okay?"

"Better than okay. I'm also not sore. Making love in a healing pod—unique concept."

That startled a laugh out of him. "Thanks. Spur of the moment and all that."

"Spontaneity is good for the soul," she murmured sleepily.

"Do you want to stay here and sleep longer?" he asked against her ear.

Her arms squeezed tight. "Only if you stay too."

"I will until you fall asleep." He shifted down slightly, grabbed the sliver of the blanket hanging off the edge, and wrapped it around her. "Just sleep."

She gave a deep sigh and closed her eyes. She fell asleep almost instantly.

Liev relaxed beside her, a slumberous warmth in his heart. It had been a long time since he'd held a woman like this. Sex, sure, but not the wonderful aftermath that came from making love with someone special.

"Liev," Milo called through the intercom that piped through their home, interrupting Liev's sated mood. "I think we may have more company coming. They just left the office after serving a warrant there."

Liev froze. "Friendlies or unfriendlies?"

"Unfriendlies."

Liev rolled over. "I'm coming. Make sure stealth is on."

He dressed quickly, his mind twisting with possibilities. "What now?" he whispered into the silence. Lani didn't need any more trouble—and neither did he. He just wanted time to spend with her. To get to know her without all the stress in their lives. And ... time to spend making love with her.

Instead he had to handle yet another headache. He dressed quickly, his movements controlled and efficient.

"Milo, did we get a notification that they were raiding the office?"

"About an hour ago. But, ... er, ..." Milo snickered. "You were busy, ... so you probably didn't get the messages."

"And you didn't interrupt me for something as important as a raid?" he asked incredulously.

Milo's voice dipped in embarrassment. "Yeah, I was a little involved in my VR unit at the same time."

"Damn it. Not the best timing." He could hardly blame Milo. This time.

He walked out to the kitchen and opened his scanner.

When the pod had first been delivered, he'd placed it into a stealth container so that any scanners from outside the building could not see inside. That would keep the pod and Lani secret. This room and the pod had another layer of stealth coverings. He'd have to bring her out of hiding at some point, but hopefully not until she was ready. His comp jangled. He opened the screen to find the Council henchmen once again at his door. His heart sank.

Liev walked over and opened the door. "Good morning, gentlemen. This is becoming a habit."

The guard held up a red comp unit.

Shit. His nerves tightened. A court order. "I presume that's for searching the premises?" He reached for the unit, read the details, and sighed heavily. "Of course it is." He stepped aside while clicking through the screen, checking to see what the orders covered. "You're looking for the source of a power surge? In my home?"

"That is correct."

Hard to believe they had secured a warrant based only on suspicion. Liev shook his head and leaned against the door. "Go for it. Although maybe you could explain to me why this supposed power surge is of interest. It's not like they don't happen many times a month."

"The Council is concerned that your brother Milo may be up to his usual tricks."

As if. Liev snorted. "Only he doesn't work at home."

At least he didn't normally. In fact, right now, Milo appeared to be putting on coffee. Good. They would all need it when this was done.

"We checked your office building already and couldn't find the power issue there." He nodded at the techs doing a quick search of the home. "This is just to follow up."

"Okay." Liev waited with casual nonchalance. Deep inside, his head was screaming with warnings. Had they found anything at the office? Was there anything to find here? He'd been so careful, but it was easy to slip up on the little things. Damn Milo for missing that transmission. Instantly he kicked himself. He'd been just as absent as Milo. That he couldn't regret. But seriously, the timing sucked.

After ten minutes, the techs all filed out, shaking their heads.

"Are you satisfied?"

The guard nodded. "We will continue searching the other residences." He motioned to the team. "Johan Strand's place is next."

"Wait, what?" Liev asked. "Why would he have something to do with the power surge? And I thought you were searching to see if Milo had something to do with it."

"We had to eliminate any chance of Milo's involvement first." He turned and walked away, presumably to go to Johan's place.

Undecided on his next course of action, Liev realized he should warn his friend, but, at the same time, the guards could find out Liev had contacted Johan, and that could implicate both of them. Again. Liev couldn't risk placing Lani in trouble.

He closed the door and reset the security before leaning against the front door. "Shit." He closed his eyes, sorting out what had just happened.

"Yeah, more trouble. All brought on by your brother."

"Whoa." Liev turned to see Charming, cleaning his paw on the chair nearby. "That's not true. Besides, you don't know anything about it."

Charming looked up, smiled, and said, "Really? Which

part?"

"It doesn't matter. I'm not arguing with a cat." Liev walked past him.

"No, you'd rather mess around with Lani, I suppose."

Liev froze. Not so much that the cat was talking or even at his words. No, it was the edge to the cat's voice. Like an older brother looking out for his younger sister. A younger sister Liev had been caught dallying with. As if the relationship was wrong—at least to Charming. He even felt heat crawl up his throat. "Are you saying Lani isn't allowed to have a special friend?"

"Is that what you are?"

The cat's tone of voice was anything but friendly. Liev looked around, hoping for some help, but Lani was sleeping and Milo, per Milo's usual behavior, had taken off. Probably gone to his bedroom. Cornered, Liev tried to think of a way out of this conversation. Then decided on the truth. "I'd like to think so," he said quietly.

Charming stared at him intently, that gaze locked on Liev's, searching, as if the cat could see into the heart of Liev. Then Charming dropped his gaze and shot one leg into the air and started to clean it.

"Umm …" Liev wasn't sure, but he would assume that he'd passed a test of some kind. He backed up quietly. Thankfully Charming didn't appear to notice. Liev checked on Lani, happy to see her sleeping soundly, and made his way into the kitchen. He contacted Johan on what Liev considered his secure line. *Need to get Milo to do his magic on that security feature too.*

Johan's face came on screen. Liev could only see gray walls behind his friend but had no idea where he was—except that he was not at home. "Are you okay?" Liev asked.

"Fine. I've secured this line, which will erase this conversation from any database. So speak freely."

"The guards just left my place. They're looking for the source of the latest power surge."

"I'm on the move. I slipped out the back and escaped." He grinned. "The guards said they were there to confiscate the pod—and anything else they deemed necessary. Or at least they are trying to. I have the pod set to self-destruct, … so, if you hear an explosion …" Johan walked forward, the scene behind his head shifting with his every step. "They will find some stuff. Although not what they are expecting."

Johan laughed, but there was a nasty edge to it. "Take care of your woman, Liev. I don't know where she came from, but you need to stop the Council from finding out about her."

Liev winced. "What do you know?"

"Not much, except from the pod. Also, I recognized your first visitor this morning from the rooftop cameras when I did a quick check around." He sighed. "Look. We live like we do for a reason. We have secrets. Protect yours. I'll take a trip. I may be gone for a while."

As Liev watched, he could see the scenery shift over and over behind his friend. "And a final word to the wise. The tagging, the unregistered pod, anything else you might think you've done to protect her, it won't be enough. You have to give her the protection of your name." His voice deepened. "Power needs more power, or you won't survive."

And he clicked off with a mock salute.

A heavy rumble carried overhead. That was likely the pod doing its self-destruct thing. Shit. Did it blow up in time, or did the Council henchmen get the information they were looking for? And, if they had, what recourse was there at this point? Liev's mind flipped to the other shocking point. Johan knew about Lani's tagging? That wasn't good. If Johan knew, who else could find out just as easily?

Liev's mind raced from one possible problem to another.

What Johan had said was true. Liev belonged to a long, powerful family line. And that was one thing the Council couldn't squash. Although his parents were dead, his uncles had kept him and Milo relatively protected for decades. Liev tried to be as independent as possible. Milo had pushed the limit, but, in a world where applications had to be made and accepted for children to exist, they were treasured. And families stood strong.

Powerful families stood for and against the government. He'd been trying to keep his brother out of any government involvement, and so far that had worked, but Johan was right. The easiest way to protect Lani was to enfold her in the family.

If she lived with anyone but Liev and Milo, she'd barely be of interest and could likely live out the rest of her life without raising any flags. But being here with them …

So the easiest answer was to set her up elsewhere away from them. Away from Liev. And that he couldn't do. Wouldn't do. Refused to do.

He'd done the best he could with Lani's fake back-ground, but how would it hold up under closer scrutiny?

Therefore, only one option remained. If he'd had two minutes to think, he'd have realized it himself.

He had to marry her.

CHAPTER 14

LANI WOKE TO the sounds of an argument. She was deliciously warm, her body limber and relaxed. In fact, she felt pretty darn good. Even her wrist. She lifted it and rotated her hand experimentally. A low-level ache set in, but it wasn't bad. She ran her fingers across her skin and pressed gently. The ache deepened, but, considering what surgery had been done, it looked and felt amazing. She rolled over and shrieked in surprise. Charming was sitting inches from her face, staring at her with an odd look in his gaze.

"Damn it, Charming. Why are you sitting here, staring at me like that?"

His whiskers quivered, but he stayed quiet.

She frowned, reaching up to stroke his back. "Charming, are you okay?"

"Yes." He paused, then leaned closer. "Are you?"

She frowned. "Yes, I'm feeling much better." She held out her wrist. "See? I'm chipped now." She laughed. "Stupid, huh?"

"He's not Lawrence," Charming said, "but how do you know he's not *like* Lawrence?"

Heat rose on her cheeks. It was stupid to be embarrassed. Charming was a cat. What did he know about relationships?

Charming snorted. "It's not been so long that my old tomcat self doesn't recognize another tomcat catting around."

She winced at that. "I know he's not. I'm not trying to relive a dream," she said earnestly. "By the time my relationship with Lawrence was over, he wasn't the same man he'd been in the beginning."

"Lawrence was always the same. You just finally opened your eyes and saw him."

Wisdom. From a cat. Wow. It would take some doing to get used to this. She tried again. "You're right. But Liev is hardly the same type of man."

"And yet ..."

She stiffened. "What's your problem with me having a relationship with Liev? Cat relationships last all of ten minutes."

"Except with you."

She smiled and reached for his chin to give him a good neck scratch. Charming was as insecure in this new world as she was. A relationship with Liev would put her baby's nose out of joint even more. His eyes crossed in joy as she continued to pet him. Seconds later, his engine started up. She lay here, rubbing Charming and thinking about her convoluted relationship with Liev.

Milo raced into the pod room. "You have to get dressed. We all have to appear in front of the Council." And he bolted away.

Fear stabbed her stomach. She curled up into a small ball. Oh, no. She couldn't do this. But she had no choice, did she?

Charming spoke up abruptly. "Remember how you always dreamed about marriage and kids one day?"

She looked at him. "Yes?"

"Well, you just might be in for a surprise." And he

hopped down and stalked stiff-legged to the doorway, his tail upright and waving in the air. He turned to look back at her. "Remember to keep your dreams fluid."

And he left.

Even more concerned now, she got dressed and made her way to the kitchen. Liev stood there, talking in a low voice to Milo.

"What's going on?"

Liev spun, smiled at her, and took a deep breath. "The first night you were here, I took you to Johan's pod. I tried to erase the information, but it caused some issues on the machine and sent corrupted data to the Council. Johan had some of the information still in the unit. When he was raided this morning, the Council gained access to the bulk of his place. He's gone traveling to avoid the Council. He had his own reasons for not wanting the Council to gain access to his place."

She shook her head, her heart calming slightly. "So we're safe?"

"No. In fact, only one way will ensure that you are safe." He paused.

Milo spoke up. "Make sure you know what you are doing, Liev."

Liev spun on him, his anger turning his face red. "You brought this on. Not me. Not Lani. Yet we are the ones taking the hit."

"You don't have to. We can find another solution."

"Really?" Liev asked, bitterness in his voice. "You've had time to utilize that magnificent brain of yours. What solution did you come up with?"

Milo looked downcast. She almost believed him. "Sorry, bro. I hadn't thought this through far enough."

"Yes, that's exactly right." Liev stood glaring at his brother and didn't look like he was prepared to stop any time soon.

"Stop the sibling stuff and one of you explain what does this have to do with me?" Lani crossed her arms over her chest, wishing they'd get to the point. "Milo said something about having to appear in front of the Council?"

"Yes. The occupants of my residence have been ordered to appear. The Council already suspects three of us are here. Therefore, the three of us will show up. It also means they'll know that you were the one in the pod." He paused. "The thing is, I don't think you are ready. Not for the Council. You could get into trouble over too many pitfalls there. You don't know anything about our way of life. About the government rules and laws we live with."

"But there is no other option, is there?" She studied his face, even as her stomach sank. In fact, panic settled in on the edge of her consciousness. "I'm hoping there is though, as I really don't want to go if I don't have to."

Milo nodded. Liev said, "My family is wealthy, powerful, and we have members in big business across most sectors."

She waited.

"With all the problems, … past, present, and potential ones racing towards us …" He took a deep breath. "The best way I can protect you is to give you the benefit of my name. I can stand before the Council on your behalf that way." He paused, then added, "There is only one way to do that."

Her heart stopped. What did that mean?

"Lani, will you marry me?"

LIEV HELD HIS breath. Inside, he wanted to wrap her up and rush her to the opposite end of the planet. Only that would just delay the same ending. They'd be found. There was no way they wouldn't. But she looked so lost. So forlorn. It broke his heart.

He walked over and tugged her into his arms. He didn't love her yet, but he knew he was well on his way to that state. But she hadn't had a chance. Not to understand life here. Not to understand her options. Not to understand what any of this meant.

"I just want to go home," she whispered, her words a dagger to his heart.

Charming hopped up onto the table and whispered, "Me too."

"I'm sorry," Liev said to them both. "That's the one thing we can't do for you."

"Well, at least not yet," Milo said. "I might be able to build a new program, but they took most of my computer equipment from the office during the raid. It will take years to recreate my work."

"Do they know what they have?" she asked, peering around Liev's shoulder at his brother.

Milo shook his head vigorously. "No, the program was set to corrupt when anyone else accessed it. My records show it's gone."

She stared at him suspiciously. "And you didn't have a backup? A half-dozen backups? Some modern way to make sure you didn't lose everything?"

He gave her a sheepish grin. "I do, but it's not that simple. It's in pieces, and everything is encrypted." He frowned. "Chances are I could put it together again, but knowing that it succeeded and that they are now looking at it, makes me less likely to even try. It could take years to make it functional. Even worse, there's no way to test if it works." He glared at Lani in a challenging manner. "Do you want to try it under those circumstances?"

She shifted her gaze to Liev. "I have to make a decision today?"

Liev winced. "We have to be at the Council in an hour."

She stared at him. "And what? We'll tell the Council that we are engaged?"

Charming snorted. "Engaged? You?"

Milo and Liev looked at each other. Milo grinned. "Nope. You'll be married." He started to laugh.

Liev growled, "Milo, stop."

But Milo laughed louder. Between his giggles, he said, "Except for the final formality, you're already married. He just didn't bother asking you."

CHAPTER 15

L ANI STARED AT the two men. One howling with ill-placed humor, oh-so typical of a teenager. And the other shuffling uneasily on his feet.

Charming, his eyes bright and lively, stayed quiet, watchful. Smart.

"Are we married?" she asked in an ominous voice. Could something like that really have happened without her permission or her knowledge? Of course it could. These two could do anything.

She studied Liev's stance. She didn't believe he'd done it for a bad reason. After all, he could marry anyone. Why her? Unless he cared about trying to keep her safe. Of course, keeping her safe also meant keeping his brother safe—so that made a kind of sense.

But that was the last reason she wanted to get married. All she had ever wanted was to be loved. For herself. Not because she was a problem to be fixed.

She gazed at the window, realizing it was uncovered. She wasn't sure she wanted to look beyond this apartment. To see what was outside. She'd loved the bit from the rooftop space, but she knew more would be out there. She'd wanted to stay inside and to avoid the reality check of her new ... reality. She was in hiding, like a victim. And she was damn tired of feeling that way.

Ignoring the two men, she walked to the window and stared out. Even though she'd seen little bits and pieces before, she almost turned around and ran back to the healing pod. With no frame of reference for what she would see outside, the thought of going out there terrified her. The odd-shaped buildings appeared even closer from here. More alien in shapes and colors. And ... the flying cars—if they were flying at all, which they weren't—at least not in any way she understood flying. The cars had no wings. They all proceeded in an orderly fashion—at breakneck speeds!

A shiver ran through her. She'd seen this all before. Something about this time ... brought the reality of her situation closer to home. It had been fun, maybe getting to the point of being exciting. But now that she had to appear in front of the Council, ... everything was suddenly magnified. This was not her world. She didn't belong here. She spun around and closed her eyes.

No way could she go out there.

She could hardly breathe. She gasped for breath.

Liev rushed over. "Easy, Lani. Take it easy. It's not that bad."

Her head shook, and the words wouldn't come. She pointed out the window. He winced and pressed a button. Instantly the light in the room darkened, as if he'd closed the curtains. Only she had heard no *whoosh* of material sliding across the window or the blinds dropping. There were so many things she didn't understand here. So many things that worked in ways she'd never seen before. Her gaze landed on Charming. Were there other pets here? Cats specifically? Dogs? Were they allowed to keep pets in this century or was that joy gone? Yet Liev seemed to be more worried about her than Charming. As if Charming was a non-issue.

Something that would horrify him.

"I'm sorry. This is just the same view that you saw on the rooftop garden." He reached out to rub her shoulder. "The blinds have been closed for the last few days. Milo opened them this morning."

"It's one thing to see *that*, out there, when I'm safe in here, but to know that I will be forced to go into that world, ... to face the Council, ... it is not easy to be so detached."

"I hate the darkened room," Milo said cheerfully. "Felt like we were living in a prison."

His high-pitched voice paired with his words made her turn her head and stare at him. His bright purple air boots shone weirdly in the half light. She wondered if he was as harmless as he liked to appear. She hoped so. He could do a lot of harm to her if he chose. She gazed at Liev. He glared at his brother, obviously disliking his word choices. Then again, so did she.

She asked Liev quietly, "Are we already married?"

"Not fully. I need your acceptance."

"But the preparation, the paperwork, the legalities?"

"All done."

She shook her head. "When did you do this?"

"This morning," he said quietly. "After I realized it was the only answer."

"After the raid." She nodded, starting to understand. "After the Council went to Johan's."

"I called Johan to warn him, but he had already slipped away. He told me about the possibility that the Council may have some information that I didn't want them to have."

"Why would your name protect me?" She shook her head. "That makes no sense."

"Only because you don't understand how our government works today. We can protect you. But I need the family to help. Once you're family, they will surround you. Shield you. You can have me represent you in front of the Council as your legal partner. I already have the papers drawn up. Then you'll be safe."

The thought of leaving the safety of the apartment made her feel faint. The thought of facing the Council brought on nausea. She couldn't face strangers. Not now. Not yet. Maybe never. She shuddered inwardly. She studied Liev's serious face. "And will you be safe too?"

"Yes. We will be too." He nodded.

"Then your logic is flawed. Because, if that were the case, you'd be protected now. You two already have the family name."

Milo snorted. "She's got you there."

"No. She doesn't understand." He shot an exasperated look at his brother before turning to face Lani. "The family has been protecting us. But, at the same time, Milo keeps crossing the line. This time, there is more than just us at stake. I couldn't live with myself if anything happened to you. When the family closes ranks around you, we can make all this go away."

"You hope …"

A weird musical sound filled the air. Liev looked frustrated for a moment. He ran his fingers through his hair. "It's time."

"Time for what?" Lani asked, looking around for the source of the music.

"Time for you to say yes or no." He took a step toward her. "Please, say yes."

She stared at him, confused, but realizing that he wanted—needed—the process finalized before she showed up at the Council. Something that mattered to keep her safe. To keep him and Milo safe. She didn't care about Milo, but she didn't want anything to happen to Liev. She hadn't known him long, but what she did know, she liked—a lot. She could fall in love with him. But that could only happen if she agreed to his plan. A plan that was deeply uncertain. But what were her choices?

None.

Damn.

"Answer one question first." She couldn't get over the feeling that she didn't know something here. Something they weren't coming clean about. And she needed them to. "Why me? I understand that stuff about picking me because I fit the parameters. But there had to have been thousands of other women who would do."

Milo laughed. "I can tell you the truth about that now that you're almost family." He pointed at Liev. "My big brother here carries around a picture of a woman. I saw it a long time ago and asked him about it. It's originally from our family archives." Milo's grin widened. "He told me that he didn't know why, but something about the woman's smile struck him as special."

She turned to stare at Liev.

Milo beamed. "Show her, Liev."

Lani walked closer. "May I see it?"

Liev frowned, then reluctantly pulled a square metal-looking thing from his pocket. He unfolded it several times before handing it over.

She gasped. "Where did you get this?"

"I told you," Milo said. "From the family archives."

Lani stared at the very same picture she'd ripped into

little pieces and had tossed into the garbage—or would be the same image except that the part with Lawrence had been cut away, leaving just a shot of her face. She couldn't believe what she was looking at. Coincidence? Fate? Destiny?

How much had her life changed in what? One day? Two days? She couldn't tell anymore.

She lifted her stunned gaze to Milo. "Based on this one photo, you brought me here?"

"That image was the start of my research. I ran the tests, probabilities, scans, more tests—and you passed—so I figured, why not do something for my brother who's always doing nice things for me?" He patted Liev on the shoulder, then turned to address Lani. "You were meant to be a gift for Liev."

Bells chimed again.

Liev looked at her, his voice low, urgent, as he said, "La-ni?"

Her gaze went from one brother to the other. Liev had taken the first step with the photo.

Milo the next.

This step was hers to take.

She swallowed, held out her hand, and said, "Yes, Liev. I will marry you."

And Charming, who'd been silent up until now, added, "Well it's about time …"

The End

Cat's Pajamas

Broken Protocols 2

by
Dale Mayer

Protocol 2:3:5. You will in no way use force to damage the life of another—particularly if those actions are to selfishly enhance your own.

CHAPTER 1

M ARRIED? TO LIEV Blackburn? Just like that? Lani Summerland's sense of humor kicked in. How typical of her crazy life. She couldn't find a man on her own in her twenty-first-century world, but was already married after a couple days in the twenty-third century. That was some matchmaking trick.

And not by choice.

Well, technically that wasn't true. The marriage part was by choice. At least it seemed like a great idea at the time. All of five minutes ago.

Lani Summerland stared suspiciously at the odd-looking adornment on her finger. It looked like a ring. It didn't feel like one. In fact, it had almost no weight to it at all. And, given the size of the deep purple rock on top, she thought she'd have noticed. Even the metal was soft, comfortable to wear.

She held her fingers splayed wide and shifted her hand in the age-old movement of women ever since rings were invented.

"Is it all right?" Liev Blackburn, her new husband, and yet still a stranger in many ways, stepped a little closer to her. The clear glass cube, or what stood in for an elevator of this time period was almost normal—but there was no way she'd become accustomed to it as it disappeared into thin air when they arrived at their destination. Not to mention it didn't follow normal pathways or tracks. In fact, it went where it was ordered to go by an invisible technology all its own.

She flashed him a quick grin. "Sure. I'm just not used to wearing big rocks that appear to be made of nothing or that adjust automatically to any size."

"It's the new alloys," Milo, Liev's brainy younger brother, piped up. "Gold fell from grace when the shortage came about ninety years ago. This was the answer. It's no different than the clothing you are wearing. It adjusts naturally to the size of the wearer."

Well, that explained the perfect fitting clothing she wore that never constrained or tugged at her or pinched her skin. Amazing. "And the supersize rocks?" she asked, playing with the rock to make it twinkle in the light.

"Most are synthetic." Milo judged his brother in a joking manner. "But not this one."

She frowned, pretty sure that the rocks in her day came in a synthetic variation as well. But they still had weight.

Then she had no time to wonder as they arrived at their destination. Her heart beat faster as she realized this was it. "Now remember. Just smile," Liev said. "Hold out your arm when requested to do so, but don't say a word unless asked a question." He shoved his arm outward to demonstrate.

She imitated his actions.

With a nod, he said, "If anyone asks where you're from, tell them you're from Felonia, and you arrived a couple days ago."

"Felonia," she repeated dutifully, dread congealing into a nasty ball in her stomach at the thought of anyone speaking to her. "Are you sure I can't just go home?" And back to Charming Marvin, who was even now resting in the pod at

Liev's place.

"I wish you could. But, after this, no one will question your presence or your absence in the future." Liev wrapped an arm around her shoulder and led her forward. From all appearances, he looked like the doting new bridegroom. She shivered inwardly at the remembered passion they'd shared. Now if only they could head off on a romantic honeymoon.

But apparently not. She managed a warm glowing smile. He was her lifeline right now. And had quickly become the love of her life.

And, for that, she'd even put up with his brother Milo. Whom she had yet to forgive for dragging her into this century. Using an amazingly advanced computer program, he'd gone back in time, snatched her up, and brought her here as a gift for his brother, Liev.

Talk about a mind-bender.

That he'd also brought Charming and had accidentally enhanced his communication abilities, which were originally intended for her, was beyond anything she could have imagined.

The cube disappeared, and Liev, his arm still wrapped around her, led her forward into a large room with a clerk standing at the ready. "Good morning. Lani Summerland Blackburn," Liev said, "Liev Blackburn, and Milo Blackburn reporting in as requested."

The clerk frowned. "Only your presence was requested. Not your brother." He glanced up, saw Lani, and his frown deepened. "Not your girlfriend."

Lani straightened in outrage. Liev squeezed her shoulders. "My wife and brother are here because everyone living in my house was requested to attend."

"Wife?" Now the clerk's frown deepened. He clicked

madly away on his weird tablet computer. Lani couldn't help but be fascinated as the lights flashed and pages shifted in a wildly erratic pattern she suspected was anything but erratic. She'd always loved computers. She hoped that she'd learn how these worked soon.

"Why do I have no record of that? I should have been notified." His voice rose slightly.

Control freak much? Lani eased out a shaky breath, trying to appear natural. As if showing up before a futuristic Council to answer for something she had nothing to do with was completely normal. She'd wanted to bring Charming with her for comfort, but both brothers had shot down that idea instantly.

Charming hadn't liked the idea much either. "Nope, this is a human thing. I'm going to do the cat thing and sleep the time away. Have fun though and ta ta till later." And he'd walked away from them, head held high, his tail straight in the air and the tip flicking in their direction.

Even now she wanted to go back and hug him. He was her only link to her old life. Then he'd always been special to her. The two of them only had each other for years. Now it seemed their family had unexpectedly grown.

The clerk finally looked up and studied her. Whatever he saw made his lips curl. "Don't tell me. She's from the outer areas. From a fringe group."

Cutting words bubbled up on Lani's tongue, but she bit them back. She had no idea what the *outer areas* meant, but she didn't deserve to be treated as a lesser person because of it.

Liev nodded comfortably. "She is."

The clerk rolled his eyes. "Whatever. I'll put her down."

Liev nodded his thanks politely and led Lani into a huge

chamber room where the ceiling appeared so high up she couldn't see the top. "Wait here. I shouldn't be long."

She reacted instinctively, reaching out to grab his hand. "Are you sure you can't sit here beside me?"

He leaned over and dropped a kiss on her forehead. "You'll be fine." He looked up and nodded his head at someone. "Here's my lawyer. Hahn Driscoll."

Lani turned as the stranger approached. He wore a uniquely tailored suit in glowing blue patterns. The styles might not have changed a lot, but the colors of today sure had. She smiled a polite greeting and shook his hand, charmed at the old-style greeting.

"Liev. Are you ready?"

Liev nodded. "I was just settling Lani here, where she'd be comfortable."

Hahn smiled at her, and damn if one of his teeth didn't wink out at her in the same color as his suit. Wow. Tooth jewelry. Her gaze widened, and her breath caught in the back of her throat. It was all she could do to not say something. Instead, she turned to look around her to see the room filling up. Several people took seats. She decided the best thing was to do the same. She watched one man sit down on a black pole that instantly widened to accommodate his butt.

Taking a deep breath, she promptly sat down on the closest pole, her breath whooshing out when it opened successfully into a seat to support her butt. Thank heavens. She took a shaky breath and smiled up at the brothers. "Go on. I'll be fine."

Milo gave her a weird finger salute she guesstimated meant something similar to *Right on* and turned and bounced forward. He'd certainly dressed up for the occasion, wearing a black-and-white striped skin suit. She shuddered at the jailbird look. It didn't matter how long she lived here; she would never wear a skin suit like that.

As if understanding her thoughts, Liev bent over and whispered, "You'd look better in that than he does." He kissed her cheek, winked at her, and walked away.

The lawyer, thankfully not sporting painted-on skin pants, waited a few steps ahead for Liev to catch up. Heads bent deep in discussion, they strode out of the room.

And left her alone.

LEAVING LANI IN the waiting room was one of the hardest things Liev had ever done. She knew no one, knew nothing about the world she found herself in, or the pitfalls that awaited her every time she opened her mouth to speak. But he had no choice. He quickened his pace to catch up to Milo, who was strolling on ahead. His brother's flagrant disregard for the rules had put them in this situation. Only Liev had compounded the situation by using his friend's healing pod to help repair the damage done to Lani and Charming from time-traveling.

Liev could only hope that his friend's attempt to destroy the pod Liev had used to heal Lani in would make today's Council visit more of a maintenance checkup than an actual investigation. He'd had his lawyer meet them here just in case, but Liev hadn't had time to brief Hahn.

The legal fees that his company paid to keep Hahn's law firm available for times like this were exorbitant. As they were checked at the door and led into a smaller chamber, Liev spotted his old friend Stephen Cavendish on the Council dais. Relief swelled inside Liev. This might have started as a witch hunt, but it wouldn't end up that way.

Stephen, young, only a junior Council member, was on Liev's side when it came to government meddling. And played the game well.

Liev smiled at his friend, relaxing even more when Stephen winked at him. This would be just fine.

Stephen opened the discussion. "I hear congratulations are in order, Liev?"

Liev beamed. "They are, indeed."

Milo bobbed at his side, his headset in his ear. He rarely spoke at these meetings. Probably just as well. What came out of his mouth usually didn't bode well for Liev or Milo.

In a genial let's-get-this-over-with-so-I-can-get-back-to-my-honeymoon tone of voice, Liev asked, "What is the problem that you needed to disturb me during my time of celebration?" He kept his face curious but amiable—at least he hoped it was. One sign of fear and these vultures would pounce.

"It's your friend Johan Strand," said one of the senior Council members. "He's wanted by the Council. When his request to appear was ignored, a team was sent to retrieve him. Unfortunately he'd set up some self-detonation on several of his equipment centers. Suspicious behavior at best." Some of the Council members nodded. "As your residence is known to be associated with him, we requested everyone there to appear here for questioning."

That's not quite the way Liev understood events to have gone down, but it wouldn't be the first time that the Council had twisted things to suit themselves. "First, Johan is an acquaintance, not a friend," Liev said in a what-has-this-got-to-do-with-me voice. "Second, I don't know anything about his equipment. Nor do I know where he is, if that is what you are looking to me for answers about." He stood tall and straight. "And my wife knows even less."

The Council stared at him. Even Stephen. Then again, Liev had always been good at playing the Council game.

Liev waited patiently. Ever since Milo had gotten them in hot water a year ago, whenever the Council wanted a question answered or needed to collect information, Liev and Milo were dragged down to appear in person. As if they couldn't lie or cheat their way through these sessions in person, like they might through a HoloKomp. He suspected that the Council ran illegal scans on every person who entered these rooms. Hence the reason for keeping Lani out. She might not pass the scans.

He needed the Council to find nothing wrong for a few more months. Then he would start asking them to back off before he involved the lawyers at a more in-depth level. As it was, today was one step from harassment. And Hahn had brought that up more than once. But Liev needed to keep a low profile while Lani settled in. No one could take a closer look at her right now.

He couldn't imagine the shock of what she'd been put through. He didn't think he'd have handled it half as well as she had if he'd been in the same situation. In fact, he knew he wouldn't. He looked around, seeing Milo and his lawyer, ... his extended family only a call away. He'd lose everything familiar and dear.

Just like Lani had.

For the first time, he had a little insight into all that she'd lost.

And how little he could do to make up for it. He'd done his best to protect her, but he could never replace everything.

"Liev?" Hahn nudged him. With a startled look at his old friend, he realized the Council was talking.

"We need to know any information," the elder Councilman, Carlson, said in a tone that demanded obedience. "Any names or locations that you may have heard Johan mention to track him down."

Liev frowned while he stopped to consider the request. "In truth, I'm not sure I ever heard him mention anyone or anyplace in particular. He was notorious for his parties, and serious talk didn't happen then, nor were any partygoers willing to engage in serious talk either."

"And yet, he mentioned the two of you going out for coffee after your last appearance here."

Liev's eyebrows shot up at the reminder. However, he answered smoothly, "He did invite me, but the coffee never happened. He wanted to see his lawyers instead, so he asked for a rain check."

That, at least, was the truth. He suspected the Council members already knew what he'd done that day. A drone would have noted his and Johan's actions at the time and would have promptly submitted a report on both men, to be filed away for future reference.

The Council muttered among themselves for a long moment. "Your answers have been recorded. Should you have any further information to offer regarding the issue, please contact the office."

A different Council member spoke. "We notice that Milo has not added anything to the conversation."

Liev shrugged. "He has nothing to say. He had nothing to do with Johan."

"Not one of the regular partygoers?" Eyebrows shot sky-high, and amused twitters rippled through the Council members.

Milo was an anomaly to them. He lived in his own

world and wouldn't have attended one of Johan's parties if Milo's life had depended on it. Milo's parties were always private with his other geek friends. Liev highly suspected they played more computer games than sex games when they were together. Milo's whole group was more active sexually in VR than in real life.

But that might also be his age or his perspective on other people. Milo was light-years ahead of others. While normal people looked into their coffee cups, wondering at the pretty pattern the cream made as it was poured, Milo had already analyzed its composition, calories, health detriments, and health benefits for everyone in the damn room, as well as who could tolerate that level of fat and who should be running in the opposite direction.

No one was like his brother.

Councilman Carlson said, "And the other occupant in your residence?"

"My wife, Lani?" Liev hated the way Carlson spoke about Lani. "You know her name is Lani. She isn't an occupant." She was so much more, but in their arrogance, they tried to dehumanize her that way.

"Is she here?" The speaker ignored Liev's comment, choosing instead to stare at him in a cold manner.

"She is waiting in the outer chamber." Liev curled his upper lip, his tone even but hard. "I speak on her behalf. All documents have been filed as per protocol."

After a moment where the men clicked away on their comps to verify his statement, the men nodded. Stephen smiled at Liev as they were dismissed.

Liev promptly turned and silently let his breath *whoosh* out. So they'd skated by safely again.

But for how much longer?

He pushed Milo ahead of him as they walked out. Now to collect Lani and get her home, safe and sound.

As he walked back into the anteroom, she no longer sat where he'd left her.

In fact, he saw no sign of her. "Shit."

CHAPTER 2

LANI SAT IN silence, watching in wonderment as the kaleidoscope of people walked by. Just like in her time, she saw a mix of races and ethnic groups. Skin appeared to come in a few more colors, like a light mauve, teal, and copper shades. She didn't know if those were medical enhancements, cosmetic changes, or something genetic. The copper-toned skins were beautiful, but the purple and pink ones were fascinating. Hair was another anomaly. It appeared as if anything went here. Colors from glittery black to Milo's wild green appeared on men in business clothing, similar to what Liev's lawyer wore.

The female in her was fascinated and a little jealous of the women here. Every color from the rainbow was represented—plus some she swore she'd never seen before. The skirts appeared to shift and almost wrap around the women's legs, as if it were some kind of intelligent material. And maybe it was. The fashions were unlike anything she'd seen before. It wasn't like old styles coming back around again. Instead, this time period had made huge leaps in terms of fashion sense. She glanced at her own interesting clothing, realizing she did fit in, but likely with a younger group than those she saw here.

Another thing that caught her gaze was the lack of purses or bags or even briefcases. How could that be? Everyone had to carry something.

Odd.

How did they carry laptops, tablets, or whatever the modern version was? Where did women put their makeup?

As she pondered life in this century, a beautiful businesswoman sat down beside her. Lani started. Dressed with severely coiffed hair in an almost purple-black one-piece skin suit, very little was left to the imagination. Lani stared. The woman's eyes were a deep emerald green. And her smile was nothing like anyone's she'd seen before.

"Hi, Lani."

Lani shrank back. Her tentative smile dropped away in shock. How did this woman know her?

"I'm Gina Stewart. Hahn is my law partner," the woman said reassuringly. "Our law firm represents Liev and Milo," she added.

Relief caused some of the tension to slip away. "Oh, they've all gone into that room." Lani motioned behind her.

The woman nodded. "That's normal." She paused, studying Lani's face intently. "But there's nothing normal about you, is there?"

Lani's gaze widened, her stomach sinking. "Pardon?"

"Oh, come on. That innocent-lost-girl look might work on Liev, but I know better." She settled more comfortably, but her sharp gaze never left Lani. Studying, probing, as if trying to figure out something. "You managed to marry one of the most eligible bachelors around. It's not as if I can do anything about that." Her smile turned glacial. "At least not right now."

Lani stared. She waited for the woman to say more. If Lani wasn't careful, this was a conversation guaranteed to get her into trouble. Like, what the hell? Was this woman jealous? Had she and Liev had a previous relationship? Her last comment sounded almost threatening. Too bad women hadn't changed with the times. Ambitious *cats* had existed in her century too.

When the other woman didn't speak again, Lani plastered a cool, confident smile on her face and said, "I'm sorry. I don't understand."

The other woman snorted and sat back, an irritated edge to her features. "Right. Fine. Be that way if you want." She looked around at the crowd. "Hopefully the men will be done soon, and we can leave."

Lani murmured something unintelligible. She was still struggling with her reaction. Relief and worry had taken over her bloodstream, and a headache like she'd never had before was building quickly. Too quickly. Where was a healing pod when she needed one?

"Are you all right?"

"I'm fine. Just a bit of a headache is all."

That brought the other woman's head around, her sharp gaze locking on Lani's face. "Why the devil would you allow one of those? Liev really fell for this back-to-natural stuff, huh? Never thought he'd be such a dupe." Gina snickered and stood. "Later."

And she walked away.

And what was that about *all natural*? Had people managed to do away with headaches completely here? But in a non-natural way? How confusing. More questions to ask Liev.

Lani was left to mull over Gina's words, her gaze on the woman's retreating back, when Gina just … disappeared. No cube surrounded her, nothing. She was there one moment, then gone the next.

Lani stared at the spot Gina had disappeared from to see a series of circles on the floor. She couldn't help thinking of the *Star Trek* movies from her day and the transporter system. Was that possible here? Or was this system even more advanced?

Other circles were on the floor, with people stepping in and out just as suddenly as they arrived and left. She hadn't noticed them before, the people traveling in such a way or that odd circle system. But where were they going to and coming from?

And how did they not crash into each other in transit?

She got shivers just thinking about it. What kind of a world had she found herself in? Her headache grew. She wished Liev was done. All she wanted was to be back home, safe in the healing pod with Charming.

And damned if her wrist didn't start to flash weird colors right then. Flustered, she dropped her arms into her lap and slapped her right hand over the lights. But they flashed brightly between her fingers. She had no idea what any of it meant. Neither had she seen anyone else's wrist start a light show.

Even as she thought that, it seemed as if everyone suddenly noticed her. Plain Jane Lani was getting way too much attention than was good for her. She tried to hide the bright lights against her belly but nothing seemed to do the job.

She searched behind her, desperately hoping for Liev or Milo to show up.

There was no sign of either of them.

Suddenly her arm was grabbed, and she was jerked up and out of her chair and pushed toward one of those weird circles. *Gina Stewart.*

"You're coming with me," the older woman snapped as

she pushed Lani forward.

Lani stumbled and would have fallen but if not for Gina's grasp on her arm. "What are you doing?"

"Shut up."

Lani pulled back and managed to get free of Gina.

Gina snorted, gave Lani a short shove, and … the room disappeared.

Oh, no. Lani could hardly swallow. Her throat convulsed, and it was all she could do to keep the food in her stomach. She didn't know what had happened, but it hurt like hell.

"Jesus, what is wrong with you?" The disgust in Gina's voice had the effect of pushing the nausea up a notch, sending Lani almost to her knees.

"I'm sick," Lani whispered, bending over and trying to take deep breaths. "Where is Liev?"

"They're almost done. If you throw up in my office, I'm charging Liev for the damages."

"It wouldn't be in your office if you hadn't shoved me in here," Lani snapped with as much backbone as she could muster, helping regain her equilibrium. "Take me back to Liev."

Gina shook her head. "I don't get it. He actually married you? I can see partying for a day or two, but marriage?" She turned on her heel and opened her comp. "Hahn, I have Lani at the office."

She clicked off her comp. "Sit down, for heaven's sake. They should be here soon."

Shudders rippled down Lani's spine. She cast a quick glance around the gleaming iridescent room. There had to be something to sit on—just not something she recognized as a chair. "I'll stand," she said quietly.

That only earned her another disgusted look. "Whatever." Gina walked out of the room, leaving Lani alone.

Thank God.

A window was open on the far side. Not trusting that she was truly alone or that she wasn't being recorded in some way, she walked over to the window, schooled her features, and looked out. Another traffic scene. This time she studied the vehicles and the pattern of controlled pandemonium. She didn't think she'd ever drive in this lifetime. The sheer speed of the chaos outside the window shook her. That she didn't know the rules of the road was one thing but she didn't think she'd ever be comfortable enough to follow whatever passed for driving rules here.

This place was just too … *out there* for her.

And where the hell were Liev and Milo? They shouldn't have left her alone. At least not for this long. She understood on one level, but on another … how was she to know about the Ginas of his world or the weird circles on the floor and the nonexistent furniture she was supposed to sit on? She hadn't had a chance to do or see or learn anything. She'd been concerned with healing enough to just walk.

She heard an odd *whoosh* in the center of the room.

She spun around, her hand going to her chest. Now what?

LIEV TURNED IN a slow circle, his gaze darting from side to side. "Come on, Lani. Where are you?"

Milo stared at him. "What did you say?"

"Where's Lani?" Liev muttered softly.

Milo's gaze widened in horror, and he spun around. And continued to spin in a slow movement as he searched the room a second time.

"Maybe she had to go to the washroom," he suggested.

Hahn approached the two of them. "I'll file a motion when I get back to the office to have any further Council meetings done by comp. It's ridiculous that we have to continue to show up in person to answer a few questions."

Liev pulled his attention back to look at Hahn. "Good. Please do that. And thanks for your help there." He watched as his lawyer walked away, the blue of his suit shimmering in the brilliantly colored crowd.

As soon as he was out of sight, Liev spun to find Milo working on his comp. "Tell me that you found her."

"There's no sign of her anywhere." Milo swore under his breath before sucking it in sharply. "Wait. Incoming."

Where the hell could Lani have gone? Liev lifted his shoulders. "Incoming what?"

Milo gasped, then choked. "Incoming message. From Charming Marvin?"

Liev turned so he could see Charming's feline face over Milo's shoulder. "Lani is in trouble. Tracking … now on."

"What the hell?" His words, even voiced low, caught the attention of curious passersby. Damn. The place was crowded. Still, their curiosity was a good reminder that anything they did and said was likely being recorded.

"Yeah, he's good." Milo clicked a few more buttons. "Got her. She's at Hahn's office."

"How the hell …" Liev raced to the ports.

"Gina took her there," Milo called out, running behind him.

He stepped into the port and appeared at Gina's office, Milo right behind him.

And there was Lani.

She stared at him in shock. When she realized he was here in person, she raced toward him. He caught her in his arms and hugged her tightly. "It's okay," he murmured. "I'm here."

She couldn't stop shaking or burrowing closer. Her arms locked around his waist and wouldn't let go. He held her close and continued to whisper comforting things in her ear. She was stiff and unyielding—terrified. He could just imagine ... and hugged her closer.

"As you can see, she's fine," Gina snapped. "Lord, all this fuss over nothing."

Milo came to Lani's rescue first. "Really? You remove someone from the Council offices without anyone's permission, including that of the woman you kidnapped, and you say it's *nothing?*"

At the word *kidnapping,* Gina gasped, and Lani burrowed deeper into Liev's embrace. "I did no such thing." Gina stormed closer, her perfect face twisting in fury. "Lani was attracting attention. What did you expect me to do?"

"In what way was she attracting attention?" Liev asked, trying to keep his own rage under control. Which was hard as Lani burrowed closer.

"She sat so damn still. So perfect. Like a statue." Gina snorted, disgust threading her voice. "She didn't move, no comp, no nothing. Just an oddness that stood out." She shrugged. "Then her ID started to flash. It was too close to the Missing Person's Alert. Like, really?" Gina rolled her eyes. "I had to stop her from making a spectacle of herself."

"So because she wasn't *you,* you figured she was odd." Milo mimicked her voice so perfectly that Liev had to bite back a grin. "And her ID could flash for any number of reasons."

"It wasn't so much that it flashed, it was the look of shock, horror, and confusion on her face that was so ridiculous." Gina glared at them. "She was fine when I first saw her. So I left her alone. Only after I returned did I realize she was causing such a commotion."

Milo narrowed his eyes. "And you couldn't leave it alone. Not because she was garnering attention, but because *you* weren't. For some reason, Liev married *her*, not you. *She* had him. You didn't. It was all about jealousy, wasn't it?" Milo snapped forward from his sixteen-year-old mental self with a wisdom beyond his years. "Liev partied with you, and you wanted more. He didn't. Next thing you know, he shows up with this natural girl and is married to her."

Gina's voice turned cutting. "Go back to bed, Milo. It's a little late for you to be up, isn't it?"

Lani lifted her head from Liev's chest and, in low tones, asked, "Can we go home now?"

He hugged her gently. To the others, he said, "You two can stay and fight if you want. I'm taking her back. She's been sick and needs rest."

"She could get that fixed. Playing on your sympathies, you know." Gina raised both hands in frustration. "Whatever." And she strode out of the room again.

Milo glared at her receding back. "Bitch."

Lani giggled. "Glad to hear that word is still used nowadays."

"Especially nowadays," Milo said with a smile. "Let's go home."

"Yes, please. By the way," she said, "how did you know I was here? Gina left a message on Hahn's comp, or whatever that thing is, but I didn't see her call you two."

"That's because she didn't," Liev said, loosening his arms

and turning her gently, nudging her from the room.

Milo bounced on his heels to his toes. "You aren't going to believe what did happen."

She twisted slightly to look him in the face. Liev kept her walking forward. "Why? What happened?" She looked up at Liev. "Hahn called you?"

Milo shook his head, almost dancing with glee now.

Liev gave a low and deep rumble of a laugh. "Charming Marvin told us."

She came to a dead stop and stared at him. "What? Really?"

They both nodded.

Her sense of humor kicked in, and she giggled.

Liev grabbed her into his arms for a hug, stepped into the same circle Lani had popped out of earlier, and led her out into the Council anteroom within seconds. Her joy was a light in his life. She had to be feeling rough enough without enduring the cutting edge of Gina's tongue, but it hadn't gotten her down. Lani was a survivor.

Gina had been a mistake years ago. Liev should never have hooked up with her. After she'd joined his lawyer's firm, their first business meeting had been slightly uncomfortable, but then he'd promptly forgotten about her and the weekend party. An easy thing to do.

To think she'd gone after Lani, regardless of her motives, concerned him. She'd said it was to protect him, to protect Lani, but there'd been no need to remove Lani from where he'd left her. And, if Gina *had* said something to Hahn, why hadn't his lawyer said something to Liev?

Liev mulled it over, not liking where his thoughts were taking him. An innocent miscommunication? Or something more sinister?

Milo's comp beeped again. The three were back in the Council anteroom, where Lani had originally been waiting for them. He led them back out through security. On the other side, Milo stopped and tugged Lani toward him. "Could you please look into my comm?"

She shot him a startled look. "What?'

He held out his arm, and the tiny screen flashed in front of her. Obediently she stared into the comp. Immediately it flashed. Then the screen cleared, and Charming's flat face filled the screen. Charming gave her a huge cat grin.

She gasped in joy. "Oh, please, let's go home."

"Right now." Liev stepped into the elevator cube which appeared to morph into a tube at some odd times. The other two crowded close to him. The trip back was fast and efficient. Lani appeared to have relaxed about their traveling system, and that was good. It was just one of many things she'd have to learn to do on her own. Just as Liev had other things to learn. Like how to deal with a talking cat who could send an alarm about Lani. What Liev didn't understand was how Charming knew Lani was in trouble in the first place.

It would be the first thing he'd ask the talking feline.

CHAPTER 3

"**H**ER VITALS HAD gone off the chart," Charming explained, in between licking the nutrient-rich cream off the plate, his tongue making little *snick, snick* sounds. "I saw a flashing button labeled Scan, so I pressed it and didn't like the results." He shrugged. "It was obvious she was upset. There were too many variables to pinpoint the reason, so I figured you should be the one to deal with it."

Charming lifted his head, pink cream dotting the fluff of orange fur sticking out in a tall cloud around his face, and asked Lani, "What was the problem anyway?"

"Oh, nothing," she said tiredly. "Just an old girlfriend of Liev's who decided to kidnap me."

Charming spluttered, sending pink cream all over the table. "What?" He lifted his head to stare at her, his shock widening his gaze.

Relieved to be home, her fear slowly subsiding now that she was safe and back with Liev, she gestured in Liev's direction. "He'll give you the details."

Charming turned to face Liev. When he didn't jump in with an explanation, Charming stalked across the table closest to where Liev stood and glared at him. "Liev, explain."

The look on Liev's face made Lani choke back a giggle. He looked like he'd swallowed a sour candy.

"What's the matter, Liev? Not used to explaining your-self, especially to a cat?" she murmured as she walked past him to stare out the window. He gave a snort, but she ignored him, choosing to study the outside world again, this time with a jaundiced eye.

Behind her, she heard Liev explain about the short rela-tionship he'd had with Gina a long time ago, shortly after she had joined the firm, working for Liev's lawyer. Damn, Lani knew that whatever happened in Liev's life before her arrival should have nothing to do with her. But somehow her rules didn't sound like they'd apply in this case. Gina wouldn't let them.

"Why would she do this to Lani?" Charming asked.

"I don't know," Liev admitted. "It makes no sense."

"Yes, it does," Milo piped up, adding, "She's jealous. She heard about your marriage just this morning, as did everyone else, and reacted badly. An opportunity presented itself, and she snatched it."

Lani winced. That woman's damn superior tone had said more about Gina than Lani cared to know. She *was* a bitch. If she'd dated Liev, that was one thing, but, according to Milo, Liev had had an affair with her. At least that's what Lani thought *partied* meant. Like, really? That was what he considered his type?

If the other women of this century were the same as the barracuda lawyer, no wonder Liev hadn't yet hooked up with anyone permanently. She wouldn't have either. Maybe Milo had done Liev a favor in bringing Lani here.

"But she didn't do anything other than take Lani to her office," said Liev, his frustration and temper showing in his voice. "It's not as if she hurt her or demanded money. It's more like she wanted to check Lani out for some reason."

"She kept calling me *natural* or something like that." Lani spun around to look at the men. "What does that mean?"

"Ha." Milo laughed. "Everyone is improved these days. Babies are born with the preferred genetic markers, so there is no illness anymore ... or very little. Brainpower can be chosen. Looks. Things like that. But it's the parents' choice of course. When the child grows up, they can also choose their own enhancements. Similar to cosmetic surgery from your day," Milo added. "Every society has fringe groups. Naturals are one of ours. People who eschew any non-natural improvements."

"So because I don't have any enhancements, I'm natural looking, so that's something to laugh at?" Lani asked. "Really?"

Charming snorted. "Some of us don't need enhancements."

Liev smiled and reached out to scratch Charming under the neck. Charming's eyes crossed with pleasure. "Not all enhancements work or are an improvement. Many times the person looked better before the enhancement. But there will always be those who have to push the edge."

"And, Milo," Lani asked, "are you one of those genetically chosen brains?"

He smirked. "I am that and so much more. Something different happened with me, and I ended up with more than expected."

"Meaning, he was likely a genius naturally," Liev said. "By genetically choosing more intelligence, our parents had no idea they'd get someone at the far end of that spectrum."

"Did they understand his nature before they passed away?"

Liev nodded. "Yes, they did. Milo could read before his second birthday and could solve calculus problems before his fourth. He hasn't stopped since."

"And you," Lani said gently, "how do you feel knowing that your parents gave Milo all those brains, but they didn't give them to you? Presumably it was an option."

"One can ask for genetic markers to be enhanced, but no one can guarantee the results. They chose different markers for me." He shrugged. "And I'm happy with who I am."

He didn't mention what the other genetic markers were and left Lani trying to guess. He'd tell her when he was ready.

She turned back to the window. What kind of world could already determine what their children would be like before they were even born? "Where is Mother Nature in all this?" she murmured. "Does she still have a role to play?"

"That's the thing about Milo. If you take ten different fetuses with all the same genetic markers like his, you won't get ten Milos. Mother Nature still rules."

That made her feel better. She hated to think that everyone was now preordained to be a specific way.

And she refused to believe this was an improvement over the rules of her old society. She couldn't argue that she'd love to be better at some things. Speed-reading was an example. She'd wanted to go back to school, had just been accepted into an IT Security program before Milo so rudely yanked her out of her life. Now that little training program would be laughable to what she'd need to learn for a successful life here.

She stopped in her tracks. Was it possible? She turned slowly, realizing even Charming was better suited to life here, due in part to his enhancements. Were there some enhancements that would help her to adapt, to learn what she needed to know to thrive here?

"Is there something you can do to enhance me too?" she asked slowly, studying their faces. "Some way for me to learn what I need to know about your society? About how to live here safely. About your government. Your monetary system. There's so much I don't know. Is it possible to get some kind of, … I don't know, … microchip downloaded to my brain or something?"

Milo stared at her in fascination. "Wow. That would be so cool."

And she realized there wasn't that possibility for her. She sighed. "Damn. If I could speed-read or something, I could whip through all the schooling of your times until I caught up with my age group. Surely I could understand how this time period functions by the end of that."

"That's not a bad idea." Liev looked at her in surprise. "Milo, you can set her up with a VR system that will walk her through the lower learning levels."

"No one does grade school anymore," Milo said in surprise. "What good will that do?"

"It'll be the little things that trip me up," Lani explained. "Things that every child will know."

"But they are born with most of that knowledge. Or they already have it by the age of five."

"So how can I get the same knowledge then? You didn't end up enhancing me. You enhanced my cat."

"Hey, how was I to know you'd bring a critter with you?" Milo protested. "I'm not taking the blame for that."

"No one is blaming you," Charming said with a sniff. "Personally, I like it."

"You would," muttered Lani. She wanted to run back

into the pod and forget about this place. Maybe she'd wake up in the morning, and this nightmare would be over. But she'd asked for that before, and it hadn't happened yet.

"I think Milo can help you," Liev said calmly. "We do have virtual reality learning modules. He also has boosters to help you learn faster and to retain what you learn. It won't be so bad. We can get you through most of the basics in a few weeks."

Weeks? With a tired nod, she walked back to the small room that had the pod. Fully dressed, she climbed inside and closed her eyes. Hot tears threatened to pour out. Instantly the pod hummed as it worked to heal her. Only there was no healing this.

How did one heal a lack of self-confidence, a feeling of being overwhelmed, and a knowledge that she would always be the stupid relative from the fringe society in which others thrived?

She closed her eyes, curled up in a fetal position, and sobbed.

LIEV REACHED OUT a hand as Lani walked past. She didn't see him, and his hand dropped away. He didn't know how to help her.

As she disappeared around the corner, he was afraid he'd seen her shoulders shake. She'd had an incredibly trying couple of days.

"Well, go fix it." Charming gave him a flat stare that made Liev pause.

"And how would you like me to do that?" he asked.

Charming's gaze never blinked. "How about the same way you fixed it last time?"

And, damn, if heat didn't climb up Liev's neck as he realized just how much Charming understood.

"How did you fix it last time, bro?" Milo asked, walking closer, as if that would help him understand the solution.

Liev groaned silently. "Never mind." He spun on his heels and hurried after Lani. He wished he could fix it like last time, but somehow he knew it wouldn't be that easy. Not now that Gina had become involved. He'd avoided her after that one weekend because she'd become possessive. Meddlesome. Unlike Lani, Gina was the kind to push herself into situations where she wasn't wanted. And laugh while doing so. But her actions today? … He'd have to contact her and sort it out. And he also needed to talk to Hahn as to why he hadn't passed on the message about Lani's whereabouts. Not for the first time, he wondered at the loyalty of those he employed.

Lani's subdued sobs reached him in the hallway. Shit.

He bowed his head. He had to stop putting her in situations where she ended up in tears. They were obviously her coping mechanism. But how sad that she ended up crying as often as she did right now.

He walked to the pod and opened the lid. He sat down at the end and tugged her into his arms so he could look into her teary eyes. "First, I'm sorry you had to go to the Council this morning."

She blinked those wet baby blues at him.

"Second, I'm even sorrier that you had to deal with Gina this morning. I'll get to the bottom of what she was up to. I promise."

She blinked several times.

He waited curiously. When she didn't say anything, he continued, "And, as for helping you to learn the world

DALE MAYER

around you, I'll take off the next few days from work to go over the basics with you. Then we can hook you up to an education system and go through the lower levels first. Milo will be able to help you learn faster."

"*Faster?*" she asked cautiously, a glint of curiosity peeking through the waterworks.

Thank heavens. "Yes, we have modules you can listen to while you're asleep, and you should assimilate the information at a rapid rate."

Her curiosity turned to excitement. "Now that would help."

He smiled. "I won't leave you in the dark about my world. I should have taken a few minutes earlier to make you understand the ports. They are in all major centers, like the Council chambers. As long as the circle is empty when you step into one, you are tagged." He lifted her wrist as a reminder of her implanted tag. "Then the ports take you home or to work. If someone is already in transit, the arrival is delayed to sequence landings in the proper order. Ports read your tags automatically."

"But I didn't go to either of those places."

"No. Gina's tags were coded for her office and the Council, as part of her work. Not everyone can use them all the time." He paused, wondering how to clarify it. "The Council is an important part of the system and requires easy access for people in law enforcement. People working in police stations, lawyer's offices, the jail system, at the parole board, and others in some related fields must have access, so they can bring someone with them. They have an override. So, even if you wanted to go home, because Gina was there in an official capacity, she would have automatically over-ruled you—unless you knew how to change the coding to come home."

"Then learning how to change the coding is what I want to learn first."

He paused. "That's not a bad idea. You were in computers before, weren't you?"

She shrugged. "Only in a small way. And nothing like your computers of today."

"No, but it shows an aptitude. And we can build on that."

Without realizing it, he'd shifted her position so she was in his lap, cuddling her against his chest. He dropped his chin to rest on the top of her head. "We will make this work."

"So many pitfalls are out there," she muttered, but her tone was softer, more relaxed.

"There are, but we can teach you."

"And Gina, is she likely to be someone I have to see a lot?" She pulled away slightly from Liev, as if withdrawing into herself.

He tugged her back. No way would he let her go. Or give her a chance to squeeze more distance between them. He dropped a kiss on her forehead.

She stiffened slightly, then melted. She wasn't completely comfortable in his arms, but she wasn't against it.

He, personally, didn't think he could get enough.

CHAPTER 4

LANI HATED IT when she behaved badly. Crying was getting to be a habit, and she had to stop it. She wasn't weak, just overwhelmed. As in, she'd hit the wall.

Sure, she'd had a shock. Sure, she'd been scared, but she also knew people, and this wouldn't be the last time she came up against someone who didn't like her presence in Liev's life. The fact that he'd married her would add to that disgruntlement and disbelief from other women.

Gina had wanted more from Liev than he'd been willing to give—she likely still did. Lani didn't know what had been on Gina's mind this morning, but Lani would just as soon avoid seeing Gina again. "I don't get how Charming sent you a warning. Even if he did get the enhancement. And I hate thinking he is superior to me now." She wasn't sure how to reconcile the amazement and jealousy she felt over that bit. "How did he alert you?" she asked Liev.

"He called Milo on the house comp. We had just returned to the room where we left you, and, with Charming's info, Milo could track you easily. Because of Charming, your wrist tag went crazy. He noticed your vitals were rising, after we left you alone so he ran a scan that set off your wrist tag. He called us after that. I have no idea how he knew to do that, but he did somehow."

She didn't know what to think. "So Charming didn't

know where I'd gone?"

"Not really. He only knew that you'd moved and that your vitals had gone *off the chart*." Liev grinned. "To put it mildly."

"Yeah, the meeting with Gina wasn't exactly a warm bonding experience."

He laughed. "Gina was never into warm or bonding. She's into what's in it for her."

"Nice. *Not*," Lani said. "You have interesting choices in women."

"Not my choice," he said almost absently.

"What?" She froze and gave him a wide-eyed stare. "You mean, Milo chose her for you too?"

He started. Then a rumble started deep inside his chest as his laughter rolled freely. "No, he didn't," he gasped when he could. "Sorry. I meant to say that I met her at a weekend party a long time ago. I had nothing to do with her after that. She called many times, but I wouldn't go out with her. Never had any intention of doing so."

"Well, guess what? The silent treatment isn't working. Because you never said no, she's still working that angle, thinking that maybe this time you will say yes."

He glanced down at her in surprise. "This was years ago. She's not still interested."

"If she's not still interested, then she's happy to get a little revenge instead." Lani did understand women. And that was something in her experience that men never seemed to get. Rejection was a bitch. And some bitches never forgot.

"I'll make sure she stays away from you."

Lani wasn't so sure. "She's a lawyer and could make a lot of trouble for us if she chose to." Lani knew, to her regret, how some lawyers acted. Not all of them were the same, but

Lawrence Blackburn, her former boyfriend in her time, and Liev's "blackhearted ancestor," as Liev had put it, had been bad enough to give her a warped perception of lawyers.

"No," Liev said with such surety that she started to relax. "She won't."

"Yeah, I hate to bother you two, but Hahn is calling, bro." Milo's voice filtered overhead from the built-in sound system. "You need to deal with this."

"Damn," Liev said. "You stay here in the pod, and I'll go talk to Hahn."

She tried to slide off his lap only to find herself being lifted, then laid down on the wide bed. He lowered the lid, clicked a few buttons, and walked away.

Immediately the pod started to hum again. Disappointed that he didn't kiss her goodbye, she rolled over and closed her eyes. Suddenly the pod opened again, and he stood there in front of her. With a heated look, he lowered his head and kissed her.

Heat licked down her spine, her toes curled, and her mouth surrendered to his onslaught.

Then he was gone.

She sighed happily, tucking up into a contented ball.

"Really? Do you have to moon around like that?" Charming said from the floor level. He jumped up and padded up toward her. The lid slowly closed over them.

She laughed. "*Moon?* I think they need to work on updating your vocabulary, Charming, for this particular century." She shuffled backward to give him more room, her hand instinctively reaching up to pet her best friend. "Thank you so much for telling the brothers where I was this morning. That was a horrible experience."

He leaned into her hand, rubbing his head against hers.

"They shouldn't have taken you out there."

"I agree," she exclaimed, "but the Council's orders were explicit."

"*Hmm.*" He padded in a circle before curling into a ball. "I wonder why?"

She tilted her head to look at him closer. "Charming? What are you wondering about?'

He started to snore.

She frowned. "Are you just pretending to be asleep?"

"No." But he kept his eyes closed, and the snores kicked in again.

"Right." He might not be pretending at this point, but he was only one step away from making it a reality. She rolled over, giving the pod access to her back.

She could feel herself getting sleepy. Nothing like nerves, shock, and then recovering under soothing warmth to wear one out.

She closed her eyes and slept.

"HAHN, WHAT'S UP?" Liev stood in front of the HoloKomp, trying to remain cool and collected when all he wanted to do was return and finish what he had started. Lani was warm, wet, and willing. And he was a newlywed. He wanted to get back to his wife.

That thought brought a smile to his face.

"I don't understand the humor in this situation," Hahn said stiffly, his gaze hardening in the holographic image in front of the wall. "Glad you think this is all a farce."

Now what? "As I don't understand the situation, perhaps you could fill me in." He kept his voice cool, professional, and just on the edge of pissed. That was the thing about lawyers; they seemed to always forget who signed their paychecks. Hahn more than most.

"Gina quit the firm. She says she can't protect you and your new wife in any court scenario. She is citing irreconcilable differences between her and ..." Hahn looked down as if reading from a sheet of paper. "Lani."

Liev wanted to cheer. That was perfect if she quit. "I'm delighted to hear that. I can't say her behavior this morning was anything but one step short of criminal."

Hahn's eyebrows shot up, even as the look of anger receded slightly to be replaced by confusion. "What? Did I miss something?"

"I have a question for you that pertains to this morning's issue. Did you receive a communication from Gina, stating that Lani was with her in her office?"

Hahn frowned. "Not that I know of. Why? Wait. Gina's office? Why was Lani there?"

"Exactly what I'd like to know. Apparently Gina grabbed Lani's arm and shoved her into a port and took her directly to her office. She treated Lani like a criminal, offering no explanation for her actions. Lani was traumatized by the actions of a woman who is supposed to be helping me and mine." His voice gained a sharp edge at the end. "I hardly see that as appropriate behavior. I left explicit instructions for Lani to be in that seat when I returned. I don't care if you don't like my instructions, Hahn, but I do expect them to be carried out."

Hahn's face shifted from frustrated to startled to worried. "I have no idea what she was thinking. She said the girl was making a spectacle of herself, and she tried to calm her down. When that wasn't working, she went back to the office."

"Spectacle?" Liev said in an ominous tone. "In what way was Lani making a spectacle of herself?"

"I don't know honestly. Just that many people were staring at her. She's odd, you know," he said apologetically. "Different."

"Natural is the insult that Gina used." And now that he had a better idea of what Gina thought about Lani, he was delighted Gina was leaving the firm. Liev watched the rush of emotions slide across the face of a man who had worked for him for a long time.

"Liev." Milo worked on the big 3-D monitor in the kitchen beside Liev and just out of Hahn's sight. Milo was always on one of the many computers in the house. He'd been clicking like a madman for a few moments; then he punched a fist in the air.

"Look at this." He punched a couple more buttons, and suddenly the feed from this morning showed up on the HoloKomp, where both Liev and Hahn could watch.

All three men watched as Gina approached Lani, sitting quietly in the chair, oblivious to Gina's approach. After a short conversation, Gina checked her watch, glancing around at the crowd. The crowd moved past Lani, but in no way was she making a spectacle of herself.

Gina left. Then Lani's wrist flashed. It was apparent that she was trying to cover it up. Gina returned, said something, then she tugged Lani upward, almost dragging her to the ports. Gina pushed Lani into the closest one. Liev's gut clenched as he watched the shock and fear on Lani's face before she disappeared from the screen.

"Jesus." Hahn's shocked exclamation came through clearly before he managed to cover it. "I don't know what was on Gina's mind, but I will be speaking with her about this."

"And will she still be working for your firm after this?"

"I had planned on asking her to reconsider her resignation." At the sound coming out of Milo's mouth, Hahn winced. "She's very popular with our clients."

"*Male* clients," Milo said in disgust. "I bet she doesn't work with any female ones."

They both watched as surprise lit up Hahn's face, before his features twisted as he considered the issue. "You know what? I think you might be correct." His lips grimaced downward. "Let me talk to her."

"And get back to me with an answer. Then I can make my decision as to how I will proceed."

Before Hahn could respond, Liev disconnected the HoloKomp.

As the screen went black, Liev turned to Milo. "Send him a copy please, and keep that recording, in case we need it again."

"Done." He was busily tapping the flat counter screen, obviously searching for something. Liev watched his brother work. When Milo went on the hunt, there was no hiding anything from him. "What are you doing now?"

Rather than answering, Milo grabbed the corners of a small window and stretched it enough for Liev to see Gina's office clearly. Then Milo switched the time clock, backing it up to when Lani should have arrived. Last, he clicked on the speakers.

Liev grinned. Milo had tapped into Gina's security feed.

After a weird popping sound, all of a sudden Lani arrived in the office. Scared and stumbling to maintain her balance—in more ways than one—she bent over suddenly, her face green.

They watched the next few minutes in silence until the two brothers arrived at the office after Charming had alerted them. At one point, Milo stopped the feed, enlarged it, and backed it up so they could replay the section when Gina sent a message to Hahn.

Lani was right, at least as far as she understood. Gina had left a communication for Hahn, but the name wasn't clearly audible. Was it for the same Hahn or a different one? Or was it a fake communication? A coded message? Liev lived in a world of corporate espionage. He didn't take anything at face value.

Milo voiced his doubts. "I wonder who she left that message for." He switched cameras and zoomed in on her wrist comp, found a series of numbers. None of them were Hahn's code. So she'd left a message for a different Hahn. Milo immediately started a search. Within seconds, he had a name.

Johan Strand.

Not Hahn Driscoll, Liev's attorney, not even another Hahn, but a Johan. Liev's old friend. One on the run himself. And one who was taking way too close an interest in Liev's affairs. With one of Liev's lawyers.

Was Johan a friend? Or not any longer? Had he ever been?

The one thing Liev knew about Johan, the man was an opportunist.

So what the hell was he up to now?

CHAPTER 5

L ANI SURFACED TO a feel-good stretch with warmth bathing down on her. These pods were something. She was so happy to be in here. Registered or unregistered, the pod was a huge help, and she was grateful. She could just imagine those with arthritis lying here after a long day and feeling the healing rays beat down on their swollen joints. Or those with physical jobs. It used to be that having a Jacuzzi tub was the best way to end the day, but with one of these babies? … Wow.

Then she had to wonder if physical work was done in this century anymore. Did labor jobs exist? And that took her to another form of labor. Did women still go through labor, or did they give birth in a pod? Or did they go to sleep and wake up with a newborn? She laughed. Most likely there was no such thing as pregnancy or labor. Kids were probably created in test tubes now.

"Did that mean computerized nannies as well? Day-care dummies? Kindergarten komputers?" She laughed. "Better not be that way. Right, Charming?"

"A cat computer would be good," he murmured sleepily. "A custom chef for cats would also work. How about a computerized cat scratcher? I do need someone to take care of me when you're not here."

"Ha." She smirked. "I am not going anywhere ever

again."

"Little do you know."

She sat up, pushing the pod lid out of her way so she could slide her legs over the side. She stopped to look down at Charming, now sprawled across the bed, taking up her spot. He was seriously relaxed. "Are you feeling better now? Back to normal?"

He lifted his head to look at her. "Still tired but better." And he dropped his head down.

As long as he wasn't screaming for food anymore, they were good. She could use some of that wonderful coffee though. She walked slowly from the pod, happy when the room looked normal and the walls stayed straight. She used the bathroom, then walked into the kitchen. And stopped.

"Holy crap," she cried out.

Charming must have heard her, for he raced down the hall toward her. "What?"

They both stared.

The countertop had been converted to some kind of large computer screen, and both brothers were bent over it, searching through various screen loads that, at the touch of their fingers, moved and shifted, changing form and colors. Fascinated, she walked forward, her gaze on the computer screen loads as they rippled past. Charming followed at her side, then jumped into a nearby chair to get a better view, his gaze locked on the colors and images as they winked on and off, mesmerized.

"What is this?" Lani asked.

"A computer." Milo looked at her in surprise. "Surely you've seen one of these?"

"I've seen many but nothing like this." She searched the massive countertop for something recognizable in terms of commands. She found none. Neither was there a keyboard. She watched pictures of offices and buildings flash by. "What are you looking for?"

"Who, not what," Milo answered absentmindedly. "Johan."

"Your friend? Why?"

Liev snaked an arm around her waist and tugged her closer. Smiling, she wrapped her arms around his waist and snuggled in. "He's the one Gina contacted in the lawyer's office. It was Johan, not Hahn."

She frowned. "Are you sure?"

"Very. We watched the numbers as she coded them on her personal comp device. We managed to get a recording. It was Johan."

She shook her head. "You guys have a feed of that room from that specific time?"

"Milo found it."

Of course Milo did. She wondered what the Council would say if they knew he appeared to go wherever he wanted to electronically, and could retrieve any information he wanted. Nothing good, she was sure.

"Milo is on our side, and that's a good thing," Liev murmured.

"I'll say." She watched the screens flash by. Up on top of the screen was some kind of counter. She didn't understand, but it appeared to be connected to the flashes.

Suddenly she heard a *beep*, and a single window surfaced and flashed.

Liev leaned forward. "There he is."

"GOOD, WE FOUND him." He watched Milo concentrate at

the screen loads that flashed faster than the human eye could see.

"No, we haven't."

"What? What do you mean? He's right there." Liev tapped the picture that had shown up. "That's his location."

"No. It's the location he's letting us see. He's not there now. In fact, I'd probably say he set that up as a decoy."

Liev groaned. "Not good." He turned away to glare around the kitchen. "What reason would he have for hiding like that? What is he afraid of? And why from me?"

Charming laughed. "The same reason you hide away. Because you are involved in something you want no one to know about."

Milo stared at Charming, considering his remarks. "In which case, Johan's likely the one behind all this. Maybe the one who actually supplies the pods." He turned to his brother. "Liev, what does Johan do?"

"Deals in trading. But I don't know what."

Lani made an odd sound. He turned to look at her, but she stared at Charming, who was already nodding. "Like Lawrence Blackburn. Part of the reason he was so oily was he used information like a weapon."

Liev stared at her. "What does Johan have to do with my ancestor?"

"Ah," Milo said. He turned back to the computer system. "That assumption is probably correct."

"What is correct?" Liev stared at the three of them. "What am I missing?"

Charming filled him in. "Johan and the pod that he freely lets his partygoers use and his disappearance all make sense if he is trading, … buying, … selling, … information."

"Ah, hell."

CHAPTER 6

LANI WONDERED WHAT kind of mess she'd fallen into. From Johan to Hahn to Gina. "I don't understand what Gina would gain by taking me to her office. If she is working with Johan what difference does it make? What purpose could they have?"

The two brothers shrugged. "I don't know either," Liev added. "Unless we weren't supposed to get there as fast as we did? Maybe someone else was arriving, and we beat them there," Liev said thoughtfully. "Milo?"

"Already on it."

Milo's fingers flashed so fast, Lani could hardly see what was happening. Her ever understanding Milo was a long way away.

"Ah, here it is again," Milo stated. "I'll let it stream longer. Should have thought to do that in the first place."

Before her was a recording of Gina's office. In silence, they watched as the video continued. Lani couldn't see a timestamp, but it hadn't been more than a couple minutes after the time she'd left with Liev when they heard another *pop*, and two men arrived.

She gasped. They looked dangerous. Unsavory. Then again, it was a law office. They dealt with the criminal element all the time. Both men wore leather skin suits with heavy boots and chains hanging from their pockets. They

205

were so typical-looking of the thugs from her day that she started to laugh.

Milo shushed her. "Let's listen."

The speaker replayed the conversation.

"Where is she?" asked the younger of the two men.

"How should I know?" said the older one. "The boss said she would be here."

She? Lani or Gina? And who was the boss?

While Lani tried to figure out what the men were talking about, Gina walked into view on-screen. She stared at the room and spun around in a full circle. In a shocked voice, she said, "Please tell me that you have her stashed somewhere."

Liev sucked in his breath. Lani looked up at him, watching as fury darkened his skin and tightened his features. But he never lifted his gaze from the screen. Lani returned her attention to the men talking.

"She wasn't here when we got here. Figured you had her in your private office." The man looked behind her. "Are you sure she didn't go in there with you?"

Gina glared at him, tiny beads of sweat forming on her brow.

If Lani hadn't been watching so closely, she doubted she'd have seen them.

"Of course I'm sure." She spun around once more. "Damn it. Where could she be? No way those idiot brothers could have gotten to her first."

"Check the log. Then you'll know for sure."

She walked over to a wall, just off-screen. The two men turned to watch her, but they weren't close enough to read the log.

"Damn. It was them." Gina turned to face the men.

"How could they have known she was here?"

Lani was confused. Gina knew Lani had left with Liev and Milo. *Why was she lying?*

"The obvious answer is, Lani told them," the first man said. "How else?"

"I scanned her when she arrived," Gina said. "She had no personal comp on her."

"Really? How bizarre is that?" Thug One asked. "Everyone has one."

"She must have left it behind at the Council," Thug Two said.

"What? So the brothers would find it and know that she's here somehow?" Gina asked sarcastically. "That makes no sense."

"Well, they knew somehow." Thug One looked bored.

"Tracker," Thug Two said. "She must have a tracker on her."

The three stared at each other.

"They wouldn't track just anyone," said Thug One in consideration. "She must be valuable."

"What she is, ... is different," Gina said. "We need to know in what way."

The two men shrugged. "She can't be that different."

"Oh, she is. We just don't know how much or why."

And the video stopped.

Silence ensued.

Then Milo exploded. "*Idiot* brothers?"

LIEV GRINNED. LANI laughed. Welcoming a chance to lighten up after all the lies and deception. "Of course that would be the one thing out of that entire conversation that you'd comment on," Lani quipped.

"I remember everything," he snapped. "I am *not* an idiot."

Liev watched Lani and Milo spar. He listened with only half an ear. His mind was consumed with what he'd heard. How did anyone know about Lani? And what did they know? Or thought they knew?

He'd been so careful. It had to be Johan, but what good would that knowledge do for him? He had his own troubles. Snatching Lani wouldn't help his case.

And why kidnap her? *Ransom?* Liev had money but not billions. As far as he understood, Johan had more money than Liev did. Johan knew about the tagging, so that was probably where the leak had come from. Liev had been afraid of problems from that corner but hadn't expected it so quickly. Or from his neighbor. Liev had done everything right. Lani should have been safe. She needed to be safe.

But apparently she wasn't even close.

Damn.

That Gina had been lying through her teeth was also worrisome. Was she trying to save her own skin so no one would know Lani had disappeared in her presence before the men arrived to take Lani away? Or was she playing a different, more dangerous game?

His mind spun. "Milo, we need to track Johan's movements, before and after he disappeared. Find out who he's been associating with, who he lives with now, who he lived with before. Details on his business pursuits. Even IDing partygoers at his house. Things like that. I hate to think he's behind all this, but we have to consider the possibility."

"For what purpose?" Lani asked him. "Would he have any concept of where I've come from really?" She lifted her shoulders slightly and dropped them. "Honestly, unless he knows the truth, and that's too bizarre for anyone to believe, what difference would my story make to him?"

"That's what we have to find out."

Milo tapped the screen, and a picture of Gina appeared. "She's the one who will know. We have to get this information to Hahn and corner her. If we show her the evidence we have on her, she'll break."

Liev saw a mature look come over his brother's features, a rare occurrence.

"I refuse to let this bitch do this to us."

"I don't know what penalties she'd face for this, but surely she'd turn on the others to save her own skin." Lani glanced at the photo. "Women like her are always more concerned about squeaking out of trouble themselves."

"True enough." Liev walked over to a blank wall and brought up his private HoloKomp system. "I'll get Hahn on the line. Milo, can you package up the section of video where the two men arrive in Gina's office? Cut it after she checked the log to see if we'd managed to get there before her henchmen. We'll show Hahn how she's been lying to both sides."

"Done," Milo said almost absently. "I've also isolated the henchmen's faces. Their tags have been shut down, so we can't identify them that way. I'll run a facial recognition program instead."

"Let's show their faces to Hahn as well," Lani said. "He might recognize them."

"Speaking of Hahn," Liev said to Milo, "make sure you initiate a body scan to see his vitals. He might be a good liar, but his body will show the effects of my questioning and seeing the men's faces."

Milo nodded. "No better lie detector in the world."

Lani gasped. "You can do all that?"

"And so much more. Watch and learn, sweetheart." Liev sent a link to Hahn. "He'll be online in a moment."

CHAPTER 7

L ANI WATCHED AS Hahn's face appeared on the wall again. On the wall yet out of the wall in a very lifelike 3-D image.

"What now?" Hahn snapped. "I'm still trying to get ahold of Gina."

"This." And Liev set the video screen to Play. "It's just after Milo and I left Gina's office."

In front of Lani, projected on a wall for Hahn to see, the two thugs appeared in Gina's office almost magically. Another holographic projection but large enough for Hahn to see. Lani really wanted to learn to use those ports. She would love to travel if it was instantaneous. She'd had some initial stomach reactions, but presumably that would get better over time. At least she hoped her physical reactions would calm down.

She studied Hahn's face, wondering at the clarity of the image that made it seem like he was right inside the room. It was on the tip of her tongue to ask. Maybe they even had interplanetary travel. Now that would be so cool. Honestly, what she'd seen outside had scared her, but, at the same time, it was exciting.

As long as she was safely inside. Though, by this time, she realized that she'd only seen a tiny portion of what the technology of today's world could do.

As the video played out in front of him, Hahn gasped in shock, his skin turning a pasty gray. Once he spoke, he didn't waste any unnecessary words. "That's Paul and Tommy Defino. They're on the run after escaping prison transport. Both are wanted for breaking and entering, armed robbery, and a host of other charges."

"Did you represent them? Did Gina? Is there any other viable reason why they'd be in your offices and communicating in this manner with your business associate?" At Liev's cutting tone, Lani turned slightly so she could see his face.

This angry Liev took some getting used to. He stood tall and arrogant, his arms crossed over his chest as he challenged Hahn. Irate but in control. Someone had messed up, and he'd know the reason why.

He handled power well. It emanated from him in long-reaching waves. He knew what he could do and how to get what he wanted in life. Something was very attractive about that.

She understood he ran the large company he and his brother founded, and that had to have molded him. For the first time, she could see the businessman who'd carved a place for himself in the corporate world.

Hahn shook his head. "No. I won't have that element in my company. I've been trying to locate Gina, but, so far, she's not answering her personal comp, her home comp, or her car's communication system. I don't know where she's gone."

Liev shot Milo a look. He grinned and shambled over to the large countertop, flexed his fingers, and got to work. Lani was torn between watching Liev verbally bat Hahn around and racing to Milo's side to watch him perform magic. She'd always had a love for technology but hadn't realized her interest was this strong. And the stuff she now saw ...

Her fascination won out, and she raced to Milo's side. He moved screen loads and clicked parts of the countertop where she couldn't see that it had any buttons. She presumed he was busy tracking down the bitchy lawyer on one set of monitors and running scans on Hahn at the same time. She could see a heat scanner but it was holding steady with only slight variations in temperature. It had stabilized on the red edge. Hahn was pissed.

Lani didn't want to cause anyone else trouble. *Live and let live* was her motto. But, if they weren't going to leave her alone, then all bets were off.

Still, she wished she understood what Milo was doing.

He pounded on the countertop, making her back up, afraid the monitor thingy would break. Instead, the huge flat display opened up like a 3-D box, rising straight up from the counter. She gasped in delight and wonder. Milo went into action, sweeping screen loads to the side and bringing up more. His hands danced in and out of the blue-green images that flowed from the box. She noted that Milo had some facial recognition software down on one side. He was looking for the missing lawyer just in a different way than his search for Johan. And Lani wanted him to find her.

She bent over and studied the pictures as they whipped by. Now he flicked the pictures like a movie stream, and the computer tossed in ones of the males from the search for the Defino brothers she'd seen in the video. Her mind saw it before her eyes recognized it.

She reached out and stabbed a picture before it disappeared off the side of the counter. "That one."

"What one?" Milo dragged it toward him and blew up the image. It was the profile of one of the men. Oddly enough, it had been the snake's head earring she'd recognized.

A long, low whistle slipped from Milo's lips. "Nice. That's the older one, Paul. Now to source his location."

Once again screen loads went flying. Just when a headache settled in for good into Lani's brain from trying to watch all the flying images, Liev turned off the video screen with Hahn and joined them.

He stood on the other side of Milo. "No sign of her?"

"Not yet. We've found him though." Milo reached up and tapped the image in the corner. As he did, Charming jumped up on the countertop. "Whoa," Milo said. "No cats on the monitor."

Charming backed up slightly to the edge but did not jump off. He stared at the images, his whiskers vibrating.

She didn't know if he planned on jumping on the flashing images or if he understood what they were looking for and could help. She didn't want to ask, but her attention was caught on Charming as he stared at the fast-paced screens in front of him. Then his paw flashed out, and he dragged an image back toward him.

"Hey, no scratching the monitor," Milo cried out.

"I didn't scratch it." Charming sniffed. "Besides, I can't. It's holographic." He released the image. "I believe this is who you are looking for." He sat back and proceeded to clean the paw he'd touched the monitor with.

Everyone leaned over the picture. The image was too small for her to see. Liev reached over and tapped it twice. The image blew up.

Gina.

Milo stared at Charming. "Wow. Like seriously good."

Liev snorted. "And who made him like that?"

Milo snickered. "Good point. We're all good."

"Yeah, right," Lani said.

"Hey, you found this guy. I didn't." Milo beamed at her, as if she were a prized student.

"Really?" Liev looked at her with added respect. "That's great. Trying to find images when Milo gets going is not easy."

She grinned. How could she not? At least she wasn't a complete loser.

Charming shot her a direct look. She flushed. Surely he couldn't read minds now, could he? He went back to his grooming. As she looked around the kitchen, what she really wanted was some of that awesome coffee. She'd come out looking for some earlier, but, with everything going on, she'd gotten distracted.

She walked around behind the men. At the other side, she studied the flat wall, looking for anything to denote cupboards, coffeemakers, or even a water spout.

And found nothing.

"LANI, WHAT DO you need?" Liev asked, circling the counter to stand beside her. He wanted to take her in his arms and kiss her, but something stopped him. Maybe it was the fact that she'd so done well with Milo.

Not everyone did. Maybe it was Charming, who'd shifted his position so he could stare right at Liev. Stupid to be nervous of a cat. But there it was.

Even odder that the cat had managed to snag Gina's picture out of the thousands floating past. Liev would have to talk to Milo about what exact enhancement he had given the cat.

"I was looking for a drink."

"Water?" He walked to the wall. "Watch." She stepped closer to see a break in the paint. It was a scrolled-style circle. He pressed his hand flat on the wall and pressed down. Instantly, a cupboard popped out. He removed a tall skinny glass and moved over several feet. While she watched, he pushed another section of wall, and a small fountain slid out with a hand attachment. He squeezed the attachment, and her glass filled with water. "See? It's easy. Every space in today's world is designed to multitask."

"Like anything new, it is easy if you know how. Is this filtered?" she asked.

"Absolutely." Like everything in their world, water was severely regulated, being one of the last few natural resources left to them. They had to protect it. But she didn't need to know that right now. She'd quickly be overloaded with information.

She tossed back the drink and held the glass out again. He refilled it and handed it over. She sipped the second glass. "Is there any chance of getting coffee?"

His face lit up. "Oh, good idea. That's exactly what we need." He turned around to make the first of what he expected would be several pots. He'd have to look into buying a bigger unit.

Yet none of the changes he would be making were anything like the ones Lani had gone through, so he couldn't complain.

He ordered coffee with a push of a button. Lani was quiet behind him. He wondered at her conspicuous silence over their marriage deal. Then he'd avoided the topic altogether. Once he'd gotten her agreement and had pushed through the process he'd left the subject alone. It was a land mine waiting to explode and needed delicate handling. He'd almost brought it up in the pod room earlier, but it hadn't been the most pressing issue then, so he'd held back. Maybe she was hoping it would go away.

Whereas he was hoping to resume the honeymoon. He couldn't help but think about the many benefits of being married. And how hot and willing she'd been in his arms. God, he wanted that again. And soon. Like now. He slid a gaze her way. She'd settled back to watch him, as he made coffee her gaze intent on his motions. And, damn, if that intensity wasn't a turn-on.

Just then, her stomach grumbled. At first he didn't recognize the sound. Then it sank in. He froze. Uh-oh. Lani had been pulled from bed, taken to the Council, kidnapped, and returned home to recuperate in the pod—all on an empty stomach. Checking the comp on his wrist, he winced and said, "You missed another meal, didn't you?"

"Two meals," Charming whined from the monitor counter.

Liev nodded. True enough. "Right. Coffee first. Then food."

Charming howled at the sound of food being placed second. "How can you put coffee first?" he moaned. "I need *foooood*."

CHAPTER 8

L ANI CHUCKLED AT Charming, walking closer to him to scratch his neck. "You hadn't even noticed that you were missing a meal until it was mentioned."

"Of course I noticed," Charming said, turning his neck for her to get at another spot.

How did a cat manage to look affronted? Lani shook her head and scooped him up. She stared down into those eyes, so familiar and yet so different now. She recognized her wonderful old tomcat in there, but, at the same time, someone different was there. Someone even better. Her heart swelled as she held him close. "I'm so glad you survived that trip."

"Me too," he whispered, rubbing against her neck. "Like what would have happened to me if you came here, and I was left locked in the apartment?"

A shudder swept through her. "That would have been horrible. You'd have died without me to take care of you."

"And yet today, I took care of you." He reared back and pinned her with a beady eye. "So I should get your share of lunch."

She laughed. "So not happening." She carried him over toward Liev, who appeared to be making sandwiches. At the sight of the thick slabs of bread and cheese, Charming moaned louder.

"With all the technology you have available, how is it you are doing the cooking?" Lani asked.

"It's a hobby." He flushed, then shrugged uncomfortably. "It's a bit of a joke to my friends actually."

"So there is an alternative."

That made him laugh. "Yes. We have machines that create complete meals now. I just don't want to have one around."

"Oh." She personally would love a machine that could do it all. Then again, if he was happy to cook, she was happy to let him.

"He's into retro stuff. Like food and cooking," Milo spoke up. "It takes work, and it's disgusting."

Lani laughed. She looked at Liev and shared a look of understanding. "Unless it's chocolate, I suppose."

Milo scowled. "Chocolate is different."

"The food is almost ready. Give me another minute." Liev reached for a large block of something. She leaned in, then realized what it was. "Oh, yum. Roast beef."

He gave her a strange look. "Did they have that in your time?"

She stared at him. "Of course." Then she frowned. "This is from an animal, isn't it?"

He looked at the block of meat and then back at her.

And she realized it was square in shape. As in, very square. As in, too square. "Oh, damn. This isn't meat, is it?"

"Meat is bad for you," Milo said from the other side of the counter. "I've told you that. Boosters are better—in all ways."

"Except that Charming is a carnivore," Lani reminded him. "And so am I."

"He could drink boosters too." Milo appeared to be

warming up to one of his favorite subjects.

Charming said in a low voice, "Let's go back to the meat."

"Except I'm not sure it's meat."

"Oh, it's meat," Liev said, "and it came from an animal but not a live one."

Dumbfounded, Lani could only stare at the block of gray stuff. "Like cloned meat?"

"Ha! More likely 3-D printed meat," Charming said with a snicker. He sniffed the air experimentally, caught a whiff, and started to wiggle out of her arms. "Except that would be old tech here. And this smells delicious."

"Hey, wait. You're going to fall." She tightened her grip.

"Let me go, and I'll jump."

He tried to sneak out of her arms, but she clamped down tight and said, "No animals where the food is. We'll sit at the table. He'll bring food when it's ready." She walked him back to the table where they'd eaten their first meal.

"I could be dead by then," Charming groaned.

"And they might happily kill you if you don't behave yourself," she snapped. "Remember your manners."

"And maybe they should remember theirs," he retorted. "Considering that we are the guests, and they are the hosts." He peered around Lani's body to stare at Liev's back. "Lousy hosts at that."

She gasped in horror. "You apologize right now. That is not acceptable. You know perfectly well that he's preparing our meal. Now be appreciative of that fact before you lose out completely, based on your bad behavior."

"*Harrumph.*" Charming stared up at her. "I'm not a two-year-old. You can't treat me like that."

Milo laughed from behind her.

She tilted her head toward the sound. "Do you hear that? That's because, although you're not that age, it's how old you are acting."

Charming's marble eyeballs hid behind his suddenly slitted eyelids. He howled deep in the back of his throat.

"Stop it. Communication is new for you. I get it." She dropped a kiss on top of his head. "That's okay. You'll get the hang of it, and, besides, you'll always be my adorable kitty."

"Oh, brother." He turned away from her to pad over to the farthest point on the kitchen table. "This could get embarrassing if you're getting all mushy."

Her laughter pealed out to ring around the room. Without warning, she reached across and scooped him back into her arms. She started to dance, like they did in their previous life, holding Charming in her arms, as if he were a human-size partner with one paw up. "It so could get mushy. Because I love you. I always have. You are my best friend. And, now that you can talk, I so want us to have a tea party and to play dress up …"

At his shocked shriek, she bent over, giggling, still holding him in her arms. He dug his claws in, probably as a punishment. She straightened, the odd giggle still pouring out. "You are too funny. I was only kidding, by the way."

"You'd better be," he threatened, curling his claws ever-so-slightly.

"Watch the nails," she said in warning.

"Why? You have a healing pod now. I can cause all kinds of damage, and you'll be just fine." He stretched up to stare into her eyes.

Would she ever get used to him being able to talk like this? She hoped so, but she also didn't want to lose the pet she'd had since forever. Emotion washed over her, and she wrapped him up tight. Against his fur, she whispered, "I'm so glad you're mine."

His engine kicked in and made the tears once again burn her eyes.

When he whispered, "Me too," that made her heart melt.

LIEV STOPPED TO watch the two interact. He couldn't believe the language coming out of Charming's mouth. Damn, he needed to corner Milo and ask him about those enhancements. He remembered Milo's slip of the tongue earlier. If he knew his brother, Milo wouldn't stop at one enhancement if he had a chance to slide more in. Considering how quickly Charming had locked on that image on the screen, Liev had to wonder if eagle vision or super-quick reflexes might have been one of the other enhancements. And that would suck for Lani if the cat had received all the benefits. Imagine knowing that your cat was smarter, faster, and more intelligent than you were.

Talk about a major turn in their relationship.

Yet he remembered Lani had snagged a picture from Milo's fast-moving stream as well, so maybe they'd both received enhancements. They could have shown up stronger on Charming, due to his size in relation to Lani's.

Liev watched the two cuddle, and, for the first time in his life, he saw something lacking in his. He'd never had a pet. He'd had a stuffed teddy bear for his first couple years, until he'd been deemed old enough to go without. And now, as he watched Lani cuddle Charming, he realized how much the cat enriched Lani's life. And quite possibly that worked both ways.

Just then, Charming's head popped up over Lani's shoulder, and that golden gaze locked on his.

Even before the cat opened his mouth, Liev knew what would come out. He held up heaping plates of food and walked closer. Charming's eyes rounded in delight, and he scrambled to get out of Lani's arms and onto the table.

"He's got food," Charming said urgently, when Lani resisted.

She laughed and set him on the table. "Let's eat then." As she took her place at the table, she asked, "Liev, can I help you do anything?"

"It's done. Not to worry. You can help next time. These are just simple sandwiches."

Milo walked past. "And I'll make boosters for both of you while I get mine."

Liev happened to be watching both Lani and Charming, so he saw them wrinkle their faces in disgust. Catching his eye though, they both grinned. Lani said, "We'll drink it because we need it, but honestly, food is more our style."

She motioned to Charming, who busily gnawed on thick chunks of ham that Liev had found for him to accompany his serving of beef as well.

"I need to get cat food for him," Liev said.

Charming lifted his head and stared at him in horror. "I eat protein. Not cat food. *Protein.* Chicken. Fish. Lamb. Mice." He stared more intently, just to make sure Liev understood the seriousness of the issue. "Understand?"

Liev raised one eyebrow and nodded. "Got it."

Chapter 9

L ANI HAD FINALLY filled up enough to know that she would make it another day. She wasn't so sure about Charming, as he'd finished his second helping and right now plowed through a third. For herself, the fatigue had returned in triplicate. The pod seemed too far away to reach, and her eyelids already drooped.

Before she had a chance to decide if sleeping where she sat for a few moments was a good idea or not, she was scooped up and carried into the tiny healing room. She snuggled against Liev's chest. "Sorry. Just got so tired all of a sudden."

"Hey, it was a tough morning for us all." He shifted her in his arms. "An afternoon nap is perfect."

She heard a series of buttons clicking, then a low hum. The healing pod. She so wanted to be in there. And, just like that, he laid her inside and dropped a kiss on her forehead. She smiled sleepily, closed her eyes, and let her mind drift off.

She heard the door shut behind Liev as he exited. In the distance were sounds of conversation, but it was far enough out of her hearing that she couldn't make out the words.

Drifting was nice, easy. She heard a weird sound, then felt something small hit her arm. She rubbed her arm, then rolled over to get more comfortable, loving the way the bed adjusted beneath her. What a marvelous invention. Several small noises outside the pod bothered her, but a buffer created by the pod's humming noise filtered those out. It was great.

But maybe not *quite* great. Her eyes opened. Something didn't feel right.

She didn't feel right.

But she didn't know what was wrong.

"Charming? Are you here?" He'd said he'd follow her in a few minutes, when Liev had carried her in this direction—but had he?

It felt like … someone was here.

As that knowledge filtered in, she realized that someone definitely was, but it was not someone she knew. Or rather, wasn't someone who was supposed to be in here.

Shit.

Her breath caught in the back of her throat. What was she supposed to do? She could slip out of the pod and make a run for the door, but it wasn't like that would be a subtle move. They'd see her. And maybe that was okay. Just because a stranger was in here didn't mean they were out to get her. Except everyone who had been a stranger so far had been out to do just that.

She could lie here and pretend to be asleep.

Gently she rubbed the sore spot on her arm.

She felt exposed. What if this person grabbed her by her feet? That thought whirled inside her head, making her almost blind with fear. Slowly she pulled her feet up toward her chest. Her breathing became raspy. The more she tried to control her breathing, the worse it got. The pod lights changed from blue to purple, and immediately more heat beat down on top of her. The pod knew she was under stress.

Her vitals had to be off the chart again. At the same time, she knew that had to be a signal to whoever was in here with her. She saw no sign of Charming still.

Would he recognize that her vital signs had gone crazy again? Or was he still eating like he wouldn't get another meal? She closed her eyes and starting calling him in her mind. *Charming, please help. Charming, can you hear me? Please, someone, come.*

She took another long shuddery breath, surprised to find she'd curled up into a fetal position. She would feel like a fool if everyone came racing into the room, and she was actually alone.

But she'd rather that than the opposite. She wondered how she could bolt out the door without getting caught.

Then a noise sounded behind the pod. *Oh, God. Oh, God. Oh, God!*

She froze. And couldn't catch her breath. She had never had a panic attack, but this was starting to be a full-on scream-for-her-life-and-run moment.

As quietly and as naturally as she could, she slid over to the edge of the pod bed.

Stiff, barely breathing, she readied her muscles and slowly pushed the pod lid open just a little bit.

Three, two, one …

She slid under the edge of the pod and bolted for the open door, screaming at the top of her lungs.

"WHAT IS THAT?" Charming sat up abruptly from his cleaning to stare in the direction of the pod room. Liev and Milo raced down the short hallway, where Lani ran smack into Liev's chest. He caught her in his arms, while trying to see what had scared her. "Milo, check out the room."

"No, no, he shouldn't go alone," Lani cried out. "Someone's in there."

"What? Impossible." Liev shook his head as he held her close. "No one else is here. It's not possible."

She shuddered in his arms. "It's not only possible, it's real. I could hear their breathing and weird noises." She slapped her hand over her arm. "I swear something hit my arm."

"What?" Liev stepped back and lifted her arm so he could see. "There's no way."

But there was. A slight red spot showed on her upper arm. He tucked her close to him and moved her into the kitchen. "Stay here." He walked to a wall and brought up his security system with a few commands. "Milo, where are you?" he asked.

The intercom broadcasted his voice. Liev set the computer to show all the occupants in his house. Immediately the gray screen lit up several orange hot spots. He easily identified himself and Lani. Charming had to be the smaller one.

And there was Milo in the pod room.

"I'm right here, Liev," Milo said as he walked into the kitchen. "Nothing's there."

Liev shut down the intercom, sealed off the pod room, and motioned his brother to come over to him. He tapped the monitor at the red image in the pod room and, in a low voice, asked, "Then what or who is this?"

Chapter 10

L ANI HUDDLED AT the kitchen table. Charming sat in front of her, but his attention was on the brothers behind her, checking out the apartment still via their computer security network. She'd rather be back in Liev's arms. A chill rippled up and down her arms. She rubbed them, wishing she understood what the guys were talking about. Had she just imagined an intruder? The pod room was barely big enough for anyone else to stand in, let alone hide.

And why hadn't she seen someone if they were there?

None of it made any sense. The fact remained; her arm stung from whatever had happened to it. Liev walked over, ran a gentle finger over her arm, and frowned. He asked, "The healing pod didn't fix this?"

"Not sure it had time," she admitted. "And I'm not going back in there until I know it's safe."

"We need to know what caused it."

"And how do we do that?" She stared down at the puffy skin on her arm. It was a tiny injury. Not worth making a fuss about. Still … "Whatever this was, my body doesn't like it."

"I'll take another look with Milo."

Charming jumped up on the table beside her and rubbed his head against her shoulder. "Hey, Charming.

Wish you'd been in there with me?"

"I hate strangers. You know that."

"True, you used to always run away." She rubbed her cheek against his head. "Except you like Liev and Milo just fine."

His engine kicked in when she kissed the top of his head.

"They are different," he said with a yawn, dropping his butt on the table and looking around with interest. "Do you think they have any leftovers?"

"Probably, but keep eating like a crazy man, and they will be forced to keep canned cat food around for you."

He looked at her through slitted eyes. "You mean, canned shrimp and tuna, right?"

She shook her head. "I don't know why they would. Besides, you loved canned cat food before."

"Sure, but they don't have that food here. And," he leaned in, tilting his head so he could whisper in her ear, "what if Milo picks the food? It's likely to be green and full of boosters."

At that, she giggled. And, boy, did that feel good. From fear to laughter in a heartbeat. She caught a glimpse of the satisfaction in Charming's gaze. "You did that on purpose." she accused.

"Did not." He twisted and started grooming his back.

"Did too," she muttered.

"So what? Someone has to do something to keep your mind off the intruder."

Intruder? It sounded way worse when he said it. More real.

"Nope. It wasn't." Charming continued to clean, sounding completely unconcerned.

So you can *read my mind?* she asked, watching him.

He gave her one of those *Duh* looks.

She sighed. Charming had at least three enhancements that she had discovered so far. "Then who was it?" she asked in an ominous tone of voice.

"Not sure," Charming said, "but I think it was a what, not a who."

Puzzled, she stared at him, wishing he'd pay attention and stop cleaning his butt. "How could that have been anything but a person?"

"Holograph," Charming said.

Wordlessly, she stared at her four-year-old cat, who appeared to understand things way beyond her comprehension.

Into the sudden silence, he paused what he was doing and lifted his head to pin her gaze with his. "What?"

"How would you know that?"

Damn if his nose didn't go up in the air before he returned to his cleaning.

Apparently she didn't warrant an answer.

LIEV STRODE DOWN the hallway, Milo close on his heels. At the pod room doorway, he stopped and gently pushed open the door as wide as it would go. He couldn't see anything, but the computer scan wouldn't have made a mistake like this.

"I don't see anything," Milo said. He almost pushed Liev into the room as he craned to see over his shoulder. "There has to be a glitch."

"I wouldn't be so sure about that." Liev stepped into the room and bent to look below the pod. He couldn't see anything with the naked eye. But ... he clicked through the screen loads on his wrist comp and found the same disturbing hot spot. Above and behind the pod.

He walked around until he was directly under the spot. He twisted his head, trying to see into the dark corner, when a light shone right on him. Startled, he turned to see Milo lighting the spot in question. Liev pivoted when something beeped behind him. "What the …?"

"It's my new toy." Milo held up the base of the light to show him the flashing buttons that accompanied the beeps. "It's a bug finder."

Liev stared at his brother before switching his gaze from the device to the high corner of the ceiling. "Bugs?" he asked in a hard voice. "Here? After all the sweeps and security measures we have in place?"

Milo leaned closer and whispered in his ear, "Probably came in with the pod."

Damn. As he thought about it, it made perfect sense. He'd been so worried about taking this step and hoping it was the answer to help Lani that he'd not run through any of the special security checks. The normal ones, sure. But who had time to consider beyond that? He hadn't had a chance to think about anything, … let alone act on the thoughts.

He stared, wondering what to do next. Milo motioned him to retreat the same way he did. Back out in the hallway, Milo closed the door and pressed several buttons on his little gadget. Liev had built-in bug sweepers that he used often. His office and home were wired to catch any that made their way inside, but this one …

He smiled reassuringly at Lani, Charming in her arms, standing hesitantly at the end of the hallway. They'd obviously followed him and Milo to see what they'd found.

"It's very high tech," Milo muttered as he popped open a

3-D screen. Then he stepped back to walk around the image. "These are the blueprints of the bug."

Liev stared. "It was inside the unit. Meant to break off as the bug was released from its hiding spot." He turned to face Lani. "The casing is what hit her arm."

"It has audio." Charming sauntered closer, making Liev back away. "So it can hear us. ... Meaning, we should be able to hear it."

Milo spun around and stared at the damn cat in excitement. "That's right. I can track it back, using its own programming code."

And damn if that cat didn't sit back on its haunches and nod his head approvingly at Milo. Liev felt like the dummy in the class—again. Milo hadn't been the easiest brother to live with. "Can you find out who sent this?"

"Not only that, I might be able to listen in on what's going on in their office or wherever they are holding the receiver for this unit."

"I didn't see a bug in there." Liev hated to bring it up, but ... "How small could it be?"

"It's holographic and invisible."

Liev, in the act of walking back to the kitchen, froze. "What did you say?"

"It's an invisible holographic bug," Milo said impatiently.

"And that doesn't sound incredibly wrong to you?"

Milo shook his head slowly, as if to clear his head so he could focus. "We have invisibility, and we have bugs and holographs. Someone put them all together."

"And that someone wasn't you?" Maybe that was the biggest surprise here. Liev had never known anyone to get the edge on Milo in a field he loved, and espionage toys were one of his specialties.

"Nah, no point in adding holograph stuff. Just a waste of time."

That almost made more sense. It wasn't a practical application. With a smile, Liev continued down the hallway, gently moving a very confused Lani ahead of him, until he realized what his brother didn't say. He spun around and continued to walk backward. "Wait? What about the invisible part?"

"What about it?" Milo was busy with his little toy.

"Have you managed to make an invisible bug?" Liev tried to hang on to his patience, but his brother could try a saint. "Like this one?"

"Not like this one."

Liev waited.

"Better." And Milo shot him a quirky grin of success. He didn't punch the air with his fist, but it was damn close.

"Better how?" He couldn't see how an invisible bug could be improved on. He waited, but Milo busily chuckled and clicked away on his fingerboard comp, matching it to something happening on his bug finder. Liev waited a moment, then nudged his brother. "Milo, how could you make a better bug than an invisible one?"

Milo looked up in surprise. "I just expanded on your idea."

As he looked to be returning to the toys in his hand, Liev quickly interjected, "What are you talking about?"

"Stealth technology. *Duh*. On a microscale."

And he walked back into the pod room, leaving Liev to stare after him in shock. He'd developed the home stealth technology system to cloak what they were doing in the company and at home. It was a military-type application, but he'd refined it for their purposes, and apparently Milo had refined it yet again. He trailed behind his brother. "So you can send in an invisible bug *and* have it receive and send data without anyone picking up its presence with any tracking device?"

Milo stopped and threw his head back in frustration. "That's what I just said, didn't I?"

Liev snorted. "Not really."

"Well, it's what I meant. Now, if you don't mind, I'd like to listen in on our uninvited visitor." Shooting Liev a dark look, Milo walked forward until he stood just below the spot. Adjusting the monitor, strange voices filled the room.

"I can't tell what's happening. There's been only static for the last bit."

"Any chance they found the bug?"

A snort came first. "Hell no. This baby isn't even on the market."

Liev cocked his head, trying to figure out who was speaking. He brought up his own comp and set up to record the next bit of conversation.

"Maybe it's broken."

"And maybe you should pull your brain out of your butt and use it once in a while."

"Watch your mouth. You might think you are the best of the best, but someone better is always out there. You can be replaced."

That sharp retort was followed by footsteps and a door slamming.

"Ass."

Liev checked his comp to find he had enough to run a voice recognition program. He started it and looked over to see what Milo was up to. He'd held up his bug finder as high as he could to the ceiling.

A weird ear-splitting sound filled the room.

And then came dead silence.

CHAPTER 11

LANI DIDN'T UNDERSTAND what was going on. A virtual invader? Like, how was that possible? It was hard to be scared of someone jumping out and attacking you if just an image. She'd followed the two brothers as they'd wrangled their way down the hallway. She had heard their discussion and then some other voices. It didn't make complete sense, but it appeared that something extra had come in with the pod. And that wasn't likely to be good.

Then the room filled with a horrific noise. She clapped her hands over her ears and crouched on her heels. Just as suddenly, the noise stopped, and the silence was almost as painful. She shuddered when something touched her. She turned to see Charming rubbing up against her leg. "That didn't bother you?"

"No, not the same way it did you."

"And I thought animals had better hearing."

"Sure we do, but I also knew it was coming, so I had time to prepare for it."

"You knew it ahead of time?" She shook her head at her cat. "How is that possible?"

And damn if he didn't give her that look that said she was too stupid to bother explaining it to. She shot a glare at his back and stood up as the brothers came out. "What was that?"

Liev wrapped an arm around her shoulder, turning her toward the kitchen. "Milo just killed a bug."

She twisted so she could see his face. "You mean, an espionage-type thing?" At his nod, she raised her eyebrows. "Are you two so heavy into this stuff that people are trying to steal information about Milo's inventions, or is this about me?"

"I don't know. Both are possible. I just don't know how they knew the pod was coming here to have something like that ready in time."

Charming galloped down the hallway in front of them. "What's to understand? The bug and pod came from the same person. If you needed an unregistered pod, they needed a bug in here to find out why!"

"That's getting old," Lani muttered, glaring at her beloved know-it-all pet.

His tail flicked in several sharp motions as if to say, *Get over it.*

"He's right though." Milo sauntered past. "It had to have been ready to go before you ordered the pod—or right at the same time. I told you it was a bad idea."

Liev pulled up short. Lani turned, about to ask him what was wrong when he said, "This is getting damn old."

She grinned. "Milo might have brought me for you, but it looks like he brought Charming for himself."

Liev's gaze widened, and he broke out laughing. "That is so true."

They entered the kitchen to find identical looks on Milo's and Charming's faces. As if reading each other's minds in tandem, they turned their backs on Lani and Liev.

She giggled freely, loving it when Liev hugged her close. "Let's go see if the two geniuses can figure this out."

Still smirking, they stepped up to the side of the big holographic monitor that the two smarties studied.

"My voice recognition hasn't found anything yet," Liev volunteered.

"And it won't most likely. You don't have the latest software."

"What?" Liev stared at his comp. "Sure I do. This was just updated last month."

"And I updated it after trying to find Gina's henchmen buddies." Milo lifted his head to Liev's glare. "What? I sent it to you. It's not my fault if you didn't do the upgrade as you were supposed to."

"There aren't supposed to be any. It's supposed to be seamless. Remember?"

Liev's deceptively soft tone had Lani searching his face, not understanding the undercurrents. "Updating computer software was constant in my world. Is that the same here?" she asked.

"No," Liev said, his voice more resigned than hard. "It's part of Milo's mockery of my retro preferences."

"Not totally. It's fun to bug you, but it is safer right now to do things manually. You know that. If we have a problem, we have to go into blackout mode. And that means taking everything off-line and updating manually."

"Damn."

Milo laughed. "See? You forgot."

"Well, I've had other things to worry about."

Milo reached out, flicked a couple of holo buttons, and pulled a holo headset out of the monitor and wrapped it around the back of his head. He brought up some white screen and, with his hands not touching the monitor or the keyboard, words started to appear.

"What the heck?" she muttered, leaning closer. "What's he doing?"

"Recording his observations and planning what to do next."

Lani shook her head. "But his fingers aren't moving."

Liev stared at her. "What does his fingers have to do with it?"

"Ah, … typing?" She gave him a look that should have made him understand the problem, but instead he grinned. "At least audio for speech."

He laughed. "Sorry, typing is old-school."

"Just like me, apparently." She watched as paragraphs of text appeared on one side of this big monitor. "So you can just think what you want onto that screen?"

"Sure. Works much better."

"I can see that." She stared, trying to figure out how it worked. "It must be set up for his neural impulses."

"Exactly." Charming looked at her in admiration. "I didn't think you could figure that out."

"Watch it," she warned. Then had to smile as his face split into a huge feline grin. "You were teasing me, weren't you?"

He nodded before turning around on the spot and lying down. Just before he closed his eyes, he whispered, "Nap time."

"I wish."

Liev reached an arm across her shoulders. "You can go back in the pod."

Wistfully, she considered the idea. "Is it safe?"

"Absolutely. Come on. I'll take you back."

She let him lead her back into the small room. "It doesn't feel the same."

"No, but it is fine. It's safe and secure. The sounds you heard were coming from the bug."

"But it sounded like heavy breathing."

"Probably just the initial sounds as it went live. The bug had no visual on it, so it couldn't see into the room. But it did have audio."

At her shocked look, he rushed to reassure her. "They didn't hear much. It just turned on now while you were in there."

"It could have been on then too." She leaned in and whispered, "You know? When …"

"No." He shook his head. "The bug would have showed up earlier on our house comp, if that were the case. I had to run all sorts of security programs with the raid and the warrant. No. It was turned on just a few minutes ago."

"Are you sure?" Because she wasn't. "What a horrible thought to think someone was listening in like that."

"They weren't," he reassured her. "It was installed in the pod, to detach at the right time."

Inside the room, he opened the pod. "I have something special to make you feel better."

She slid him a sideways look, wondering what he meant by that. But he appeared to be studying the computer dashboard on the pod. "Go ahead and lie down," he said, his fingers dancing on the keyboard.

Desperate to have the soothing sensation the pod could provide, she scrambled inside and immediately felt better. She had to trust that the Blackburn brothers knew what they were doing.

Then again, she didn't have much choice.

LIEV WAITED UNTIL Lani had stretched out in the pod. He needed her to relax enough to be back in here. Afraid or not, she still needed the pod and likely would for a long time to come.

He played a gentle music track and set the pod to give a massage.

She moaned. "I don't know what you did, but it feels wonderful."

"It will massage whatever surface you lay on the pod. So a back massage or a chest massage."

"Then I'm good here for a long time."

He smiled. "It will help you to sleep too." He backed away toward the door when she asked, "You're sure it's safe?"

"I'm sure. Just rest."

He waited a few moments, studying the small room and realizing how unimpressive it was. He could fix that. He could also make the room bigger. His head reeling with ideas, he snuck out of the room and headed directly to the big computer.

There, working on the opposite side of Milo, he brought up the dimensions of the apartment. He had paid extra for the adjustable space, and, so far, they hadn't used it all. He enlarged the space of the pod room, incorporating the bed she'd slept in the first night to make a bedroom big enough for Lani and the pod. As much as he'd love to have her in his bedroom—she was his wife, after all—he wanted that to be her decision. So until that time, ... he opened the decorating program, studied the settings, and selected a Pacific island hideaway. He started the program, hoping she was asleep already. Otherwise the changes might freak her out. He should have thought of it earlier.

As it was, he realized he'd better check up on her. He

quickly raced down to the room and watched as the colors changed and as the holograph appearance shifted so the pod was in the middle of a South Pacific island. The walls also slowly adapted to the new parameters he'd set, allowing the imagery to have more punch. He thought the sand was a nice touch. He noticed that Charming had followed him into the pod room.

"*Ohh*, a litter box." Charming jumped in.

"No! That's not a litter box," Liev whispered in a harsh tone.

"Looks like a litter box." Charming walked forward and sniffed. "Smells like a litter box." He turned in a circle and started to dig. "Feels like a litter box." And he squatted.

"No! Don't do that." Liev hurriedly opened his link to the comp programming back in the kitchen. "Program. No sand. No sand!"

Too late.

Charming flicked his butt, lifted his nose in the air, and sighed happily. "Nice litter box." He studiously buried his mess, then bolted past Liev.

Liev groaned. "I can't believe you did that," he yelled after Charming. "You know better."

"Who knows what better?" Lani stuck just her head out from under the pod, frowning at him. "I was asleep. What happe—" She stopped. Her eyes went wide, and she gasped. "Oh my. What happened in here?"

"It was supposed to be a surprise."

"It's a fantastic surprise," she exclaimed. "But why? How?" She pulled herself farther out to stare in happy amazement. "We're not really in the South Pacific, are we? If we are, I'm all for staying here."

He smiled at her innocence. "No, we aren't. But, if you

want to go, just say the word."

"*Word*," she cried out happily, bouncing on the bed inside the pod. "Word. Word. Word."

He stepped over Charming's heaped sand pile and opened the pod. "Sorry. I didn't mean today. Later we'll travel. A lot of things need to be taken care of here first."

She stared up at him, lying back on the pod bed. "Really? It's not expensive?"

His eyebrows shot up. She really had no idea what kind of wealth he and his brother had accumulated, or that she herself had, for that matter. "Let's just say it's definitely doable." He thought about the benefit of taking her where no one else would know who they were, until she learned more about their world. "And it might not be a bad idea. I'll have to think about the ramifications."

"No, you have to work. I understand. You can't just take time off whenever you feel like it."

She really didn't understand. He needed to fill in her education and fast. "There's a lot you need to learn about the family business, but, for the moment, I can work anywhere in the world. I can show up to work in holographic form. That's how I attend most meetings. Yes, we have offices, as you know, but, if I want to spend a month on the top of a mountain in a resort, that can be arranged as well. I can also use special ports to come back to work on a daily basis if I choose."

Her eyes went even wider as she absorbed what he said. "Everyone can do that? Not just rich people? 'Cause wow!"

He laughed. "Not everyone. Obviously, if you are in a field that requires your presence, then you can't take off all the time. But this is normal in the business world, and it's common to port from one place to another this way. Go for lunch in Europe with a business partner or attend a meeting in South America in the afternoon. Time zones can be a bit of a problem though."

"I bet," she said with feeling. "And there must be currency issues."

"No, we now have a global currency and a global financial group that keeps track of the international monetary scene."

"That makes sense," she said slowly. "In my time, there was talk about doing something like that."

"It happened somewhere around the same time that English became the global language."

"Do you still have banks?"

"Financial centers, but you can access the same one all over the world. Makes traveling much easier."

"Do you have to pay to use ports?"

"Oh, yes, like the internet, we pay for usage. It's expensive, but nothing like plane traveling would have been in your time."

"That's a relief." She smiled up at him.

And damn if that simple movement of her lips didn't make his groin tighten. "First, you need to heal." He went to close the lid of the pod, letting her go back under. "Then we can explore. I want to show you a lot of things here. It really is a magical world."

"Wait." She pushed the pod lid back up. "Can you join me?"

"What?"

She gave him a slow sexy quirk of her lips. "Remember the last time?"

"Oh, God, yes, I do." He hesitated, hating that he felt like he needed to ask. What if she said no? "Are you sure?

You need to rest."

"I believe we went over this once already. Sex in a healing pod helped in many ways."

Part of him wanted to correct her use of the word *sex*. It wasn't just sex for him. He didn't really want to know if it was only that for her. He hoped not, but this was not the time to discuss such things. Not if he wanted a chance to make love to her again.

She smiled, a warm, enticing smile that heated his blood. Damn, she was something.

He grabbed his shirt and tugged it over his head, tossing it to the far side of the room. "Make sure you miss the litter box," she whispered with a smirk.

"Ha. It's gone. Bet Charming didn't know that the rooms clean themselves."

And didn't that make her stare. "They what?"

"Absolutely. Housework is a thing of the past."

"My past, apparently." She reached out a hand and stroked down the front of his thighs, pausing before slowly climbing back upward.

His hips surged into her palm, willing her to explore further.

"Remember last time? You said I could have a turn?"

He'd barely thought of anything else. "Yes," he muttered, struggling to open his pants and to then step out of them. He finally managed to stand in front of her, his eyes watching her face as she studied him with a fat grin.

"So let's trade places." And she scrambled out of the pod to stand beside him. He was now fully nude, and she was fully dressed. And didn't his knees start knocking? He wanted this. Damn, he wanted this very much. He lay down on the warm bed, self-conscious for the first time as his erection stood tall and proud. He watched her watch him. He waited with bated breath as she reached out a hand and grasped him gently with one hand. He groaned softly and closed his eyes.

When he felt her wet tongue, he almost lost it. "You do that again, and it'll be all over before we've even started."

She gave a low throaty laugh. "Oh, I don't think so."

CHAPTER 12

S HE LOVED THAT he lay here so accepting. With all the problems she'd brought with her, he'd done his best to keep her safe. And now he trusted her like she'd never had anyone else trust her. And Lani wanted to make it good for him. For them both. She took her time stripping off her new clothes, loving the feel of his heated gaze, his appreciation. He had the ability to make her feel beautiful with just his eyes. When she pulled her midriff top over her head, finally as bare as him, he sat up and reached over to cup her breasts.

"Hey," she teased, "I thought this was my turn to run the show."

"Too late," he said thickly. "I can't wait. I need you now." He tugged her forward until she rested on top of him. "I swear I've been waiting for you forever."

Sliding his hands up to clasp her head gently, he pulled her down for a kiss.

And what a kiss it was. Fireworks and liquid heat fought for supremacy, lighting up nerve endings while melting her insides. Lord, he was a hell of a kisser. And she had to admit, an odd sense of homecoming was attached to this moment. As if she'd been waiting for him too. And didn't that train of thought take her down a direction she had not considered. He was here, and so was she. That was good enough for both of them right now. And she wanted him. She'd never been a one-night-stand type person and didn't plan on being one now.

Besides, he was her husband. And they'd yet to have a wedding night.

"Do you have a bedroom?" she murmured when she could.

"Of course." He reached up to clasp her head and tugged her down for more drugging kisses. She twisted sinuously against him, dragging her breasts from one side to the other, then flexing her hips and pressing her pelvis hard against him. He moaned, sliding his hands down to grab her hips and ground his pelvis up against her.

"You know that we could try out your bed one time."

He smiled beneath her lips before moving to trail kisses down her throat. "Next time."

She tilted her head back, letting her long blond hair fall down around them. "That's what you said last time."

He laughed and flipped her over to lie beneath him. She stared up at him in wide-eyed surprise when he came down on top of her, just where she wanted him.

She spread her legs, making a place for him. He settled in deeper. She arched beneath him, offering her breasts. He bent his head, tugging first the one, then the other, into his mouth and suckling. He stoked the fires until she twisted beneath him, crying out, "Liev, now."

"Not yet."

"Now." She wrapped her legs around his thighs and gripped him tightly. Then she wiggled beneath him.

He roared, lifted his hips, slid his hands down to hold her hips steady, and plunged deep.

She gasped at the invasion. At the fullness. At the right-ness. Again. A tiny corner of her mind worried that it was dangerous to think that way, but the rest of her reveled in it. All her life she'd been trying to find her place. Trying to find her home in the world. Apparently she'd just been behind the times.

Liev lifted his hips, pulling back and back and …

She dug her nails into the smooth rounded muscles of his buttocks to stop him from slipping away from her completely.

He drove inside.

She wrapped her legs around him as he set up a rhythm that she was desperate to match and more frantic to increase. He picked up speed. Throwing her head back, she held on for the ride.

Inside, her blood heated as her body raced to the finish line.

She twisted her head, crying out as tiny explosions went off, but she wasn't quite there. He lowered his head and claimed her lips, his tongue slipping inside as he drove in one last time. His body stiffened above her, and he threw his head back, a long and low groan sliding out from deep in the back of his throat.

Then she wasn't aware of anything more as her own body exploded.

NICE. ACTUALLY A hell of a lot more than nice. Liev lay listening to the strong, steady beat of her heart. The pod started humming around them. The lid was still up. He wondered if it had the ability to take over and help even when it hadn't been closed. Then to his amazement, it dropped into place and set up healing rays all around them. He'd never heard of them being able to open and close on their own, but it didn't really surprise him. It was, in fact, very helpful.

Especially right now, when he couldn't possibly move.

"Wow." She sighed happily, her breathing only slightly calmer. "You are *soo* good at that."

He grinned, loving the lighthearted intimacy with her. He tugged her up close and closed his eyes. How had Milo known that this was what he needed? That he missed loving someone. Being part of a special twosome.

His kid brother was many things. Intuitive was the one thing he wasn't.

As Lani nestled closer, her leg sliding over his, he could feel her body settle into the gentle rhythm of sleep. That she could trust him after all that had happened made him feel good. He knew she'd had little choice over these major changes in her life, but he hadn't forced her into this step. And, although he needed her legally bound to him to keep her safe, she hadn't seemed to have a problem with that.

He twisted slightly so he could look down on her ash-blonde head. Who'd have thought she'd find a way into his heart?

He almost winced at the thought. He hadn't thought to find a partner anytime soon. He'd looked for one years ago and gave up when all the relationships seemed superficial and dull. He'd made what he thought were a lot of friends back as a young adult, but the friendships hadn't lasted, and the girlfriends had disappeared even faster.

He'd always been looking for something … more.

Dropping a kiss on Lani's head, he realized he might have just found it.

Chapter 13

L ANI WOKE UP, cozy and comfortable with the sound of surf breaking close to her head. Her eyes popped open to find Liev's decorating system still in place. She loved it. And she would so enjoy being part of his world with these types of perks. She pushed the pod open and sat up.

And laughed.

The sand was gone. Instead a long deck stretched from her pod out into what appeared to be water. She couldn't imagine it being real water, but Charming had apparently used the fake sand just fine, so who knew?

She tilted her head back to see blue sky and sunlight shining high above her head. This decorating stuff was incredible. She not only could see the surroundings but she could feel a gentle breeze and even smell the heavy blooms of the tropical flowers. She spread her arms and flopped backward in delight. "I love it here!"

"Ha. I wondered when you'd get around to saying that."

She laughed and rolled over to see Charming, walking gingerly along the deck, as if the water would reach up and grab him. He did so hate water. "You won't get wet, you know."

He glared at her. "What was wrong with the sand here? It was perfect."

"Ah, except I don't want the pod room to be your litter

box. If I have to adapt, so do you."

"What can I say?" He hopped lightly onto her pod bed. "It was done in a weak moment. A nostalgic moment."

She shook her head. "As much as I can understand that …"

"It's done, so forget about it." He head-butted her. "Think about loving me for a bit."

She stroked his beautiful fur. "As if I don't love you."

"Maybe, but it seems like you are loving Liev a little more."

"Not more than you!" She gasped in horror. "Never."

"Aha! So you do love him." He half fell, half sprawled on her.

She barely noticed his body landing on hers. Her mind was spinning with his words. And that *L* word. Did she love Liev? How could she? She didn't even know him. But she'd already acknowledged that she knew him better than her major asshole ex—and she'd loved him, or so she had thought.

Damn.

"Stop thinking so loud. You're disturbing my beauty sleep," Charming grumbled. "With all your activities, you might want to grab some shut-eye as well."

"Hey."

"If you're going to be kidnapped, you'll want to look your best. Just sayin'."

She bolted upright. "Why did you have to say that?" she wailed. "How am I supposed to rest now?"

"Seeing as how you forgot that you have bad guys chasing after you, I thought a reminder would be appropriate."

"Did you and Milo figure things out while I was resting?"

"*Resting?*" He turned his head and narrowed his gaze. "Is that what you call it?"

And damn if she didn't flush. "Hey, be nice."

He snorted and stretched out, showing his belly. She sighed and reached over to give him a little more love. "I wish I knew what was going on."

"Milo found out a bunch of stuff. Go check with him. And, while you're at it, we must have missed a mealtime in there somewhere."

"You wish."

"Hey, you satisfied your hunger. Now help satisfy one of mine."

Considering he'd been fixed before she ever got him, it seemed a reasonable request. Besides, she could feel her stomach starting to grumble too. "I'll see." She searched the island hut for her clothes, amazed to find them at odd places but fitting into the scenery, as if she truly were here. Once dressed, she stopped at the doorway for a final look and smiled. "Charming, this island look is perfect for us."

"Only if you bring back the sand."

"Not happening." She partially closed the door as she walked out. The hallway was still the same. She had to wonder why Liev didn't decorate the apartment as something more glamorous. Surely it could be a palace on the inside instead of this normal boring old apartment? In the kitchen she found the brothers, heads bent, studying something on the table.

No. It seemed to be the tabletop. What the heck? She hurried closer. It was another computer of some kind. "What is this?" she asked.

Milo lifted his head to stare at her, but his gaze appeared unfocused.

She switched her gaze to his brother. "Liev?"

"It's a new tracking system we've been working on for military applications." He grimaced. "Technically you're not cleared to see this."

"Oh, fun. The problem is, I already have." She sat down beside him on the bench and grinned when it widened to give them more space. "I do love the future, especially the decorating system you have in this place. Although why you haven't changed all the rest"—she waved her hand outward to encompass the kitchen—"I don't know."

"Milo doesn't like change. Or rather, we can't agree on a change that suits us both."

Milo turned to stare at him. "I'm not a kid anymore. If you want to redecorate, go for it."

"We tried it once. Remember?"

"Hey, you wanted the place to look like some creepy haunted house, and I wanted it to look like a science fiction flying ship." He shrugged. "So we did nothing."

Her jaw dropped. With difficulty, she managed to pull herself together. "You can do that?"

"Well, you have to pay for it, but the motto of today's world is that *Everything is available—for a price.*"

"Wow. Okay, things have really changed." She nodded to the table that wasn't a table. "Did you guys design this table too?"

Milo frowned. "Why would I care about designing furniture? That's so old hat. Anyone can do that."

"So this isn't a real table? You just designed the computer that sits on top of it?"

"Ah, you mean the fact that it's part of the table. Today, you can place computers on any kind of hardware."

Liev started manipulating his side of the 3-D image

again.

"What are you looking for?" she asked him.

"The missing lawyer. She's the key to this mess. If we could talk to her …" Liev trailed off.

Lani frowned. "Didn't Charming find her?"

"Yes, but she's dropped off the grid again. We tracked her until she just … disappeared."

The big screen on the side wall opened up, and Hahn appeared to step through. "Liev, are you receiving calls?"

Liev pushed back his chair and walked over. "Hahn. What did you find out?"

"There's no sign of Gina," he said nervously. "We've tried everywhere and got nothing. Her mother hasn't heard from her either." Hahn's face twisted as he said the last part.

Lani stood in view of the holoscreen.

Hahn turned to look at her. "I think the answer lies with your wife, Liev. Maybe if I could ask her some questions."

Liev immediately shook his head. "You can give me your questions, and I'll see about asking her, but Lani's not the problem. Gina is."

Milo nudged Lani off to the side. He lowered his head and whispered, "He can't see you here. If you stand in that square"—and he motioned to where she'd been on the floor—"he can see you."

"Oh, sorry. I didn't know." She lowered her voice. "Can he hear us too?"

"Only if you are in that box."

"Wow." She could imagine the technology being very helpful in many cases, but it sure seemed like an invasion of privacy to her. Or was it? Hahn had asked if Liev was receiving calls. Maybe that was the same as asking permission. "Does Gina live with her mother?"

Milo shrugged. "No idea."

"Maybe we should find out. After all, if she does, and her mom hasn't heard from her, maybe something bad has happened to Gina. Maybe she didn't run off. Maybe she was punished for failing to grab me."

Milo cocked his head to the side, then reached into his back pocket and pulled out his weird fingerboard computer. After tapping on the silver machine for a few moments, he smiled and said, "She does live with her mother."

Liev, distracted by Milo, turned to look at them. "Does that matter?"

"Depends if she's in trouble with whoever she was to deliver Lani to. Chances are, failure is unacceptable."

Liev's jaw clenched. "Hahn, have you checked the hospitals for a woman fitting Gina's description, either dead or alive?"

"Oh, dear." Hahn's face twisted up.

Lani thought maybe it was because of the unpleasant media attention that his firm might receive if that were the case. Then her attitude toward all lawyers was awful since she had worked with Lawrence, the king of all asshole lawyers.

She sighed and tried to remind herself that Hahn was likely a very nice man. Just because Lawrence and Gina weren't didn't mean all lawyers were bad. Good ones had to be out there, right? She just hadn't met any. Except maybe Hahn. And the verdict was still out with him.

Milo shouted, "Yes! Found her."

Liev turned to face his brother, while Lani tried to see what Milo's comp said. "She's in the morgue on Cronan Street."

"Morgue." Lani's stomach felt queasy again. Gina could have had an accident, but Lani couldn't quite believe it. She was afraid that these people were playing for keeps, and failure was not an option.

LIEV HATED THE look of fear on Lani's face. He pulled up the information Milo gave him and got into the databanks to give him a visual of the body. Sure enough, it was Gina. He showed the headshot to Hahn, watching the shock, the fear, then the lighting-fast calculation wash over his face as he tried to figure out the best way to play this.

"She must have had an accident. Although why they wouldn't have notified me, I don't know. Or her mother." At the mention of Gina's mother, Hahn's face twisted once more. "Her mother will be heartbroken."

Liev continued to read the file. "She came in with her tags missing and minimal clothing." That caused Hahn's eyebrows to shoot up.

"And showing signs of torture."

Silence.

Hahn exploded. "What the hell did she get herself involved in?"

"That's something I expect your help in finding out." Liev continued to read the file. "Her body was dumped outside the hospital."

Hahn dropped his gaze, but his shoulders shook. Lani didn't know if he was upset by the news or if he'd had a personal relationship with Gina and was affected on more levels than she'd first assumed. Regardless, finding out one of his employees had been murdered had to be difficult for anyone.

"Liev, I have to do damage control. Let me know when and if you find out anything else." Just like that, he blinked off.

Lani stared at the spot on the wall, wondering how long it would take before she got used to that.

"So much for his help." Liev shook his head. "Milo, can you get into the Council files to see if they have any further information?"

Milo walked over to the countertop and brought up the big 3-D unit and started clicking.

"Also didn't we find some of the bad guys' photos on the facial recognition program?" Lani asked. "Did that help at all?"

"We're running their list of known associates, trying to find out where they might be located."

"And then what?" Lani asked. "Do you have police you can call on for help?"

Milo shook his head so fast, his long mohawk looked to be in the middle of a major storm. "No. We've crossed the line. We have to handle this ourselves."

"And can you?" she asked, studying his face.

He looked at her, showing his inner wisdom and maturity. "We have to. A lot is at stake here."

She didn't know if he meant her or more but decided some information was better left unknown.

She felt helpless. They had so much to do. Normally she'd have made tea or coffee or pulled together a simple meal; yet it appeared at the moment that she couldn't even do the simplest of things.

She hated that.

She walked over to where Liev had gotten her water before. She placed her hand where he'd placed his and pushed slightly. Instantly a water fountain slid out from behind the wall. She grinned in delight. Now if only she'd watched how he'd made coffee. How hard could it be? Exploring the things she'd watched him do, she managed to open the cooler and to pull out some cheese for a sandwich. At least it would be a sandwich if she could figure out where the bread had gone. She remembered their first meal with a big chunk of cheese and meat. Back in the cooler, she found something that appeared to be meat. She pulled it out and turned to ask Liev about bread.

Instead, he stood in front of her with a large loaf in his hands.

She smiled and snatched it from his hands. "Next time, show me where you got it from." He tapped the counter in front of her, and a cupboard rose up. She grinned. "I do love all this cool technology."

Milo stopped what he was doing, looked at the shelving, and glanced back at her. "What technology? That's a simple cupboard."

She shrugged. "It's more advanced than anything I've seen."

"Right." He gave a small headshake and returned to what he was doing.

She studied the cupboard, looking for other food that she'd recognize. Some were recognizable. Most were not. While the men went back to work, she busied herself opening packages and tasting food. One looked like crackers but tasted like cardboard. Another had brightly colored images of food all over the package but gave no clue as to what was inside. She read the instructions to find it was a synthetic supplement. Yuck. Must be something for Milo.

The bread was good though. She could really use a slice while she rummaged but couldn't even find a knife to cut it with. Finally, in frustration, she began systematically placing the palm of her hand on every surface she could find and giving a light push. Nothing happened for the first few tries, but she persisted and was delighted when she opened one cupboard, then another, and another. She investigated all the contents and realized the third one had a mother lode of utensils. She grabbed a knife and cut herself a slice of bread. She turned to study the cooler trying to remember how to open it. She pressed at various places but to no avail. The door would not open.

Ignoring the snickers from behind her, she said, "Open." *Nothing happened.* "Open sesame."

Still nothing, but the laughter behind her grew. "Open, please."

Silently, the cooler opened. She turned and threw an accusing glare at the two snickering males and said, "You just programmed it to do that, didn't you?"

Milo nodded, a wide grin splitting his face. Liev walked over. He reached out a hand and hit a hidden spring. The cooler door closed.

"No, wait."

"Now you open it."

She reached out and touched the same place he did. It didn't work. She looked at him with a knowing glare.

"Again." He smiled. "A little harder this time."

Success. She grinned and reached in for butter. "What is this?" she asked about a big package wrapped in paper.

"Steaks for dinner."

"Oh, yum." She could really use a steak. "With baked potatoes and a salad?"

"If you like. Do you need more right now?" He motioned to the thick slice of bread she was eating.

"I'm fine, but Charming is hungry again."

Liev rolled his eyes. "Of course he is." He walked to a side cupboard. "I ordered this today. It's premium cat food."

"Oh, thank you." She watched him open some kind of odd package and pour a premeasured dose into a bowl. It didn't look like cat food, but it did smell like it. It had an unmistakable smell, once you dealt with it more than once. Still, Charming should approve.

She hoped.

She walked back to the pod room, carrying a bowl for Charming, Liev following. "I love the South Pacific theme. It's stunning."

"I was hoping you'd like it. If you don't, we can always change it."

"Later," she smiled. "After I'm bored with the concept. If I ever get bored."

"My bedroom is a Swiss chalet."

"Really?"

He grinned. "Let's feed Charming and maybe I'll show you."

The look in his eyes sent a shaft of heat right to her toes. She murmured quietly, "I think I'd like that." She'd love to spend a private hour or so in his bedroom.

As they opened the door to the pod room, she gasped. Instead of her South Pacific island getaway, the room had been filled with cat trees and cat ledges, walking up and down the walls. Including a dozen cats apparently sleeping on various beds. Over all the scenic sounds was heard a deep rumble of a snoring cat.

"What the ...?"

Liev laughed. "Hey, Charming, I don't suppose you were planning on sharing this meal with all your friends."

The snoring stopped. Charming raised his head, his nose

sniffing the air. "Program revert."

While Lani watched in amused surprise, her pod room turned back to the South Pacific hut. "Wow."

Charming stood, stretched, and walked over to them. "I'm so weak," he moaned.

"Ha. Not so weak as to set yourself up right at home." Lani scooped him up and tried to cuddle him, but he wanted nothing to do with her. Instead, he scrambled out of her arms to land softly on the floor in front of his food bowl. He immediately burrowed his head into the food. Lani took a step back. "Amazing, Charming. You've picked up everything so fast."

He lifted his head and pinned her with a marble glare. "And why wouldn't I? Nothing here is hard to understand or learn."

She sighed. "Says you."

"It would be easy for you too. You just need to do things instinctively instead of overthinking everything." With that pronouncement, he returned to eating his meal.

"He's right, you know? Everything nowadays is meant to be intuitive and easier to do, minimizing time and effort."

She shook her head. "Then why is it we haven't sorted out who killed the lawyer and why she was after me?"

He winced. "That's a good point. Before I show you my place, instinct is prodding me to go see what Milo has found."

CHAPTER 14

WHILE LIEV WENT to check on Milo's progress, Lani stayed with Charming until he'd finished eating, then she bent to scoop his dish off the floor when the pod started to make weird sounds. It often made similar sounds when she was in it—but not like this. This one had a weird metronome sound to it. She called out. "Liev? Milo? The pod is making weird sounds."

In seconds, the two men rushed toward her. "It's probably nothing," Liev said. But his face said otherwise.

Milo circled it, his hands full of his gadgets. "Okay, this is not good. It's a tracking device." He pushed a button, and a weird *splat* sounded, like a power outage. "Not anymore."

Lani released her pent-up breath she hadn't been aware of holding. "Why didn't your bug finder pick this up earlier?"

"I think it was triggered after the first one was destroyed. Like a backup system. While it wasn't active, I couldn't have picked it up."

She didn't like the sound of that. "What if there's a third bug that will start when it realizes this one stopped working?"

"It's possible but not likely. Still ..." Milo attached the bug detector, its lights flashing to say it was working, right on top of the pod. "That will take care of anything else."

With that, he returned to his study of the pod, looking for the now-defunct bug. "I did tell Liev that the pod was dangerous."

The other two trailed behind him.

"You said a lot, but you didn't exactly leave me much choice," Liev snapped.

"And I, for one, am very appreciative of the pod," Lani added with feeling. "It's helped a lot. Though I can't say it feels very safe, and I'm not sure I want to sleep in here any longer."

Liev tugged her close. "You don't have to."

Milo rolled his eyes. "Can we stay on topic?"

"On topic, I just want to sleep," Charming said from behind them. "Who can rest with all that racket going on?" he grumbled.

"I thought you were eating," Liev said suspiciously.

"I was eating. Now I want to sle—"

A heavy pounding sounded at the front door.

"Milo, I thought stealth was on?" Liev ushered Lani into the pod room. "Stay here," he said to Lani and Charming. "Don't come out until one of us says so."

And he closed the door in her face. A final *snick* made her scoop up Charming and whisper, "That last part didn't sound very good."

"He locked us in." Charming stared at the closed door in shock. "That's bad. Like, really bad."

"Why is that?" She figured it couldn't be that hard to get out. It seemed like everything was either hand- or voice-controlled.

"Because the food is on the other side of that door." He turned until his flat face was pushed tight up against hers, his eyes round with horror. "We'll starve."

"MILO, FIND OUT who is here."

As usual, his brother was way ahead of him. Being naturally distrustful, Milo had set up multiple programs to keep the world out there—right where he wanted it. He valued his privacy. More than that, he detested the invasiveness of the government.

Liev walked toward the front door, when Milo said urgently, "Wait. It's one of the thugs from Gina's office."

Ah, shit. Liev froze. "Now what the hell are we going to do?"

"I don't know."

Liev shook his head, not happy with Milo's answer. "The Defino brothers shouldn't know that we are home. Stealth is on and active. No heat seeking, no audio, no power surges being registered. As far as the outside world is concerned, we are not home."

"Unless," Milo said, "they were the ones listening in on the bugs. Then, of course, they know that we are home. And, if that last device was a tracker, they'd have traced the pod here anyway."

Liev winced. "Then make sure stealth is on in the pod room, and let's see what this guy wants."

"Don't open the door," hissed Milo. "He might have come here to kill us."

That was a possibility as well. But Liev had other options. He opened the wall comp. "What do you want?"

"The girl," came a hard flat voice.

Liev closed his eyes. Damn.

"Give her up."

"Or else what?" Liev asked, deceptively calm. He stared at Milo, who was waving his hands in the air in a wild manner.

"She's nothing to you. But she's worth a lot of money to us. You already have money, and, with her, we will too."

Liev frowned. "That makes no sense. She is worth something to me. She's not worth any money to you. How could she be?" He managed to work just the right amount of helpless confusion into this voice.

"I'm not getting into an argument with you. I have orders."

"Orders from whom?" Liev watched as Milo finally stopped panicking and started calling someone—anyone— for help. He hoped Milo was calling the same people who hassled them all the time. It was only fair.

The big wall screen beside him opened up to show Milo sending a live feed of their visitor to the same department handling Gina's murder case. At the same time, Milo sent a feed from Gina's office showing the same Defino brother with her that morning that was here on their doorstep. Liev didn't know if any of this would happen fast enough, but, if the cops came, … he didn't want Lani anywhere around. Or Charming. And that damn pod needed to stay hidden.

Suddenly the male outside the door sneered. "Called the cops, have you? That's all right. You can't stay in there all the time. She's the one I want. Give her up, and I'll leave your freak of a brother alone."

A frightened squeak behind him said Milo had heard that bit.

Just as suddenly, their visitor disappeared.

Liev turned to Milo. "How long have we got before the police arrive?"

"They're almost here."

And, sure enough, the alarms sounded. Within minutes,

a small force had arrived at the door.

Liev had to open up this time. He faced the officers, "Sorry, gentlemen. You just missed him."

"We need confirmation of the material that was sent to the department."

Of course they did. Resigning himself to a long couple of hours, he opened the door and let the men in. They had ComBots with them. Using combat robots was standard procedure when apprehending anyone considered dangerous. At least the authorities believed him about the thug. If that guy had had something to do with Gina's death, then he was very dangerous.

Liev immediately considered getting a ComBot as a security guard to help keep Lani safe, just in case he wasn't home.

He waited off to the side as Milo confirmed the video footage and explained via HoloKomp to the Council Security officials how he'd come into possession of the feed and why he hadn't turned it over earlier.

They all appeared satisfied with his explanation about not knowing about the dead woman until her partner called to see if she'd been in contact.

Just when he thought it was over, the person in charge handed over more orders. Both he and Milo were to appear in front of the Council.

Now.

Chapter 15

Lani held her breath as she heard heavy footsteps approach. Other people were in the apartment besides the two brothers. It bothered her to be locked in the small room, but, at the same time, if the stealth mode meant what she thought it meant, no one would see this room either.

That should keep them safe. The pod itself was illegal, so even finding that would cause Liev big trouble. She was a whole new dimension of trouble for him.

She didn't want that for anyone. If anyone knew the truth about her, she'd never be allowed to stay with Milo and Liev. No, the best thing she could do was learn to blend in. To be one of them.

"Charming, is there anything that will help me learn how things work here?"

"Time?"

"We don't have time," she said urgently. "I need to fit in. I have this horrible feeling that Milo and Liev are in trouble."

Charming studied her, but his thoughts appeared to be far away. "There is no comp in here, is there?"

"I have no idea." She spun around. "Comp, turn on."

Nothing.

Charming spoke up next. "Audio from the rest of the apartment *on.*"

Immediately sounds of people moving through the rooms filled the air. Lani shuddered and squeezed Charming tight.

"We are to take you down to the Council right now."

"Why?" Liev asked. Lani shivered at the barely contained anger in his voice. "Why are we going back to the Council when we were just there?"

"More questions need to be answered."

Then Lani heard no more talking as they all filed out of the apartment.

Charming stared at Lani. "They've gone back to the Council without saying anything to us."

"They couldn't," she said absently. "He didn't dare speak to us."

"I will contact Milo then." And damn if Charming didn't hop up onto the pod and push some buttons on the unit that Milo had left humming away in the background.

"That's a bug finder. Not a comp."

Charming shot her a look. "They are all computers, and here all computers can communicate with each other."

"Oh." Of course they could. It seemed like everything here communicated with every other thing. The damn coffeemaker probably talked to the house alarm and vice versa. "So you can talk to Milo?"

"Of course. So can you."

"I'd like to talk to Liev."

"His comp is on Silent mode."

"Oh, but Milo's isn't?"

"His is never off. He's receiving my message now."

"Is that safe?"

"Probably."

She didn't like the sound of that. She also wished she

could go outside and double-check that the apartment was empty. But what if it wasn't?

Then she heard it. The sound of a door opening. She couldn't help herself. She stared up at the ceiling as they heard audio of someone else entering the house.

Charming froze, his whiskers quivering.

He tapped the comp very gently, as if afraid that the very tiny *clicks* could be heard. The unit in front of him flashed an answer back. He swallowed, looked at her, and said, "It's not the group who was just here. It's someone else."

She closed her eyes. "That can't be good."

"Milo says to not make a sound. Stealth is on, but ..."

She grabbed Charming, the comp unit, and crawled underneath the pod.

She didn't know who the unknown visitor was, but nothing about this situation was good. "Did Milo say if they were on the way home?"

"They can't yet. He says he's sending help."

She thought about that. "I wonder what that means."

"No idea." He added slowly, "I wonder if they are bringing food."

LIEV GLARED AT the Council. "What was that question again?"

"We wish to know where you obtained copies of these videos." Off to the side, the videos of the two badass henchmen entering Gina's reception room were displayed.

"It's obvious where we got it. We do consulting security work for Hahn Driscoll's office." Liev didn't like where this was going. Sure, he and Milo had crossed the line by showing it to the police, but, as they were looking for a murderer, he hadn't thought they'd crossed the line that much. "Why is this an issue?"

"Because," the speaker said, anger putting an edge in his voice, "if you accessed the private feeds from the lawyer's office, what else might you have obtained and why?"

"Nothing other than the regular security feeds. Which is funneled to Hahn's primary security company." Liev tried to stay calm, but he was damn worried about Lani. "I don't understand what this has to do with anything."

"We have a murdered lawyer, who, prior to you sending this feed, is known to have spoken to your wife before her disappearance."

"No. My wife had nothing to do with this. As we've shown, Gina was still alive when we left. The conversation with those two men proves that."

"Except that, since both you and your brother are known to have exceptional skills with anything electronic, so you can't actually prove that you didn't doctor this feed." He pointed to the feed frozen on the wall, one henchmen's face stopped with his mouth open. "For all we know, this man was there visiting the lawyer earlier in the morning, and you just made it look like their visit was later."

"Good Lord. You actually think that we had something to do with Gina's murder?" His voice rose at the end. "That's preposterous."

"Why is that?"

Liev could hardly formulate an answer. How did one prove that he hadn't done something? "For one, I have an alibi. I've been home with my wife and my brother all day. Besides, what possible reason could I have for hurting Gina?"

"Gina?" This comes from one of the other Councilmen. "You have a personal relationship with her?"

"No." Liev shook his head. "No. I knew her early on as she joined Hahn's firm but not well."

"But she wanted to know you better? She might have pushed you. Hard. Became a little too pushy. Maybe you told her to back off. Maybe she pushed back. You argued, ... and things went from bad to worse."

Liev stared wordlessly at the four men staring down at him. He wanted to rage and scream at them for their blatant stupidity. "You have this all wrong."

"That's not what this man says."

Liev turned to stare, shocked as a very sober and sad-looking Hahn walked in. "Hahn? You're the one accusing me of hurting Gina?"

Hahn's dour face turned even more sober. "I didn't want to believe it, Liev."

"But you just can't help yourself." Liev's cynicism kicked in. "This is your attempt at damage control? Place the blame on my shoulders, then you and your firm don't have to take the fall for a rogue lawyer. Won't have to reassure all your clients that she didn't sell out all their secrets?"

Milo stared at Hahn. "Wow. Slick move. Of course, it won't work."

Hahn's gaze hardened. "And why is that, genius?"

"Because I'm pretty sure, if I were to access your office, we'd find a string of communications showing that Gina was alive after we left her office. *Your* office. The office you have full access to. The office you pay your primary security company to do whatever you want. The office where you can screen potential clients to do some of your dirty work."

Hahn's face became a picture of innocence. "I had nothing to do with the death of my colleague." He managed to look outraged, yet grieving at the same time. "How dare you accuse me of such a heinous crime?"

"Oh, but it's okay for you to accuse us?" Liev was back to being stumped. At the same time, his mind raced in circles, looking for something, anything, the one thing that would get him off the hook. "Then let us take a look at your communications." He dared Hahn.

Hahn raised an eyebrow. "Of course. Here." And he dropped his comp onto the table in front of everyone. "I have nothing to hide."

Milo snatched it up, clicked a few buttons, and lifted his gaze to stare hard at Hahn. "It's a brand new phone."

"Yes, sorry. I lost my other one yesterday afternoon."

"Of course you did," Liev mocked. "Coincidental timing, I suppose."

Hahn stared at him blandly. "It still links to my office and home. Whatever."

Milo continued to *click* and *click*. Liev hoped he found something useful. His brother's head was bent like always when he was focusing on a new project. "Find anything, Milo?"

"Yeah, I did."

Hahn stiffened. "Impossible. There is nothing to find."

"Well, not on the phone. But I tracked it back to the office."

Milo looked up with a smile and hit Play. Gina's voice could be heard easily. "You know very well why I'll be late for dinner." She sighed. "Dear boy, I need to meet someone. This is going to be an easy open-and-shut deal. No worries."

"Somehow, whenever you say that, it works out to be the opposite."

"Then come with me so I'm not alone. That way, we can go to dinner earlier, and that will make for an earlier playtime." On that last note, she dropped her tone, oozing a very low, suggestive sexuality.

Milo clicked on something, and the feed froze.

Liev said, "So, Hahn, would you care to change your story? After all, you are now the prime suspect. You spoke to her well after we did."

"That means nothing," he blustered. "And that conversation could have happened a while ago. In fact, I'm pretty sure that it did."

"Oh, I'm sure she was always wheeling and dealing with *someone*. However, by your own admission, this phone links to both your office and home, and it's a new phone, so you spoke to her after you got it. Which you said was late yesterday afternoon. So technically, you were the last one to speak with Gina."

Silence.

CHAPTER 16

L ANI CROUCHED LOW, making herself as small as she could. The South Pacific theme was open and empty. Kinda hard to hide here. She had no idea who walked the hallways outside the pod room, but, from the sound of the heavy footsteps and the pounding on the walls, no doubt someone was.

Her nerves were shot with every hard *thump* on the wall. The intruder was looking for her. She knew it deep inside. And the fear choked her. She couldn't take a breath. She clutched Charming so tightly to her chest, she doubted he could breathe either. She closed her eyes.

Thud. Thud. Thud.

She shuddered and buried her face into his fur. "Please keep us safe."

Thud.

They had to be following the signal from the tracker before it was fried. Charming shivered in her arms. She squeezed him tighter.

Then the door opened. She gasped silently and shrank lower.

"Bloody hell. Here it is. How the hell did they hide this place?" The stranger walked in. From her position under the pod, she could only see his boots. Leather. Heavy. High. Studded. One of the Defino brothers. The boots were meant to instill fear. And they succeeded. She was terrified.

From the quivering flesh in her arms, she presumed that Charming felt the same.

The footsteps circled the room one way, then returned the other way. Back in front of the door, the boots stopped. "Damn." The boots shuffled slightly. As if he were standing in one place and looking the place over. "Who'd want a pod on an island? Stupid people."

His hands hit the floor, and he bent down to look under the pod.

And Charming attacked. He flew at the stranger, claws out, slashing and slashing, … and yowling.

"Holy shit. What the hell?"

Charming howled again and dashed away, only to come back and jump up again, this time going after the man's face. Footsteps sounded as the stranger—she thought it was the older thug—raced out of the room.

Charming gave chase.

A horrible alarm set off, filling the halls and making the walls rattle. Lani cried out and slapped her hands over her ears. "Oh, make it stop."

She scrambled out from under the pod, raced to close the door, and stopped. She couldn't leave Charming out there alone. He could be hurt. In danger. But the horrific noise was worse with the open door.

"Charming," she whispered. No way he'd hear her with that alarm going off.

Damn. She snuck into the kitchen, but she saw no sign of him. Scared to be too far away from the pod room, she snuck back and called for him again.

Still nothing.

On the floor, she found a comp unit. It wasn't one she

recognized. She picked it up, wishing she understood how to use it. After tucking it into her pocket, she went to close the pod room door when she heard, "Hey, open up."

She pulled the door wide open. "Charming!"

He jumped into her arms. She shut the door with her hip and hugged him close. After a cuddle, Charming dug his claws into her arm. "Ow! What was that for?"

"You have the intruder's comp," he said, jumping from her arms to the top of the pod, whacking at her pocket. "I can see the corner of it. It has to be that comp. Let me see it."

Feeling ridiculous but willing, she laid it down on the slightly rounded top of the pod and held it steady for her cat to use. Boy, if any of her old friends could see her now, they'd lock her up in the loony bin. Then again, she would have been living there permanently after the last few days anyway if she tried to explain what had happened to her. "What are you trying to do?"

"See his connections."

She frowned. "As in, who he worked for?"

"And when he last had contact with that lady."

"Gina?" That might be helpful, but she wasn't sure how, since she was dead now. But, if they could find the person behind all this, she'd be happy. Maybe then she could settle in to learn about her new world. "Do you think the apartment is empty now?"

He shrugged. "I think so."

She walked back to the door and opened it. Everything was quiet. Maybe too quiet? She really wanted to make sure the damn intruder had closed the front door. All kinds of security was in place—but she was pretty sure the front door had to be closed for any of it to work.

Milo said he was sending someone to help them. Surely they'd be here by now?

Leaving Charming to work the phone awkwardly with his fat paws, she crept toward the front door. And stopped. A man approached the open doorway. Then she realized who it was. *Hahn.* Liev's lawyer. Still in his blue outfit.

"Thank heavens you're here," she exclaimed with a big smile. "The place was broken into. We've been trying to reach Liev and Milo and can't seem to get through."

"You did get through. The alarm on the place sent an automatic alert to them. That's why I'm here." He smiled with relief and held out his hand. "I'm so happy to find you safe. Hurry now. I'll take you to Liev."

"Oh." She was so happy to see someone she recognized. She raced toward him.

He was just outside the door. As she reached it, a clear shield of some kind came down between her and Hahn.

A look of sheer frustration washed over his face.

"What the …?" She reached out a hand but realized the shield had a charge of some kind. She'd get a shock. "Hahn, what do I do?"

"Shut it off from the inside." But the peculiar look on his face made her realize this was something she should know how to do.

"He changed it recently," she lied. "I don't know how. He never got a chance to show me the new system."

Anger swept over his face. He turned to look behind him. "You need to hurry, before someone comes."

She studied the wall beside her. She assumed another virtual comp was hidden in here with the controls she needed. But, even if she could open it up, there was no guarantee she could shut this down.

She needed Charming.

And didn't dare bring him out here where Hahn could see him.

"I can't figure this out."

"What the hell? How could he possibly want you when you haven't got even basic computer knowledge?"

His disgusted tone bothered her, but the building rage on his face bothered her more.

She stepped back. "You have no reason to speak to me like that. Our relationship is none of your damn business."

He glared at her.

And she realized this shield was all that stopped him from reaching through and grabbing her.

He wasn't here to help her at all.

He was here to kidnap her too.

LIEV OPENED HIS mouth to answer yet another question from the speaker of the Council. His own lawyer, Hahn, was now under suspicion. Hahn had excused himself, saying he'd be contacting his own lawyer. At that point, Liev had thought that he and Milo were in the clear. That they could go home. He'd been wrong.

His comp went off. He pulled it out, disregarding the frown on the Councilman's face. "Sorry, gentlemen. That's my house security system." He clicked through his signals. An alarm notice sent shock waves through his system. "My place has been broken into. I need to go. My wife is alone." He turned to Milo. "Move. Lani is in trouble."

Milo already headed to the door. Liev ran toward him. "Excuse us, gentlemen …"

With Milo ahead, they raced to the portals. Liev barely

made it into the same one as Milo. "Are they okay? Can you contact anyone? Lani? Charming?"

"I'm trying. But it's not as if either one is trained to override the lockdown system."

Shit. Liev winced. He hadn't done enough to help Lani. She was in a terrible position. And he'd made things even worse. Again.

His heart pounded in his chest. He could only hope they'd make it home in time.

The port opened, and the elevator closed. They were back home in seconds.

They raced around the corner, his breath caught in the back of his throat. He stumbled to a stop.

The front door was open.

And the blue shield was on.

Shit.

He came to a sliding stop, hitting the brakes just in time. "Damn it."

From behind him, Milo said, "I'm working on it."

"Work faster ..." He tried to peer through the waves of blue electricity and thought he saw something. "Charming? Is that you?" He looked around to make sure no one else could hear him. "Milo, is that Charming sitting on the other side of the field?"

"Give me ... one ... more ... second." A loud *click* sounded. "Got it."

The blue screen disappeared.

Liev rushed forward, over his threshold, into his entry-way, surprised when he heard a new voice behind him.

"And now I've got you two. Better yet, I've got her."

Liev came to a confused halt, looking behind him to find Hahn, just inside the threshold of his home, holding a laser gun to Milo's back. Milo, his comp still in his hand, had his arms up high over his head.

"Now, Liev, get the girl. I don't have much time."

"What is this all about, Hahn?"

"Did you hear me say, *I don't have much time*? I'm supposed to deliver her within the next fifteen minutes or the delivery will be late. Late does not cut it with these guys."

"Who?"

Hahn's face darkened. "No more talking. Get her, or I'll kill your brother. These guys mean business. Gina failed, and look what happened to her."

Liev turned his shocked gaze toward Milo, who stood helpless in front of him.

"Get her," Hahn repeated.

How could he? How could Liev hand over Lani? Yet he couldn't put his brother in danger.

"Tough choice, huh? Brother over lover? Too bad. It's not a choice. Hand her over, or you die too."

"He doesn't have to hand me over." Lani's cool voice drifted toward them. "However, I'd like to know who you are planning on delivering me to and why."

Hahn relaxed now that Lani was here with them. "I don't know. And it doesn't matter. They get whatever the hell they want."

Lani stepped past Liev. He reached out and grabbed her. "Wait."

"No. There is no waiting, Liev. There is no choice." She tugged her arm free and walked toward the open front door.

Hahn grabbed her and shoved her ahead of him while keeping the gun still trained on Milo.

"Don't bother trying to follow me," he snapped. "You don't want to be where I'm going." Bitterness swept over his face. "Hell, I don't want to go there myself. But that bitch put me in the clinch now. So it's you or me ..."

Liev stared, his mind racing to find something, ... anything that would save the situation.

Hahn sidled up to the doorway, shoving Lani outside. With one last warning glance at the brothers, he backed up several steps into the doorway.

Charming—quiet and unassuming Charming—sprang into action, jumping high up on the wall and slamming a paw into the 3-D monitor. Instantly the electric screen flashed.

As Hahn crossed the threshold of the doorway, ... as the electronic shield surrounded him, he was fried instantly.

The system flashed and sparked ... and shorted out.

Milo raced past Liev, deeper into the living room, crying out in horror.

Liev could only stare.

"Jesus," Milo whispered, now at a standstill. "Charming, did you mean to do that?"

"Of course." He walked closer to what remained of Hahn's body. Charming proceeded cautiously, then caught a solid whiff and reared backward. "Oh, gross."

Liev skirted the remains on the floor and quickly disengaged the shield. Lani stared at him in horror from the other side.

"It's okay," he reassured her. "It's off."

She didn't look hysterical, but Liev wished she would be—then he wouldn't feel so bad about his own reaction. He shook uncontrollably. With a cry, she ran inside without looking at the floor and threw herself into his arms. "I was so scared. So scared," she whispered against his neck, squeezing him hard.

"So was I," he murmured, holding her tight against his chest. "Oh, God, Lani, so was I." He backed up, keeping her with him. "Let's get you into the back of the apartment and away from that."

"Gladly," she muttered.

He led her to a big comfy chair that shaped itself around her. "I have to deal with this first. Then you can tell us all about what happened."

"And we need to get something for Charming too." Charming jumped up on her lap just then, and she wrapped her arms around his furry body and cuddled him. "He's my hero today."

"He's everyone's hero. As soon as the police and those … remains are gone, we'll get him anything he wants."

"Food?" Charming poked his head up over Lani's shoulder. "Food would be good."

"You got it, little guy. I might even be able to get that for you right now." Liev walked to the wall and opened up a cupboard full of cat food. "What do you want? Salmon, tuna, chicken …"

"Anything," Charming said, "anything but … barbecue!"

The End

CAT'S CRADLE

Broken Protocols 3

by
Dale Mayer

Protocol 3:2:2. You will in no way misuse your authority or position or the trust placed in you— particularly if those actions are to selfishly enhance your own authority, position, status, and/or wealth.

CHAPTER 1

LANI SUMMERLAND BLACKBURN walked restlessly through the living room and kitchen. Her new life two centuries in the future had taken a strange and ugly turn. The problems besetting her since her arrival should have been over—instead things were likely to go from bad to horrible. Figures. Murphy's Law had somehow followed her to this time period. Like, how did that work?

She was desperate to calm the tension vibrating through her. The police had come and gone. As for the lawyer who'd tried to kidnap her, his remains had been removed. Life supposedly could now return to normal. Whatever that meant. She had no normal left. This time jump had come with no warning or preparation for what could happen next.

Life had hit her sideways, and she was still sliding. She'd done the best she could, and Liev had been a godsend. Then again, he'd been the reason she'd been plucked out of her nice happy little life into his—as a gift for him—compliments of his uber-brainy kid brother.

Since she'd first arrived, they had had nonstop trouble. From horrible pain to debilitating exhaustion to heated passion between her and Liev. That last part had been a bonus. But between that and the people coming after her, life had been a dangerous roller coaster.

And she needed off.

As they still hadn't gotten to the bottom of this night-marish kidnapping scenario, they weren't safe yet. And, if anyone found out that the time-travel trick had resulted in her overgrown Persian cat now talking like a fluffy Ein-stein—and getting worse every day—would more people be after her and Charming Marvin? More than likely they'd both be locked up in a lab for the rest of their lives. That was so not going to happen.

Was it any wonder she needed a break from this stress?

Determinedly, she turned to face Liev. He sat, his chin propped up on his fingertips. Eyes closed, deep in thought. And she could just imagine what was going on in his incredible brain, one that matched his incredible body. Sex aside, Liev had turned out to be a hell of a good man. She walked closer.

"Are you okay?" She sat down beside him, happy when he opened his eyes and smiled. Something was still so weird knowing that this man was her husband. They'd only known each other a few short days. He'd married her to keep her safe; yet now she couldn't imagine life without him. Her cheeks heated as she remembered some of their best times together.

His gaze warmed. He cocked an eyebrow and mur-mured, "What are you thinking about?"

She gave a slow, intimate smile. "Good times." She paused, then added, "And I was wondering about …" She let the words trail off, not sure how to phrase it.

"What?" He reached out and slowly ran his fingertips up and down her arm. "If you need something, you only have to ask for it."

"I need to get away. From here. From all this nastiness."

He frowned and damned if a bit of fear, insecurity maybe, sat in the back of those deep purple eyes.

"Not from you," She reached out to stroke his cheek.

The shadow in his eyes lightened, and he sat back to study her.

"I was just thinking that I have a lot to learn. We need time together, yet people are after us."

He nodded. "All true."

"I was wondering if we could go away for a week or two. Where it might be safe for you to take me out and to show me life here. Where making a major gaffe won't attract much attention. Where we could spend a little time together. Where every move won't be watched. Where I can learn ports, and shopping, and ..."

He held up a hand. "I get the idea."

"It's a great idea," Milo piped up. "We could all use the break."

Liev faced her, a question in his eyes. She gave a small laugh and nodded. Of course Milo could come. And no way would she go without Charming, her walking, talking miracle feline.

"A good idea as long as we all go," Charming said, as if reading her mind. "It's too dangerous for us to split up. Besides"—he hopped up on the back of the chair and butted his head against her shoulder—"who'd look after me?" His huge golden eyes stared at her in worry.

"Not going to happen." She stroked his silky back, leaning over to kiss the top of his head. "I wouldn't go anywhere without you."

"Or Milo," Liev said with a laugh. "It's a good idea. We both have a few things to take care of first, not to mention deciding on where to go. In theory, we could leave tomorrow."

She brightened. "Thank you. That would be perfect." She grinned, thinking about how easy that had been and added, "Besides, today is almost over."

Charming snorted. "What time are you on? It's barely after lunch." And he gasped, his eyes rounded into huge glowing marbles. "*Lunch.*"

"No," Lani said. "You had lunch."

"But I had an early lunch, and that means it's snack time." He turned his flat face toward Liev and deepened his tone. "You did order treats for me too, right?"

"Wow." Lani rolled her eyes. "It's hard enough for poor Liev to adjust to a talking cat without that same cat trying to order him around. Remember your manners."

"Ha. He's doing fine." Charming shot a leg into the air and proceeded to clean the back of it. "Soon he might even start obeying those orders."

She smiled and reached out a hand to stroke her four-year-old pet.

"Liev, as much as it's a good idea, I think we need to solve this problem first," Milo said. "The leads are hot right now. If we leave, these assholes will go under, and we might never catch them."

"I was actually thinking about sending you three away, and I'll stay here and deal with this," Liev answered.

"Oh no." Lani shook her head, adding in a flat tone, "All of us or none of us."

He frowned. "Milo has a good point. This has to stop." He reached over to cover her hand. "If we leave, they'll just be waiting for us when we return."

"So we solve this first and then leave. Personally, I'm thinking a beach." Charming dropped and sprawled along the back of the couch. "I'd like some more sand."

Lani snorted. "Maybe you could just get a litter box instead." She exchanged a laughing look with Liev, remembering the last time Charming had come close to sand. "If that's the case," she said, returning to the problem, "what must we do to resolve this mess permanently? I hate the idea of always looking over my shoulder."

"It seems to have started with Johan. We need to find Johan and whoever was behind my lawyers' attempts to kidnap you. Hahn said that Gina had gotten him into this trouble, and *they* probably tortured Johan's name and location out of her. So we also have to find her killer. I'm hoping the two are the same man or group of men."

Johan was Liev's friend who lived in the top apartment—or used to. Lani had never met him. He was on the run from the authorities now. "Okay," she said. "That makes sense, but how we do that?"

"That's my part," Milo said around the straw in his mouth, as he sucked up something bright green. "Finding them, in theory, is no problem, but stopping them is."

"Because we don't want to involve the authorities?" Lani asked.

"Partly, but they are involved already," Liev said. "Two dead lawyers cannot be glossed over." He reached out and tugged her into his lap. "We need you safe."

"I need all of us safe," she muttered, "but how?"

LIEV CUDDLED LANI close. He'd do anything to keep her from harm. Had already done several things he never believed he would have done. But they'd been necessary. "We're good at what we do. We'll find the responsible parties." He squeezed her gently. "I promise."

When she looked up at him with those huge eyes filled with uncertainty, he repeated, "I promise."

Milo came up behind him. "Sounds like it's time to get back to work." He brought up the big countertop 3-D monitor.

"I need treats first." Charming groaned. "I can't help you until I regain my strength."

Lani laughed. "Ha." She nudged Charming's large sprawling belly. "You're getting fat."

"I am not fat. Well, maybe a little, but I'm cuter this way." He stretched out a right paw and offered the underside of his belly for a scratch. When she obliged, he moaned.

Liev shook his head. "He's something else. I'll put on coffee and help Milo."

At the sound of coffee, Lani swung around so he could get up. He laughed. "You are as bad as your cat. Your treat is just in liquid form."

She stretched out on the space he'd vacated and smiled. "In that case, we both deserve treats."

"Finally." Charming moaned, as if in major pain. "Treats. I need treats."

Milo snorted. "How about a booster? Whoa! What do we have here?"

Liev raced over.

Lani twisted to lean over the back of the chair. "What did you find?"

"I'm not sure." Then Milo pinched his lips, and his hands moved faster and faster.

Liev stepped back and watched his brother work. It was rare to see him in the zone to this extent. His brother was sheer magic. And, when he was on the hunt, he was lethal. His hands flashed. The screens shifted too fast for his eye to see what they were. The monitor buzzed with the speed of the activity. It blurred in front of him. Then Milo made a slashing motion with his hand, and everything froze.

Lani made a strangled sound from behind them.

Liev could only imagine what she thought. Nothing even close to this in terms of home computing had existed in her time. Bigger, faster, and more complex computers were at his office, but not by much. By the very nature of Milo's genius, his baby brother needed tools available at all times. And typically the best that could be had. That meant building their own supercomputers. Not a problem, but many of their inventions went way past computing. That's when they got into trouble with the Council and the cops.

Milo leaned closer.

Liev stepped in to look. "What is it?"

"An intersection of paths."

"Whose paths?"

Milo tapped the top of the screen, drawing Liev's eye to the faces. Both Defino brothers' images sat on one side. On the other side sat the two dead lawyers, Gina and Hahn.

"So you've tracked all their paths?" Liev asked Milo.

"To this one spot." Milo tapped the monitor frozen in place. "At the old shipping docks."

Liev frowned. "That's the turf I'd expect from the Defino brothers, but not the lawyers."

"Except," Lani interrupted, "Hahn said something about not liking where he was being forced to take me to." Lani walked closer to study the screen. "So maybe that's the headquarters. The boss man would be in a location like that, wouldn't he?"

"Only part-time," Liev said. "They'd have a home base somewhere a long way removed from that hellhole. Likely at the topmost end of the scale."

Her face fell. Then lit up again. "That would make sense. Could that be Johan? He lived pretty well in this building. You have no idea what he did for a living, but it sounds like it was just on the edge of legal."

Liev shrugged. "If we could track his path to the same area, then I'd say definitely. But as he's gone underground ..."

"What about his known friends and associates?"

"He doesn't have any." Milo looked at his brother. "Does he?"

Liev looked from one to the other. "I don't know. I don't know him that well."

"Then maybe that's where we should start looking. Everyone in his circle. See where those paths intersect?"

Milo raised his eyebrows at Lani's suggestion. After a quick glance at Liev, he swept his hand back the other way, unfreezing the monitor. Immediately the screen loads flashed and sparkled as they moved at light speed.

Lani faced Liev. "I guess that means he's on the hunt again?"

Liev smiled. "Seems like it."

"So does that mean coffee and treats are back on the menu?"

With a smile at their tenacity, Liev walked over to the wall, where he started coffee. "I guess it does."

While he waited for it to finish, the house alarm went off. Lani gasped, her hand going to her chest. He reached out to her. "It's all right. We have company. That's all."

She took a deep and shaky breath. "Okay. I'll go back in the pod room then."

"You don't have to." He was already walking toward the

door. "Not if you don't want to."

"Actually, I wouldn't mind." She gave him a wan smile, reminding him how tired she was. What she'd been through already today. "A short nap, with Charming, would be nice. I'm feeling *peaky*."

"Okay then." He watched her carry on down the hallway; Charming, somehow knowing what she was up to, followed close behind. Lani looked tired, melancholy. Taking her away from all of this was a great idea. She'd only been here a few days, but they'd been brutal. The alarm went off again.

"Liev? Are you answering that?" Milo asked.

Giving his head a shake, he said, "I've got it."

At the door, he looked outside. Damn, another Council henchman. At least the suit and close-cropped hair denoted henchman. He could only see the back of the guy's head, since he appeared to be looking behind him, as if waiting for someone to join him. Not unexpected considering the break-in and death this morning. But Liev had hoped it would be over, at least for today. Like Lani, he was tired and fed up. The alarm sounded again.

Gritting his teeth at the visitor's arrogance to keep hitting the alarm, Liev went about accessing the security system. The alarm went off one more time. "I'm coming. You don't have to keep pressing the damn button."

Finally he unlocked it and pulled the door open. And stared in shock at the man standing in front of him.

Johan.

CHAPTER 2

LANI OPENED THE healing pod. Charming hopped up and froze. His whiskers quivered. She sat down on the side and yawned. She had to admit, she really could use a nap. The morning had worn her out. She slumped backward, spread her arms, and closed her eyes. She giggled when she felt the pod automatically shift and move under her as it adjusted to her sideways position. "Nice, huh?"

Charming didn't answer. She ignored him. She was so tired. The pod was always so welcoming. Nothing like warmth on your back to soothe and ease the tension inside. She was one step away from falling asleep now.

"Lani?" Charming asked.

"*Hmmm?*" She rolled over and tucked her knees up higher. "What?" She yawned and felt herself drifting deeper and deeper.

"Did you hear who just arrived?"

"No." And she didn't care. Her body relaxed a little more. Boy, she needed this. Just as she drifted off, she heard Charming's response.

"Johan."

The word percolated through her brain, then slammed into her consciousness. She bolted upright, barely missing the pod lid as it lifted automatically ahead of her movement. She hadn't had a chance to think with so much going on, but, upon reflection, it seemed like the pod was doing more things. As in learning her, adapting to her and her likes and needs.

Nice.

And creepy.

"Did you say that was Johan at the door?"

"Yes." Charming stared at her, his eyes impossibly round. "Why would he come here?"

"No good reason that I can think of." She sat on the edge and worried about the problem. "Can we hear the conversation?"

"Audio on," Charming said.

Immediately Liev's voice slipped through the ceiling. "Johan? I don't understand. Why are you here?"

Milo didn't give Johan a chance. "Whatever his reason, it's a bad idea."

"Milo, give him a chance to explain."

Silence.

A strange lilting voice rasped, "Thanks for the opportunity, Liev. And, Milo, for all your brains, you need to learn a little more about human psychology."

Charming snorted. "Why? He's got brains, and that means he doesn't need anything else."

"That's not true," she whispered. "And we should probably be quiet in case they can hear us."

He shot her a look of disgust. "Whatever." He lay down, rolled over, and curled into a tight ball.

"Great. You wake me up, and now you get to sleep." She glared at the sleeping cat. "How is that working for you?"

"Quite well. If you'd be quiet, I could actually get some rest."

She threw herself down and curled around the bright

orange body, hugging him close. "Do you think I should go out there?"

"No. Absolutely not." The alarm in his voice reassured her.

"Right. That's not a good idea, is it? Then Johan will know for sure that something is odd about me."

Charming shuddered. From his twisted-up position, he opened his eyelids and glared at her. "DO NOT GO OUT THERE." He lifted his head, as if to make sure she was listening. "Liev will handle it. Johan knows we are here. Let them deal with it."

"But"—she stared down into the flat face—"what if the brothers are in trouble and need our help?"

"Not going to happen." He closed his eyes and went back to sleep.

"It might." She lay her head next to his. "You never know."

"I know." He snored gently.

"But what if you're wrong?"

No answer. She closed her eyes and relaxed. Before she realized it, sleep swept her away.

LIEV STARED AT his old friend and wondered what the hell had happened. The fun-loving guy was gone. This man had a hard edge to him, a well-used look to his face, and his eyes? It seemed they'd seen too much. A second closer look showed heavy bruising on one side of his neck. He held himself slightly hunched over, one arm protecting his potentially damaged ribs.

This was not good.

"What happened to you, Johan?" Liev waved him inside,

watching his friend move gingerly.

He winced. "I look that bad, huh? I could use my damn healing pod right about now."

"Sit down. I'll get you a drink." Ignoring Milo's disgust and instinctive wariness, Liev poured a stiff drink into a glass and brought it over to Johan. "Here."

Johan took it gratefully and tossed it back. He shuddered and then said, "Thanks, I needed that."

"I can see that, but why?"

His friend slouched back, stiffened, then straightened slowly.

"You're hurt," Liev said quietly. "Is it bad?"

"No. Just took a beating. On an ordinary day, no problem, ... but I blew up my pod." He gave Liev a lopsided grin. "Don't suppose you'd like to return the favor and let me borrow yours?"

"No," Milo snapped. "For all we know, you're behind the problems we've been having."

Johan's eyebrows shot up. "What kinds of problems?" He looked at Liev. "I told you to marry her to protect her."

"I did."

"Well, congrats, man." Johan slapped Liev on the shoulder, then groaned at the resulting pain it caused. "That's great. You're a married man now." He shook his head, like he couldn't believe it. "She must mean a lot to you."

"She does."

"When do I get to meet her?"

"Never," snapped Milo. "Someone is after her. We're making sure she's safe."

"Why the hell would anyone want to kidnap her?"

Milo narrowed his gaze. "I didn't say *kidnap*."

Silence.

Johan put up both hands. "Hey, I'm not sure what's going on here, but I have nothing to do with whatever is happening. I've been on the run and got into a little trouble myself."

"Why?" Liev asked curiously. "What happened to you?"

"I thought I took everything I needed with me. Instead"—he grimaced—"I left something behind. I'm here to retrieve it."

"Have you been up there yet?"

"No. I was hoping to use your tube to get there, take a quick look around, grab what I needed, and then scoot back down here undetected." At Liev's surprised look, Johan added, "I could go through the little rooftop garden you use."

Liev shook his head. "And here I thought that area was private. Secret."

"Nothing is secret anymore." As he spoke, he stared straight at Milo. "Haven't you learned that yet?"

Milo stared back at him silently, not showing any give in his expression. After what they'd been through, and the secret experiment Milo had accomplished in bringing Lani here, keeping his work private—top secret—was paramount. Milo would do anything to protect his inventions. And, if Liev didn't quite trust Johan, no way Milo would.

He was suspicious of everyone.

Yet, Liev had to concede, Milo appeared to have taken to Lani and to Charming just fine. More than just fine. Maybe he'd run compatibility tests across everyone's profiles. Yet another thing to ask his brother.

Later.

Liev refocused on the issue at hand. "You can use the tube to get to the rooftop."

Milo started to protest, took one look at Liev's glare, and shut up. He stormed from the room.

"He's not a happy chap," Johan noted.

"We've had a rough morning." Talk about an understatement. Liev half expected to see more Council henchmen here soon enough. Not to mention cops. They would have more questions. No way they wouldn't. Hell, Liev had a lot more questions himself. He studied Johan carefully. "So you had nothing to do with the bug that came in with my healing pod?"

"What?"

His shock was real at least.

"Don't you have an automatic bug sweeper here?" Johan's lips twitched.

"Yes, we do. But the bug was built to detach at some specific time or at a prearranged signal, then move to a different location in the room."

That shut Johan up. He sat back slowly and stared. After a long moment, he shook his head. "What the hell. Whose bug is that?"

"Milo is tracking it down. At the moment, we have no idea but suspect it belonged to the Defino brothers."

"That's not good." Johan stared into space, but didn't sound surprised at the brothers' name. Then they had a long rap sheet. "I had my pod customized, you know? So it would only transmit specific innocuous data to the database."

"Really?" Too bad Johan hadn't mentioned that fact earlier. It would have saved Liev a lot of worry. "That's a great idea."

"Not good enough. Something still went wrong. It did make me a popular fellow for a long time though." He grinned, a rueful smile of remembered parties and women, ... so many women. "I had the same person rig it that you bought yours from."

"How do you know who I got it from?"

A harsh laugh slid out of Johan's throat. "Only one supplier has the audacity to do something like this."

"Do you have a name?"

"Nope. No one does."

"Damn." Liev walked over to the window. He wasn't getting much help here. If he knew Milo, his kid brother would already be out searching the airwaves for information on Johan. Nothing like siccing someone who didn't trust another to dig out dirt on them. "Paul Defino broke into my house today."

"What? I didn't hear anything about that." Johan stared.

"Oh, you will soon. My lawyer was killed during the mess."

"Wow." Johan let a long slow whistle slide through the room. "Okay, now *that* I definitely don't know anything about."

CHAPTER 3

L ANI DRIFTED IN and out of the pod's warm healing rays. Some of the conversation from the other room filtered in. Not enough to truly understand what was going on but enough to stop her from going into a deep sleep. *Figures.* She yawned and rolled over to face Charming in another attempt to drift off.

He stared at her. And damn, those whiskers were quivering. His large globe eyes stared into hers, and his small ears peeled back along his head, as if to hear better.

"What's the matter?"

"Johan says it's not him."

"What's not him?" She blinked, trying to process the short, terse message. "None of the mess is?"

Charming gave a small headshake, sending his fur billowing out.

She frowned. "Then who is behind all this?"

"No idea. And we need to find out."

"Agreed." She lay here, thinking, when Johan's voice filtered in again.

"Are you sure I can't use the healing pod? Just for a few moments. I'd sure like to feel better. Honestly, besides the jaw, I'm pretty sure a couple ribs are broken." His painful gasp could be heard.

It didn't sound like he was faking it. And that made her

feel guilty as hell.

"Sorry, Lani is sleeping in it."

"Sleeping? Dude, she should be warming up your bed, not snoozing in a healing pod." Amused envy laced Johan's voice. That sounded more like the party-giving Johan that Lani expected to hear. The sexy party animal looking to score and not understanding his buddy's reticence.

There was a heavy silence. Lani winced. If the guy was hurt, it was the right thing to do to give it to him. Did she get up and walk out, as if she had just woken up? How else would they know she was awake and willing to leave the safety of the pod? "Charming, can you contact Milo?"

One eyelid slid open. How did Charming manage to look insulted? "Of course."

She didn't want to be seen. She didn't want to meet any more strangers. Any more bad guys. "Can you tell him that I'm leaving here and going to Liev's room, so the pod is free for Johan?"

"Yes." Charming stood and arched his back. "If that's what you want."

"Are you coming with me?" She sat up gently and slid to the side of the pod. "Or are you going to stay and visit with Johan?"

He gave an odd mewl that she took for a snort, then he jumped down. To the speaker system, he said, "Message for Milo only." She stared as he said, "Lani and I are switching to Liev's room. The pod is free for Johan." He twisted, gave her a look, and, when she didn't understand, he sighed. "Open door. Stealth to remain on."

The door opened silently.

Damn. She hadn't even realized the door was voice-controlled. Hating the things she didn't understand, she motioned for him to go first. "Lead the way so we can't be seen."

He shrugged. "Configure to keep us in stealth." And he walked out.

She followed, a low burning irritation with a touch of envy washing through her. "How am I ever supposed to get used to you knowing how to do all this when, only a couple days ago, you didn't even talk?" she muttered.

"We've been over this. I could always talk. You're the one who just learned how to understand." He groaned. "Now if only you'd learn the rest of this stuff faster."

He ran down the hallway, and she had to pick up the pace to keep up with him. With his tail in the air, he looked like a normal feline. Under that pouf of orange fur, he was anything but.

Still, that mess could be laid at Milo's feet.

Charming disappeared up ahead. She entered a room and came to a dead stop. The door closed silently behind her. She gasped. She was inside a huge chateau-type room that could have come from anywhere in the Swiss Alps. The open beam structure with log walls and wood details were awesome, but the huge bed on a platform beside a roaring fire really got to her. "Is that fire real?"

"As real as anything here can be." Charming padded over and tilted his face up to catch the warm rays.

She had to see for herself. It was, indeed, warm and cozy. She felt safe here. Comfy. She smiled. This was gorgeous and said a lot about Liev. She turned to warm her back and studied the huge bed. The coverings appeared fluffy and light. Maybe down-filled. But she suspected it was as much of an illusion as anything else here.

An illusion she wanted to believe in. The idea of sharing

that huge bed with Liev? Luscious!

"Pull your tongue back into your mouth." Charming stalked to the huge bed and hopped up. He sank into the middle and turned around several times before lying down. He yawned. "This will do nicely."

"Ha. Who said that's for you?"

"Losers weepers," he replied, using an old phrase from back in her time.

She stared at him. "How is it you can adapt so quickly? Why are you not bothered about how different things are here in this time?"

He lifted his head. "What's different? Bad guys. Good guys. Kidnappings. Murders. They are the same in both times. The technology is more advanced—and so it should be. But honestly it doesn't look like humanity improved much. Besides, I only need food, love, warmth, and a cozy bed to keep my world balanced." He closed his eyes, then opened one. "It's the same for you."

Was it, she wondered. "I need to be safe."

"And you will be. Soon."

MILO CLICKED AWAY on the comp in his hand, essentially ignoring Johan and the rest of the conversation. Liev studied his brother for a brief second. Then returned his gaze to Johan. Who looked to be fading. "Do you want to retrieve your property and come back? The pod will be waiting for you."

He didn't know why he made the offer, but it seemed the right thing to do. He sensed an odd stillness come over Milo, before his clicking started in earnest. He was up to something.

Then again, so was Liev.

Johan struggled to stand, his face wreathed in smiles. "Thank you. I surely appreciate that. I'll be back in a few minutes." He staggered down the corridor to the front entrance.

Liev walked behind him. At the door, he asked, "Do you want company?"

Johan paused to look at him, considered the suggestion, then shook his head. "I'll be fine, and it will be better if you aren't seen with me. It will just get you into more trouble. Stay here and stay safe. I'll be back before you know it." And he entered the tube and disappeared. Liev stepped back inside and reset the security.

"How long do we have?" Milo asked from behind him.

"Maybe ten minutes." Liev turned to face him.

Milo had secretly followed his brother and Johan down to the hallway. "Then we'd better get moving."

"Moving where? What are you up to?"

"Setting up video in the pod room," Milo said.

Liev stared at his brother as he raced into the room where Lani lay sleeping. "Why? Wait. Don't scare her."

"She's in your bedroom. Charming told me that they'd moved so Johan could use the pod. Lani felt guilty."

Raising both hands in the air in surrender, Liev ran to catch up. Since when had Lani moved? "How did they even know about Johan being hurt?"

"Charming turned on the audio in the pod room. They heard the whole conversation."

"Sweet." He entered the room to find Milo tinkering with the comp on the wall. "How long do you need?"

"More than ten minutes," he muttered, tapping the console quickly. "I'd really like to know why he wants to use the pod. Oh, he's hurt all right. But, while he's in here, is he going to retrieve information on us? Will he send messages from our location? Is he really badly hurt? Or did he pay someone to rough him up to add some weight to his story and to get him into the pod?"

"He looks hurt. I'm sure the pod would help heal him." Any number of pods were available to Johan, but not as many were unregistered. If he used a registered pod, then his name would be sent to the databanks. He could expect a convoy of ComBots and police to be at his side within minutes. Here, he could stay undetected.

"Do you believe his story?" Milo asked.

"No. I don't." Liev added, "But it is quite possible that he is looking to retrieve something he missed from his place."

Milo shrugged. "I don't trust him."

Liev said, "Neither do I."

CHAPTER 4

LANI CURLED UP in Liev's bed. It felt wonderful. And yet so right. Special. Illicit. Which, considering she was married to the man, was just plain stupid. She sank a little deeper into the covers, enjoying the feel of Charming kneading her belly. They'd had lots of mornings in the past where it was just the two of them. Time together to enjoy a late morning spent in bed. Time to spoil each other and to gain the comfort each offered so freely. Times had changed. In more ways than one. "It's been tough, hasn't it, Charming?"

The kneading paused. "In some ways."

She smiled. "It's nice that we can really talk now."

"Yep."

"Do you think ..." She had to stop. What she was going to say sounded stupid.

"What?"

"Nah, it doesn't matter."

"Except, if it's bugging you, it does matter."

She gave a small laugh, startled at the wisdom coming from his mouth. "I shouldn't let it bother me."

"And again, that has nothing to do with it. Just because we shouldn't think about something doesn't mean we don't. And, if it's in your mind, then far better to share it."

True. She said in a thoughtful voice, "I just wondered if

any of the enhancements Milo added to our transport came to me. Or if you got all of it."

"Them."

"*Them?*" She twisted slightly to look at him. "You mean, you received more than one enhancement?"

"I don't know that. I do know he added more than one. It's Milo. How could he resist?"

"Yeah." She sank back into the pillows thinking about it. "He'd think it would all work out perfectly as he had planned anyway."

"Of course, and, for the most part, it did."

"Does it bother you that you are communicating at the level you are now?"

"Yes. It's just much harder to get my beauty sleep," he grumbled from somewhere in the center of the curled-up ball of fur he'd become. "Everyone wants to talk."

She smirked. "Sorry. I'll be quiet again."

"Yeah, but not for long."

Reaching out a hand, she gently stroked along the curve of his back. "Maybe not, but I do love you, and I'm so glad we're together."

His purr hit diesel-engine level in seconds.

Content, she lay here and dozed, wondering what other enhancements Milo had added to the two of them—or just Charming. And had they worked? Supposedly there was a high incidence of failures with enhancements. Apparently Mother Nature still ruled.

The door opened. Liev walked in and looked around. "Hey, how are you feeling?" he asked, after spying her in his bed.

She realized he had to be worried, considering she could barely be seen under the mound of covers. "I'm fine. Just tired." On cue, she yawned. "Is Johan in the pod?"

"No, he's gone to his place to retrieve something. He'll be back in a few minutes."

"Okay, at least it's ready for him."

"Thanks for that. We did use his pod when we needed it, so …"

"Understood. It's the right thing to do." She shuffled back up against the headboard, so it was easier to see Liev. She was surprised to see him standing in the middle of the room. "Uhm, I hope it was okay to move in here? I know I didn't ask, but I wasn't sure what else to do."

"Of course it is," he rushed to reassure her, yet stood stock-still.

She stared at him, loving the warmth that filled his huge eyes. "Good. Then why are you standing in the middle of the room like that?"

The heat in his eyes flared. "Because I don't dare get any closer." His legs brought him a step closer regardless. He clenched his fists.

She raised an eyebrow. Her toes curled.

He dropped his gaze slowly down her face and neck to rest on her breasts, plumped up from the bedding she'd tucked around herself to keep warm. "Because joining you in here is exactly where I want to be, but Johan will be back in a few minutes. And Milo is working on something that might need my help."

That made sense, and it reassured her. "You should hurry back."

He swallowed hard. "Working on it."

But he stayed frozen in place. Then, with a low groan, he said, "I'm leaving. I'll be back soon."

She raised her other eyebrow. He raised both hands in

frustration, turned on his heel, and raced out. She grinned. "Nice to know he's just as affected as I am."

"You're both idiots," Charming murmured. "Now do you think I could get some sleep?"

LIEV TORE OUT of that room before he jumped into that bed and made love to Lani. He'd dreamed of her in his bed, lying beside him. Lying under him. On top of him. Any position would work as long as it involved Lani.

"Whoa, Liev. What's going on?" Milo stood in the hall-way studying him. "Is everything all right?"

He winced. Definitely time to control his unruly thoughts and wayward body. "I'm fine. Just realized you might need some help." Yeah, as lame excuses went, that one topped the cake.

And, if the look on Milo's face was anything to go by, he agreed. "*Right.*" He walked toward the kitchen. "Maybe coffee? Or a cold shower?" he murmured as he slipped past his brother.

"Ha. Coffee will be fine."

"I'm not so sure. You don't need more stimulants," Milo said, a grin on his face.

Liev glared at his brother. "No, I don't. But the coffee would be good regardless. I'm sure Lani would love some after all the attempts to get her a cup just to keep getting interrupted. And maybe we have time for a cup before Johan gets back."

He walked over and pushed the button, choosing an espresso blend. He might not need the stimulant, but he could use the shock to his system. Lani was a powerful drug all on her own.

"Speaking of which, I expected him back already."

Liev turned around to face Milo. He frowned as he looked down at his own comp. "How long has it been?"

"Fifteen going on sixteen minutes."

Liev made the mental calculations in his head. "He could have trouble finding what he needs to find. If it's even still there. He's hardly late yet." He walked over the counter and the big 3-D screen. "Did you track his movements?"

"No tracks to show how he got here. Unfortunately. Then again, he's spent a lifetime living this way. As for where he went, he did take the tube to the top floor. From there? I don't know."

"Can you hack into the system? See if any working computer eyes are in his place that we can access?" Liev thought about what Johan had said before. "Johan said he had eyes on most of the building. Said he recognized the guy who came to give Lani her tags. Knew the guy who sells the unregistered healing pods."

"Did he now? *That* you did not mention before." Milo got busy. "Would have been good if you had."

"It never occurred to me. We do the same with Johan. Well, *before* we may have."

"Yes, but he didn't come in today through the normal channels. He's keeping track of us all but not letting anyone see his tracks. And that's not allowed."

Liev grinned. Milo had a huge competitive streak. He also lived on the airways and knew how to traverse the electronic world better than anyone Liev knew of. Milo's ability to dig himself in until he found what he was looking for spoke to his stubborn nature. He had a lot of bulldog in him.

A good trait when it came to hunting. Liev left Milo to

it and took a moment to check the huge backlog of emails and business issues waiting on Liev. He'd been slacking these last several days, and some things he couldn't ignore any longer. He buckled down to deal with the easiest and fastest of them. It took twenty minutes to take the cream off the top, delegate a huge portion of the other issues to his staff, and skim over the rest. Feeling better now that he knew what was backed up, he turned to the coffee he'd forgotten about. Pouring two cups, he carried one into the bedroom for Lani.

And found her sound asleep.

He stared down at the sleeping beauty curled so innocently in his bed. All he wanted to do was slide under there and curl around her.

She rolled over and opened her eyes.

He smiled gently. "Hey, did you enjoy your nap?"

She smiled sleepily. "Did you come to join me?"

"I wish." He lifted the cup in his hand slightly higher so she could see it. "I did bring you coffee."

Her eyes lit up. "That's a wonderful second-place prize." She shifted back and up, and he realized she was fully dressed, not exactly the image his mind had been busy creating. And reminded him of another oversight. "I need to get you new clothes."

She winced. "I'd appreciate it. I've been washing my underwear in the sink and leaving it to dry overnight. But one outfit does not last forever."

"Do you like the style? I can give you others, but that style looks lovely on you. And it's easy to grab you a half dozen of the same."

Her gaze widened. "Yes, please."

"Your wish is my command." He turned and walked toward the side wall of his bedroom, where he brought up the clothing program. He quickly repeated his clothing instructions but switched up the colors. As an afterthought, he multiplied the outfit by seven. That should work for the moment.

As he stacked up the goods on the bed, he got a transmission over the home security system. The robotic voice said, "A request for help has been received."

Liev straightened. "What? Who?"

"Johan Strand."

"Damn. Is he hurt?"

"I have no further information from the sender."

"But he's alive?"

"At the time of transmission."

"Well, that's something." He hated that the first thing through his mind was that Johan was dying. There'd been too much death lately. He raced out of the bedroom and into the kitchen. "Milo? I have to go check on Johan. He's sent out an alert for help."

"I'm coming with you."

"No, you need to stay here with Lani."

"Lani will be locked in here. You need backup."

That his kid brother saw himself as Liev's backup was touching and funny as hell, but Milo had proven that he could be helpful in many situations. Given the choices, Milo was correct. As long as Lani stayed inside, she'd be safe. Liev could set the security system to alert him if anyone approached. And that was a hell of an idea. "Thanks, Milo."

He ran to the front door, set up the alarm, and stepped out, Milo at his back. The two stepped into the tube and took off for Johan's apartment.

The tube disappeared as they arrived at their destination. Johan's door was locked down tight. Liev motioned at Milo to follow him to the small rooftop garden. They couldn't hear any sounds from the place. That in itself was unusual after hearing Johan's endless parties. Liev stepped over the small divider and carefully worked his way around to Johan's big rooftop patio. The place was dark and silent. The big double doors stood wide open, also unusual, but good for Liev and his brother. He wanted to race inside and call out for Johan, but Liev's instincts stilled his tongue. He felt an eerie sense that they weren't alone.

He knew the layout pretty well. He slipped inside and slid along the wall to the left. Johan's bedroom should be down the same side of the apartment. Liev couldn't hear anything, but neither could he see anything. The darkness was absolute.

Milo motioned toward a large black bar set near the middle of the room. Nodding, Liev crouched down and made his way to it.

Then they heard someone rustling around in the room next to them.

But was it friend or foe?

CHAPTER 5

L ANI SAT UP, threw off the covers, and slid her legs over the edge of the bed. Beside her was a large stack of clothing. Different colors and designs, all appearing to be pieces of the same outfit he'd given her last time. Liev had dumped them beside her before racing from the room. He had called back as he left, "These are more of the same. Later we can sit down and pick you out different clothes."

Now she wondered at his words. Sit down and pick out some clothes? Did they have stores anymore? Or only online stores? Did he design something himself? Or did he use a design program? Input her coloring and measurements, and, voila, a whole new set of clothes? Hit the Print button, and there they were?

She paused at the idea. That almost sounded possible.

Spreading out the clothing, she smiled at the bright colors. They were the same design as the one she currently wore but with a fresh look. She loved them. A deep bronze top and milk chocolate pants were her first choice. The array of matching sexy underwear made her cry out in delight. She dressed quickly. She folded the dirty clothes and laid them off to the side, then restacked the remaining outfits. She looked around and realized that, of course, she saw no visible dressers or drawers. Everything would be sunk into the walls. Or compressed in such a way as to open upon command.

Multitasking space, he'd called it. Cool idea.

And it made for a nice clean line in the room. There was little clutter, just open warm space.

Leaving the clothes stacked on the bed and feeling like every other woman with new clothes, she walked out with a skip to her step.

And found the men missing.

She wandered through the kitchen and large sitting room, with no sign of Liev or Milo. She frowned. If they were with Johan, she preferred to stay out of sight. After a moment of indecision, she refilled her coffee cup, delighted that she'd learned that much here and returned to find Charming. In the center of the bed, Charming opened one eye and stretched out a paw. In a lithe move, he rolled over onto his back.

"Charming, I can't find Milo and Liev. Can you tell me where they are? Without alerting anyone else in the place?"

He rolled over again slowly and sat up. "Audio on."

Silence.

She kicked herself for not having tried the same thing. None of this was instinctive yet. "If they're in the pod room, with stealth on, will you be able to hear them?"

"I don't know." He tilted his head and said, "Audio on in pod room."

More silence.

"Locate Milo and Liev."

A weird robotic voice said, "Liev and Milo are not on the premises."

Lani gasped. "How? When? Where are they?"

Silence.

"Oh, come on. You must track them," Lani snapped.

"Stealth is on."

"On their personal comps too?" She doubted that.

"No."

"Then send a message and ask them where they are." She added as an afterthought, "Please."

Charming made an odd sound.

She turned to look at him. "What?"

"Oh, nothing. Just good to see you learning how this system works."

"I wish," she said. "Then I'd be able to contact Liev directly."

Like magic, Liev's voice whispered from somewhere in the ceiling, "Lani, we're in Johan's place. He sent out a call for help."

"I was just worried. I couldn't find you," she admitted.

"We'll be home short—"

And his voice disappeared.

Lani stood beside the bed and called up at the ceiling. "Liev? Liev!"

No answer.

"Contact Milo," Charming instructed the house computer.

"Communication has been disrupted."

"Ya think?" Lani turned around in a slow circle, staring up the open-beam construction as if it would magically answer. "What can we do?"

The house system said, "We must wait for communication to be re-established."

"Can you tell me if their vitals are okay?"

"Their vitals are fine."

Walking toward the kitchen, she breathed a sigh of relief and raised a trembling hand to her temple. "Good, then they aren't in any danger."

"I did not say that."

"No. You didn't." She frowned, her heart sinking. "Are they in danger?"

"I don't know that."

"Of course you don't. Then who does?"

"This might help."

Lani turned around, surprised to see Charming on the kitchen counter. "What are you doing up there? No cats on the kitchen counters. Remember?"

His *get real* look left her gasping. "I'm trying to open the 3-D computer. We can track them visually in Johan's apartment this way. See if they're in trouble. Also see if they're alone."

She watched him study the granite-looking countertop. "The problem there is, we need a scan of Johan's place with that heat-seeker scan thing on." She looked surprised at the words that came out of her mouth.

Then again, so did Charming. With an odd look her way, he turned and clicked one slightly larger white spot, and damned if the 3-D computer didn't form above the counter, with Charming in the middle of it. His fur filled with the accompanying static charge, and he immediately looked like an orange cotton ball—megasize.

She laughed. "Get out of the monitor, idiot," she said affectionately.

"Hey, how was I to know it would appear instantly? There should be a three-second time delay for me to shift position."

"Well, be sure and tell Milo that. He can program that in for you."

"Ha, I'll do it myself."

"Ah, Charming, that might not be a good idea."

"Too late," he groused. "Besides, we live here now. Everything needs to be adjusted for us too."

"Right." Fascinated, she watched as he closed the system, then tapped the same white dot and moved off to the side.

He beamed at her, his marble eyes glinting through the fluff. "See? Not so hard after all."

"Wow. I look forward to seeing Milo's reaction to you tinkering with his computer."

"He'll be fine with it."

She doubted it, but that was Charming's headache, not hers. Besides, Milo gave the brains to Charming. If she had received them, she'd have respect and common sense to go with it, … she hoped.

Charming studied the multilayered holographic images in front of him. "Do you know how to find the building?" she asked.

"It *is* the building."

"Oh." She knew that. *So not.* Now that he'd pointed it out to her, she could see the different floors. Shifting her gaze to the top floor, she saw myriad yellow, orange, and red glowing places. "What are those?"

"I think those are the brothers."

"Maybe two of them are, but then who are the other two?"

LIEV CHECKED HIS comp. The house comp was listening in, but he'd gone into Silent mode. Undetectable even by the house comp. That meant Lani couldn't contact him, but any calls from her right now could get them killed. He lifted a finger to Milo and pointed to the right. Milo turned his head and frowned.

Crap, Milo didn't understand. Liev looked around Johan's lavish apartment. They'd found Johan on his bed, hurt and apparently worse than he'd been earlier. As they'd walked across the apartment to him, they'd heard someone approach from the other side.

They'd been in hiding ever since.

"Damn it, Johan, I asked you where it is. If you don't tell me, I'll have to hurt you for real."

A weird mechanical voice with a feminine tone. Liev shook his head. How was that possible?

Johan groaned in response.

"If you hadn't set your pod to self-destruct, you could be in there healing by now."

"So you can torture me more?"

"Sure. That works."

Liev couldn't see the speaker, and the voice, although familiar, sounded odd.

Milo whispered in his ear, "Voice mask."

Liev considered that. Did that mean they were dealing with a man after all? That was the more likely answer.

"What do you want to do?" Milo asked.

Damned if he knew. He had to help Johan. He could identify his attacker, and maybe they'd finally get to the bottom of this mess. That thought alone propelled him down to the room beside Johan's bedroom. He glanced inside. It was a spare bedroom. Totally bland. Odd that Johan had left it that way. In today's world, he could have turned it into so much more with just a flip of a button, so why hadn't he?

Milo joined him, glanced inside, and winced. "Boring."

"And that's what's wrong here. Johan's lifestyle was anything *but* boring."

"So why this?"

Liev nodded.

Milo lifted the bug detector that he'd grabbed on the way out of their place and turned it on. He ran a sweep, but nothing stood out.

Liev stared at the space and wondered. Then realized it was a holograph, like he'd done for Lani's private island. Johan had deliberately made it to look like a dull, boring bedroom. So what was underneath? He slipped inside, motioning for Milo to join him. He closed the door slightly so that the flash of the house comp wouldn't alert anyone, then with half an eye on the hallway, he quickly stopped the cloaking program.

Milo gasped.

Liev turned to see an incredibly high-tech computer layout. He spun around and turned the cloaking program back on. This was what the intruder was after. And, if he was willing to kill Johan for it, Liev wanted to make sure he didn't get his hands on it.

A scream split the air. *Johan.* Liev, knowing it was the wrong thing to do, but couldn't help himself, raced to his friend's aid. He tripped around a corner and dashed into the bedroom where Johan had collapsed. Liev heard the sound of running feet as the intruder bolted outside. Liev ran to Johan's side, but Johan waved a hand at him. "Get him."

And he collapsed again.

Liev followed the sounds of running feet. Time was of the essence. If the person managed to get to the port before Liev … "Milo," he screamed, "shut down the port."

For a small apartment, it seemed to take forever to make it to the front door.

Just as the port vanished.

"Shit." He circled the port area, hoping that the attacker might have left a clue.

"Sorry, bro. There's some kind of fail-safe set. I didn't have enough time." Milo's aggrieved tone brought Liev back to his senses.

"Not your fault." He walked back to Johan. His friend looked bad. Like seriously bad. "Call for a Medivac. He needs more help than a pod."

"He's past it, bro. Look at him. He's not breathing."

"Damn it." Liev checked Johan's vitals. "Come on, Johan. Stay alive. Please." He lifted one of Johan's eyelids, but there was no response. No pulse. No breathing.

Milo stepped up and pressed his comp to Johan's tags. No responding beep, only a hum that sounded fainter and fainter, … before completely dying away. "Sorry, Liev. He's gone."

As the words left his mouth, the apartment doors slid closed, and a steel cover came down, sealing them both inside.

"What's happening?" Liev asked.

"The system just registered Johan's death. It's gone into a complete lockdown."

Chapter 6

WATCHING THE ORANGE dots on the big monitor was like watching a horror movie, knowing that something bad was about to happen but being unable to stop it. Lani watched the heat blobs move, crouch, and run. One appeared to be lying down, and another one stormed around. "Can we identify who these people are?"

"Not everyone." Charming pointed a claw at the two crouching. "I'm thinking those are the brothers. The one lying down will be Johan and the other one? ... Yeah, that'll be whoever Johan was calling for help about."

"You think he's a bad guy."

Charming shot her a curious look. "Is there anything in this picture that makes you think this is a good scenario?"

She studied it. "No. It looks creepy as hell."

"That's because ..." He paused midsentence and leaned closer, his whiskers quivering. "Oh, what's going on?"

She leaned forward. "That doesn't look good." The two men who crept farther away had gone down one side of the apartment, away from the other two, and had stopped inside a room of some kind. She could see a change in the energy field, but then it switched again. "What was that all about?"

"I don't know, but Johan is in bad shape and deteriorating rapidly."

She switched her attention to the prone figure and realized the heat signature, the bright orange and red colors of the others, were muted in his case. Almost faded. Something happened suddenly, and all three mobile orange dots ran in a straight line. She gasped as the first man was almost caught, but dove into … something … and disappeared off her screen. "Where did he go?"

"I'm trying to track him, but I'm afraid that might be hard to do."

"And look at Johan. His color, it's almost gone."

"The color itself will last a little while. It will take hours for his body temperature to drop so low that no color will show up."

"I'm presuming that the other two left are Milo and Liev?" At least she hoped so. She watched them go to Johan. Suddenly, as if someone flicked a switch, the entire floor of the building disappeared. It was still there, but now it only showed as a solid black bar. As if the entire floor had disappeared.

"What did you do?" she cried out. "Bring it back."

"I didn't do anything." Charming tapped the console several times, only nothing changed. That floor existed but only as a black bar. Charming sat back, stumped. "Something must be going on up there where the apartment is no longer visible."

"That's not good. Johan is in really bad shape. He needs help."

"He's past needing anyone's help. He's dead."

She gasped. "Are you sure?" she cried out. "Maybe he can still be saved. They have wonderful medical advancements here. Maybe it isn't too late."

"Oh, he's dead all right. That's also likely what triggered this blackout. Consider the secretive type of business that

Johan was in. If anything happened to him, especially on his premises, some kind of fail-safe must be in effect to protect the contents. Or ... to catch the killer."

"But the brothers are stuck inside." With a dead body, and, boy, did that part creep her out. "Can they get out?"

"Nah, I doubt it. It's probably locked down until someone, a prearranged someone, comes to remove information from the premises. Likely what Johan had come back to do himself."

She stared at him. "Like more bad guys coming to make sure sensitive information isn't recovered by the wrong people?"

"Something like that." Charming wandered over the counter and sniffed toward the wall. "Is there food in here?"

"Somewhere." She barely listened. Who could think of food at a time like this? "We have to help them. They're innocent, but whoever comes to deal with this situation will suspect that Liev killed Johan."

Charming looked at her. "True, Milo doesn't look like he could kill a bug. Now Liev, that's a different story. That man looks like he could kill."

She shook her head. "What are you talking about? Liev isn't dangerous."

"Nah, of course he isn't." He snorted. "Unless his family or business are being threatened." He motioned with a pudgy paw at the monitor. "If I hadn't seen for myself that Johan was already in trouble and that a fourth person was there, I'd be wondering if Liev hadn't taken care of Johan himself."

"No way he'd do something like that," she cried out. "Where are you getting that from?"

"Uh, maybe from that can-do-what-needs-to-be-done

attitude he gives off without even trying." Charming sat his paunchy bottom down and glared at the monitor. "I like him just fine, and the fact that he likes you is helpful, but it doesn't change the fact that, when threatened, Liev will do what needs to be done."

"That's a good thing," she said gently. "That's something to admire."

"So is killing when killing needs to be done." And he slid down to lie on one side where he proceeded to clean his paw.

She stared at him, his words rippling through her mind. There were times when killing was a good thing, and, if Liev was capable of protecting her from the kidnappers, well, it was a really good thing for her. Although she hoped it wouldn't come to that. Even if Charming didn't think so. "He's a good man."

"Yep, he appears to be."

"It's not as if you wouldn't kill for food."

He pinned his beady eyes on her. "I have killed for food. Why do you think I catch mice? To keep them as pets?"

She grinned. "You could go back to that. It would be good for you. A form of exercise and, just think, you wouldn't need to wait on other people to feed you. You could feed yourself."

He made a strangled sound that came from deep within his throat. "If there were mice in this day and age, I'd consider it. However, what I won't consider is exchanging my killer skills for the food that they serve me on a regular basis. Where's the sense in that? I'd do both. Not the one that takes effort at the expense of the one that is easy." With a shake of his head, he went back to cleaning.

She returned to staring at the blacked-out apartment on the top of the monitor. "We have to help them."

"I agree. Do you have any idea how?"

She winced. "We could go up there and try to open the door."

He hooted. "Really? That's the best you've got? Knowing a little about this system, chances are good you won't even find the place. It'll be on stealth mode under heavy lockdown."

"We have to do something. They'd help us." She thought about it. "Maybe we could call whatever lawyers are left at Hahn's company."

"They won't come here after two of the lawyers were killed, one on our doorstep."

"Then we have to help Liev and Milo ourselves."

LIEV HAD ALREADY done a second search for a way out that they might have missed. No such luck. From the furious pounding Milo was doing on his comp and the wall computers, he wasn't having any better luck. "This is not good," Liev said under his breath. "Johan's computer system is our best bet. Plus, I want to see what he was hiding."

"I'm working on it," Milo said. "He's got to have an override for this system."

"Yes, but it's likely to be controlled by someone elsewhere. When Johan's tag said he was deceased, this lockdown was instantaneous."

"Something important must be here. Otherwise there'd be no need for all this security."

"Information and possibly items." Leaving the main room again, Liev tossed back, "Let's keep an open mind." And he returned to the spare bedroom, Milo right behind him.

"Right." Milo reached a hand past him and clicked off the mask hiding the room's interior. Instantly the high-tech computer room showed up. Milo whistled. "Like there is some seriously good stuff here."

"Sure, but what was he into? Was it legal? Was he working for himself or for someone else? And, if it's someone else, then we need to know who."

"The system might not load with this lockdown happening." Milo had the system booting up, when he said, "Or it might send a signal to someone that we are here."

"I don't want to hear that. We need in. And fast."

"I'm working on it. You take point."

Liev stepped closer to the secondary system, surprised to find it similar to what he had in his place. Johan had to be into something secretive. Had that been what had gotten him killed?

"*Hmm.*"

"What did you find?"

"This system is connected to another system. It's trying to boot me out."

Liev waited. His brother wouldn't take that kindly. He'd be working his ass off to beat this asshole at his own game. It would also increase the danger of staying here. The need for the other party to secure this place and to retrieve or destroy what they needed was now paramount. And … he glanced over at Milo. "Careful in case of a self-destruct order."

"Oh, there will be one, but there's a reason it hasn't gone off yet. The assholes monitoring this place need something from here first."

"Right." That made sense. That kept them alive for a little longer. It also guaranteed that a retrieval team was on its way.

And they were stuck inside.

CHAPTER 7

L ANI STRODE DETERMINEDLY to the front door. They
could do this. So what if she didn't know how to use the
elevator-tube thingy? There had to be stairs. Even in her
century, every place had two exits. Stairs made sense.
Charming sat at the door, waiting for her.

"Good." She scooped him up and held him firmly.
"Let's go."

"Door open," Charming said. Only the door didn't
open.

Lani reached out and put her hand on the door. Nothing. "Open door."

Still nothing. "It's not coded to our voices."

"Damn. Now what?"

"We stay here?" he said hopefully.

"Nope." She turned to stare at the wall and the huge
computer screen in front of her. "It means you need to add
our voices or use an override system."

"Oh, great." He puffed up his chest. "As if that is a two-
second job."

She smiled. "It would be for Milo."

He spun to glare at her. "That's not fair. I don't know
the system, and he does."

With a laugh, she said, "True enough. So how about five
minutes?"

But he was already busy on the comp. He spun around triumphantly. "Done."

She hugged him tightly as the door opened. She stepped through, hoping she'd done the right thing. The tube surrounded her instantly. Like, how did that work? "Johan's place."

And they took off. "Shit," she said against Charming's furry head. "I will never get used to this."

He snuggled closer. "It's cool. But a little freaky."

"A lot freaky." And, as suddenly as the tube started, it stopped … and disappeared. Looking around carefully, she realized they were alone. Good. She led the way, with a couple wrong turns, to the rooftop garden. From there, she could see the whole city ahead of her. She was getting slightly more used to the scene now. It didn't scare her as badly. But it would be much more comfortable if Liev were with her. Just the thought of being left without Liev terrified her. *So not going there.*

She turned in the direction of Johan's and tried to figure out how to make her way onto his patio. Charming jumped free from her arms and raced ahead. What was easy for a cat, however, … was not as easy for her. But she made it over the cement-looking barrier and dropped safely on the other side. With only one scraped knee, she walked across the patio to the large doors. She didn't know how to get in. Steel-looking shutters hid the glass. She saw no handles. No levers. No locks. No windows. The place appeared to have locked down, like a bunker underground. She couldn't do this. "Charming, we're in trouble."

"Ya think?" He trotted alongside the house as far as they could go, until there was no side to be on. The wall dropped away to the vast city below. "That's definitely not the way."

He turned, retraced his steps, and went around the other side. Following behind, she realized that led nowhere either. "So where are the fire escape doors?"

At Charming's odd look, she explained, "The second exit in case of fire so that the inhabitants can get out safely."

"Never heard of it."

"Well, I have."

"Not in the building codes of this time."

"Well, I doubt that they've managed to do away with fire, so there must be a way in or out—especially in these fancy places."

"They'd port in and out. It's fast and efficient."

She stared at him. "You know what? That's a damn good idea. I'd have a port in my house too. Actually I'm pretty sure Liev mentioned that. So why can't they port out?"

"It won't be coded for them."

"Ah, that tagging thing again."

She backed up several steps to get a better look at the building. Tall peaks and round domes, it looked like part of a duct system from her time. Then maybe a lot of those were ducts for the rest of the building. She bit her lip. Could they get in that way? Or better yet, could Liev and Milo get out that way?

"I don't like the look on your face."

She shrugged. "I was just wondering if we could get in there via the ducts or pipes." She waved at the odd structures. "Whatever they are."

"Not a good idea. We could end up anywhere."

"True." She turned to look back at the spot where the entrance should have been. "What about us porting in?"

"Not coded for us," he repeated patiently.

"Then how about the vents again ..." She studied him.

"Maybe you could get in."

He looked at her askance. "What? Why am I the guinea pig?"

"Because you're small, you can get into places I can't."

"I told you to lay off the bread and cheese," he murmured with a sideways look.

"Did not." She glared at him.

"Did too." He moved over slightly, as if out of kicking range.

"Yeah, you'd better move," she said in a temper. She considered his innuendo. "Am I getting fat?"

"Oh, brother." He plunked down his butt with an exaggerated sigh. "In truth, you could use some flesh on your bones."

"Not going to happen." What a stupid conversation. And, with a cat, no less. "And it doesn't change the fact that you can get into places that I can't."

"Agreed, but that also means that Liev and Milo can't follow me back out, as they are as big as you."

"Bigger."

And, boy, did he give her a look. She loved him dearly, but since he'd learned to talk, … she turned her back on him. "True that they can't follow you back out, but you could bring them something that will allow them to break out again."

"It's not a prison, and I can't carry a crowbar. Remember? I'm a cat."

"Glad you remember that." Still, he was right about being limited in what he could carry. "It would have to be something small to fit on your back."

"Like, treating me as a pack animal, … a, a, a *donkey*?"

His horrified tone made her laugh. "Exactly. Like an

ass." Still giggling, she wondered out loud, "What could they possibly use in there that they wouldn't have taken in the first place?"

"Milo's new personal stealth port."

"What's that?"

"A port he can take anywhere, coded for him. So he can move in and out anywhere he wants to."

"Why wouldn't he take it with him yet?"

"No need for it. They accessed the place like normal. They probably figured they'd exit the same way. Plus the personal port is not in the testing stage yet."

"It might be a great time to hit that stage. As in here and now to get Liev and Milo free." She couldn't think of anything better. "But, yeah. I can see how that would be a hot product for the masses."

"Some are on the market but not as transportable as this one." Charming scratched behind his ear. "Milo's portable model is ready, but he's working to interact stealth technology with it. Another military application that will make them a ton of money."

She could just imagine. It sounded ideal for military use, but she'd hate for just anyone to get their hands on something like that. No one would ever be safe. "Do you know where it is?"

"Sure. In the kitchen. He's got it on his bug computer doohickey."

It took her a moment to translate what that meant, but she remembered Milo's unusual little computer. "Wouldn't he have that on him already?'

"You'd think so, but he left it on the kitchen counter. They must have been in a hurry when they left." Charming walked to a spot in the sun and sprawled down sideways.

"Not doing anyone any good anyway. I can't carry it in."

"But, if you could, do you think you could take it to them?"

At that, he slumped to the side and laid out flat. "Of course. But I'm not going back down to Liev's apartment to get it."

She glared at him. "Well, I'm not risking being separated from you as well. The chances of losing you are too great." She bent, scooped him up into her arms, and stormed back the way they came. Thankfully the door to the apartment was still open. Maybe that wasn't a good thing considering other strangers. She walked straight to the kitchen and turned in a slow circle, looking for the item. "Charming, where is it?"

He reached up, batted her cheek to get her attention, and then pointed to the counter, back against the wall. The *doohickey* blended in perfectly. She picked it up and studied it. "It's so small. And it weighs nothing. You could easily carry it, if we can figure out a way to affix it to your back."

"True. That won't be easy."

"We need something to tie around you to hold it firmly in place. It doesn't need to stay in place for long, but we can't lose it either." She faced Charming. "Is this like a prototype, the only one that Milo has?"

Charming nodded, a grimace in place. "You better not lose it. Milo will never forgive you."

"Hey," Lani replied. "I've—more or less—forgiven him for time-traveling me two hundred years into the future." She shifted her stance. "So he should remember that we did this to save him and Liev."

"*You.* Not *we.*"

"Charming Marvin Summerland Blackburn! *We* are a

family. *We* work together. *We*, as in the four of us."

"Like *The Three Musketeers*, plus one?"

"That's better. Now help me think."

Charming sighed loudly.

Lani knew her baby was all heart, just under that crusty outer shell he sometimes projected to protect that soft heart of his. Luckily Liev had figured that out too. Of course Milo could care less about all the outer stuff but was totally impressed by Charming's brainpower. So it worked out all around.

"A harness would be better than something that ties," Charming stated.

"Ha. Glad to have you on board with my plan. The carrier will have to be something of a compromise, as I don't know how to make anything here and don't have any tools, like a needle and thread so ..." Her mind raced. "Elastic would work."

"Like they have that here."

Lani glanced at her own clothing. "True." And then she remembered. "But I have my old clothing." She raced into Liev's bedroom, but her twenty-first-century clothes were no longer here. Right, the pod room. She jogged over there. They had wasted enough time.

There, in a corner, she found her pile of clothes that she'd been wearing when she had arrived in this era. And in that pile ... was her bra. Her new clothes had one built in. She studied her old bra, wondering if she could make it work without cutting it up, somehow salvaging it—remembering how much Liev had liked it—but there wasn't another way, as far as she could see. She ran back to the kitchen where Charming and the small gadget sat. She opened the bread cupboard and pulled out a knife and went to work.

Ten minutes later, she raced back to Johan's place, carrying Charming and the portable port.

"I look ridiculous," Charming snapped, twisting inside his quickly tied harness—one bra cup around his belly with the new device nestled inside.

"You look great." She lowered him on the patio. "In fact, it's very stylish."

"Ha, you're just saying that so I'll do this."

"No, you need to do this to help Milo and Liev."

"I know that." He took several awkward steps, his tail flicking in sharp movements. "But you could have made it so I didn't look fat."

LIEV HAD ALREADY searched Johan's premises twice, looking for a way out. A different control server, something that would allow them to escape. Time was running out. They would have visitors soon. And, if anyone found him and his brother here, they'd soon find Lani and Charming. Not good.

He paced behind Milo and bit back the words threatening to tumble free at any moment. Milo had already snapped at him several times.

Liev had searched through Johan's communication center and had been shocked. Something that was hard to do.

He and Milo liked to keep things secret. But this? ... This was scary stuff. Johan had dirt. Like major dirt on a lot of people. Liev had been horrified when he'd found the file that had his name on it, with damn-near everything detailed, including every girl he'd partied with on the list. Milo's information had been more detailed in that it had a specific set of inventions he'd created and was in the process of creating. That's what scared Liev. How had Johan known? Bugs at his place? At his office? Kept a team watching their every move. Milo will be pissed. Liev pointed out the file to Milo, who went very, very quiet. Next thing Liev knew, the information was streaming at an incredible speed. "I presume you're copying all this."

Milo nodded and held up a small storage device he always carried. "It's downloading on this and will corrupt the original when done. We don't have time to sort through it all right now."

"Have you found a way through to shut down the other system?"

"The system is not on here."

Liev sat back and thought about that. "I wonder if Johan knew."

"I don't think he did. Johan's system could have gone into lockdown any time they wanted it."

"So why didn't they do that before he booked it? Even right after he left." And then Liev understood. "They missed that window. There'd been no warning. But they set a trap in case Johan returned. So, as Johan was looking for whatever it was, he tripped a warning alarm, notifying the other computer, the one watching Johan's computer. And had a henchman here in seconds."

"Maybe, or maybe his death tripped it, like we suspected all along. Any physical or virtual tripwire or whatever could also have been set off by Johan's attacker. Once he knew Johan was dying or that we were here, he—or his partners— could have set it off remotely. For all we know, that was only stage one. Several other levels of defense are likely to come."

"Or it could be that's all there is. We'd be left here to die of starvation."

"Not likely. It would take too long."

They stared at each other.

"We need to get out of here." As the words left Liev's mouth, they heard an unidentified sound.

"Shit," Milo said, his fingers moving faster. "I need just a little more time. And why the hell didn't I bring my comp?"

Liev snuck over to the doorway and worked on the panel. He set up the same decorating disguise that Johan had originally. Instantly the same boring spare bedroom shone and damn. ... Liev stared in shock. ... He saw no sign of Milo. He quickly reverted the program, and Milo appeared again.

Deep in concentration, Milo wasn't affected by the change. Liev switched it on once more, and Milo disappeared again.

Cool. And technology he needed himself.

Now if only he could manage to do the same right now.

A long scraping sound came from somewhere overhead. "What the ...?" he whispered. "It must be a rodent."

Milo's voice came through in an eerie whisper. "We don't have rodents."

"Then what is it?" Liev studied the ceiling.

A crack appeared—and not one as part of the bedroom camouflage but there nonetheless. And seconds later, Charming poked his head through.

"About time I found you."

CHAPTER 8

L ANI WAITED IMPATIENTLY outside Johan's place, hating
the fear rippling down her body. She hated being alone.
She never used to have a problem with it, but now that she
was in a strange world where so many things could go
wrong, she had additional fears. And some of the worst ones
were running through her mind right now. *Please let
Charming be safe. Please let him find the brothers.*

She blew a strand of hair out of her face, and, with her
hands on her hips, she slowly counted to twenty. When she
hit twenty, she continued to sixty.

"Okay, he should have reached them by now." And if he
had? Then what? According to Charming, Milo would be
able to port them into their own home from Johan's
apartment. What about Charming? Would he come back out
here to find her in the rooftop garden area, or would he go
home with the brothers? And what was she supposed to do?
Return to Liev's apartment or wait here? Damn it. Why
hadn't she gone over these details with Charming?

She shifted her weight from one side to the other and
looked around nervously. What if someone else came while
she was here waiting? And damn if she didn't hear a sound
behind her. She dashed around the side of the building and
hid.

The air tensed as odd noises crackled.

Hearing sounds but not being able to see was bad. Her mind conjured up horrible scenarios of all bad things gone wrong. Her breath caught in her chest. She flattened herself against the wall, eyes closed, ... and something brushed against her legs. She screamed and danced in place.

"Ouch. Knock it off, will you? Someone will hear."

Charming! She snatched him up and clutched him in her arms. "Charming," she cried out. "You scared me to death."

"Ha, you scared me with your screams," he complained and head-butted her.

"I'm so glad to see you." She buried her face in his fur, trying to get her pounding heart to calm down; then she remembered why he'd gone in. She lifted him higher so she could see his face. "Did you make it in?"

"What about me? Are you glad to see me too?" Liev's warm, caring voice reached her.

She lifted her head, saw Liev standing in front of her, and dashed into his arms. They closed securely around her. She shuddered, then realized that Charming was squirming in the middle of the hug. She let him down before standing up to wrap both arms around Liev. Slightly behind him, she could see Milo grinning like a crazy man.

Hell, they were all crazy.

"I was so scared," she whispered.

"I wasn't feeling all that good myself." He dropped kisses down her temple and along her cheek. "Thank you for sending Charming in with Milo's personal port—a brilliant idea, by the way." He squeezed her slightly. "As you can see, it worked."

Tears burning her eyes, she tilted her head back. "I'm so glad." She glanced around the rooftop, where they were all so visible, and said, "Can we go home now?"

"Yes, absolutely."

Keeping an arm securely around her shoulders, he led her around to the tiny rooftop garden and to the main elevator.

Once inside, she breathed a sigh of relief. She held up one shaking hand and laughed. "I hadn't realized how scared I really was."

"To be expected." He squeezed her shoulder gently. "I can't believe that you did that."

"Ha. Thank Charming for that."

"You both did that. It was brilliant to choose Milo's personal port, but then you figured out that the building's ventilation system would get you around the physical lockdown. And when you put it all together, using Charming as your delivery vehicle, that was sheer genius."

Milo bobbed his head. And this time it wasn't because he was listening to his headset.

She smiled and straightened slightly under Liev's—and Milo's—admiration. Out of the corner of her eye, she could see Charming puffing up too, his head held high, as they returned home. "I am just so glad it worked. I don't know what I would have done if it hadn't."

"We'd have gotten out somehow," he reassured her.

She wasn't so sure, but, hey, she was willing to believe anything at this point. Everything was good. Well, almost good. "What about Johan? He didn't make it."

Liev flinched. "I don't know what to do about that. It'll be hard to explain to the cops how we found him and not explain how we got out."

"True. Even if you could explain Charming, you wouldn't want to explain the new port system that Milo is developing."

Liev smiled at her insights. The elevator vanished, and they walked to the apartment.

Lani noted the front door was now closed, reminding her. "Maybe you could show me how I can close this door and open it, from both the outside and the inside," she said. "While we did several trips in and out between the two apartments just now, we had to leave it open."

"*Hmm.*" Liev was focused on the front door. "The door is closed now. So presumably it closed automatically after the time-lapse control was triggered."

That made sense. As much as anything here did.

Liev shared a look with Milo; then he nodded to his brother. Milo worked his wrist comp, and the door slid open.

Stepping inside, she watched as Liev secured the door behind her, then she opened her arms and collapsed against him. She hugged him tight. "Please, don't leave like that *ever* again."

He cuddled her close. "I'm not planning on it." He dropped a kiss on her forehead. "I think you need to sit down and relax."

"I'm thinking a nap in the healing pod might be a better idea. I'm seriously wiped out. Still not accustomed to the environment here."

"Good idea. You do that, and I'll start dissecting the information Milo stripped off Johan's communication center."

She walked to the pod room, calling behind her, "Was much information there?"

"Lots. But we don't really know what it all means yet."

"Right. I'll leave you to it then."

At the pod, she crawled inside and sighed as the humming started, lulling her to sleep.

LIEV WATCHED LANI as she slept. He let out a heavy sigh. She'd done so much with so little, and it looked to have completely wiped her out. And they were a long way from being safe. As long as she was in the healing pod though, he could work on the next step. "Milo, make sure the stealth is on in the pod room," he said as he walked into the kitchen. "She needs some downtime, and I want to make sure that she can't be found."

Charming pinned him with that look Liev was starting to hate. The look that said he was falling down on the job of taking care of Lani. Liev could hardly argue. Lani had been in nothing but trouble since Milo had snatched her up. And she'd been the one to save him in more ways than one. His relationships with women had been superficial in many ways. In all ways, if that was possible. Until Lani.

Nothing was superficial about his feelings for her.

"Hey, lover boy, I could use your help here."

Liev gave himself a mental headshake. "I'm here. What's up?"

"Look at this," Milo said. "It seems like whoever was monitoring Johan's presence at his place came from the Council."

"And that would only be if he was a prisoner out on bail."

"Normally, but we're dealing with a corrupt Council. So I've searched the databases and find no sign that Johan did time or has a criminal record of any kind anywhere."

"But it would begin to explain the secret life that Johan liked to live." Liev studied the square holograph, tons of images moving faster than his eyes could interpret. "What are the chances that Johan had a criminal record, and it was wiped?"

"The odds are pretty good. At least I'm inclined to think so. Considering he was as cagey as he was, his history is a little too clean for my liking."

"That's what I was afraid of. But why would the Council be onto him?"

"That's the million-dollar question."

Charming yawned. "Someone in the Council is bad."

Both Milo and Liev stared at him.

"We already know that," Milo stated.

Liev nodded. "But how do *you* know that, Charming?"

"Think about it." He rolled his eyes, as if speaking to peons instead of peers. "Johan's been reporting, willingly or unwillingly, to someone in the Council. Only someone with power could wipe Johan's criminal history clean. So someone in the Council is doing this for the benefit of the good for all or for the benefit of himself. Knowing people, I'd say he's doing it for himself."

"Listen to him." Milo snorted. "He's making sense."

Charming raised one long-haired eyebrow and peered down his short nose. "Of course I am."

"Besides"—Milo grinned—"I'm all for anything that makes the Council the bad guy."

"But there could be other answers. We have to keep an open mind." Although Liev couldn't think of one. And it was galling to think a cat had seen it first. Liev added, "It won't be just any one Council member. It will be maybe all four of the senior members, covering for each other."

"Or the Council is keeping tabs on things they shouldn't be, making deals with criminals," Milo suggested. "Or blackmailing criminals into working for them."

Liev tilted his head back and stared at the ceiling, his thoughts a jumble. "If Johan's pod is the issue, then it affects us a lot. If this is something Johan was into by himself, then we are only involved at the edge. And that could mean we can stay quiet, and no one will know anything. We're just afraid someone would know something. But they might not know anything."

"The real questions are, how to find out who knows what, and then what do we do to protect ourselves."

Charming added under his breath, but loud enough for the others hear, "And our food."

"I'm locking down this material from Johan and keeping it in a deep dark hole where no one can find it."

Charming stared at him. "Except for you guys, right? It's not blackmail material, but it might keep someone off your back if they know you have this ace in the hole."

"Ace in the hole?" Milo asked curiously.

"An old phrase," Liev said absentmindedly. "An archaic one at that." He pulled out his comp. "The lockdown of Johan's apartment makes sense if the Council was the one forcing Johan into collecting dirty information. We're presuming he was doing it for them, to a certain extent, enough to keep them happy, but he could have just as easily been keeping plenty back to screw with them."

Charming sat back. "I like that last part."

"So do I." Milo grinned. "So let's see what else I can find."

An alert sounded through the apartment, followed by a robotic voice saying, "Stephen Cavendish requests a call."

Milo looked up slowly. "Oh? Interesting."

"Yeah, let's see what he has to say." Liev flicked the buttons to open the communication system. Instantly Stephen's face and shoulders popped out of the HoloKomp. "Good to see you, Stephen. What can I do for you?"

"Sorry, this isn't a social call. We have alerts coming from your building. A death and rodents."

Milo froze. He picked up Charming and walked him down the hallway to the pod room. Liev heard the door open and close. "Sorry to hear that. Anyone I know?"

"Johan Strand."

With what he hoped was a suitable look of shock, he said, "Johan? He's deceased?"

"Apparently. A Medivac team has been dispatched. Someone anonymously reported the death. But we have no idea who it was."

Liev raised his eyebrows. That alert had to have come from the intruder who escaped because Milo didn't send one with Johan dying suddenly. "I have no idea who that would be. I was under the impression that you were searching for Johan, but he was on the run."

"And apparently he returned and was living quietly under everyone's radar."

"What can I do to help?" Liev asked.

"I need to know everyone's whereabouts for the last four hours."

Liev narrowed his gaze and felt his temper simmer. Not to mention the fears arising as well. "Are we suspects in Johan's death too?" he asked incredulously.

"Not at all. However, the Council wants to clarify who reported Johan as deceased."

"Well, it wasn't me. Or Milo or my wife."

"There are signs that someone from your apartment accessed the rooftop from your elevator. Several times, in fact."

Liev tilted his head. "Yes, that's quite possible. My wife's cat got loose today when we were trying to fix the front door after Hahn's death. She had taken her cat up to the little rooftop garden a couple days ago, and she figured he might have gone up there again."

"I need to speak with her."

"And why is that?" Liev's voice deepened with anger. No way would he force Lani to speak to the Council. "Particularly when the documents are in place for me to speak on her behalf."

CHAPTER 9

L ANI WOKE UP slowly. The heat from the pod was a
welcome relief from her earlier stress. It felt like she'd
slept for hours. Chances were good though that it was less
than a half hour. She felt decent. With a yawn and a stretch,
she pushed the pod lid open and swung her legs around. The
room theme was still the Pacific island. She swore she could
hear the surf as it rolled out in the distance. Could smell the
flowers. Maybe they could leave and go to a Pacific island for
real in a few days.

Or somewhere else. Anywhere else would be good. She
needed a few days away. Milo and Liev could do with a break
as well. Charming probably wouldn't care where they went,
as long as food came with them.

She smiled at the thought of her baby. He slept, snoring
gently beside her. He'd done so well getting in and out of
Johan's apartment. He'd been quite the hero, saving the day.
She hopped off the bed and wandered to the kitchen. Food
and coffee were topmost on her mind. As soon as she'd
imagined herself sitting on the island with a cup of coffee in
hand, she'd been lost.

The kitchen appeared silent, until she made it around
the corner and saw Liev in a discussion with someone on the
HoloKomp. She didn't recognize the male holo image and
had to remind herself that Liev ran a huge corporation that

she knew nothing about. He interacted with hundreds of people. He had to get caught up on business sometime.

A pang of guilt hit her. He was behind because of her. Milo was busy doing something on the big 3-D monitor, both also appeared to have an ear tuned to the ongoing conversation.

That stopped her on the spot. She now tuned into the conversation too. And stopped herself from gasping, slapping a hand over her mouth. Milo grabbed her arm and tugged her to him. "Stay out of sight and be quiet."

She nodded mutely. "Did they find Johan?" she whispered.

"They know about his death. Presumably they will be sending someone to investigate further. They want to speak to you about what you saw."

Her eyes widened, and she shook her head. "Hell no." Then she winced. "Unless it helps you guys. I didn't really see anything."

Liev left the square on the floor, designated for Holo-Komp conferences, to sidle up to his wife. "And, if you could tell them exactly that, I'd appreciate it," Liev said from beside her. "I've told them that you went up to the rooftop garden to search for your cat that got loose. It's not like you could see much from there, but if you could tell them the little bit you do know …"

He let his voice trail off and raised an eyebrow. She nodded. And took a step toward him. He held out his hand and drew them into the HoloKomp square. "Stephen, my wife, Lani."

Lani, suddenly shy, smiled. "Hello."

Stephen's face split into a broad grin. "Hi, Lani. Couldn't believe it when I heard this guy finally found the woman of his life."

Her smile brightened as Liev wrapped a possessive arm around her waist and pulled her close. "That I have."

"I'm sorry," she said, addressing Stephen. "I really didn't see much up on the roof. I wasn't focused on anything but my cat."

Stephen nodded. "Understood. But can you tell me if you saw anyone? Anything?"

"Oh, no. No one was up there. And the place was quiet." She opened her mouth to add that it was dead quiet and managed to choke back the words. But Stephen looked at her oddly, as if waiting for her to say more. Compelled to add something else, she said, "The place was locked down and silent."

"When you say, *locked down*, what do you mean?" Stephen asked curiously.

"It had steel doors all around. The other time I caught a glimpse of it, I saw a lot of glass everywhere. This time I couldn't see any glass."

Stephen frowned. "Interesting."

"It could have been just window coverings inside. It looked different from the last time I saw it."

"Thanks. I'm glad you found your cat."

Her smile this time was bright and happy. "Thank you. Me too." She stepped away from Liev, smiled at both of them, and said, "I'll leave you to your business."

"You're a lucky man, Liev," Stephen said.

Lani wanted to believe genuine admiration was in his voice, but she didn't know him. And everyone she'd met here so far had been less than what they had seemed.

She backed away and circled around to meet Milo. Charming had woke up and had joined them too. Bending close to Milo, she asked, "Was that all right?"

"Perfect." Milo reached forward and tapped the screen in front of him. "Look."

"What am I looking at? I can hardly see what you're pointing out with everything else going on." With every side of the monitor showing different images and all overlaying atop each other, it was confusing to see what he indicated.

Milo made several adjustments, and the monitors on three sides went black. In the center was a series of boxes with orange spots. "That's this building, isn't it?"

He smiled and nodded, then pointed to the spots around the middle of the building. "That's us."

How freaking fantastic was it that he could shift perspective like this? Then her gaze shot to the rooftop and the blacked-out apartment. Only it wasn't black any longer. An orange dot appeared … on top. "And who is that?"

"We don't know."

"But you can find out?" She shot him a sideways look. "With the tags and visual stuff you guys do here, I'm sure you have it figured out."

"His tags appear to be undetectable, and he's wearing a mask."

"*Oooh*, interesting." She studied the spot. "Maybe he's just running something that interferes with the signal." Feeling Milo's sudden start, she glanced at him. "What? What did I say?"

"You could be right." He leaned his hands on the counter and stared at the display. "If he is running interference, then I should be able to bypass it." He frowned, then his fingers moved faster. "It could take some time though."

"Or don't bother. Wait until he leaves and track him then. Surely you can identify him from that point."

He snorted. "Say what?"

"Why try to bypass it? He had to arrive from somewhere. Can't you track him backward and check his tags from his earlier position?"

"Only I don't know which way he'll leave, and, if he ports out, then he'll disappear faster than I can track him."

She shrugged. "True. I thought maybe you gave him only one choice. But then all this is beyond me." She watched Liev end the conversation. The HoloKomp disappeared. She walked toward him, catching an odd look on Milo's face as she did so. She raised an eyebrow in question, but he shook his head. She reached Liev's side. "Is everything okay?"

"As good as it can be." He tugged her into his arms. "You look much better after your nap."

"I feel better." Her stomach grumbled. She gave a tiny laugh. "Sorry. It's been a while since I've eaten."

"I'm hungry too," Liev added. He turned her toward the kitchen, where his brother worked. Charming, awake and alert, watched them with hungry eyes. "Yes, Charming. I'm making a meal."

Charming flopped to his side and rolled over in ecstasy.

Liev laughed. "That's the closest I've seen you to looking happy in a long time."

"You haven't fed me in a long time either," he moaned. "*Food.*"

"Ha." Lani smiled. "Now you can be patient while Liev cooks."

"Shrimp would be good," Charming said, with a long-suffering groan of hunger.

"Cat food is what you're getting."

"That works." He sat up and proceeded to clean his paw.

LIEV SET ABOUT making a hot meal. He'd ordered salmon earlier, thinking that might be the kind of meal Lani would love. He knew that Charming would if no else cared for it. Lani made coffee and watched him prep the fish.

When the meal was almost ready, she set the table, asking Milo, "Are you going to have a booster drink with us?"

He looked at her blankly. "Why?"

"So you can join us for the family meal."

He stared as if that were a foreign concept.

Liev grinned and smacked his kid brother lightly. "Yeah. Come join us."

"Not now. I'm on the hunt."

"Hunt for what?"

"This asshole."

"But you know where he is." Lani walked back over to the comp. "He's still showing up at Johan's place. So what's the big deal?"

"Hey, I'm just taking note of your suggestion and taking it one step further."

Liev looked up from plating dinner. "Really? What did she suggest?"

"To only give this guy one escape route, so we could ID him." He grinned, that boyish look Liev loved and hated at the same time. "I figured we'd use Johan's equipment to pick up anything we needed to know. Like this guy's comp number."

That didn't sound so bad. "And what good will that do?" Lani asked.

"If we can ID him, we'll figure out who he works for."

"Or not, considering the Defino brothers are still out there, and one of them is likely to be in Johan's apartment right now." Liev set the plates down. "Stephen is sending in a team."

"When?" Lani asked.

Milo laughed. "Right now from the looks of the orange spots shooting up to the rooftop. Looks like we'll get to see some fireworks soon."

"Except we can't see anything."

"Then come here and watch. I'll plug in the video."

And, sure enough, the inside of Johan's apartment showed on-screen.

And the intruder, dressed in black, paced back and forth.

Chapter 10

LANI HATED THE suspense. They needed to know who was in Johan's apartment. And what that person might want from there. Lani was more concerned about what they might know about her—if anything—and what they would do with that information.

"Lani, come and eat."

She spun around, completely forgetting that Liev had cooked a meal. Then her stomach reminded her. With a last look at the comp, she took her place at the table. And couldn't stop staring at the scene unfolding on the screen.

"Milo."

"Yeah?" But his voice was distracted as he watched the screen.

"Bring it over here," Liev said. "Then we can all watch, without getting a kink in our necks."

Lani's attention was caught by his words. "Bring it over?"

And, sure enough, Milo arrived at the table, and suddenly the big 3-D monitor sat at the side of the table where they could all see. "I had no idea you could do that!" she exclaimed. "That's totally awesome."

Liev smiled. "It's fun seeing things from your perspective." He pointed to the see-through image. "We get blasé about our technology."

"You have no idea how much you've advanced." Her gaze was caught by the orange blobs surrounding the top apartment, with the intruder still inside. "And then, in some ways, nothing has changed."

"The criminals are more sophisticated, but they still exist."

"Crime is everywhere," Milo said. "Then again, what do you expect when the Council is corrupt as well?"

Lani lifted a forkful of hot food, then gasped as she watched the team enter, surround, and attack the intruder. He collapsed to the ground, and darned if that hot spot didn't slowly fade to yellow.

She put down her fork, suddenly sick to her stomach. "It was fascinating to watch—like a movie—but, at the same time, I just realized that a person died. It's not so nice now."

"And I'm glad to hear you say that," Liev said in between mouthfuls. "This monitor allows one to see what wouldn't normally be seen, while allowing the viewer to distance himself from the reality." He took another bite. "But it's not a vid. It's real life."

"Good thing it was a bad guy." Charming finally lifted his head from his bowl of food and proceeded to clean his face. "And this bad guy would have killed us."

"But we don't know that," Lani protested. "He might have been a nice guy and not out to hurt us."

All three males stared at her.

She sat back and sighed. "Okay, so that's not likely. But I don't want to be so complacent that someone's death is not a concern."

Liev reached across the table and grasped her hand. "That's not likely to happen."

"Good. Please remind me of this conversation later."

"I will." He gave her hand a squeeze and then released it to resume eating.

"I'll remind you too." Charming gave her a fat smirk.

"I can do without your input, thanks."

She polished off her dinner in silence, her gaze watching the rest of the drama in Johan's apartment play out. The team of orange blobs collected the injured intruder and were moving down the building—at a slower pace. "Surely they could move him out of there much faster?"

"Actually they could." Liev frowned. He got up and walked over to his wall comp. Lani watched the orange blobs stop about midlevel. She gasped. "Are they here?"

An alarm sounded.

LIEV HAD PLANNED to ask Stephen about the raid, ... when the alarm went off again in his apartment. He quickly told Lani and Charming to go to the pod room.

She had a puzzled look on her face, but she scooped up Charming as requested. At least she no longer panicked as she had earlier. Good. When she'd entered the pod room, he double-checked that stealth was on to keep her presence secret. Then he turned off the alarm to his front door and opened it.

ComBots. A robotic retrieval death team. Or, as some called them, ... death squads.

"What can I do for you?"

"Identification required."

"I am Liev Blackburn."

"Acknowledged. We need this man identified." And a body bag was thrust forward.

Liev blanched. "Why me?"

"We need to know if you recognized him from the earlier altercation."

"Let me see his face."

He expected to have the body bag opened, but instead a tablet was shoved under his nose, a large image of a dead man on the screen. "That's Johan Strand."

"Thank you." And the ComBots retreated.

Liev stepped outside. "Wait. Who is in the bag?"

"You just identified him," the leader said.

"No," Liev snapped. "I did not. I identified the face on the tablet, not the body in the bag."

"Same man."

"No." He shook his head. No way in hell they were the same man. He didn't know what was going on here, but they were trying to pull something, and he didn't want his identification of one dead man to be mistaken for the identification of another dead man. "I need to see his face."

"We cannot allow that."

"Then my identification does not stand."

"You have already identified him."

The ComBots were only computers. Advanced computers, but not conversationalists. "No. I identified the picture on the tablet. I need to see the face on the body in the bag to confirm."

"We can't allow that."

"Yes, you can. And I have Councilman Stephen Cavendish's permission."

The ComBots buzzed, as if forwarding the request to the Council.

"The Councilman cannot be reached."

"Well, he gave me permission." Liev walked closer. As much as he didn't want to look at any dead man's face in reality, he did want to know who was in the bag. The ComBot turned and conversed with another bot. Liev walked closer. He turned his back on the bots and quickly opened the bag.

"Stop. You cannot do this."

"Too late. I have done it." And it was not Johan. "This is Paul Defino. Older brother to Tommy Defino. This is not the man on the tablet. I repeat, this is not Johan Strand." He turned, anger building inside him. "Where is Johan Strand's body?"

"We do not have it. This is the only body that we have collected."

"Why did you not collect the other one?"

"There was no other body to collect."

CHAPTER 11

L ANI HAD BARELY relaxed in the pod when Liev opened the door. "Lani?"

She poked her head out. "I'm awake. What's up?"

"That was a death squad of ComBots. They have one of the Defino brothers, bagged and tagged. Dead."

"So that's who was up there? Interesting."

"Even more interesting, Johan's body was not there, according to them. They, being robots, can be ordered to do one thing, then reprogrammed to forget what they did. But it appears that whoever is behind this is hiding Johan's death."

He walked closer and pushed open the pod lid higher so she could swing her legs around and hop off. "They are gone. I've been trying to reach Stephen, but there's no answer—anywhere."

She winced. "That always sounds so ominous. I was hoping that they'd caught the bad guy, collected poor Johan, and now we were safe."

"I'm hoping that's exactly what the situation is, but I can't be sure of anything at this time. It's almost bedtime, so maybe Stephen got word from the team and now has turned off his comp."

"I'm not sure I can sleep now." She walked with him down the hall to the living room. "I am tired but more wired. Wondering when this will all go away."

"I wonder what happened to Johan."

"Are you sure the death bots didn't remove his body?"

"They said they didn't. If they did, they didn't let me see it. I only saw one body bag, and that held Paul Defino." Liev slipped a hand up the nape of her neck and gently massaged the tight muscles. "I'm sorry there have been so many issues since you arrived."

"Apparently many were caused by my arrival." She moaned gently as he stopped, turned her around, and dug in his fingers to knead deeper. "Where's Milo?"

"Retired for the night."

Her insides perked up. She looked over her shoulder and gave Liev a fat smile. "So does that mean we are alone?"

"Not quite," Charming said. "But I'm heading in to lie beside the fire, so don't mind me."

She laughed. "We won't. Keep your ears shut."

"I'll sleep instead. Just don't wake me."

She watched as her baby sauntered toward the hallway into Liev's bedroom. That was where she wanted to go.

"He not only talks but thinks, has words of wisdom, and can solve puzzles," Liev said. "He's quite a puzzle himself."

When Charming had disappeared from sight, Lani turned to face Liev. "Now are we alone?"

His smile quirked. "As alone as you want to be."

She ran her hands up his bare arms, loving the feel of his silky skin. "Good. And it's late. So …"

"So …?"

She raised her eyes to his. "Bedtime?"

"Absolutely." A slow smile quirked, lighting a fire in her heart. "Back to the pod or …"

"Or … your bed?"

He lowered his head and kissed her. "Definitely my bed."

In a move that shocked a surprised squeak out of her, he scooped her up as if she were no bigger than Charming.

Snuggling close, she yawned. "You live a crazy life."

"It's your life too." He walked toward his bedroom, nudging the door open with his foot. Sure enough, the fire burned bright. Overhead, the big timbers affixed to the ceiling sprawled the length of the room. She shook her head. "This is so amazing."

"Glad you like it. I can change it, if you'd rather have a different scene."

"No," she cried out. "This is perfect."

He walked over to the bed and softly dropped her in the middle of the big poofy comforter. She laughed. "I love this. It seems like forever since I spent a night in a bed."

"It has been forever." He turned away to lock the bedroom door, then glanced at the big plush rug in front of the fire, where Charming slept. "Charming, in or out?"

All they heard was a heavy guttural snore.

Lani added, "He'll be fine in here with us. He's a heavy sleeper."

"Good. Two's company in the bed, but three is a definite crowd."

"I'd get used to it if I were you. Charming has always slept in the bed with me."

"Not right now. This is the time for just the two of us." He walked to the side, and, while she missed what he'd done to make it happen, a large series of built-in shelves and hooks appeared, where he hung his clothes after stripping them off. She sat up, wondering what they did with laundry. "Do you have a laundry service, or do you wash your own clothes?"

He paused momentarily as he took off his wrist comp. His shoulders started to shake. He turned with a silly grin on his face. "Haven't you figured it out yet? We don't do menial work anymore."

Her mouth dropped open. "None?"

"None."

"You cooked," she accused. "And cleaned up."

"Did I?"

She stopped and had to think. No one had washed dishes. She'd assumed that Milo had cleared the table, but she hadn't seen that happen either. So really she had no idea. "You don't do laundry? Dishes?"

"No. I'll show you the kitchen cleanup tomorrow. But I can show you the laundry process now. Hand me your clothing, and I'll hang them up. That's it. It will be clean and ready to wear again in the morning."

Her mouth gaped open. "That cupboard will wash your clothes?"

"It's like a mini dry-cleaning service inside." He stood completely nude in front of her, as unconscious of his nudity as she was conscious of it. Then again, she'd have to be dead to not notice. "Do you want to try it?"

"Oh, yes, please." Trying to be as natural stripping in front of him as he was with her, she stripped down to her skin and walked over. He showed her where to hang up her items. When done, he closed the closet and pushed a small button. "Do this every night, and every morning the clothes will be clean and ready to be worn. If you don't do it all the time, it stacks up, and you have to stand here and do this over and over again."

"Marvelous." Lani turned to him and smiled brightly. He opened his arms.

She stepped into them, loving that they instantly closed securely around her.

LIEV PULLED BACK slightly so he could look into her deep blue eyes. She was so beautiful. So natural that he couldn't imagine any enhancements that would improve what Mother Nature had given her. She wouldn't agree, but that he'd found was the way of women. Maybe people in general.

"What are you thinking?" she asked, a small shadow sliding into her gaze.

She didn't know him well enough to understand his actions, the nuances of his voice, yet she stood before him, as bare as the day she'd been brought into this world, with such trust, and he felt his heart swell. "I was thinking that I am the luckiest man alive." And damn if his voice didn't drop to a hoarse whisper. He closed his eyes and set his chin on top of her head as his emotions choked him. "I don't know why I am so blessed, but I truly am grateful that you are here in my life, in my arms tonight."

She snuggled closer, the brush of her nipples against his chest a sweet torment, the slide of her arms around his chest a delight. When she laid her head against his heart, he thought he'd cry. Instead, he crushed her against him and held her tight.

She deserved so much more. And he planned on giving it to her. He gently picked her up and carried her to the bed. In some weird sense of tradition, a night in his bed meant the start of their married life. A wedding night for just the two of them.

He flipped back the covers and lay beside her. Instantly she turned toward him. God, he loved it that she wanted to be here with him. Not just some party where everyone came to have fun with anyone, not because he was wealthy and eligible, but because she wanted to be here with him—because she cared.

Heat rolled through him. He needed that. Needed her.

Her hands slid up his chest to cup his face. He shuddered. "Are you all right?"

"Yes," he murmured. "Just a little overwhelmed."

"Same here." She kissed him gently. "I came a long way to find you, Liev."

He shuddered again, her words finding all the lonely places in his heart and filling them.

"I've missed you all these years," she whispered against his neck, her breath warming him to his toes. "Where were you, Liev?"

She dropped more kisses on his chin, then on his neck, before moving to his collarbone. A trail of heat, then ice followed as she drifted her way down his body. He wanted to tell her to stop. Wanted to pleasure her, but the words wouldn't come out. The need to be, to exist, as is, with her like this, ... it was too strong.

She propped herself on one elbow, then pushed him from his side onto his back and slowly worked her way downward.

"Let me," he said in a low voice. "I want to make this special for you."

"Oh, it will be," she assured him, a tiny smile playing at the corner of her lips. She slid her hand down. "Besides, you promised me."

"Later," he said, but, when her hand closed around him, he cried out.

"This is my time," she murmured, dropping kisses down

his chest and across his ribs. "My turn."

And then she found him with her mouth.

Liev thought he'd died. Lani's mouth was so wet, so sweet, and so damn hot, he almost couldn't hold on. He was afraid to move. Afraid she'd stop. And afraid she wouldn't. He didn't want this over too soon. She scraped her teeth down the long length of his shaft.

He lifted his hips and groaned.

Then her mouth was gone. He opened his eyes to find her carefully shifting over him, straddling his hips. She grasped him gently in one hand as she found her position.

And lowered herself.

His groan rumbled free. He couldn't help himself. He reached up and grabbed her hips to hold her steady, and he lunged upward, grinding his pelvis against her. She gasped and threw her head back, tightening her inner muscles.

He shuddered at the delicate internal massage. "Oh, God," he whispered. "Lani, you feel so freaking good."

She laughed, a wild abandoned sound that ended on a low moan. She leaned forward, dropped a tongue-dueling kiss on him, and started to ride.

He was a goner. In heat. In lust. In love.

And that no longer scared him. Emotion overwhelmed him. "Lani," he cried out.

"I'm here, Liev," she whispered. "Just let go."

"Not ... without ..." He flipped his head back and forth, the tension coiling tighter and tighter. He didn't want to let go. He wanted this to last ... forever. "Not without ... *you*." And he couldn't hold back. His body exploded, his hands holding her hips in place as he ground as deep as he could go.

Through the haze in his mind, he heard her cry out, her

thighs holding him tightly. He shuddered. When she collapsed on his chest, he held her close against his heart. "I think I'm in love."

She froze. Then a tiny giggle slipped free. "Only *think?* 'Cause I don't have any doubt."

He rolled over, still inside her, and pinned her underneath him. He stared down into her beautiful luminescent eyes, so full of joy, satisfaction, and, … yes, … love.

"Neither do I," he whispered. "I don't know how I got to be this lucky, but I love you, Lani. So very much."

And he proceeded to show her all over again.

CHAPTER 12

A LONG TIME later, warm and happy, Lani rolled over and cuddled up against Liev.

His strong arms wrapped around her and pulled her even closer. He kissed her forehead before dropping back in exhaustion.

Good. She'd worn him out too. She smirked.

"I heard that," Liev murmured against her hair.

"No, you didn't."

"I felt it."

"Now that's possible." She waited, wondering if she should ask.

But Liev, ever sensitive to her needs, asked first. "What's on your mind?"

She shifted so she lay, arms crossed on his chest, chin resting on top. Where she could look into his eyes. Where she could see the truth. In a serious voice, she asked, "Did you mean it?"

His eyebrows shot up in surprise, but his eyes warmed all the way through. Even as satiated as she was, her body quickened at the heat glowing from his heart.

"I meant it. All of it. All the way."

She closed her eyes. In spite of herself, a tear leaked from the corner of her eye. She swore she was done with the bawling, but the depth of the feelings in his voice? … Well, she didn't think anyone had ever cared for her like he did.

"Please, don't cry." He pulled her higher up on his chest so he could kiss the tear away. "I didn't mean to upset you."

"You could never upset me by telling me how much you care." She smiled, blinking rapidly to stop more tears from rolling down her cheeks. "I was just realizing how much I want this. How much I missed out on when all my friends had loving relationships, and I didn't."

"I feel the same way. I didn't want to be with everyone and yet no one. I wanted to find someone to love, someone who'd love me."

She made a face. "I hate to say it, but it looks like we owe Milo our thanks."

Liev laughed. A deep rumble rolled through him, making her sigh with delight. "That we do, but we won't tell him just yet."

He flipped her over, and she whispered, "Tell me again."

"How about I tell you *and* show you." He paused one moment, before adding, "I love you, Lani Blackburn."

And then he lowered his head and kissed her.

HOURS LATER, AN alarm shuddered through the apartment. Liev bolted from bed.

Lani woke up beside him, a cry on her lips.

"Alarm on low."

Instantly the sound stopped.

"Liev," Lani said, now that she could be heard, "what's going on?"

"Intruders."

She gasped, clutching the covers to her chest. "What?"

Liev bolted out the door, even as he hopped on one foot

trying to get into his pants and calling behind him, "Grab Charming and hide in the pod room."

He couldn't stay to make sure she obeyed his orders. Milo was stumbling through the kitchen when he arrived. "Any idea who it is?"

"No." Milo yawned but brought up the security system. "I also don't know if it's building-wide or just us."

"Find out." Liev headed to the front door and his wall control panel. "The exterior is secure. I can see no breach anywhere." He called out to Milo, "I can't see what's triggered the alarm."

"Uh, Liev?"

"Yeah?"

"Can you come here?"

Exasperated, Liev gave the panel one final look, but it didn't have anything new to offer. "Coming." He bolted to the kitchen. There was no sign of Lani along the way, so he hoped she'd hidden as he had instructed.

In the kitchen, he came to a skittering stop. Milo faced him, and so did Lani, who'd managed to get completely dressed. Behind them both stood the younger Defino brother, Tommy Defino.

"What the hell?" Liev approached slowly, his hands partially up. "How did you get in here, Tommy?"

Tommy glared, his lip curling. "You're not the only one who's good with technology. The world is full of geeks. Just not so full of guys who can get the job done." He smiled a too-shiny grin. "Like me."

"And what job is that?" Liev studied the man, looking for some weakness. The asshole was cocky, confident. In fact, he looked too damn confident. This wasn't the first time he'd broken into someone's house, even a high-tech one like his. But under that veneer was anger, fear, and maybe a hint ... of ... desperation.

And that made him dangerous.

"Besides, you didn't use technology to get in here. Our scans would have alerted us. So how else?" While he waited for an answer, he studied his brother's face. Milo kept rolling his eyes to the left. Liev casually checked out Lani's pinched face, then carried on to the counter, where Milo was motioning.

Lani snorted. "When I left the door open earlier. You snuck in then, didn't you?"

"Well I did, and left a device behind so I could get in again when I wanted to, like now."

Damn. That made sense. The system had been off while Lani was outside rescuing him and Milo. This kid could have snuck in and found a place to hide his device until he found the best time to return.

And Tommy nodded and laughed. "You geeks seem to think you're so damn smart. Sometimes the easiest way is the best way to do something."

Milo made a sharp movement with his head. Liev saw the large 3-D computer was up and running. The hot spots showed who was where in the building. It took him a moment to realize that Johan's place was once again occupied.

"Your brother already died in this building," Liev said in an even tone. "Are you sure you should be here?"

Tommy narrowed his gaze. "Like hell he did." Tommy turned slightly to look at the shutdown HoloKomp center behind him, as if wanting to call his brother.

"I saw his body myself. The ComBot death squad retrieved him." Liev realized the kid didn't know. "I'm sorry."

"I don't believe you. He's on a job." Tommy shook his head. "He'll check in when he can."

"Except something went wrong." Liev would hate to hear news like that from a stranger. "Sorry."

"Like hell. Paul is good. Better than anyone I know. You're just messing with me." He snorted and waved something around.

Liev's gut clenched. Shit. The guy had a laser gun. With a wave of his hand, he could cut a person in half. Lani wouldn't have a hope of escaping. She didn't even know what it was. "What do you want?" Liev asked in a cold voice. He smiled at Lani to reassure her, but his mind raced. What the hell could he do to protect them all? He took a step forward.

"Whoa. That's close enough."

Milo made a sharp movement of his head again.

Liev glanced at the monitor screen. He studied the three figures in Johan's place, then motioned toward the moving images. "Those are the ones who killed your brother. Most likely another death squad ComBot looking for the information Johan has secreted away."

"What? Like hell." Tommy waved the gun around again and grabbed Lani's arm, pulling her back a step. Lani lost her balance, only righting herself at the last minute when he shoved her forward again.

"Leave her alone," Liev snapped, his voice hard. He clenched his fists.

"Or what?" Tommy sneered. "It's not like you can do anything. She's coming with me."

"Why?" He needed to keep the asshole answering questions. He had to find out where Lani was being taken, not that he'd let her leave. … He just needed an opening.

"What about me?" Milo asked.

Liev was happy to have the distraction his little brother added to this confab. They had to stop Tommy from leaving with Lani.

"I don't know anything about you. Unless you're worth something, you get to die along with Liev here."

"So you know me," Liev interrupted, "but I don't know you. Interesting. I presume you took care of Gina?"

"What do you know about that bitch?"

"Only that she was a bitch," Milo said. He'd shifted closer to the monitor.

"That she was." Tommy pushed Milo slightly away. He fell toward the counter and pushed something on the monitor, a move so slight it was almost unnoticeable. Liev did notice. Milo had unlocked the computer system. What was he up to?

Charming sauntered into the kitchen.

Then the balance of power shifted.

Lani gasped. Liev watched, waiting with a fatalistic attitude, knowing that something was about to give.

Casually Charming hopped up on the counter by the monitor. He started to clean himself.

Like any ordinary cat.

"That is one ugly cat."

Uh-oh.

Charming froze. His whiskers quivered. He turned to stare at Tommy. In a low voice, he snarled, "What did you say?'

Liev groaned.

Lani rushed to talk. "Poor baby, you've still got that horrible hoarse voice." She rounded on Tommy. "How dare you say that about my cat?"

The poor guy's jaw worked. He frowned, his shocked gaze going from Lani to Charming and back again. "Did that cat just talk?"

"You're losing it." Milo laughed. "How can a cat talk? Get too many bangs on the head, by any chance?"

Tommy glared. "Shut the hell up."

Behind Milo, a series of weird beeps started.

"What's that? What did you do?" Tommy raced to the monitor, dragging Lani with him.

Charming scurried backward out of the way. Liev looked at him suspiciously. Charming gave him a bland look back. What the hell had he done?

Milo studied the computer. Liev caught a grin on his baby brother's face before Milo wiped his face clean. So Charming had done something good. Could they be so lucky?

"Turn it off," Tommy snapped. "Hurry up."

Milo reached over and tapped in a code. Instantly the unit silenced.

Tommy relaxed. "That's why you shouldn't have pets around computers. They'll fry the circuits."

"This one is particularly bad." Milo smiled. Charming snickered.

Tommy stared at Milo suspiciously before switching his gaze to Charming. "Should throw the damn thing out the window."

"You'd do that?" Lani rounded on him. "What kind of a horrible person are you? Animals are innocent. They don't deserve that type of behavior." She poked her finger into his chest. "What kind of an asshole are you?"

"The asshole with the gun. Now lay off, lady." He spun around, his glare angry and frustrated. "What kind of a house is this?"

"A good one," Lani said with a sniff and lifted her nose. "Unlike the one you live in."

Tommy shook his head. "I don't know why the boss wants you. I wouldn't want to be anywhere close to you."

She deliberately stepped closer. "Yeah, how about this close?" She took another step. "Or this?"

"Stand back. I mean it."

Liev watched, fascinated, yet simultaneously worried as hell, as Lani, her temper up now, shoved her face into Tommy's. "Why should I? You can't hurt me. The boss paid you good money to make sure you don't. So are you going to defy your boss and hurt me?"

Tommy winced at the thought.

"Yeah, I didn't think so."

Liev wanted to wince too, because Lani wasn't thinking. Tommy could just as easily hurt them … or use Charming against her instead to get her cooperation.

As if reading Liev's mind, Tommy swung his arm out wide, bringing the laser gun around to bear on Charming.

And Charming jumped.

CHAPTER 13

C HARMING LANDED ON Tommy's arm. Claws dug in deep. Tommy screamed. And the laser gun went flying.

Milo jumped for the gun.

Liev jumped for Tommy.

Lani jumped for Charming.

"Get it off me," Tommy screamed, dancing backward, half bent over, and still shaking his arm. Liev pinned him against the counter, twisting Tommy's free arm up and behind him.

"Charming, let go." Lani tried to pull Charming off the man, but Charming was not interested. "Please, Charming. You'll get hurt."

"*He's* getting hurt?" Tommy screamed hysterically. "What about me? I'm the one who's been attacked."

Milo snickered. "Then you shouldn't have threatened Lani. The cat is very protective of her."

"You guys are nuts. Do you hear me? Bat shit crazy!" This last bit he delivered at the top of his lungs.

"Ha," Lani snapped. "You're the one who attacked a poor defenseless cat."

"What?" Tommy stared at her in shock. "I didn't attack him. He attacked me. And that makes him anything but defenseless."

"Not the point. You insulted him first." With Charming

now safe in her arms, she cuddled him close. "Ignore him, Charming. He's just being mean." Charming popped his head over her arm to glare at Tommy, and damned if he didn't stick his tongue out at him. She caught his move out of her peripheral vision and glared at Charming. He raised an eyebrow and pulled it back in.

"Did I just see that? Did you just see that?" Tommy cried out. "That cat stuck his tongue out at me."

"You really need to lay off those recreational supplements." Milo laughed. "Natural is fine but not in the doses you've been indulging."

"What are you talking about?" Tommy groaned. "You all belong in the nuthouse."

"Right, and you're the one making crazy talk about a cat," Liev snarled.

That shut him up.

Lani watched from a safe distance as Milo handed the gun off to Liev, who then held it on Tommy, as Milo checked over their intruder for weapons and communication devices. When Milo pulled Tommy's personal comp from his pocket, he stepped back and started clicking away on it.

"Hey, that's mine," Tommy protested. "Don't mess anything up."

Milo rolled his eyes at him. "He's got both Gina and Hahn in his address book, and yes, here's Johan. Just like we found on Paul's comp.

"Hey, how did you get my brother's comp?"

"He conveniently left it behind here," Liev snapped, "when he broke in while we were dragged off to the Council."

"So that means nothing. Johan is behind all this bullshit."

"Then you're left holding the bag—in big trouble, kid—because Johan is dead, as is your brother, Paul," Liev said, his voice icy and hard.

Tommy froze. "What?"

"I said, Johan is dead. As is your brother."

"That can't be. No." Tommy shook his head. "Paul said to come here and to grab Lani. How Johan said she needed tags. And we know what that means. Paul had an argument with Johan about it, when Paul tried to retrieve the information for the Council. Johan wouldn't tell Paul where the info was. Only someone else was there. Paul barely escaped that time, so he had to go back."

"That argument finished Johan," Liev stated with some heat. "He'd been hurt before. Your brother must have given him the final blow to his injured body. So the Council did away with Paul for his failure to keep Johan alive long enough to find the information the Council wanted and then for not getting that data on his own." Liev paused, glaring at Tommy. "As far as the others in Johan's apartment, *we* were the others in that damn apartment. Your brother escaped from *me*," Liev snapped. "And, no, I don't know what *needing tags* mean. What does it mean?"

Tommy shook his head, trying to absorb the facts as they flew at him. "It means that she's not from here."

"So, she's from somewhere else," Milo said. "What's the big deal?"

"They are eradicating the fringe groups. You know that."

"No," Liev corrected. "The Council is isolating the fringe groups to live in one area, where they can't cause as much trouble."

"Talk about naive." Tommy snorted. "Look. They just dispatched a large group of them a few months back. When the alert came through on the tagging for Lani, they figured she'd escaped. She'd cause them a ton of damage if she spread the word."

Lani stared. "Are you saying someone committed mass murder, and they think I got away? And now I'm going to blow the whistle on them?" Oh, this was not good. Like, so not good.

"Who did this?" Liev asked Tommy in a hard voice.

But Milo answered, "The Council, of course."

And Tommy nodded. "They did. And they can't have anyone know what they did."

"Why kill these fringe groups? Were they terrorists?" Liev asked.

"That's what the Council will try to convince everyone," Tommy explained, "but they weren't. They were people who didn't want to live under the Council rule. They lived a more natural life."

Instantly Lani felt a connection to them. "Those poor men."

"Women and children too," Tommy added. "The Council was especially clear about making sure the breeding stock was taken out, so the problem couldn't continue."

Lani burrowed her face into Charming's lush fur. How terrible. Centuries in the future and genocide was still a problem. In her own country yet. She didn't know what to say.

Liev did. "Do you have any proof?"

"Johan had it. He was trying to make a break from being under their thumb. They blackmailed him into monitoring everyone." Tommy nodded at Liev and then at Milo. "Like you two. He didn't want to tell them about Lani here, but they saw the information from his pod, and they found out anyway."

LIEV HATED THE ring of truth in Tommy's words. This explained so much. Tommy no longer looked like a major badass. Instead, he looked like a punk who had made a wrong turn and didn't know how to make the right one to get the hell out.

Liev took a look at Lani. How was she taking this revelation? True to form, she had tears collecting in the corner of her eyes. He just didn't know why. Fear? Agony for the victims? Something else?

"That's a horrible thing to do," she said in a harsh whisper. "Those people just wanted to live their life their way."

Tommy nodded. "I agree. But you're dead meat regardless. The council can't afford to let you live."

Liev realized that Tommy believed Lani had escaped the massacre, and—if he did—others would too. She was marked. Unless this was resolved, ... and fast, ... there'd be no end to this hunt. Ever.

Except they had Johan's material. He spun around to look at Milo.

And his kid brother—as usual—was way ahead of him.

"You do realize the Council killed your brother?" Liev asked Tommy. "They couldn't leave him alive with what he knew about the genocide. They've already—or someone has—killed Gina, Hahn, Johan, and now your brother."

Grief filled the young man's eyes. "I was hoping you were lying. I haven't heard from Paul since last night. He was on a retrieval mission at Johan's."

"Retrieving what? The info on Lani?"

Tommy shook his head. "They had the pod scan on Lani, from Johan's pod, but it was too corrupted. That's why they need Lani in person, to run their own scans. But the Council knew Johan had something else. The data Johan had on the Council."

It all made such terrible sense. "And what will they do with you, now that you've failed?" Liev asked in a gentle voice. He wondered who had beaten Johan so well that he was inches away from death. Then again, thugs were easy to find and even easier to hire. It could have been one of many. All hired by the Council. Or rather, all blackmailed by the Council. Liev doubted Tommy knew about any of those "contractors," outside of his brother.

Tommy shook his head and said in a gloomy voice, "I'm dead already. The final act just hasn't happened yet."

Milo turned to look at him. "Run. Surely you can find a place to go where you can be safe."

Not likely, but Liev waited for Tommy's answer.

"No. I have no place to run to. All the Councils are connected. I could go to the other side of the planet, and they'd find me within a day."

"Unless we find a way to stop them first," Milo said.

Tommy looked up at Milo, a tiny bright bit of hope in his eyes. "What good would that do? You'll just throw me to them anyway."

"Did you kill anyone?" Lani asked out of the blue.

"Me? No." He looked shocked at the suggestion. "I'm good with computers." He shrugged. "I've committed many a break-in though. That will get me off-planet jail for life. And it's not fair. We were ditched early in life by Mum and had to fend for ourselves afterward. A little hard to do and to stay honest when you're trying to stay out of the system and have no family to turn to."

Liev nodded. And that was the biggest issue. No family to take them in and to give them a home. Without it, life could be a little grim. Hell, a lot grim.

Tommy confronted them. "So what will you do to me?"

CHAPTER 14

LANI HEARD THE challenge in Tommy's voice. She carefully placed Charming on the table with a whispered warning, "Be quiet." He shot her a hooded look. She wasn't sure what he meant by that. She wanted to believe he'd be good, but there was no guarantee.

Ever.

Not with Charming.

Giving him a stern look, she walked over to Liev and slipped her hand into his. He squeezed her hand and tugged her up close. She murmured, "What can you do, Liev?"

"I'm working on it," he said with light humor. "Give me a minute."

She watched Tommy shift uneasily. Milo was back at the big computer. Now that Tommy had been disarmed, he'd lost his bravado. He just looked sad. Worn out. "How good are you?"

"At what?" He looked confused.

She glanced at Milo, whose face had twisted in thought. "Milo?"

"I'm thinking."

She groaned. "Could you two think a little faster please?"

"What difference does it make?" Tommy slouched against the back counter. "There is no going back for me."

She wanted the brothers to step up and to give the kid a

break, but she didn't know enough of how life worked here to make that happen. Maybe the kid was a major badass and needed to be slung out onto some horrific planet all alone. What did she know? "Liev, can you help him?"

He glared down at her. "And why would I want to do that? He broke into my house and tried to kidnap you, besides threatening to kill me and Milo, not to forget about tossing Charming out of a window sixty floors up. Where in any of that does it say he deserves my help?"

"Because he didn't succeed, and he really had no choice himself."

"But he did in the beginning," Liev argued, his jaw stiff with anger.

"Did he?" She waited. She didn't know Liev as much as she'd like to, but she knew him better than he thought. He was a good man. With a good heart. A ruthless businessman, yes, but not at the expense of endangering people. He'd help Tommy if he could. If he saw a reason to.

"Oh no." He shook his head. "I know that look. No. We're not saving the world."

"I didn't ask you to save the world. Just one small part of it." She widened her gaze at him. "We couldn't save those on the fringe."

He closed his eyes and groaned. "Really? You're going there?"

She smiled. Milo laughed, then said, "She has a point."

Liev shook his head. "No. No, she doesn't."

"He's good," Milo said quietly, with a head tilt toward Tommy. "We could use him."

"Is he?" Lani asked, her hopeful gaze on Milo's features. He nodded. She switched her attention to Tommy. He was slumped with apparent disinterest, like he'd never known there to be anything but a bad outcome in his life.

"It doesn't matter how good he is, when he can't be trusted." Liev's hard voice brooked no argument.

But Lani had to admit to feeling perverse. "How do you know that? I imagine loyalty and trustworthiness are the two main requirements in Tommy's life up to now." She turned toward the very confused man, staring at her like she'd lost her marbles. "Or am I wrong?"

"No," he said in a rush. "You're not. They mean everything. Or I'd be dead by now."

She nodded, facing Liev now. "See?"

"No," Liev said in exasperation. "I don't see." He raised both hands in frustration. "He's a criminal. I can't change his history. The law wants him. The law will get him."

"I actually did my time. It's my brother who's ... was ... wanted by the law. Then the Council said I hadn't done all my time. Only I did. But because they said I hadn't ..."

"Juvie?" Milo asked, busy clicking away on his damn computer again.

Lani didn't know if he was helping the situation or playing games, but she wanted someone to do something. "Milo?"

"Yeah," he answered, distracted.

"What are you doing?" she asked.

"Looking at his record."

Tommy started. "You aren't supposed to be able to see that."

Milo snorted. "I'll look at whatever the hell I want to."

Tommy stared from one person to the other. When it was Lani's turn, she gave him a bright smile.

"Milo?" Liev waited for a response from his brother.

"Says he did his time. Was released four years ago. Model prisoner. Time off for good behavior."

"And they said that was revoked because I moved back in with my brother, who was a known criminal."

"That's not fair," Lani cried out. "You paid your debt to society. And he was family."

Tommy shrugged. "The Council said it wasn't enough. It's not like I can argue. They have all the power."

"Too much power apparently." Lani twisted slightly to face Milo and Liev. "Can you help him?"

Milo grinned. "I don't think Liev wants to. Tommy here was all set to screw with us. You in particular."

"Only because I had to." But he stared at Lani in fascination. "I've never met anyone like you."

"Not going to either." Milo almost danced in place with his secret.

But that was one secret that could never be shared.

LIEV STUDIED THE awkward young man in front of him. He wanted to slug him and hug him, for all that he'd tried to do. Liev couldn't help comparing Milo to Tommy. If Milo and Liev hadn't had the benefit of their extended family, where would they have ended up?

Likely the same damn place as Tommy. Considering Milo's seriously scary computer skills, they could be running the underworld by now. That brought a tiny smile to his face.

But that didn't change the fact that Tommy was dangerous. And alone in the world. "Tommy, how old are you?" Liev asked him.

The younger man's eyes narrowed. "Twenty-two. Why?"

Of course he was the same age as Milo, and Paul, his

older brother, would likely have been about the same age as Liev. With Paul dead, Tommy was completely alone. But that didn't make him someone worth rehabilitating. Paul, his brother, had been a hard case. Several steps further down the crime path than Tommy. Was it too late for him to be saved?

Lani shifted patiently at his side, and Liev realized he really wouldn't have much choice, now that Lani and Milo had aligned their positions regarding Tommy. "He'd have to give over all the information he knows, sign a contract as to what he would honor, and should he break that contract ..." Liev deliberately added an edge to his voice.

Tommy's eyes lit up. "I'm not sure what you're talking about here as an end result, but I'm sure looking for a way not to go back to jail or to have to face the bosses."

"And just who are the bosses?"

He swallowed. Looked from one to the other. "Paul dealt with him. *Them.*"

"But you know who the bosses are, right?"

"They are all on the Council. But one is handling this Lani issue. He's the one we dealt with."

"Who? And is he the one who killed Gina?"

He winced. "We think so. But I don't know who he is. Besides, he commands many contractors. We were supposed to snatch Lani here, but, when we couldn't, Gina was blamed. Then they put the pressure on her partner."

"Hahn Driscoll, the attorney. Who came here to grab Lani himself after Johan had bailed?"

"Yeah, the bosses want her bad."

"Alive?"

Tommy nodded his head vigorously. "They need to know who escaped with her."

"Right. And would torture the information out of her if necessary." Shit.

CHAPTER 15

LANI MADE COFFEE again. Tommy was hardly a visitor, but the males sat at the table, discussing what was to be done, and would likely appreciate the coffee. And she had quickly become addicted to the stuff herself. Tommy was dishing dirt on everyone he knew in an effort to show his good intentions to clear himself. She felt sorry for him. He'd had it rough. He'd done the best he could, but now he was at a crossroads.

What he did from here on out would be dangerous and would change the course of his life. With his permission, Milo had run every kind of scan he could on Tommy while everyone had watched. And Milo had fixed some kind of emotion detector on the poor guy too. Lani felt horrible about that one. The last thing she would want was to have her emotions scanned or detected.

That Liev had never mentioned such a thing to her hopefully meant that he had trusted her at least that much from the very beginning.

"What's the matter?" Liev spoke quietly behind her. "Do all the tests we're putting him through bother you?"

"Yes," she said with feeling. "Especially the emotion one."

"We have to make sure he's telling the truth. Our lives depend on it."

She nodded. "I understand. I hope you guys never feel you need to do that to me though."

He laughed and tugged her against him. "Never. You're honest all the way through." His chest rumbled behind her head. "Besides, that's one of the tests Milo already checked you on before he chose you."

She stilled. "Really? How? I wasn't even here yet. Even so, how could he know for sure?"

"We have much more sophisticated ways to detect stuff like that now," he said easily. "Honesty is big for Milo. And, being in business, for me, it's even bigger."

"Me too," she said with feeling. "Particularly after your blackhearted ancestor."

He dropped a kiss on her head.

"What's to be done with Tommy?" she asked.

"I can't say for sure. Depends on whether we can catch the Council with what they are doing and stop them, or if we have to go on the run."

She tilted up her head. "Really? The latter sounds horrible."

"I am hoping that won't be necessary. The trouble is finding the information, then going above the Council to get them charged with criminal behavior, as well as letting the public know. Above the Council are only a few older men. They are supposed to be the watchdogs over the Council. But are they really?" Liev shrugged. "We won't know until we get to that point."

"Doesn't Milo already have that incriminating information?"

"Milo grabbed everything he could off Johan's system, but that doesn't mean he'd recognize the information when he sees it. I'd expect Johan to have it secured and barely identifiable. The material is too dangerous."

That made sense. "So is Tommy going to help Milo look for it?"

"Something like that. We know the material is encrypted. And breaking that encryption is likely to be the toughest part. Apparently Tommy's skills have to do with code breaking. That's how he and his brother have been so good with breaking into houses. Tommy manages to bypass security codes easily, letting Paul gain entry, like he did here to find the pod room and you and Charming."

She smiled. "Sounds like Milo has found a kindred spirit."

Liev dropped another kiss on her head. "The biggest issue is, do we trust him?"

"No. Don't do that at this point. Yet he's got a lot of reasons to expose the Council himself."

"And that's partly why we're running the tests."

"If he holds up his end of this, and we do expose the Council, what about Tommy then?"

Liev shrugged. "I don't know. Maybe if we get a new Council, they will give him a medal. They'd certainly look at his criminal past with a more judicial eye than the current Council. He's being blackmailed into following their illegal orders now."

"Hopefully he'll come out fine."

"Chances are good." Liev looked over at Milo and Tommy, their heads together as they looked at the huge holographic monitor. Liev looked like he wanted to say something but stopped.

She nudged him. "What?"

He smiled down at her. "I'm not making any promises, but, if Tommy's any good, we could probably use him in the company. *Keep your friends close and your enemies closer* type of thing."

"So find the information. Blast it out to the world so everyone knows what the Council did. Make sure it can never be buried as yet another bureaucratic secret. And we need to tell someone about the Council's involvement in Gina's and Paul's and Johan's murders, but who?"

"I'm debating talking to Stephen."

"Your friend on the Council?" At his nod, she coughed lightly and said, "How can you know for sure that he's not a part of this?"

Liev's face scrunched. "I can't. That's why I'm still thinking about it. I don't want him to be involved, but who knows if everyone is or if it's only the four top-tier members."

Tommy twisted around to look at them. "I wouldn't trust anyone on the Council. They're all privy to what goes on there."

"But Stephen is new. He hasn't even gotten full status there yet."

"He's too close to the top to be trusted. His meteoric climb within the Council makes me suspicious."

"You think he's been handpicked to climb that hierarchy because of his involvement in the corruption?"

Milo piped up. "Everyone in the Council will be involved. There's no way not to be."

"Except they need a fall guy," Tommy said. "What better way than to blame the new guy?"

"Or what better way for the new guy to cement his position than to arrange for the deaths of those interfering with the Council's plans?" Lani asked.

"There is that." Liev glared down at the huge computer.

"How can we find out who is involved and who is not?"

LIEV HOPED STEPHEN wasn't involved. This was too important a mistake to make. He walked closer to Milo. "Any progress?"

"A little. I think we found the files, but Johan's layered it with different encryption techniques. We're still working our way in."

"Okay, I'll make some phone calls." Liev hesitated, still thinking. "See if there's anything I can find out on Stephen's history."

"You're probably better off checking the government files," Milo told Liev, "and scanning them to see if they've been doctored."

Tommy stared up at Liev. "You guys can do that?"

"Sure," Liev said. "We're just not supposed to."

Instead of calling a few people he knew, Liev walked up to the computer on the kitchen counter. Everything looked normal in the building, and Johan's apartment was once again empty and dark. Liev might need to make a trip up there, just to see if the latest round of ComBots had discovered the cloaked high-tech room and computers and had somehow accessed them or carted them off.

He bored into the government database and did a quick sweep of Stephen's files. Liev scanned the information. Everything confirmed what he already knew about Stephen. It wasn't surprising. Liev had gone to business school with Stephen, and, even then, he'd been full of political idealism. Liev had been the opposite. He'd been full of commercialism and was all about protecting Milo and his inventions.

Stephen's records were all just as Liev thought, but this

was surface stuff. Lani would expect him to do more. Damn it, he wanted to prove that Stephen was okay. Beyond any doubt. So Liev kept digging, using Stephen's middle name too. Nothing unusual in any direction. No leads and no red flags, which was to be expected. Stephen would be covering his tracks professionally, if he was involved in anything wrong. He'd been active in a few political rallies as a young man, nothing to raise eyebrows over, just enough to make him "normal." … And that's what bothered Liev. On second glance, his buddy looked a little *too* normal.

Scowling, he went deeper.

And suddenly things got interesting.

Lani walked over and handed him a cup of coffee. He'd forgotten she'd even made it. He smiled his thanks.

"Did you find anything?" she asked.

"Maybe." Liev rubbed his eyes. "Signs that he might have had his fingers in a few gambling pots I hadn't known about."

"Bad pots?" she asked. "Or just a little recreational gambling?"

"A lot of money lost." He kept reading the information on the screen. "A hell of a lot of money lost."

"Maybe he had to replace it? And the Council offered him a way to do that?"

"Or they used his gambling debts against him?"

"Or they put that into his file to keep him compliant. He's in good financial standing everywhere else and his credits are excellent so no red flags there."

Chapter 16

"TO MAKE HIM go along with their plans? That could be possible." Lani didn't know the man, but it would be nice to think that not everyone here was an asshole.

The HoloKomp beeped. Liev walked over to stand in the weird square on the floor that tied in any visuals and audio into a holocall. Lani watched from a safe distance as Stephen's face came through the wall. From the corner of her eye, she caught Tommy's shrinking motion. Interesting. She flipped back to Liev, who seemed to be carrying on an animated conversation in silence. He must have muted the audio.

She turned around with raised eyebrows. Milo said, "Stephen has the conversation on double security levels."

"So it's serious." She sat down beside them. She leaned toward Milo and whispered, "Can you lip read?" He grinned and held up a finger to his lips, then tapped his ear. She realized that he was listening in on the conversation anyway.

Smart boy.

Standing, she walked to the table where she'd placed Charming. He'd long since disappeared, but she was hoping he was close by. He wasn't. She went to the pod room, but there was no sign of him. Remembering the beautiful fire he so loved, she headed toward Liev's bedroom. Her bedroom now, she supposed, only it didn't quite feel like it yet.

"Charming, you in here?"

"Over here."

She turned to find him balancing on his rear legs on the back of a chair, his front paws on the wall, studying the wall computer there. She understood today was all about the technical age, but literally a built-in computer was in each room. She'd never seen what this one could do, but, since it was in Liev's bedroom, she doubted it did less than any other one in this apartment. In fact, as Charming spiked out a long claw and touched another part of the screen, she realized this one was similar to the one in the kitchen counter. Maybe they were all the same, and she only saw parts of them.

She asked Charming about that.

"Yes, they are all part of the same computer. You can pull out a section to look at via holograph at any place. They all have the same capabilities."

"And what are you doing?" She tried to see for herself, intrigued by the different screen loads he had open.

He said, "I'm looking for a list of those killed in the ongoing genocides of the Naturals."

"Why?"

"Because maybe it will give us some idea of who is behind this."

"You think someone did this to their own people?" She shuddered. "That's a terrible thought."

"And yet your species seem to delight in finding ways to hurt each other even more."

"I was hoping that the future would be more developed," she muttered.

"It is, but people appear to be more stupid."

She had to admit, from what she'd seen so far, Charming wasn't far from wrong.

A long list appeared on the screen. "Any names we recognize?"

"Not yet."

The list scrolled on endlessly. She hated to think of so many people killed over the years, simply for being different. It was nothing new, but seeing the names of all those people brought tears to her eyes.

Suddenly Charming reached out and snagged the screen.

It stopped, and one name enlarged, supersize.

Stephen Cavendish.

LIEV HAD JUST closed the HoloKomp when Lani dashed around the corner of the kitchen. "Liev, come into the bedroom, please."

He raised an eyebrow, shrugged at Milo and Tommy, and followed her. Once inside, she closed the door so he could see the computer better. And what Charming had highlighted.

Liev swore under his breath. "It has to be a different Stephen."

"Does it?"

"It says he's deceased."

"How hard is that to fake?" Lani asked.

"To fake a death? Hard, but not impossible. Taking over someone's life? That's much easier to do."

"And the only reason to do that is to hide who he really is." Lani studied his face. "You're thinking he might have had something to do with the genocide and is now hiding?"

"I'm not thinking anything," Liev protested. "Okay, I'm thinking plenty of things. I'm trying to figure this out. Like, maybe this is a relative of Stephen's. There are too many unknowns."

"Then we need to make them knowns," she said. "What does your gut tell you about Stephen?"

Liev shook his head, his mouth set in a firm line. "I do trust him. I did anyway. I have trusted him all along. He's saved me and Milo several times while we stood before the Council. Maybe he did so many other times without us even knowing about it."

"So," Lani said, "you only have doubts now that you have dug this stuff up?"

Liev nodded.

"Then invite Stephen here and just ask him in private."

"That's not happening. Councilmen don't just travel around casually. They come with full ComBot units."

"Then figure out how to get him to come alone or to meet him elsewhere—just the two of you—so you can find out the truth. But stay safe too. It seems like he's at the center of this."

"And yet this deceased Natural might be a completely different Stephen Cavendish, not even related."

"Same birthday," Charming announced. "But everything else looks different."

"It would have been changed to hide his history," Liev muttered.

"So …" Lani nudged him.

He ran his fingers through his hair. "I definitely need to talk to him. I'm just not sure how."

"I suggest you send him an encrypted message saying, 'I know everything,'" Charming said, "And have him meet you somewhere private but secure."

Liev stared at Charming. "For a cat, you're damn smart."

"Only because of Milo," Lani said absentmindedly.

"And you're not going alone. Take Tommy to watch your back and Milo to make sure Tommy is actually watching and not stabbing you in the back."

He snorted, then admitted, "I hate the idea of leaving you alone."

"We're better off here," she said with a sweet smile. "All hell breaks loose when I leave." She reached out a hand and stroked his forearm. "Better you go, deal with this, and come back."

"Then I'd better get it set up now." And he headed out to join Milo and Tommy.

It was the last thing he wanted to do. But, if his friend was involved in this mess, then Stephen was in for an ugly surprise.

Friends or not, if Stephen was involved in Lani's kidnapping, Liev would fry him.

CHAPTER 17

I T WAS OUT of Lani's hands now, and she watched as everything happened in front of her eyes. After Milo encrypted the message, using a dialogue code common among the Naturals group, Liev sent it off.

They hadn't had time to prepare for the next stage when an answer came immediately.

Meet at Station 42, Zone 6.

Milo immediately searched for that location. "Interesting. It's an old hangout for the Naturals before they moved out. It's deserted and hasn't been used in decades."

Tommy shook his head. "That's what the records say, but it's not empty. A heavy criminal element is there."

"Then don't go," Lani cried out, facing Liev. "I don't want you to get hurt."

"We don't have much choice."

"Yes, you do," she argued. "You don't have to go to that location. Change it to someplace safer. One where these two can be with you. And one where you will all be safe."

Milo said, "She's right, you know?"

"Make it a public place," she said. "An art gallery? A huge shopping complex."

The men looked at her. She rolled her eyes. "Okay, so I like reading about places like that, but think of something along the same line. Or ..." She smiled. "Both of you port where no one can find you. Go to a ski chalet, where you can be alone and talk."

Milo brightened. "I like that idea. Give him the coordinates—a set he can look up—then we'll meet him there."

Tommy got up and walked over to the window. As he passed Lani, she saw pain and grief in his face, and she felt for him. He'd just lost his brother, and now his life had taken a complete shift. Adjusting would be hard.

"Why not just send him to Johan's place?" Charming asked from behind Lani.

Lani quickly glanced at Tommy, to see if he had heard her cat talking out loud, but he was staring out the window, his back hunched. She turned to the others. Thankfully, Tommy was far enough away, and maybe too engrossed in his grief, that he couldn't hear Charming talking.

Milo turned to Liev. "That's an even better idea. We can track you, and everything can easily be recorded."

"And we can help from here." Lani loved the idea of Liev staying close.

Liev nodded. "That's the best plan yet."

"Then send him an updated message and get the meeting place changed," Lani urged. "At least Charming and I can keep watch from here and help out if need be."

Milo added, "Remember. We don't know if Stephen is on the good side or the bad."

"True," Lani said, "but he responded—and damn fast—so he's interested."

Milo walked out of the room and returned a few minutes later with a cloud of tiny colorful dots in his hand. "Here. Swallow."

Lani watched with interest. That Liev swallowed the items without asking questions said a lot about them.

Tommy had turned around, and even he didn't raise an eyebrow. So this was a common occurrence. She assumed they were trackers of some kind. Knowing Milo though, it could be so much more.

She sat in the background, as messages were fired off and as Milo prepped his brother and Tommy. "Tommy and I will be going up there earlier and will be in the spare bedroom under Johan's camouflage. I'll bring my new invention, and I'm setting up a smaller one for you to take as well, Liev. In case of trouble, it will be best for all of us to have an escape route."

"I hear that," Tommy said.

Lani loved how Tommy had gone from being a bad guy to a good guy. She just hoped he didn't blow this second chance. The Blackburn brothers would help him, but, if he screwed up, … Liev would kill him.

Hell, she would too. Lani shifted restlessly.

"*Psst.*"

Damn, that was Charming. She walked to the bedroom and closed the door. "What?"

"Make sure Milo sets up that emotion scanner for Stephen. Might help see what the truth is."

"Oh, good idea. But I don't think it's portable."

Charming snorted. "Hell, everything is portable here."

She glanced down at her beloved cat. "Charming, you look tired."

"Of course I'm tired. It's not like there's any chance to catch up on all our lost sleep."

"I hear you there." She yawned unexpectedly. "I'm really tired too."

"So let's go for a nap." Charming's gaze brightened. "They can go do their super-secret spy stuff, and we can sleep."

"But someone has to keep an eye out to make sure Liev is safe."

"Ha. He's willingly going into that locked-down prison called Johan's apartment. If he screws up, I'm not going back in there after him."

"You won't need to. Milo is taking that portable-port thingy you delivered last time."

"Good. Nice to know I won't be called on to save the day again. Being a hero is tiring." He pinned her with a glare. "And works up an appetite. I'm feeling better, but you're really slacking in the meal department."

"Hey, no one else is complaining of hunger."

"My stomach tells me it's time for breakfast. Besides, it's breakfast or lunchtime or dinnertime somewhere in the world."

"Lani?" Liev gently pushed the bedroom door open. "Stephen has agreed to the new location. Milo and I are going up there now to set up. Are you going to be okay here?"

Charming glared at him. "We'll be fine if you'd let us sleep."

Lani shook her head. "Don't mind him. He gets cranky without his beauty rest." She smiled brightly at Liev, feeling anything but on the inside. "We'll be fine, but what about Tommy? And what do we do if things go bad?"

"I was thinking about leaving Tommy here in that case." He tugged her into his arms.

She wrapped her arms around his waist and whispered, "I don't want anything to happen to you."

"Ditto. But I also want a life where we don't have to worry about anyone else coming after us. Looking over our shoulders all the time will not be fun."

"Can you take Tommy with you and leave Milo here?" She bent back to look up at him. "Or send Milo back right away and make them switch places?"

"That's possible. I'll talk to Milo."

"Also Charming suggested running that emotion scanner on Stephen."

Liev nodded, smiling at them both. "Milo's got it ready to go."

AND TALK TO Milo he did. Inside, outside, upside, and downside, and his kid brother still wouldn't budge.

"I'm not leaving you up there," Milo snapped. "No way."

"What about Lani?"

"You're my brother. It's your back I'm watching."

"And, as your brother," Liev said, concern for Lani a hard lump in his throat, "I'm asking you to come back and look after Lani."

Milo shook his head, the huge mohawk wafting in the wind. "No. I'll make sure you are safe so *you* can look after her. That's the best thing I can do for both of you."

And that was his final word.

Tommy butted in. "Look. I understand that you don't know me." He paused and winced at the looks from Liev and Milo. "But I do have some experience with this brother stuff."

Now that much was true. Liev could hear the sorrow in his voice and could see it in the way he swallowed before continuing.

"I get that you can't fully trust me yet, and we didn't

have a good start, but you have your tests and scans to know that I'm telling you the truth when I say that I mean you and Lani no harm. I want to find out who is behind all this and to stop it." He took a deep breath and added, "I'd like my life back."

Liev glanced at Milo, who was studying the comp screen in his hand. Milo looked up and nodded. Meaning Tommy was being honest. That helped, but this was the worst time to be wrong.

Still, it's not as if Liev had much choice here. His kid brother who had no fighting experience and couldn't hide that damn mohawk to keep himself out of danger, a criminal to watch his back—whether he went with them or stayed at home—and a girl from centuries ago who would be watching his progress with her talking cat.

He had a killer headache coming on. And it would only get worse. He was also out of time.

"Here, bro. New prototype field equipment. Your new PP." Milo grinned. "No superspy should leave home without it."

Liev stared at him. "My what?"

Milo grinned. "The new personal port. Don't you like the name?"

"It's not the one we'll market it under."

"That's your problem. I just create this stuff."

"You guys are lucky," Tommy said. "I'd love to be able to invent stuff like this."

Milo looked at Liev, a question in his eyes.

Liev rolled his eyes but gave in ... slightly. "We'll see about that, if we all survive this night."

Silence.

Liev glanced at Tommy and was surprised by the hope

in his eyes. The kid was like a big puppy, staring at the first bone in his life. And too afraid to hope that it might be for him.

Damn, his life had changed.

CHAPTER 18

L ANI SAT IN the kitchen, hugging yet another cup of coffee. Charming was in the bedroom, monitoring Liev's and Milo's progress from there. He was also monitoring Tommy.

Charming—her secret weapon. Tommy had no idea what he'd be up against if he ever attacked her.

She smiled. Then wiped it off her face. She had nothing to smile about. Not until Liev was back again. She should be able to hear his conversation under normal circumstances, but, as Johan's place was still in that weird steel lockdown, they couldn't get audio. She could only watch the figures in the apartment, and that made her insides quiver. Before Liev and Milo left, Milo had quickly explained that the only reason they could see that much was because of what he'd placed inside Johan's apartment last time. She didn't understand it, but it all sounded super cool.

As long as Liev stayed safe. She wished he'd made this a holographic meeting, but apparently Stephen wanted to confirm whoever he was speaking to in person.

It made sense, but it also made the meeting more dangerous. She took a sip of her coffee and watched Liev's healthy orange splotch on the monitor move around. She understood the other weird looking color was Milo and that he'd done something to mask his presence. He'd wanted to get back into Johan's system for another look. The information he might find had to be incredibly valuable … and dangerous.

These two lived a dangerous life and didn't even appear to notice.

A second orange splotch appeared beside Liev. Shorter, not as orange. "He's arrived," she said excitedly.

Tommy leaned closer for a better look. "I wish we could identify him."

"Maybe we can." She shrugged. "But I'm not sure how." The two splotches seemed to merge, then separate, then merge again.

"Uh, now that looks odd."

"What here doesn't look odd? Are they fighting? Or dancing?" she said, trying to inject humor into the situation, even as her voice wobbled.

"I think …" Tommy stopped, then said in a quizzical voice, "… they are hugging."

"Really?" Her tension eased. Maybe it was Stephen. "Liev said they were good friends."

The two appeared to be standing, facing each other, talking. She watched and waited and waited. Nothing shifted. Then one started to pace. Stephen, the shorter blob. His color darkened and flares fired off his body. As if he was seriously agitated.

Then he calmed down. And Stephen disappeared.

The light-blue-colored splotch that was Milo joined Liev, then they both disappeared.

The next thing she knew, she was staring up at Liev's bright purple gaze and his open arms.

She ran into them, loving when they closed securely around her. Thank God he was safe.

LIEV HELD LANI close to his heart. All that worry and nothing had happened. Thankfully. He'd told her it would all be fine, but, until it was over, and he was back safe and sound, she wouldn't believe it.

But it was all good now.

"What did he say?"

Liev grimaced. "He thought I was Paul or Tommy here." He motioned at Tommy, standing by the far window. "Stephen already knew that these two were doing special jobs for some of the Council but hadn't figured out who exactly they were working for."

"So Stephen's a good guy?" She waited for his warm smile and nod. "Thank heavens for that." She paused for a moment. "So where does that leave us?"

"Stephen is looking at the Council to help clean house." Liev took a deep breath. "He was fast-tracked into the Council by the elders to find proof of Council wrongdoing."

"A mole!" Charming danced gleefully in place. "So he knows that they are corrupt."

"*Shhh*," she whispered, stealing a glance at Tommy, but he stared out the window, oblivious to the new voice.

"Stephen knows how corrupt they are," Liev said. "He also knows what they did to Tommy, Paul, Gina, Hahn, and Johan. All of it."

Tommy stood up. "And ... will he do anything about it?"

"Yes, but not until we get to the bottom of this. He is trying to link Gina's murder to the Council. At least as far as having ordered the hit."

"And by whom?"

Liev winced. "I don't know if I believe him or not, but

425

he seems to think that Hahn did it."

Milo's shocked gasp was loud.

Lani turned to him. "Do you agree or disagree?"

"It's possible." He scowled. "But I'm not sure. I found a lot of information on Johan's computer that I hadn't really looked at because I didn't realize what it was. It's the background information on the Council members and some of their blackmailees. Johan was trying to research them."

"Did he find anything?"

"Hahn had family in the Naturals group. But he had distanced himself from them years ago—about the same time he was accepted into law school."

"And Stephen?" She glanced from one brother to the other.

Liev nodded. "Stephen was also from the Naturals, but he's years younger than Hahn, so never crossed paths with him. Stephen was one of the few who left for schooling. He was a teen at the time. When he found out that his friends and family had all been killed, he tried to keep his past a secret. He had no idea that he had supposedly died in that particular genocide, and, when he saw his name listed, he just pretended the name was a coincidence and did his best to hide any connection to the group. About a year ago, some Council documents were sent to him, he thinks by Johan, proving that the Council had killed his family."

"Why didn't he say something to you and Milo? Surely he could have asked for your help."

"He wasn't sure what we were into. Milo got into trouble a year ago, for trying to build his first time machine, and he blew out all the power in the city. It was a terrible blackout that caused untold damage to various services and financial institutions. It was an accident, and the Council never could prove it was him, but they always suspected him nonetheless. It meant that Stephen didn't dare approach us because we were already under the Council's watchful eye. It would have looked suspicious, and his actions would have been questioned."

"So now what?"

As he opened his mouth to reply, a boom blasted through the room. The force of the noise picked Lani up and threw her against the counter, like she was a dishrag. Liev was thrown in the same direction, landing half on top of her. As she gasped for air, he rolled over and jumped to his feet— and stared into the unblinking lens of a ComBot standing six inches from him.

His breath sucked in, and he saw the ComBot wasn't alone. A full-on tactical team had been sent to his place.

He tensed. That type of action was saved for the worst of the worst.

As he turned to help Lani, the ComBot said, "Do not move."

Liev froze. His heart still slamming against his ribs, he stared back at the ComBot. "What is your protocol?"

"You are under arrest. For treason."

Chapter 19

ONCE AT THE Council building, Liev, Milo, and Lani, along with Tommy off to one side, were shoved into the main chamber. Liev stood stiff and tall in front with Lani, her knees knocking, slightly behind him. She had no idea what the charges stemmed from but thought it had something to do with Tommy's presence in Liev's place. Harboring a criminal or some such thing.

She glanced over where Tommy sat, his arms pinned behind him and a look of defeat on his face. For Tommy, this was bad. Last strike and all that. Her heart still pounded away in her chest, and her palms continued to sweat. Who was she kidding? She was terrified herself. And she was worried about Charming. She hadn't had a chance to say anything to him before they were ported out of the apartment.

Did he even know what had happened?

She'd never trust the authorities in this time period if they could appear in someone's home, swoop them up, and bring them here without just cause.

Liev had tried to explain that it had something to do with terrorist charges, but no way in hell they were terrorists.

He'd told her to not worry, but she couldn't see how to avoid it. His lawyers were dead, and, if others were left to man the firm, they were likely corrupt. His best friend was dead, and he'd been blackmailed into doing criminal activities at the Council's whim, where Liev's other friend was part of this same Council that had had them *retrieved.*

Suspicious, indeed.

Yet strangely, Milo had been allowed to keep his personal comp. He'd been working away on it ever since. Liev had also been able to send several messages. If she only knew who he'd contacted, she might feel better.

She hoped it was that powerful family he'd alluded to. Liev could sure use some help right now.

A commotion at the door heralded the arrival of a dozen suited men. All in black. She almost smiled with relief to see men dressed in power suits and not skin suits.

She stepped forward and slipped her hand into Liev's. He smiled down at her. "It'll be fine."

"You said that already," she muttered.

He squeezed her hand. "And I meant it."

"What kind of place allows that kind of invasive maneuvers without just cause?" she whispered. Several ComBots stood beside her.

One turned to explain. "You are charged with terrorism. You no longer have rights."

"Then, since you entered our home without warning, without a search warrant or any other legal process in place, you are now charged with terrorism," she snapped.

The ComBot looked at her. Then looked at Liev, who was trying to hide his smile, and then back at her. "That is not possible."

"If what you did to me is possible, then what I am doing to you is possible," she cried out. "Or have you not heard of a citizen's arrest?"

The ComBot stared, then lifted his hand unit and asked

for direction.

A computerized voice answered, "You are not under arrest. Man your post."

The eldest of the Council members—Liev said his name was Carlson—stood up. "Lani Summerland Blackburn. Step forward."

Lani whispered to Liev, "Do I have to?"

"Yes." He gave her a gentle nudge.

Fine. Then she'd do it her way. "Lani Summerland Blackburn, following orders like a ComBot." And she took two steps to stand front and center. A choked twitter rustled through the room.

"You mock us?" Carlson put on glasses and studied her. After a moment, he frowned and took them off again.

She glared at him. "Can't run your secret scans on me, huh?"

Silence. His face reddened. "You will show respect here, young lady, or face the consequences."

Lani didn't know where her anger came from; something more like rage bubbled up from deep inside. "Respect? For you? For a corrupt Council? For men who have ordered repeated genocides of a complete group of people for no other reason than they chose to live life differently?" Her voice rang out. "This group of men, this Council, you included, ordered those executions, the annihilation of all the Naturals."

The Councilman slapped a hand over his heart. The other Council members gasped, fear and anger building across the group so strongly that she felt their waves of emotions. Carlson straightened, fury building on his face, but Lani stood tall, not backing down.

After all, she'd been ripped out of her twenty-first-century home, watched as her cat received the knowledge enhancements she had desperately wanted for herself, and still she'd made the best of it by finding her love of a lifetime in Liev two centuries down the road. She had made *that* work. ... Now this? This *corrupt* Council threatened to take it all away from her?

She had nothing to lose.

"You will not hide your murderous soul from me or from the rest of the world. You will not hide your ordering of the slaughter of men, women, and children—the fringe group you call the Naturals—at the flick of your stuck-up, white-ass finger."

Shock hit the Council members.

She rolled right over them as they opened their mouths, and words ripped out of her from deep inside the pit of her gut, her voice filling the massive chamber. "The world will know of your black hearts and even blacker actions. You had Gina Stewart murdered. Because of you, Johan Strand is dead. And Hahn Driscoll is too, as is Paul Defino. You abused your power and position to corrupt this place—a place of goodness, of fairness—and this place full of people who want nothing more than to live fulfilling lives free of your corrupt rule. How dare you, sir."

Lani had run out of steam, but her ire kept the stick in her backbone in place as an overwhelming silence filled the great hall.

She lifted her chin. She'd be damned if she'd back down now.

Stephen stepped up onto the Council dais. His calm, very serious voice carried in the silence. "Lani Summerland Blackburn, these are very serious charges. Do you have proof to back up your accusations?"

She smiled directly at Carlson, an icy movement that had the man twitching on the spot, the others cringing for what she'd say next. For all her anger, this was a pivotal moment in history, and she, Lani Summerland—no—Lani Blackburn, would make sure it was done right. It seemed this world was desperately in need of a champion. And it had found one—in her. "I was hoping you'd ask that."

She spun and stared at Milo.

He'd changed her life so much, and she'd gradually forgiven him for everything he'd done these past few days—but, if he couldn't produce the material she needed at her fingertips right at this moment, she would kill him herself.

The ComBots wouldn't get a chance.

He'd be dead before they ever reached him.

"Milo?"

He nodded and clicked away on a few buttons. Instantly a huge—as in, back up several steps before she became part of the monitor display and ended up looking like a female version of Charming's electrified cotton ball—*huge* monitor display materialized.

A video of the slaughter, memos of the orders, names of the dead, emails and texts, all implicating the four top-tier men on the Council in front of her, rolled in an endless display for all to see. A growing murmur of horror swept through the audience.

"Send this out to the world, Milo," she ordered. "Take over every goddamned computer and vid screen in offices and in homes, on computerized ads, and any other place where it can be viewed across the world. Bounce it across every satellite in orbit. Let the people see how power corrupts. Let them see how these four men have shamed their positions, how they have lied and cheated and killed in the name of their own heartless selves."

"In progress," Milo said. "It's streaming out to the world now."

"Stop him," Carlson screamed. "ComBots, stop this. Remove these criminals from the chamber." The Councilman stood tall, waving his arms around. "Return this chamber to order. I command you."

The ComBots stared back but did not move.

Lani grinned. Probably Milo's doing. She turned to look at the ComBots, standing like a solid army at her side. "Good. You should never follow orders that are just plain bad."

She looked around to find everyone staring at the huge display of data. Horrible mind-numbing numbers, showing a data compilation of a humanity-gone-wrong. She spun back to face the Council and found a team of ComBots standing behind the four men on the Council.

Stephen stood off to one side. She caught his eye. He gave her a smile and saluted her.

Her gaze widened, and she became flustered.

A sound started in the chamber. First low and quiet, then it quickly built in volume. She didn't understand the noise at first over the buzz from the massive monitor at her side.

Then she recognized it.

Clapping.

She turned in a slow movement to find the Council chambers filled to overflowing with men and women of all ages. And they were all clapping. More than that, they were all staring at her.

Her astonished gaze went from face to face. Maybe she was slow but really? Were these people clapping for her?

Her gaze landed on Liev, pride swelling his chest, a wide grin on his face, as he clapped harder than anyone.

Milo. Tommy. Stephen. They were clapping for her.

Tears crept into her eyes.

Maybe she could do something special in this lifetime after all.

She smiled through her tears and waved.

The crowd erupted into cheers.

LIEV COULDN'T BELIEVE that calm, quiet Lani had stood up to the Council, talking, … no, … berating, as in damn-near shouting as she hurled accusations, heaping shame on the Council that had never faced verbal opposition like this before.

The Council had had so much power for so long that they were accustomed to complete obedience, and that had been the chink in their armor. They didn't know what to do with her.

Or how to stop her.

When she hooked Milo into showing everyone the damaging evidence, even the ComBots had shut down. Although Liev cast a suspicious eye at Milo. He might have been behind that too.

This Council was finished.

The individual members would pay heavily for their crimes against humanity. Lani was right. These men had defiled their way of life. Committing the ultimate sin in the name of power.

Stephen was a shoo-in as a member for the new Council. That was a good thing. He was a fair man.

Liev had been incredibly angered at being hauled down

to the Council like a common criminal. Sure, he'd crossed the line—or at least dipped his toe over the line. He'd had to protect his own. That wasn't justification. It was an explanation. He knew why, and the reason still stood. If need be, he'd do it again.

But to see Lani stand so defiantly before their most honored—and corrupt—government system and to systematically rip them to shreds, publicly exposing their grievous deeds to the world? ... Well, he wanted to thank the ComBots for bringing him, ... them, ... here.

To have a front-row view to watch the fall of the Council.

This was a great day.

And to think Lani had brought about the necessary change they'd so badly needed.

Innocent Lani, who'd been dubbed a Natural for no reason of her making, ... had picked up the cause and sought justice for her fellow man.

He'd never been prouder.

And she'd never live down this moment.

She'd become an icon now.

Milo, he knew, had already sent the video of her speech worldwide. Maybe a dangerous thing to do, but, after this, she wouldn't need to hide anymore—except from her adoring fans.

She wouldn't need to cringe when someone spoke to her. Everyone would assume she didn't know much about their world because she had been part of one of the fringe groups. And being one would no longer be a negative trait. She'd elevated the fringe groups to equals. Something they'd never likely understand as they didn't care.

But it was a good thing—especially for her.

Lani had been amazing.

When the clapping started, Liev had been one of the first to join in. When she'd lifted a hand in the air to wave, he'd cheered with the crowd. He'd loved her before this, but now his heart swelled and was ready to burst.

To think he'd worried that she would not find her place in his world. Instead, she'd shown the rest of the world what really mattered.

Respect. Honor. Justice.

Truly, he loved her, this beloved woman of his.

He stepped forward, cheers ringing through his ears, and tugged Lani into his arms.

Dimly, in the background, the cheers resounded louder and louder in approval. He picked her up and twirled her around and cried out to the world, "Damn, I'm a lucky man."

She wrapped her arms tight around his neck, her breath warm and sexy against his ear as she whispered, "And I'll keep reminding you of it every day of our lives."

He roared with laughter and squeezed her tight. Just then his wrist unit beeped. He glanced over to see Charming's face filling the screen. Liev smirked again. "Lani, look who wants in on the action."

He watched as she caught sight of Charming's face, a huge smile breaking across her beautiful features. "Charming," she cried out.

"About time you contacted me," Charming said, pouting. "You left me all alone."

"I'm sorry. I didn't get a chance to tell you." She rushed to tell him. "The ComBots took us away within seconds."

He sniffed the air, his flat nose going sky-high. "And you couldn't tell me when you had a chance? Jeez, I had to find out from Milo."

"We're coming home," she said. "Soon."

"Sure you are." He scowled. "Like you promised to never leave me alone again?"

"I didn't want to. Honest."

She gave Charming a breathtaking smile so full of love that Liev felt a twinge of jealousy. But he rejected it. There was room in her heart for both of them.

"I'll make it up to you," she said. "I promise."

The cat eyed her carefully, and Liev frowned. Was something devious moving in the back of Charming's big marble eyes?

"Okay, I'll forgive you, if ..."

She frowned suspiciously. "If what?"

He beamed a huge crafty smile at her. "If you bring me home something special. Tuna or shrimp would be good. Lobster?" He flopped to one side in front to the monitor. "You've been gone so long that I was afraid you weren't coming back. I'm starving ..." He moaned. "*Feeeed meeeee.*"

The End

CAT'S CLAUS

Broken Protocols 4

by
Dale Mayer

Protocol 4:6:12. You will in no way use our history to recreate that which we know to be detrimental to our society—particularly if those actions are to selfishly enhance your own authority, position, status, and/or wealth.

CHAPTER 1

"W HEN IS CHRISTMAS?" Charming asked.

Lani Blackburn looked at her beloved orange Persian cat and grinned. It was a little hard to have any respect for his vast intelligence when he was upside down, four paws to the wind, and twisted in a bizarre curl.

"Remember? They don't do any of those old holidays anymore."

"So? That's them. Then there's us." He snorted out a sneeze and flopped over on one side. "And the two don't have to be the same."

Sometimes the darnedest things came out of that cat's mouth. And where was this all coming from? "Are you missing the holidays?" She quirked her lips and laughed. "You hated the noise, the company. Really howled when I sang Christmas carols."

"Ha!" He rolled over to glare at her. "Anyone would howl at your singing."

While she was still gasping at his barb, he continued, "I liked the tree. It was fun. Adored the tinsel." He grinned evilly. "Loved the cookies."

She remembered the last Christmas in Technicolor memories. Charming climbing up the pathetic fake tree, until it collapsed on top of him. The problem of him constantly trying to eat the tinsel and her finding the tinsel and plastic needles everywhere, but the cookies? … She groaned out loud. "You used to take a bite out of every one."

"I had to see which one I wanted," he said in such a reasonable tone of voice that she had to laugh.

"Christmas tree? Tinsel?" Liev, Lani's husband, who was technically a couple hundred years younger than her, sat down on her chair with her. She grinned, as the furniture stretched and sprawled to accommodate the extra person. That never got old. Her *husband*—and what a trip that still was to say or to contemplate—held a mug of something hot.

"Is that coffee?" she asked accusingly. "And you didn't bring me one?"

He leaned over and kissed her. "I brought enough to share."

"*Blech.*" Charming rolled over in such a way that his butt was presented.

"Charming, don't you fire that thing," Liev warned.

But gentle snores were already working up and out of her beloved dust ball of a cat.

"Christmas," she murmured, images of past holidays floating through her head. She didn't even know what time of year it was right now. They were currently on a Pacific island paradise. After all the hell they'd been through getting here, she'd wanted nothing more than to crash in peace and to recuperate after her time-traveling side effects—something that was taking longer than expected.

Her body still hadn't fully adjusted to her new surroundings or the atmosphere a couple centuries in the future. Neither had Charming's. And their original trip here to this time era hadn't exactly been a fun one—or one she'd agreed to. But Milo, Liev's genius kid brother, had devised a computer program that had snatched her from the twenty-first century and dumped her here two hundred or so years later, practically in Liev's arms as a gift for him. Thank goodness she'd been holding Charming at the time. Milo had added enhancements for her to better adjust to her new life, only he hadn't known to adjust his calculations for Charming. As a result, Charming had been given enhanced communication skills.

Lani wished she'd have gotten something because not only could Charming talk but he was a wizard when it came to the latest technology.

He matched Milo perfectly.

Affectionately Lani glanced at Milo. His massive mohawk was orange now. She couldn't help but wonder if it wasn't to show his solidarity with Charming. She wouldn't put it past him.

Both Liev and Milo had decent relationships with their family, but it was distant. Then again, that might have been because of genius Milo's work. The security around the two men was something else. Milo had a seriously scary brain. When he'd created the time-travel program that had hauled her out of her life, he'd created a hell of a mess.

Now he was working on something else. Genius was to be allowed at all times, as Milo had created some amazing inventions, but genius also needed to be watched. Up until now, Liev kept tabs on his brother, like a hen trying to keep track of twenty chicks. It worked but not well.

"What are you doing, Milo?"

"Research."

"Of course," she said patiently. "Research on what?"

She tugged Liev's mug toward her and took a sip. The one thing they did wonderfully well in this century was coffee. Lord, it was good. Travel was another one. Planes had been relegated to the annals of history, as the dirigibles had been in her time. Now they could punch in a code and walk through a portal. She loved that.

And she'd quickly fallen in love with her new husband. Their relationship was in its early stages for them though. A honeymoon phase, so to speak. Still, as honeymoons went, it was pretty great, once they'd gotten over the attacks, attempted kidnappings, and murders that had arisen after her time-travel event.

She smiled.

"What's that look for?" Liev glanced at her, his eyes warming.

"You. Us." She loved that about him. He hadn't had much long-term relationship experience before she'd landed almost literally in his lap, but he'd blossomed since.

So had she. She felt blessed to have him in her life.

Maybe the other two felt the same as well. The four of them made up their family unit. She knew a few people she might one day learn to call friends, but, because of the many pitfalls in this new life waiting to trip her up, she was hesitant to get cozy with anyone. After all, the conversations were limited to keep her past a secret. Then again, she'd also gained some notoriety recently, and many people had heard of her by now.

How weird was that?

Cool too. She'd been transformed from a number in a city of big numbers to someone special here.

She'd still rather trade it all in for the ability to navigate the minefields that awaited her. She didn't understand the most basic things here.

"Christmas."

Milo's distracted voice pulled her from her musings.

"Christmas?" She shook her head. "You don't do any holidays anymore, do you?"

"No. Too many protests from dissident groups all the time. As the protests became more violent, we had to ban more and more of them. Now they don't exist."

Holidays gave people something to look forward to, something to celebrate. Who in a normal workforce didn't love the thought of getting an extra day off because the holidays were coming? And the thought of family and friends gathering for Thanksgiving and Christmas—two of the biggest holidays in her time—made her reminisce about the past.

It was sad in a way. No special neighborhood gatherings or celebrations had happened since she'd arrived here. Families apparently tried to get together on a regular basis, but she could easily see how that would go by the wayside very quickly as everyone's lives ramped up.

The thought of missing Christmas put Lani in a melancholy mood.

She had great memories. Even alone with Charming, they'd had fun. She'd put treats on top of the tree, and he would climb up the needle-covered branches time and time again. Sometimes it worked well and sometimes not so well. she'd laughed a lot, sometimes cried, but they'd had each other. Lani had had Christmas parties at work too. Yeah, those memories brought a wince to her face, but at least they'd been memorable.

"What was Christmas all about?" Liev asked, his tone curious.

"Togetherness," she said instantly. "Family. Friends. Rejoicing in the experience of being alive and sharing what you had with others."

She smiled reassuringly at him. Okay, so it was a little smile, but her lips did twitch, so it counted. Liev worried about her. Always. He was wonderfully considerate. And she loved every minute of it.

A huge diesel engine kicked in. She glanced over to find Charming grinning at her upside down. She reached for him and rubbed his tummy. "You loved the turkey dinners."

"And the gravy."

She didn't think it was possible, but Charming's grin widened. Then his eyes turned huge. "Is it lunchtime? Did I miss lunch?" He rolled over and snapped to his feet. His gaze locked onto poor Liev, and, if Charming could have mentally forced Liev to get up and feed him, he would have.

A side effect of the time travel.

Her appetite was not as ravenous as Charming's, but now that Charming had brought up food, her stomach growled in sympathy. Charming turned to look her way, and his grin widened. He knew Liev might ignore her cat's demands for food, but he'd never ignore Lani's.

"Fine, food it is then."

"Thanks, Liev." She accepted the still half-full mug of coffee from him and sat back. Another great thing about her relationship was that Liev loved to cook. In a world of automatic food, it was his hobby. He cooked the same way people in her time did. Not her, of course. She'd had a penchant for fast food and pizza, whereas Milo had a preference for those disgusting health shakes.

She shuddered just thinking about them. She and Charming had been forced to drink them in the beginning to help them recover. Not fun.

But now, with Liev looking after them as well as he did, she knew they'd both landed on their feet in a clover patch.

Life was good.

LIEV WANDERED INTO the kitchen to sort out a meal for everyone. *Everyone* being the four of them. Milo might join them, but he ate like a bird. Charming, on the other hand, ate like a tiger. So odd.

Still, Liev hummed in the space he'd had renovated to suit his needs, which essentially mimicked his kitchen at home, and pulled out the makings for big thick sandwiches on fresh bread. As he cut the bread, his mind drifted to the Christmas issue. Not only did his century have no religious or fun holiday traditions, like Lani had grown up with, but no celebrations to look forward to either, like she'd also mentioned. He vaguely remembered seeing something about the holidays in his history lessons. That had been a long time ago. He'd most likely downloaded them and assimilated the information into his brain without considering the significance of it. As it had no relevance to his life at the time, he had stuffed it back into his deepest memories. Now, he not only wished he'd paid more attention but he wondered just what he'd missed out on himself.

His childhood hadn't been lonely per se, but it hadn't been overwhelming with love and fun either. He'd taken over Milo's care at an early age after their parents' death. That had taken all the fun out of his life. Milo even seemed to have stopped his mental development at the age of sixteen. And that took a lot of patience. With Lani joining their tiny family unit, Milo had mellowed out and had fallen into line in many ways, accepting the feminine rules without argument. Lani even convinced him to join them for meals, so they could have family time.

Liev hadn't really understood what that meant, but he cherished the time she'd carved out for the four of them. Yes, he included Charming in that group. Good luck keeping him out. They did have to work on his manners though. Lani tried, but, any time she got distracted, Charming would sneak food off her plate and scarf it down before she had a chance to stop him. Even when Liev doubled the cat's portions, Charming would still pull the same tricks.

As a result, Liev had dialed down the portions—much to Charming's disgust. Even now, Liev could feel those huge golden orbs locked on his every movement as he made lunch. He had made an egg salad yesterday, which remained in the fridge. It was an old-fashioned recipe with pickles in it. He'd had to scrounge those from a specialty shop, and it had cost a fortune.

At least he had one of those.

And as long as Milo continued to devise the wild and wonderful things he invented, that wouldn't change anytime soon.

"Lani, Liev is daydreaming again," Charming tattled.

Liev shook his head at Charming's not-so-subtle way of saying Liev was slow to bring the food to the table. Lani might be working on the cat's manners, but a lot of improvement was left to be had. Liev grinned.

He and Milo had both lived a bachelor lifestyle, and, wow, had that changed.

In a good way—at least for Liev. He glanced at his kid brother to see him muttering like crazy over his screen.

Liev frowned when he realized that the screen on this side of the monitor had been blacked out, so no one could see what Milo was doing. Studying his genius brother's features, Liev figured Milo was just deep into his research and turned back to making lunch. Bringing out a fresh pineapple that he'd paid an exorbitant price for, Liev quickly prepped it and portioned it out.

"Lani said she'd trade her egg salad for my pineapple," Charming piped up with a hopeful look.

Liev shook his head. "I wasn't giving you pineapple to begin with."

"Then I'd better be getting more than my fair share of egg salad," he groused.

Liev grinned like an idiot. How had his staid, stressed-out, overworked life become this combination of a loving, laughing lifestyle instead?

Just lucky, he guessed.

"Milo, come join us. We're sitting down to eat," Liev said, as he finished plating the food.

"Be there in a minute."

Liev walked to the table and held the plates up until Lani made it to her seat. Otherwise Charming—precariously balanced on his back legs—would have tried to take the plate with the bigger portions.

When safe, Liev placed the plates down and took his own seat.

Minutes later Milo joined them, one of his nasty all-natural green good-for-you-if-you-can-get-it-down concoctions sitting in front of him.

Liev caught sight of Milo's gaze and followed it back to the opposite side of the table. He stared in horrified fascination as Charming tore into the pile of chopped eggs on his plate. Bits and pieces were spilling off his chin and back onto his plate, much of it falling onto the surrounding table.

Even Lani stared.

Charming finally noticed. He lifted his head, surveyed

the mess, rolled his eyes, and tried to clean it up a little. Then, as if realizing he would just make more of a mess soon, he shot them a dirty look and went back to eating the way he'd been before.

"Just one big happy family," Liev murmured.

"And aren't you blessed?" Lani laughed.

"I so am."

Chapter 2

T HEY WERE ON vacation, a beautiful isolated spot along the ocean. Liev had told her the location but the geography had all changed now so the name Broger Islet meant nothing to her. The cabin, which had already been remodeled by Liev looked like so much was the same yet was so different.

She loved being near the coast, walking along the beach, swimming in the water. The lack of people. Privacy for the family to sort themselves out as to what the unit would look like long term. She loved it all. Yet even here she had her schooling to do. Even more important now.

Later that afternoon, after a dizzying amount of elementary-level schoolwork to get her acclimated to her new surroundings, Lani's mind once again wandered in the direction of Christmas. It wasn't as if she couldn't do without it, but it would be nice to have a few of the better things from her old life incorporated into her new one. Christmas was one of them. But she didn't need the trappings of the old holiday to make a day to celebrate. She wasn't sure she needed the same date. That was nostalgia talking. They could just pick a day and have it then. Besides, she wasn't sure what day Christmas would equate to today. She supposed the super-duper computers of this twenty-third century could tell her. Hell, those things could tell her what the weather had been in the city she'd been born in on the exact time and date of her birth. Not to mention every other demographic piece of information available.

The Christmas idea percolated in the back of her mind. She wouldn't have to make a big deal out of it. And she wasn't sure Liev or Milo would be on board with such a concept, but Charming would love it. And, since she loved him, maybe, just maybe, she could make it happen for him.

After the others saw how much fun it could be on a small scale, maybe they'd want to do something bigger next year.

She grinned. The issue had been decided. She'd make Charming a Christmas celebration. There may not be the same religious or commercial aspects to it, but one thing would be the same. She, no, *they* all had a lot to be grateful for, and Christmas was a wonderful time to give thanks. Hell, Thanksgiving would be wonderful as well.

She stared out at the lazy sunset as it slowly dropped, her toes curling into the warm sand. She'd lost track of time. The days of the week, the calendar for the months. The years never had clicked for her, and now that she was centuries ahead of her time, she really couldn't get any perspective.

But this was a place to start. Maybe she could do something special for Valentine's Day too. She bet Liev or Milo had never celebrated such a thing in their lives. Well, she could do something. As she glanced at their Pacific beach home, humming with techno geeks inside, she wondered if she could do something in secret. Or did that just mean everyone would know?

And whose help could she employ to make this happen? It was not as if she had friends to enlist, and she didn't dare let Milo in on it. Like any teenager, regardless of his twentysomething status, he couldn't keep a secret. Especially from his brother. As she mulled it over, she wondered if she could somehow pull off a trick and surprise them all.

Her mind turned back to the fancy computer equipment Milo had put together for her to learn about their advanced high-tech lifestyle and newer customs. She found it hard to believe that she still only worked at the elementary-school level, while Charming had pranced in a half-dozen times, listened for one-quarter of the time that she did, and now listened to university-level stuff.

"If I could wish for one Christmas gift, it would be for enhancements of my own, so that I could learn faster and could retain more," she muttered.

"Ha. No Christmas gifts here. Remember?" Charming wandered in front of her and down at the water's edge, where he stared hopefully into the water that teemed with fish.

"You just ate," she said in exasperation. "Besides, the fish know you. They aren't stupid enough to get close again." And know him, they did, but not in the way he might want to remember. He thought of himself as a big bad hunter, but his last attempt had him going for an unexpected swim. She grinned at the memory of the soaked orange ball and Milo's solution to stick him in the upright dryer. Poor Charming. He'd looked like a puffer fish for hours.

Charming, as if understanding what she was thinking, spun and glared at her.

Instantly she wiped the smile off her face and glared back at him.

Injured pride kept his back stiff and his tail upright as he stalked back inside. "Isn't it time for you to get back to primary-school lessons?" he tossed back snidely.

She gasped. "That's just mean."

"Bite me." And he stomped inside.

Maybe she wouldn't make a Christmas celebration for him after all.

LIEV HATED TO leave Lani even for the day, but he'd avoided showing up in the office for too long. He'd have to change that.

He couldn't help but wonder if this was a good time for her to try a few hours on her own. She'd been doing so well. He knew she was frustrated with her slow progress in their education system and her lack of enhancements, but it wasn't exactly something they could order off the shelf. They had to customize it for her.

And that meant it would take a bit of time.

Milo appeared to be in one of his resting phases, as compared to his brilliant driven-to-get-a-concept-from-his-head-into-form phase. Maybe they had all needed a break after the stress of the past few weeks. They'd return home soon, but Liev needed Lani to adjust emotionally and philosophically to her new status. And what a status that had been. From obscure in the shadows to a celebrity of sorts. That phase would calm down, but, every time she opened her mouth to answer questions from her adoring public, she was in danger of blurting out something that would reveal the truth of her background.

The education system they'd dug out of the archives wasn't ideal, but, as it ran independently without connecting to the other computers or the government system, it was perfect for her right now.

Except it was slow.

And they didn't have much time.

Chapter 3

L ANI RUBBED HER eyes. The stupid computer was giving her a headache after only a couple hours. Why was it so hard to figure out when Christmas—if they still had that particular holiday—would be in today's calendar? She'd been through several databases and had been overwhelmed with links to follow, but the actual term *Christmas* appeared to have been deleted from their history. She'd entered *Easter* and *Thanksgiving* and *Halloween* and got the same response. Outside of a short description of what each of the holidays were historically, no further information existed on the type of celebrations that took place or when it officially happened. She just didn't get that.

Was she the only person left in the world who knew Christmas was December twenty-fifth? Then again, that had been the day for her, but she remembered European consultants who had worked at her old company for a while, and they celebrated an earlier day in December. She found no mention of any of these holidays in the twenty-third-century computer systems. This time period hadn't just made the holidays illegal, they'd wiped them out completely.

She snorted. Sounded like the same thing they'd tried to do to her people. Or rather, the Naturals, the people her name was now associated with. Given that she'd only been trying to do the right thing, it was nice that the association gave her a reasonable cover for her continued ignorance of the way things worked here, as the Naturals were a fringe group who'd lived their lives disconnected from mainstream society.

She was rather hoping to be further along in her adaptation into her new life, but living on a Pacific island didn't give her too many opportunities to learn.

And, with Liev so quickly producing clothes and other necessities while she watched, she wondered if shopping could happen otherwise, like at malls, small boutiques, or even online. He said it did, but he didn't understand why one would bother, when he could just input it in a program, and it would instantly use her form to model each design on the monitor. The ones she liked, he only needed to push a button, and damn if the printer didn't just create it for her. She'd had to stop him at one point. She'd been enthralled and had loved the dresses, the different underwear. He'd been all over those too. But she felt guilty about the added expense. She didn't know how much all that cost, but she could only wear one outfit at a time.

When they had arrived on the island, he'd made a dozen different bikinis, each one getting less and less material, until she was afraid to look at the next one, in case it was a single G-string. But he'd outdone himself on the tropical skirts and sundresses. Even now, she'd only had a chance to wear half of them. She loved it.

But he had the ultimate control on her wardrobe. She didn't. If she were shopping in a store, it would be a different experience. And one she missed. She knew his income was much higher than most other people's in this place, so not everyone would have access to what he did, but she was delighted that he did. She had said she needed a pair of slip-on sandals to walk on the beach, and he'd downloaded a program and let her choose between a half-dozen different designs. Then, when she was just about to make a choice, he decided that she needed to try them on the sand to see which ones she loved and proceeded to create them all.

She glanced at the white stretchy sandals she carried in her fingers. That was the other thing. One size fits all. Like the furniture, when anyone stepped into her sandals, they automatically adjusted to fit the foot. God, she loved this stuff. She'd tried to get Charming to stand in one of her sandals when she'd first gotten them, but he'd been too smart and had given her one of those looks that said, *Do you think I'm stupid?*

Yet all this technology was precisely the problem. How could she even begin to give Liev a gift when not only could he make and buy anything he ever wanted but there was nothing he wanted?

Milo was the exact same. It wasn't like Lani was an artist and could paint him something personally. She could hardly bake them a special dessert, when Liev ruled the kitchen and all the ingredients. She might enlist Charming's help there, as he was known to successfully steal from the kitchen, but she knew that Liev wasn't fooled as to his outgoing inventory. He just let Charming get away with it.

She really wished she had a creative streak. If she could write, she could write a special poem for Liev. It could be intimate and personal.

Lani sighed. There was nothing she could give to these two brothers. They already had everything.

THE WALL HOLO shut down as Liev pinched the bridge of

his nose. Maybe he did need to return to the office for a few days. It shouldn't be happening, but it seemed like the place was falling apart on him.

"Trouble?"

Milo stood behind him. Liev turned and gave his brother a reassuring smile. "Not really. I'll just have to show up at the office more often. When the boss is away and all that."

Milo nodded even as he curled his lip. "Figures. At least say hi to Tommy for us while you're there."

"Will do. Reports say he's doing well in the training program. Should be ready to start full time in another month or so. How are you doing on that personal portal device?"

Milo shrugged. "Haven't been working on it."

Liev's eyebrows shot up. "Why not?"

Milo shifted his weight and tucked his hands behind his back. Then he shrugged. "Got sidetracked."

"Damn." Trying to keep Milo on track was a full-time job. He was into the creation process and much less the detailed final stage required to make something user friendly enough that it could be brought to the market. He constantly wanted to leave projects when it hit the tedious stage. The new shiny idea always beckoned him away.

"Christmas," he said in a low tone.

"Say what?" Liev walked closer. "Did you say, *Christmas?*"

"*Ssshh.*" Milo shot him a warning look. "Charming is too damn smart. He'll hear you."

Running a hand through his already-tousled hair, Liev stared at his brother, trying to figure out why Charming would give a damn. "What about Christmas?" he whispered, playing along.

"I was trying to research the holiday. And, like, nothing

is there to research. It's not right," he complained. "We should have access to all information. Not just what they want us to know."

"Ah." Now it made sense. Milo, being the brain he was, was offended that some information had been secreted away, so he couldn't learn about it.

Yeah, that wasn't good. Best to nip this in the bud.

"Take it up with Stephen," Liev suggested. "Lani has shaken things up a lot within the Council, but I warn you. I doubt that sufficient change has happened to make enough of a difference yet. Especially with regard to the flow of information—particularly archived information."

Milo looked undecided, then muttered, "I'll think about it." And he walked away.

Liev stared at him in consternation. Milo *thinking* about anything could mean everything, from making the company millions to destroying something major, depending on which side of that decision he landed on.

Just then, Liev's holo beeped, and he had to return to the mess at work.

Now if only Milo would concentrate on *his* work. Life would go so much smoother.

Chapter 4

L
ANI WOKE EARLY the next morning, careful to not wake either Liev, who slept soundly at her side, or Charming, who snored on his back—all four paws to the wind—at her feet. It was almost impossible to do anything on the sly in this house. Still, she escaped to the kitchen and brought up the big 3-D counter computer. Entering several commands, she left it humming and went to the coffeemaker, setting it to make a wonderfully rich cup to start the morning.

With cup in hand, she walked back to the computer and studied the information. *Great.* One wasn't allowed to buy real trees in this world now. Didn't that figure? She looked outside at the palm trees just waking up under the bright morning sun and frowned. She was not going to decorate one of those. She would as part of the larger design but not for the actual Christmas tree. She sent out more search requests for fake evergreens. She didn't dare search for Christmas trees. That much she'd learned already about her new home. Not only would it likely trigger alarms somewhere, the search could easily send a trigger email to Milo and Liev. So not what she wanted.

She waited and watched. She'd logged in as *Liev* deliberately, so that no one would know what she was up to.

There.

The screen flashed with several options. Now were any

of those good ones? She mulled over the options and prices, saved two to consider later, and carried on searching for lighting. That almost made her give up. What on earth did any of those terms mean? Whatever happened to simple LED lights? Or the colored glass lights, the racing lights? Were they all gone? And, if so, what had they been replaced with?

Frustrated, she closed down that search and tried to find decorations. But that was too broad a search. She needed to narrow it without mentioning *Christmas* or *holidays*. She tried *tree decorations*. Then *ribbon style decorations*. Then *glass balls, painted wooden miniatures*. Too much and too many choices, and yet nothing came with hangers. She frowned, cleared her search pages, and shut it down. Damn it. There had to be an easier way to find stuff.

Even ordering, shipping, and storage had to be dealt with, but she wouldn't have to worry about those if she couldn't find anything. She walked outside with her coffee and considered asking one of her three male family members for help, then immediately tossed the idea. She wasn't ready for her secret to be spoiled yet. Her fighting spirit had been pushed to the forefront now. There had to be something she could do.

As she looked around the bushes and trees, she envisioned lots of little lights, maybe ribbons, maybe little glass balls. Who knew once she got started? She just needed to find the stuff. Or maybe she could make some. She used to make some wonderful origami. She could do a few of those for the tree—but not tons. And it still didn't nullify the need for a special tree and lighting.

"Couldn't sleep?"

Liev sat down on the top of the deck, a mug of coffee in

his hands. She sat beside him. "Just a lot on my mind." His searching gaze bore into the side of her cheek. She linked her arm with his and laid her head on his shoulder. "I'm fine."

"Good. I'm glad to hear that." He dropped a kiss on her forehead. "Anything I can help with?"

She shook her head. "I've just got a few things to work through."

He wrapped an arm around her and hugged her. "If you need to talk …"

"I know. It's not major, and it's not serious. I just want to do something and have to figure out how."

His face twisted with effort, and she knew how hard it was for him to hold back. To not push. To not pry. "You did a great job with Milo," she said.

His eyebrows flew up, and he stared at her. "Really? I can't say that I see it myself."

His droll tone made her giggle. "It couldn't have been easy."

"No. Nothing with him is easy. Not even when it's supposed to be."

She laughed. "He's a good soul."

"True enough."

Sitting together in the morning dawn, it was hard to find anything wrong with her world.

"Breakfast? Surely you didn't forget to call me for breakfast." Charming's plaintiff cry wobbled toward them.

Lani turned to see him sitting in the doorway. "Hey, big guy."

His jaw opened into a huge yawn. "Is this what morning looks like?"

She grinned. "Yes. And stop kidding around. You're often up at this hour."

"Only while I'm getting a snack or a drink or something ..." He sauntered forward until he reached her. He lifted his nose and smelled the air experimentally. Then he shuddered. "Still smells too fresh. Too real. Too *morningish*."

She stroked his back. "You'll survive."

"Yeah, I will." He dropped to his belly and sprawled sideways across the deck, his head hitting it with a *thud*. "But I won't like it."

She scratched his belly, and damn if a wave of love didn't wash through her. He was so special.

He rolled onto his back and stretched his legs up as far as they'd go and offered more belly.

In silence they sat, enjoying the morning.

Until a roar came from inside.

She winced. Surely it hadn't been her searches earlier on the computer that had brought such a reaction from Milo? *Surely?*

Out of the corner of her eye, she caught Charming's expression before he jumped to his feet and disappeared around the bushes.

Milo came storming out. "Who was on my computer?"

Ah, shit. She immediately apologized. "Me. I'm so sorry. I was just trying to do some research."

Liev tugged her close. "Milo, she has to have access to a computer somewhere. Just because you're here doesn't mean all the computers are yours."

She risked a glance at Milo to see him grabbing his mohawk with both hands and pulling it in frustration. "They don't have to be *all* mine ..."

"Then what's the problem?" Liev asked in a no-nonsense tone.

"*Arrgh*." Milo spun on his heels and left.

Liev chuckled. "Don't worry about it. He's a little possessive."

"A little?" She worried about what evidence of her activities she'd left behind. She didn't really want them to know what she was doing, but, if Milo wanted to know, he could find out easily enough.

Feeling despondent and not a little crowded by her lack of privacy, she stood and walked down to the water.

"Don't worry about Milo," Liev called to her.

She tried to smile back at him, and, seeing the worry on his face, she knew her smile attempt was a giant failure. "I'm fine. I'm just going for a walk."

She sensed his indecision as she walked away. She wouldn't mind a few minutes alone. She should just ask him for a computer of her own. They probably had dozens in the place back home. The problem was that they were all connected somehow, so, no matter what she did on one, they'd know about it on the others. What she should have done was use her school computer. That wouldn't have brought any raised brows. It was older and only used for training. Meaning it hadn't been used for years before she came around.

Too bad she hadn't thought of that this morning.

Charming raced up behind her and passed her at a steady gallop, his tail flying high. She ran past him and startled him, causing him to book it. Laughing, she gave chase. They ran down the beach until she couldn't run anymore. When they'd first arrived in this world, all kinds of exertion had tired her out. Just walking across Liev's apartment had exhausted her.

Now look.

"We're doing so much better now, Charming."

He grinned up at her, his jowls flapping in the wind as they slowed to a walk. "Much better. I really like it here."

"I do too."

"But I wouldn't mind a weekend at a log cabin with that whole Christmas look."

"And that's something we could probably arrange quite easily." She amended that. "Maybe."

He brightened, then a bit of worry traveled into his gaze. "Not that I want to be outside in winter or anything. That would be cold, wet, and nasty." He gave a mock shudder.

"Then what's the point?"

"The fire. The log cabin. The looking out the window to see a winter wonderland."

The way he said it almost made her nostalgic. "I can ask Liev. It might be possible."

"Great. Race you back." And he took off.

She watched him go, too tired to give chase. She hadn't realized they'd traveled so far down the beach. If she didn't run back, it would take a good twenty minutes of walking. Oh, well. Maybe the walk would be good for her.

Or it would have been, but she'd really tired herself out on that run.

Damn it. She almost wanted to sit down and wait for Liev to find her. Walking in the sand was especially hard. She trudged forward, feeling her energy drain lower and lower with every step.

Finally she sat down to rest.

LIEV LOOKED UP from his monitor for the twelfth time in hopes of seeing Lani returning. The island was perfectly safe. He had no worries there. But, with the ease of portal travel, anything could happen.

Charming wandered in and jumped up on the desk.

"Hey, when did you get back?"

"A while ago. Why?"

"Did Lani come back?'

Charming plunked his butt down on Liev's tablet—the only thing on the desk—and stared at him. "I don't know. I ran home, and she was walking behind me." He frowned, the furry ridges above his eyes slashing downward. "Is she not home?"

"I don't think so." Worried, Liev walked outside and stared down the length of the beach. In the distance, he saw her sitting at the edge of the water. His stomach twisting, he started toward her. What was going on? This was a side of Lani he'd never seen before. And he didn't like it. She was always so happy, so balanced. The peacekeeper, when Milo and he went at it. She added calm to the troubled waters and her laughter to long tough days.

He walked steadily toward her, so that she had time to see him coming. If she wanted time alone, he didn't want her to feel like he was intruding. But he didn't want to give her too much alone time either. Normally he and she could talk about anything. And did. They had no secrets. Not with Lani. He loved that about her. She was so honest. So transparent.

So he really wanted to know why she was acting like this.

It had started after Charming's offhand remark about Christmas. He hoped she wasn't missing her old world. He'd deliberately helped Milo destroy the time-travel program and related equipment that he'd used to bring Lani here. It was too dangerous to have around where someone could steal it and pervert it for horrible purposes. They'd had to destroy it.

But it had also made sure that she could never go home. He didn't want her to go home. She was his wife in all ways. But especially in his heart.

As he came closer, she looked up. And smiled. A look that went straight to his heart. She was direct. So honest. No wonder he loved her.

"Hi."

"Hi," he responded in a lighthearted tone, his gaze intent. "How are you?"

"Tired." She laughed. "I raced Charming down the beach, but we went farther than I realized." She motioned to the water, as still as glass in front of them. "I started back but got tired, so I decided to sit a bit and enjoy the view."

He plunked down beside her. "Have to still guard your strength. You're doing so well, but it doesn't seem to take much to remind you that you aren't fully adapted."

"So true."

"Do you want to stay here longer or come back where you can lie down?"

She stared out at the water, then back at the distance she had to go and sighed. "It still looks so far away."

He hopped to his feet and held out a hand. "Come on. Nap time."

Laughing, she got to her feet and grasped his hand.

With a big grin, he swung her up into his arms, and, whistling a light tune, he carried her home.

CHAPTER 5

$\mathbf{A}$FTER A NASTY fortifying shake from Milo, she curled up on the hammock outside and napped. God, what a life. As great as it was, she still needed to find her place in this new life. But, as this last incident showed, whatever she ended up doing couldn't require too much of her, or she'd never recover. And Liev wouldn't allow her to work; she was sure of it. Money wasn't the issue, and, as someone who had worked all her life and had worked hard for every penny, this part was easy to get used to. At the same time, she felt almost useless. Liev looked after her completely.

In this century there was no manual housecleaning anymore. No laundry. No cooking, unless one chose to do it. And dishes were also extraneous. For the first time, she was really free to do whatever she wanted to do.

Lying on the hammock, she pondered life in this new age. She needed a hobby. Or to volunteer somewhere. Maybe she could help Liev or Milo in their company? No, not help Milo. He was way past her ability to be of any help. As for Liev, he had hundreds of employees.

He didn't need another one—especially an unskilled one.

She needed to find something to fill her day. But maybe not just yet.

This Christmas thing could take enough of her energy.

Now if only she could solve it. Given that Liev and Milo were busy working, she slipped into her classroom area and pretended to pick up her headset and get to work on her lessons.

Instead, she started working on her computer, the one Milo had set up for her studies. Idle thoughts at first; then she got serious about shopping. She really wanted this whole Christmas thing to happen. Money wasn't such an issue—she had some that Liev had given her. She didn't want to ask him for more, but honestly these prices didn't make any sense. They seemed outrageous even after she took into account the inflation for over two hundred years.

She sighed and wondered what it would cost to do this. Would it be possible to just rent decorations? Could Liev's parents have any stashed away anywhere? No, not likely. Still, maybe the rental suggestion was an option. She quickly searched and found hundreds of rental options.

But nothing even close to what she wanted.

Parties. That's what she wanted! *Party supplies.* At least it would give her a place to start. She started with a wide search, then narrowed it and narrowed it and came to ... nothing. Absolutely nothing. Were no parties had here in this time period either?

She looked around and sighed. It was lunchtime, and damn if she wasn't hungry again. She'd join them in the kitchen and ask the brothers how the whole party-rental thing worked.

Unfortunately they just looked at her.

"*Party?*"

The delicate questioning tone of Liev's voice had her stopping to stare at him. "What's wrong with the question?"

Milo's wide foolish grin had her slapping herself up the

side of her head. "Oh, my Lord. I don't mean parties like Johan's type of party," she cried out. "I meant like a birthday party. An anniversary party. A graduation party."

They stared at her, glanced at each other, then turned to stare back at her. Liev asked, "Birthday party?"

"Graduation party?" asked Milo, a curious look on his face. He got up from the table and walked over to the nearest computer. She knew within seconds he'd have found out all the information available to be found. "So you weren't raised to celebrate your birthdays?"

They shrugged in unison.

She sighed. "No gifts? Birthday cake? Friends over to have a great time together with? No?" The brothers just sat here and stared at her, like she was talking a different language. As she sat back in shock, she realized she was.

They had no idea what she was talking about.

She opened her mouth to ask another question, when the noise of an alarm filled the air.

LIEV RACED TOWARD his wall holo unit as the alarm continued to resound throughout the small house. He had no idea what was wrong, but his computer system had been compromised.

He reached the main machine to find Milo already working away furiously, his face in grim lines. If there was one thing in this world that petrified Milo, it was that someone would steal his inventions. "Milo, what have we got?"

"So far, not much. Looks like something on one of our computers has triggered a kickback on the government bots."

"*Hmmm.*" That made no sense. "Still, I thought we

stopped anything like that from happening with the new patches."

"Should have. But something somehow has raised the alarms."

"Is someone trying to hack in?" Liev had his 3-D screen up and busily searched the red lines that showed where the problem was. "It's coming from Lani's old education system."

Milo snorted. "That makes a stupid kind of sense. That old unit hasn't been used in decades. It probably shorted out. At minimum, it would be using old codes, and that likely would have triggered all sorts of alarms."

"Time to ditch it then."

"Shouldn't have brought it into service in the first place, but the educational software material was on old tech, so it required old-tech hardware to work." He glanced at Liev. "She should be done with them by now, right?"

Liev frowned. "I'm not sure she is."

"I'm not," Lani said in a dry voice. "I'm about halfway."

Milo stared at her, gave himself a mental shake, then went back to working on the computer. "Half is fine. We might need to download the material and put it on a new medium for you though. I can't have it triggering government security bots."

"No, I suppose not." Lani grimaced.

But Liev caught the wrinkle of embarrassment on her face. He hated that. She'd been through so much and had done so well. How could this possibly be easy on her? "You're doing just fine, you know?"

"Ha. It'll take me months to get up to speed on the useful stuff."

Milo shook his head. "Take your time. This stuff is all

about our system and how we function in it, so that should be the priority for you."

Liev was happy to see that Milo's enthusiasm had perked up Lani. Milo being the supergeek, he was used to having much less intelligent people around him. He often got frustrated when they couldn't reach his level of genius with a concept he was working on, so he often worked alone. Then it almost always took a translator to bring it down to the level of the minions in the world. Liev was often that translator. Not the same IQ level as his kid brother, but Liev was no slouch. Still, that awareness of how smart Milo was helped Liev to understand what Lani was going through because Liev had gone through it himself all his life. "Maybe we can find an easier system for her."

Milo nodded absentmindedly. He was already back at work.

Leaving the computer, the breach fixed, and the alarms no longer going off anywhere, Liev walked over and gave Lani a hug.

"Does this mean I can't use that system anymore?" she asked in a low voice.

"It would be better if you didn't."

He wasn't sure from the distant look in her eyes if she was upset that her education would take a temporary hiatus or if something else was going on behind those beautiful eyes. Again, there was a wall, a distance between them, and he hated it. "Lunchtime?" he asked.

"Ha! We didn't even have breakfast," Charming accused. He hopped up on the countertop and glared at Liev. "Did you really think I wouldn't notice?"

"Funny, one of the cans of salmon had been opened and tossed in the recycler earlier," Liev snapped and turned

Charming's words back on him. "Did you think I wouldn't notice?"

Charming's flat nose went up into the air. "That was *really* early this morning. It was hardly breakfast."

Milo piped up, "Maybe we should check him for parasites."

Charming howled, "What?"

"Hey, it happens to all of us." Milo barely held his grin back. "Your excessive appetite could be a symptom."

"Excessive? My appetite isn't excessive. I'm a cat. What would you know?" Charming stalked toward Milo, his fur standing out at odd angles. Then his attention was caught by something dashing across the 3-D monitor.

"What the—"

Milo cuffed him lightly, and he shut up. Plunking his butt down on the counter, he watched the screens dance by.

Liev frowned. It was very unusual for Milo to actually hit anyone, softly or not, let alone Charming. But what was even more unusual was for Charming to take it.

Under normal circumstances, Milo would be fending off claws and teeth for that attack. He glanced at Lani to see her reaction, but she was staring down into her empty cup. She hadn't even noticed.

And that was another anomaly.

Worried, he led her over to the big easy chair, waited until she'd curled up, and it had expanded to suit her, and then watched in amazement as it stretched upward, as if to cup her. He'd never seen the chair do that before. Lani was enclosed, curled in a ball, with her head resting on the top, as if this were normal.

And maybe it was. Liev just hadn't seen it happen before.

He took the empty cup from her and walked past the other two, still staring at the monitor, on his way to get her a fresh cup. He nudged Milo and nodded toward Lani.

Milo turned to look. He reared back slightly, frowned, looked at his brother, then back at Lani and the chair. He lifted his shoulders in bewilderment. Charming, never one to miss something going on, studied Lani too. Then, being a cat, he jumped down, raced to Lani, and jumped up on the back of the chair, where he lay down by her head. Instantly his engine kicked in.

CHAPTER 6

"PROBLEMS?" CHARMING NUDGED her neck when her hand stopped moving on his back.

"Not really, just ... stymied." She loved that word, and it suited her mood. She wasn't as much frustrated as she didn't know how to move forward. And still keep her surprise a secret. At least not now, she couldn't do this alone. Therefore, she might need someone's help. And how could she do that when she wanted something no one knew about, where the concept was so foreign that she couldn't see how to explain it to anyone other than her family without letting on about her secret history? And that had to be guarded.

So what to do?

Maybe give it up, but that really wasn't what she wanted. They had a calendar here, but it wasn't what she was used to. It was part of her next lesson, and, of course, she'd managed to delay that all over again.

They had so many wondrous things here and, sure, apparently a lot of get-togethers, just not as she knew them. Parties like Johan's had probably been around during her century, but she hadn't participated in the swinging-singles' parties or group sex activities. Those she was certain were part of Johan's *party* definition. Apparently Liev, like any healthy male, had also participated—at least initially. Thankfully he'd decided they weren't for him. But it left her wondering about what she wanted.

If she were to bring it up, she'd be reminded of her weakened state still. And, after this morning, that was still true. But maybe not in a few months from now. She could be fully healed—although portal travel still caused her stomach to revolt. Not as bad as the first couple times but still more than she liked, so traveling wasn't an easy solution. Given the amazing times, she shouldn't complain.

Without realizing it, another heavy sigh escaped.

Charming nudged her hand. "Hey. If you are depressed, the best way to get out of it is to be with your pets. I'm your pet, and I need more attention."

She looked at him, and that same big wave of emotion swept through her. She cuddled him into her arms and hugged him tightly. Outside of his initial yowl, his engine kicked into supertanker mode and rolled through the room. "I'm not depressed. I'm just looking for a way to fit in."

He reared back and gave her a beady look. "I told you to lay off the extra treats, you know? If you'd listened, you'd have no trouble fitting into stuff."

Behind her, she heard Liev's strangled laugh. She shook her head in exasperation. "I am not having trouble fitting into my clothes." She glared at him. "I'm having trouble fitting into this life."

He jumped from her arms to the floor, took a few steps, and launched himself up to the counter. "Whatever. If you do need bigger clothes, Liev can adjust the program, you know. Just saying …"

"Charming, that's not very nice." But damn if her hands didn't slip down to her waist and on to her hips, manually judging if she'd gained any weight. Catching his smirk, she glared at him. "It's all right if *you* are useless. You're just a cat, but, in my old world, I worked every day. I don't know what to do with myself now."

Liev studied her.

She raised both hands in frustration. "I know. I need to heal. I need to fully recover. Otherwise I'm a handicap in the workforce. I guess I was thinking I could do something."

"Then find it and do it." Milo's head had lowered as he studied the bottom portion of his monitor. "That's what I do."

She glared at him. "That's not the same thing."

"Well, it is. Find what you want to do. And do it." He stared at her like she was simple, which—compared to him—she was.

"And how do I find what I want to do?"

That made his eyebrows fly upward. "If you don't know the answer to that, how do you expect anyone else to tell you?" He shook his head. "*Know thyself.* Remember that phrase."

She groaned. "You can be so irritating."

"*Hmmmph.* Just trying to help." He pulled out his weird headset, plugged it in, and tuned her out. She knew the words would be showing up on the screen, going directly from his mind to the computer. The technology fascinated her. She'd been good with computers but not gifted, like so many of her coworkers had been. And they would be completely blown away by Milo's talent if they were here.

She had hoped for a future in computers and had quickly come to realize that the only way for that to happen was to receive enhancements to help jump her education forward, like Charming had gotten. Otherwise, it meant years of study, and, by then, she'd have to catch up again, as the technology here advanced so fast.

Liev walked to her, bent down, and dropped a light kiss on her lips. "If you come up with something, no matter how far-fetched it might sound to you, tell me, and I'll let you know if our world has anything similar."

She brightened. "Thanks. That's a great idea."

He led her back to her old education unit, which now looked like some space-age doorknob. "This is what we've set up for you." He quickly showed her how to use the unit. "Give it a try, and see how you do."

Right. So much for feeling like she had a light at the end of her tunnel. She needed to focus and get out of elementary school. Everything else, even ordering stupid decorations, depended on it.

LIEV STAYED LONG enough to make sure Lani was fine with her new computer setup. She'd really been doing well. Considering she was still having these moments of weakness, something Charming didn't appear to share, it was all good otherwise. Charming ate so much more than she did, so maybe lack of nutrition was the answer. She hated Milo's booster drinks, though they were full of wonderful things for her. But she was a foodie like him, and Liev could under- stand her not wanting to live on the shakes.

Walking back to the main room, he caught Milo and Charming, their heads bent together, whispering. He frowned. Those two conspirators were bad news when they got together. "What's up?"

Milo looked back at him. "Nothing."

Yeah, right. He groaned silently. Just then his office called, reminding him of all the pressing issues he'd been avoiding while on vacation. Yet that had been part of the deal to coming here. He'd take as much time off as possible but head into the office when it was unavoidable. And today it was unavoidable. After a quick call, he said, "I'm heading to the office for the rest of the day. Looks like I'll have to go for several days in a row to sort out some problems."

Milo gave him his attention. "Bad?

"No, and nothing that affects you. Mostly staffing issues and more government troubles from the new Council forming."

"If you talk to Stephen, let me know. I've been trying to reach him, and he's not answering my calls."

Liev didn't bother answering. He knew that a lot of people avoided Milo at times. When he wanted something, he could be very bullheaded about getting it. If Stephen had had the time to deal with Milo, Stephen would have responded. But, with the fall of the old Council—thanks to Lani, Milo, Tommy, and Johan—Stephen's life had been overtaken with responsibilities as the new Council was being formed.

Liev wanted Stephen to be part of the new Council, but Liev had no guarantee of that happening yet. If ever. The government system was in flux. It was all good, but, just as a lot of corruption had been in the last government, it was all too possible the same problem would exist within the new one. Liev almost wanted Stephen off the Council so that he'd remain part of the government watchdog unit. Someone had to keep the others honest.

Liev opened the portal and stepped into his office. And damn if people weren't already lined up waiting to speak with him. It would be a long day.

CHAPTER 7

L ANI DID AS many of the learning modules as she could before her head started pounding. She hated to admit it, but Milo's shakes were one of the best answers for that. They tasted disgusting but took the edge off the pain immediately, and, usually within ten minutes, the headaches were gone for good. She walked to the main room to find him and Charming busily working on some kind of joint project. She could hear them muttering something about government regulations and firewalls. She rolled her eyes. Nothing the two of them liked better than hacking into stuff they weren't supposed to hack into.

"Hey, Milo, any chance of a small dose of that headache remedy?"

He glanced up, his gaze unfocused. His eyes cleared, and his head bobbed. "Sure." He headed into the other room, his fluorescent yellow-and-black striped pants hurting her eyes. He looked like a bumblebee. Fashion sure had changed. At least Liev was more conservative, but Milo didn't appear to know the word.

He came back with a huge glass of pink stuff. She groaned. "What part of *small* drink did you not understand?"

"The part that says you are trying to avoid your boosters."

Charming snorted.

She glared at him as she accepted the glass. "That's not fair. If I want the headache to go away, I'll have to drink all this, won't I?"

"Absolutely. Just think. If you'd had this earlier, you wouldn't have a headache now."

Morosely, she stared into the pink depths and wondered why there couldn't be a bright pink pill she could take instead. "Why don't you, with all your brilliance, take this liquid and turn it into a capsule, so people could just swallow it?"

"You *are* going to swallow it." He gave her that *you are a simpleton* look again.

"Yes, but, if all this nutrition was packed into one pill, I could swallow it in one gulp and not have to taste it and suffer. This is painful."

"Hey, I made it cream-soda flavored for you this time."

Oh, no. The last time he'd flavored something, it had tasted like a cross between boogers and bubblegum. She tentatively took a tiny swallow and almost barfed. "This is really disgusting," she gasped.

He shot her a look, then went back to work.

Well, she'd asked for it, and it did work, but damn, she'd hoped for something about one-tenth this size. She pinched her nose and proceeded to guzzle it down. Out of the corner of her eye, she watched Milo and Charming high five each other, hand to paw. She stopped drinking. "Really? How childish."

On cue, both of them imitated her by pinching their noses and drinking from an imaginary glass.

"Oh, all right." She poured the rest of the drink down her throat, then ran to get water to clear her mouth. "There. I drank it. Okay?"

Both males beamed at her, like she was a star pupil.

"Now that I did that, can you show me how to do something?"

Milo stared at her warily. "What?"

"How do I order a gift for Liev? You don't have stores that I can walk into. I could possibly order from online stores, but everything is in Liev's name. All the accounts bill him, and I don't want to bill him. I want to pay for this myself."

He looked at her curiously. "What do you want to order? And, if it's for Liev, why wouldn't he order it himself? Plus it makes no sense for you to pay for it if it's going to be his." Confusion rippled across Milo's features.

Charming, however, was rolling around on the counter, laughing. He understood because he'd come from her century.

Patiently she said, "I want to give him a *gift*. That means, I want to pay for it and give it to him. It's special, and I don't want him to know about it ahead of time."

"*Special.* What is it?"

She shrugged, embarrassed. Because she had no idea what to give Liev. He was a man of means and yet simple tastes. But she might be able to find him an old-fashioned Christmas cookbook or something. Speaking of which, she didn't think they had physical paper books anymore. At least she hadn't seen any. "Don't you have books anymore?"

He shook his head. "Only in museums. You can get everything in holo or digital, and they don't degrade over time."

"Crap." She had to find another way. "If I wanted to get him a cookbook, where would I find one?"

"A cookbook?" Milo rolled the idea around in his head. "Online."

"But then he'd know I ordered it, right?"

Milo nodded. "And he'd get a notification of where he could pick up his holo and how to store it for easy retrieval."

"And if I want to buy him a real cookbook?"

Milo shook his head. "You can't. You could possibly make one. The printer would do that, but why would you?"

Yeah, why would she? *Because* she was looking for something Liev had never had.

"Where could I find the recipes I want to put into this book to print?"

That earned her another sideways glance. "On the computer."

She sighed. "Right. So ... do you think there might be a computer, some software, that would allow me to make such an archaic thing?"

He shrugged. "Sure. Many hobbyists do similar stuff. Those books have videos in them and 3-D images. I might have some free software around."

"Do I have to pay for the recipes?"

Another odd look came her way. "No. They are on the computer."

"And by that, you mean, free for anyone to use."

He nodded.

Well, at least she had a place to start.

LIEV RACED HOME, an hour late and fed up. But he knew Lani and Charming needed dinner, and they were a long way from being self-sufficient. Besides, caring for Lani was one of the highlights of his day. He hoped he didn't have to be physically at work too many more times, but the messes accumulated if he didn't show up.

The kitchen was buzzing when he walked in. He stopped in shock. All three were in the kitchen. And, if his eyes didn't deceive him, he was pretty sure they were … cooking? Interesting way to act on a holiday. Then again, it's when people often had time to try a new hobby. It also appeared that Milo had shifted the kitchen to mimic theirs at home. It was easy enough to do. And if he'd locked it in, then they could access their kitchen contents from here by opening a cupboard and reaching for the item they wanted. It also meant they could send their new purchases bought while on holiday in their house from here. Made traveling so much easier.

That would likely blow Lani's mind.

A little hard to tell as Milo was trying to show Lani the just-add-water food, and the look on her face would have made Liev fall in love with her if he wasn't already. She looked like she was about to upchuck. She shuddered and turned away. "There's food in the fridge. We can make sandwiches, if nothing else."

"Why bother? That's just as bad for you as this instant stuff. You should just have shakes and be done with it. I'm not hungry. I haven't been hungry in hours."

Liev didn't let anyone know he was here. He was too fascinated at this unique view of the family dynamics in his absence.

Milo brought other boxes of brightly colored instant food out of the cupboard. "You know this stuff was good enough for Liev before you came. Why isn't it good enough for you?"

Liev followed Lani's and the cat's movements. When Lani almost crawled into the fridge, looking for something edible, the sight of her delightful rear end pleased Liev immensely. Then Charming sidled closer to the fridge, and, in a loud whisper directed at Lani, said, "Don't listen to him. Anything that comes in a box can't be good."

She backed up slowly, her arms full, her hair flying everywhere as she tried to maneuver out of the cooler. "Don't worry, Charming. I won't be eating that stuff. Now you, on the other hand ..."

"Ha." Charming turned, rose up on his hind legs, and batted a cupboard above his head. The almost-impossible-to-see door opened, revealing stacks of canned cat food. "I'm stocked up."

"Wow. It that all just for you?"

Lani tried to peer into the cupboard, but Charming stood in front, his front legs outstretched and his head moving to stay in her face so she couldn't see. "Yes. It's all mine. Just in case the end of the world comes."

She giggled. "Charming, at the rate you eat, these won't last you one week."

He glanced at the cupboard fearfully. "Really?" And Lani snatched a couple cans while he wasn't looking.

"Hey, those are mine."

"They are canned salmon. Not cat food. *Canned salmon*—people food." She read the label off to him and then held it up, so he could read it himself. Something he was incredibly proficient at.

"Hey, I ordered that for me."

She stopped and stared, but Liev noticed she didn't put the cans back. "You know how to order stuff?"

It was his turn to stare. "Hell yeah."

"Don't swear," she said absentmindedly. "Can you show me how?"

A crafty look came over his face. "If you put the cans

back."

She hesitated, obviously torn, and Liev understood something he'd missed up until now. Although her needs had all been met, she hadn't had much choice. She hadn't been able to peruse the shops and order something she wanted. Hell, he'd designed her clothing for her at home and hadn't even considered there might be something else she'd like for herself.

He couldn't remember even asking. He'd been so wrapped up in taking care of her that he'd forgotten to ask what she wanted.

That was something he'd fix. But, for the moment, he wouldn't do anything to disturb this comic relief playing out in front of him. It was exactly what he needed at the end of a shitty day.

CHAPTER 8

"**I** NEED BOTH these cans," Lani scolded. "Don't be greedy. We can order you some more."

His flat face scrunched up, and he said in a pitiful voice, "What if the end of the world comes before it gets here?"

She rolled her eyes. "Like that'll be an issue. Deliveries are almost instantaneous here."

He gave her a fat grin. "Then order your own, and it will be here in time for you to eat it for your dinner."

She glared at him, loving and hating that her cat could argue her into circles. "I'm making something simple for Liev. He's had a tough day, and I want to do something for him tonight."

Charming gave a big nod of approval. "I like the idea of you making food. But you can have one of Milo's shakes and just use a single can for Liev."

She glared, spun around, and slammed the cans onto the counter. "I'm taking two."

"Greedy," Charming muttered. But he immediately headed to the kitchen comp, pulled up the big 3-D monitor, and started pressing the holoscreen with his fat paw. Milo sat open-mouthed throughout the whole thing.

Lani lifted her head and saw Liev partially turned to where Charming had been. He must have heard at least part of the argument with Charming, and she was sure a heated bright pink rolled across her face.

As she watched Liev's shoulders shake as he tried to contain his mirth, it bubbled up and out to bounce across the room.

"Well, I'm glad someone enjoyed that," she muttered.

Liev strode across the short distance, snatched her into his arms, and twirled her around. When he put her back on her feet, he reached up, cupped her cheeks, and gave her a resounding kiss.

When she was free again, Lani laughed. "And here I was thinking you must have had a crappy day, and I was trying to do something nice for you." She pointed to the cans of salmon on the counter. She glanced down at them and froze. Damn it. She spun around, pointing her hand at her cat. "Charming, put that can back."

He slammed the cupboard shut and turned to glare at her. "That's what I was trying to do." His head high, he hopped off the counter and stalked to the big chair in the living room. She swore she heard him mutter, *Thief*, as he passed her.

She groaned. "Is this what a mom with little kids at home feels like while the daddy is at work?"

Liev chuckled. "Probably. Although that scenario is likely not as much fun as this one." He gave her a second kiss. "And thank you for thinking about dinner. We can have salmon sandwiches if you'd like, but I did pick up something to bring home." He motioned to the box on the floor.

Charming's head popped up over the top of the chair. "Food?" He bolted in the direction of the box, beating Liev by seconds. Charming rubbed all along the sides, his nose in the air. "I can't smell anything."

"That's because it's in a special case." Liev lifted it and

carried it to the table. He did something that made audible *click*s and removed the lid.

Lani gasped. "Oh my. What is that?"

"It's roast beef with all the vegetables." He smiled at the look of awe on her face. "When I realized I'd be late, I ordered this to come home with me."

She smiled. "It smells heavenly and sure beats takeout as I know it."

Liev pulled out plates and cutlery, then proceeded to serve the ready meal.

Charming danced in his place, his eyes glowing with eagerness. Lani got up, walked to the counter, grabbed the lone can of salmon, and placed it on his plate. "There. You wanted it. Now you can have it."

LIEV LOVED IT.

He could watch Lani and Charming for hours. A warm rosy glow filled his heart. This was the family he hadn't realized he wanted—needed.

They'd just finished dinner when the wall unit beeped, indicating a call. He turned to check the caller. "Stephen."

He walked over to the circle, turned on privacy mode, and answered the call. Lani and Milo cleared the table, one eye on the conversation. Lani couldn't hear the conversation unless Milo let her. Liev made a quick motion, so his brother would do just that. With the two of them listening in, out of the sight of the screen, Liev said, "It's nice to see you, Stephen, but given the lateness of the hour, I gather something is wrong. So what's up?"

"Your number has been coming up as having restricted searches going on and bouncing off our firewalls."

Liev frowned. For one, no need to do that as both he and Milo were perfectly capable of bypassing any of the government firewalls to search for any information they wanted, yet this could be part of the trouble they had earlier. "That doesn't sound right."

"I know. Like you guys would make that mistake, right?" Stephen ran a tired hand over his face. "I guess I'm thinking this might be Lani attracting attention without realizing what she was doing. I'd hoped she'd caught up with our technology and our laws by now after living with you two but maybe not yet. It's a lot to assimilate."

Liev shook his head. "She's not quite there and most likely was looking for something that she had no idea would cause alarms."

"I'm sorry, but they do cause alarms," Stephen said, spreading his arms. "How damaging could it possibly be to have people learn that our ancestors celebrated holidays, religious and otherwise?" He shook his head. "It boggles the mind to think they felt it was so dangerous that no one should be allowed to know about it."

A contemplative look filtered across Stephen's face. He leaned back and said slowly, "The thing is, although taking a look at that issue is on the agenda down the road, it's not today's problems. And those are much bigger." He tilted his fingers under his chin and continued to work through his thoughts out loud. "Maybe down the road I could use someone like Lani to go through the archives and sort out what information is dangerous and what isn't, based on her unique upbringing. That would at least cut down on the billions of files for the panel to make a final decision on." He laughed. "Right now my problem is actually pulling together a panel. When I got into this, I had no idea what kind of mess I'd be taking on."

Stephen's face broke into a wreath of smiles. "There she is. Hi, Lani."

Liev was startled when an arm slipped around his waist, and Lani stepped into the circle. He always tried to keep her out of the political scene, but, after putting herself front and center during the last debacle with the old Council, and in such smashing style, she'd made history herself.

"Hi, Stephen. How nice to see you." She beamed up at him. "And I accept."

Stephen frowned in confusion, then his face cleared as he understood what she was talking about. "Good," he said, his eyebrows raised in surprise. "Great actually. It can't be today or tomorrow, but it'll be in a couple months. I'll call you in and see about setting up security for you ..." He stopped and laughed. "Forget that last part. Liev's company now keeps the security intact. He can set you up with the archives. Just not yet," he rushed to warn her. "I'm in a bit of a pickle right now."

"I'm sorry if I helped cause that pickle," she murmured. "I was looking back on some of the history I hadn't learned about and started searching for information to help fill the gaps." She added in more formal tones, "My apologies."

Stephen shook his head. "No worries. I'll mark this down, and I'll get back to you about our archives in a few weeks." He grinned. "That would be an excellent way for you to fill in the gaps of your education legally." And, with that, he rang off.

Chapter 9

T HE SECURITY FIELD around her disappeared as Liev closed down the system. She wasn't sure of his reaction to her butting into his session or the work she'd agreed to take on. She'd had Milo's help, and she'd done what she felt was right, so why did she feel like she'd done something wrong?

Because, of course, she had brushed up against personal and government restrictions. "I'm sorry," she said abruptly.

Liev shook his head and tugged her into his arms. "Don't be," he said. He dropped his chin on top of her head. "It's minor in the scheme of things that could go wrong and highlights an inherent issue with the way the government has controlled the flow of information from the public."

Damn right. "And they need to stop it."

"Great volunteering to take on the archives, Lani," Milo said, admiration and maybe a hint of jealousy in his voice. "It will be a heck of a way for you to get comfortable with our system."

She nodded. "A system that is wrong in its current form."

Liev looked down at her. "And because it's wrong, you'll champion it into being right?"

"Someone has to." She smiled up at him. "Since it won't be for a few weeks to a few months, that should give me enough time to get caught up on the missing information I need to know."

"I can help too," Charming said. "You can work from home, and, between us, we can figure out their problems."

Liev rolled his eyes, but Lani was nodding. "That's a good point. Only the two of us know how controlling your society has become. There was some secret stuff way back when, and hackers got into most of it, but that was nothing like the things you guys seem to have deemed dangerous."

"That you know of. Maybe more will be in there than you want to know."

"Maybe." She wasn't concerned. "I also wanted to do something that would help me fit in." She grinned. "Being raised in and having escaped the slaughter of the Naturals makes for a great cover."

"And helps you to better connect to Stephen, as he's in the same boat."

She pondered that. "Then I think my education about the Naturals needs to be beefed up, so I understand what he's talking about, if he brings it up."

"That's a great idea." Liev looked to Milo. "Can you make the adjustments to her program?"

"Absolutely," Milo said with a wide grin. "This will be great. Now we'll have an inside man in the government." At Lani's confused look, he added, "Or should I say, inside *woman*."

LATER THAT NIGHT, Liev, knowing how tired Lani had been earlier on, nudged her to bed. Charming had left them a long time ago, preferring to crash on his Pacific island hammock in the bedroom with the glass floor, so he could dream of all the fish beneath him. Liev wasn't sure what he'd do with one if he actually caught it. It wasn't like it came ready prepped in a can.

Speaking of which, he needed to remember to cancel Charming's earlier order of salmon. Knowing that cat, he had likely gone overboard and ordered dozens of cans to make sure he survived a little longer. Liev shook his head. Talk about an end-of-the-world mentality.

Lani yawned when she came out of the bathroom. She walked to the far end of the bed and crashed.

He'd hoped for a little time alone with her. Just the two of them. Instead, she appeared to be ready to sleep. She flipped onto her back, then rolled to her side. He smiled and crawled in beside her. He could fix this.

She turned into his arms, her lips already reaching for him. He was a lucky man.

He kissed her with all the emotion he felt for her welling up inside him. She responded immediately. It had always been that way between them. Right from their first kiss.

His hands caressed her, like the precious gift she was, only she wasn't having any of it. She shifted restlessly, pressing against him, a whimper catching at the back of her throat. Then she wrapped a leg around him and thrust upward. Oh, Lord, she was killing him. No, she was bringing him to life.

"Love me," she choked out. "Love me now."

Her words hit him in the heart. She was like a furnace, and he was the fire inside her. He shuddered, then reached down to tug her hips into a better position. He pulled down his pants and kicked them off, then eased into her, slowly, achingly, hearing her moan as he filled her.

Heat rolled through him, swamped him. He loved her so

much. She called out his name, then pulled his head down and gave him the hottest of kisses.

Damn. He never wanted this to stop, never ever, ever, but he couldn't stop the need driving him forward. He drew back, just an inch.

"No!" she cried out. "Don't pull away."

"*Shhh*. It's too fast," he said. "I have no control tonight."

Her laughter was wild, as wild as he felt inside, with the passion consuming him.

"Can't you see?" Her eyes were bright, her cheeks flushed. She wrapped her arms around his shoulders, pulling him down against her. "Neither do I."

The fire inside him blazed, and he made a noise he didn't recognize. Primitive. Possessive. Passionate. Unable to hold back, he plunged once, twice, and once more. She called out his name as she pulsed against him, around him, then called out his name again.

He was a goner, losing control. He threw his head back as he came apart, rejoicing in her cries beneath him, until her cries died down, and he fell into her embrace. Both of them shuddered with emotion and completion and the wonder of their love. They stayed like that for minutes, their breaths slowing, holding each other tightly, a sheen of sweat on their bodies, not ready to let go.

"I love you." Her voice was languid and sleepy, her body relaxed.

"You're my heart," he said and kissed her tenderly.

"*Mmmm*." She was half asleep in his arms.

He let her go, and she snuggled onto her side of the bed, her breaths slow and steady. With a gentle smile, he eased to the side, then tucked her in.

She was exhausted.

He, on the other hand, was wide awake. Happy. Invigorated.

And he wasn't quite ready to sleep.

He walked back out to the living room and brought up the main computer.

Considering Stephen's earlier call, he hacked his way into the government databanks and behind their privacy laws and security guards. There he searched out the information Lani had been looking for. Though he didn't understand why she'd search for something she'd already experienced many times over.

As he read through the information, he shook his head at the government. Anything religious had been locked up. Except that Christmas apparently only had a religious overtone for some people. The others had taken to it as a fun celebration.

He checked his mail and made sure there were no new issues at work. Just as he was about to close down the computer, he noticed the symbol on the top right corner. *Saved searches.* He frowned. He hadn't searched for anything recently and never saved them. One never knew when a system would get hacked. In fact, the computers deleted all information and ghosted all tracks at the end of the day. That was the standard operating procedure. Wondering what Lani was up to, he clicked on her saved searches and sat back with a heavy sigh.

She was missing her old life. Here was evidence. She'd spent hours trying to find things like Christmas trees, decorations, LED lights—whatever they were. Bringing up the other government information, he cross-referenced the information so he could see what she was looking for and why. When he was finally done, an idea formed in the back of his head.

But was it a good one? If she wanted to do something, did she want to do it alone?

And, if he stepped in, would that ruin it for her?

CHAPTER 10

L ANI WOKE EARLY the next morning, but the household
was already up and busy. She wandered into the kitchen
in search of coffee—and found Milo and Liev wearing
business suits. She stopped. "Going somewhere?"

Liev looked up, saw her, and walked over to kiss her
good morning. "Hey. Sorry, we both have an early morning
meeting."

She nodded. "Okay. How long will you be?"

She hated to be alone in his world, but this gave her the
freedom to work on her gift for Liev. She didn't have
anything for Milo and couldn't even begin to imagine what
she could give him either. But, when she saw him and his
shiny black pants with almost glow-in-the-dark white dots
on them and his orange mohawk, she had the beginnings of
an idea, ... if she could find what she needed.

That only left Charming to find something for. And that
was minor. With his endless stomach, anything food-
oriented would be perfect.

And, while the two were gone, she and Charming could
work this ordering system just fine.

She smiled up at Liev. "Feels very homey, sending you
off to do a day's work."

He grinned that lopsided grin of his. "It had better not
be all day. I expect that Milo will be home in a couple hours,

and I'll be home by midafternoon." He hesitated, glanced around the room, and said, "If you need anything ..."

"We'll be fine," she said, pointing to the portal. "Go. Take care of business, and come home when you can. We'll be fine."

A small frown of concern appeared on his forehead, but he dropped a second kiss on her lips and walked through the portal. Milo waved at the two of them and followed his brother to the office.

Lani picked up Charming and danced around the room. "We're alone."

"And ...?"

She laughed, plunked him on the counter, and poured a huge mug of coffee. "I have plans, and you are needed to make them all happen."

He preened. "Of course. That makes perfect sense."

And because he was such a perfect ass of a cat, she poured him some cream too. Then she picked up her coffee and said, "Follow me."

It took him about twenty minutes to figure out her cookbook stuff, and, before long, she was copying recipes that she remembered from her childhood—or rather recipes that sounded like the ones she had had as a kid—putting them into a book program, and voila! She ran to the bedroom where Liev had set up a temporary office, a room that housed the printer while on vacation.

"Oh, my God. The book is on material." She held up the cloth item and shook her head. "This is not what I want."

"At least it's washable that way," he said with irrefutable logic.

"True, but I want paper, or whatever passes for paper in

this time, with lots of glossy photos."

Charming looked at the printer, made a few adjustments, and back they went to the main computer. It took four more tries before she got something even close to what she wanted. And then, while proofing it, she found several errors and had to fix those. When the final product was in her hand, she laughed and ran outside to sit in the sun and to look at it. "Thanks, Charming. It's exactly what I wanted."

"Yeah, but you said it was for him." He rubbed against her. "Why would he want that? Besides, it's not like any good recipes are in there for me."

She grinned. "Ah, but now I'm not limited. I can do what I want and create as many of these as I want."

He sprawled on the deck beside her. "As you wish." And he promptly fell asleep.

Crap. She needed to know more about the ordering stuff. As she glanced at him, she realized she could work on some of it alone. The men could be home at any time, and she desperately wanted to hide the evidence of their work. She ran back inside, hid the book with her clothing, and dashed to the computer to write down the rest of her instructions, so she could recreate her morning's work later. Feeling as if she had accomplished a lot, she cleared the computer's memory.

It took a few moments before she realized she was in the clear. Except … for the failures. The projects that hadn't worked out so well.

She ran to throw everything into the recycler. Just as she was done, both Milo and Liev strolled back in. She stood with her hands behind her back and wiped the guilty look off her face.

She hoped.

LIEV EYED HER in amusement as he walked toward her. He had no idea what she was up to, and that was fine. She was entitled to her privacy.

But he was curious. His gaze was drawn to the recycler and the flashing lights on the side. Something she'd put in there was being processed—just not very well. Then again, she had little experience with recycler jams. Still, to point it out to her now would be awkward and might destroy whatever surprise she had been planning. He kissed her lightly. "I'll get changed, then prepare us some food. I'm starving."

She backed away and took a quick glance in the direction of the bedroom. His curiosity ramped up another notch.

He went into the room and shut the door. After a quick shower to help wash away the distaste from his last meeting, he finally walked through the bedroom looking for new clothes. He couldn't stop himself from looking around, wondering what she was up to. Her face was too open to hide anything. He reminded himself it was her secret, and he'd have to wait until she was ready to share.

He walked to the kitchen and pulled sandwich fixings from the fridge. Neither Milo nor Lani were around. He frowned, checked the time, and reassured himself he hadn't been gone that long. He walked outside to the deck, sure that Lani must have gone to her favorite spot, the hammock. Instead it was empty too. Worried, he walked through the place, looking for his family.

Ten minutes later, he was frantically punching codes on the locators to find out where Lani and Milo had gone.

And where the hell was Charming?

That damn flashing light on the recycler caught his eye as he stormed past. He opened the machine and out popped Charming, spitting and hissing, like the cat he was.

"Charming!" He heard the alarm in his voice. "What happened to you, and where are Lani and Milo?"

Charming hopped to his back feet, his front paws punching air and his eyes glittering with temper. "A bot took them. Walked right into the kitchen, didn't even say a word. He just threw something around Lani and Milo, and, the next thing I know, he'd shoved me in there." Charming spun around and glared at the recycler. "He could have killed me."

Liev stared at the machine and then at Charming. The whole point was to kill him. Clean up so no one was left behind to set up an alarm about the missing two. They hadn't known that Liev was here. Now was this a sanctioned ComBot, or was this something else again? He strode to the holo unit on the wall, put it in secrecy mode, and called Stephen. When his buddy's tired face came on, Liev quickly explained.

Thankfully Stephen started punching numbers, then shook his head. "It's not us. We don't have an order in place to pick up either of them."

Signing off, Liev went to the big kitchen computer Milo had set up in the rental and turned on the trackers. Damn. According to this, Lani and Milo were still on the island. He stared outside, sorting this out. Why would anyone come here, take prisoners, and not leave the island?

Unless they were waiting for Liev to show up.

Shit.

Chapter 11

LANI COULD SPIT, she was so mad. How could Liev and Milo have such advanced technology and yet be so prone to break-ins? It was one thing if this was a government-sanctioned raid and retrieval, but it wasn't. No way this guy was legal. Hell, he wasn't even human. Or was he?

She eyed him closely. He appeared to be a cross between a bot and a man. Big beer gut with a mechanical hand—maybe two mechanical hands. She couldn't tell with the other one. And he was big. Surely no human would have taken Charming and dumped him in the recycler, like this bot had done. That was just wrong. The only reason she wasn't in full-blown panic at the thought was because she had seen that it was jammed. At the time, she'd been more concerned that Liev would be the one to notice and try to unjam it, but now she had bigger things to worry about. Like this asshole.

And then there was this weird location. Like inside a really badly designed cabin, where the builder had run out of materials. It kind of matched the kidnapper.

Milo asked in a mild voice, "What do you want?"

"Money, of course."

Milo raised an eyebrow. "And how will this help you get it?"

Lani wanted to laugh. Their kidnapper had tried to kill

Charming, and that talking cat was worth a fortune. This guy wasn't too bright. "Who are you?"

"Buck's the name. And make-a-buck is what I do."

She stared at him. Surely he didn't mean making little bucks because that was just gross. The man was a mountain of bits and pieces and, from the looks of it, android bit and pieces. Nothing was attractive about him with his huge bald head and grimy beard that fell to the middle of his oversize paunch. Maybe her feelings showed on her face, because he snarled, "What's the matter? Never seen anyone make an honest living before?"

She reared back. "An *honest* living? Is that what you call kidnapping?"

"Sure. Hell, if you rich folk weren't so busy ordering stuff all the time, we wouldn't be able to track you, would we? Huh? Think I don't know you're stockpiling for some event? Well, I don't need much, but I can resell anything that you do have. Takes me nothing to turn a buck on the black market."

She had no idea what he was talking about. "So why are we here if you wanted stuff from inside the house?"

"Ha. Because I figured that, with you two out of the way, I could go back and see what else you might have there that I could use. I saw some mighty fine electronics."

Milo bristled.

"Yours, huh?" Buck grinned. "And, if you've got that kind of equipment, then you've got money. And, if you've got money, then I want some."

"Then take us back," Lani said, "and we'll give you the little bit we have."

She was desperate to rescue Charming. And she had a little money—not that she was into paying for blackmail or kidnappings. Besides, shouldn't Milo have protection from guys like this? She eyed Buck suspiciously. "Who do you work for?"

He snorted. "Why would I work for anyone? I'd have to share the profits then, wouldn't I?"

Good point. And she didn't think, from the looks of him, that he was doing too well in this business. She watched Milo as he studied him. Evidently the man didn't pass muster because Milo turned away in disgust. Yet she and Milo were both chained by something odd. Buck had thrown this loop around them in the kitchen, and that had been it. He'd yanked, and they'd been transported here.

Wherever *here* was.

She managed to press the buttons that she could feel ever-so-subtly under her skin. One should be an alarm for Liev to find her. She was actually surprised he hadn't already arrived. Then again, he didn't know where they were. Maybe this was a different planet for all she knew. He also might not know yet they were missing.

"So let us go. We'll all go back home, and you can take anything you can carry."

He glared at her. "That's likely to be a trap."

"What?" She shook her head. "How can it be a trap? We're both here."

He pondered the issue. "Nah, I'll return alone. Scope out your stuff, figure out how to move it all, and then come back here for you."

"Wait. Where are we?" she asked, hearing the urgency in her voice. Now that he was ready to disappear, she was afraid of being left alone forever. They'd die like this.

"Ha." He smirked. "That's for me to know and for you to find out."

Then he lifted his wrist unit, fiddled with the dials, and appeared to vaporize in front of them.

She turned to face Milo. "Any great ideas of how to get out of this mess?"

He nodded. "Maybe. But we need to get free first."

"Great. And how do we do that?"

He shrugged. "No freakin' clue."

LIEV WATCHED LANI'S trail end in the middle of what was supposed to be a large open field at the edge of the beach. He stood here, tracker in hand, and studied the empty spot. He shook his tracker, just to make sure it hadn't somehow been damaged. But it still read that Lani and Milo were both in front of him. He frowned and considered the options. If they were here, as the instrument in his hands said, then they were under some kind of camouflage. He knew that a lot of thieves used a similar device. Liev had had no need for one, so he hadn't looked into it any further. Now he realized he should have. Knowing the enemy's equipment was standard advice for anyone. Given that he was in the security business, it was even more important. He sighed. There'd never been enough time.

And how about now?

He could almost hear Milo's mocking voice. Liev had to presume that they were here in front of him, but he couldn't see them. Was their kidnapper with them? And was it one man, like Charming had said, or were more here helping him? Neither were great options.

The thought of Charming alone in the house worried away at the back of his mind.

If the kidnapper returned to the house, he just might kill

Charming this time. The cat had already ended up in the recycler, so round one had gone to the bad guy.

Charming wanted a rematch, but was he in a position to beat someone like this? Plus, if the kidnapper figured out that Charming could talk, then he'd become one of the stolen goods.

Liev lifted his communicator and whispered to Charming, "You there?"

"I'm here. Weird sounds coming from the other part of the house though."

Ah, shit. The kidnapper had come back, probably to clean out the place. Liev didn't give a damn about the equipment. Milo had everything set so the equipment would self-destruct if it left the property without a special password.

Still, Liev didn't dare let anything happen to Charming. Lani would kill him if that happened, but neither could he leave his wife and brother in the kidnapper's clutches.

"Stay hidden," he ordered Charming. "I'm going to see if I can find Lani."

"I thought you already did that," Charming snapped. "You've been gone for at least twenty minutes, and the locator led you right to her. What have you been doing all this time?"

In the small screen of the communicator, Charming gasped, turned to face the doorway, and went quiet for a long moment, long enough to worry Liev. Finally he turned back to face the communicator. Anger rippled through his orange fur. "I think the kidnapper is in the kitchen."

"Charming, stay away from him," Liev said in alarm. "Hide somewhere safe. He dumped you in the recycler once. Remember? Next time he's likely to kill you outright." Damn. Liev hated being torn like this. With one more warning for Charming, he said, "And, for God's sake, don't let him know you can talk."

Charming's angry face peered into the communicator. "I won't. You get Lani and get back here."

And he disappeared from view.

Chapter 12

L ANI KNEW IT would be only a matter of time before Liev found them. But that didn't mean Liev had found Charming. This Buck asshole would also return soon. Potentially with everything he wanted from the house. Just as scary was the fact that he could surprise an unknowing Liev. And that wouldn't be good either. If they were all captured, no one but Charming was left behind.

Stuck in the recycler.

She tried to think of a way to get out of this damn lasso. "Milo, surely you have something to disrupt the electrical wave on this stupid tie-down strap."

Milo turned to stare at her. "What would that do? We'd still be tied up."

"Would we? Without the current, wouldn't this thing drop to the floor?"

He snorted. "It's not the current. This is memory cord, and, even when disconnected from the source, it will hold its position."

Damn. Was nothing ever easy here? "Then hack it."

He groaned and dropped his head backward. "And how do you expect me to do that?"

"How the hell should I know? I don't want to just sit here."

"Why not?" He closed his eyes and added, "Liev will be

here soon."

"And what if this asshole surprises Liev and catches him too?"

Milo froze, then relaxed. "Nah, Liev is too smart for that."

She hoped so, but this was damn irritating. "Are you really saying that, with your bag of tricks, you can't get us out of here?" When Milo stayed silent, she couldn't help but needle him and that competitive part of him. "Bet Charming would find a way."

She watched Milo's placid look fire up into outrage. "Hey, that's not fair."

She shrugged and waited. When she glanced over again, he was assessing the loops around his chest and shoulders, then the big square block in the center of the shack. She wasn't even sure they were inside a building. "Any idea where we are?" she asked out loud.

"How can I figure this out if you keep talking?" he said.

"Oops," she murmured but smiled and sat back. Her wrist started to flash. "My communicator is going off," she said. With a sigh, he turned to look at her, saw the same lights as she did, and raised an eyebrow. Then a crafty look came into his gaze. "Told you that Liev would find us."

"Maybe and maybe not." She couldn't help worrying. "What if it's Charming?"

"And what's wrong with that?"

"Maybe Liev is still in trouble." She sighed and wished Milo would move that incredible brain of his in the direction of getting them out of here.

She opened her eyes and idly studied the room. It almost looked like a tent but with some support at the lower portion of the wall. Except ... she leaned forward. "Is that trees and water I see?"

Milo turned to look the same direction and whistled. "This is a camouflage unit."

"Yeah, like I know what that means," she muttered.

"It means, Liev won't see us, even if he is looking for us."

"What?" she cried out. "How do we tell him then?"

Milo, as if finally considering this to be serious enough to warrant his full attention, nodded to the weird box in the middle. "That's keeping the camouflage in place."

"So ..." She really wondered if boy genius here was that smart sometimes. "How do we put it out of commission?" She struggled to free herself, but, no matter what she did, the ties kept her arms bound at her side and her feet in place. She tried to hop forward and managed to move slightly, then the ties seemed to understand what she was trying to do and stopped her. "Is this stuff like intelligent or something?"

"Yeah. That's what makes it so special. You can do something once, but then it learns."

"Great." Giving it some thought, she relaxed completely, as much as anyone tied up in the middle of some kidnapping mess. She felt the ties relax. Counting slowly to three, she swung her arms in front and held them straight out. The ties immediately pulled them back to her body, but ... just the upper half of her arm. She now had the use of her lower arms and her wrists. And that meant her communicator.

She quickly turned it on. Sensing Milo's interest, she focused on calling Liev.

"Lani?"

"Yes! Milo and I are in some kind of special camouflage unit and tied with a strange cord that won't let us go." She took a deep breath and tried to control the excitement threatening to raise her voice. "I have no idea where we are, but you have to help Charming. The asshole who kidnapped us stuffed him in the recycler."

"He's out, and he's fine." Liev's voice deepened. "The kidnapper is in the house now, so I don't know who to feel sorry for—Charming or the kidnapper."

Lani gasped. "Oh, no. I have to go save him."

"Hang on," Liev said. "I think I'm seeing something here."

Lani turned to see Milo doing something weird with his locator unit on his wrist. She knew hers was a plain Jane locator, but she'd never seen Milo's in action. A weird glow surrounded his whole arm.

"Milo's doing something, but I have no idea what. His arm is glowing blue."

"Oh, perfect."

"Perfect?" As much as she loved these two guys, they really needed to work a little more on their damn explanations.

"He's required his unit to go to maximum power, and, when that happens, his unit will go to the closest power source and drain it."

"Oh." Even the expanded explanation didn't help much. She watched as the walls wavered, then sparks flew, and suddenly their ties dropped, and the tent mirage disappeared. She spun around.

And there was Liev. They were standing in the field by the beach, only ten minutes from the house.

She laughed and ran into Liev's open arms.

CHARMING WAITED AROUND the corner. He had the

computer up, with the video on, to make sure he had something to show for his efforts. He wouldn't let this guy take anything of his. Maybe something from the others. They had lots. He, on the other hand, didn't, and he needed everything he had. And more.

He crouched low, out of sight, and watched the intruder search the premises. He eyed the electronics. That couldn't be good. How could Charming order more food if this guy interrupted the supply chain?

A strange rumble filled the small house.

The hair on his spine stood up straight, and he hunkered lower.

Then a huge crate appeared in the kitchen.

"Woot! Now this is more like it," the intruder crowed, as he walked around the crate. "This is the order I was alerted to. Now ... what is it?"

Charming's gaze went to the symbol he finally noticed at the bottom corner of the crate.

Shock and horror filled him. Then came the anger.

He searched the area around him. And spied the automatic tape thingy they'd used to wrap Lani's gifts for the brothers.

Charming grinned. That crate was his order. And no one—especially this intruder—would steal from him.

"THANK YOU SO much." Lani smiled up at him. "I hated being tied up."

"Thank Milo," Liev said. "He figured out how to destroy the mirage."

He was right. She'd been frustrated with Milo's acceptance of the situation, but, once he'd focused on the problem, wow.

"Then again, Lani prodded me into it. She wasn't into waiting for you to show up and save her." Milo ran past them. "She's a pain in the ass most of the time."

"Love you too," she yelled. But he was either too far away to hear or couldn't be bothered to answer.

"Not as much as I love you." Liev grabbed her hand. "Now let's go stop this asshole."

They raced up behind Milo, who had stopped just outside the house, his head turned to hear better. Liev kept Lani slightly behind him as they approached. "Milo, what do you hear?"

Milo snorted. "Listen for yourself."

Liev turned his head to hear better but didn't need to. Damn if a male wasn't screaming and hollering for help. "What the hell?"

Lani gasped. "Charming!" She ran past the other two.

"Lani, wait!" Liev raced after her. Damn that girl. She always raced in where angels feared to tread, and the minute anything was wrong with Charming, she was there for him.

Then again, that was one of the things he loved about her. She'd do the same for him and Milo too. They were a family—as she'd often pointed out—and family took care of their own.

With Milo alongside him, Liev closed the distance between them, just managing to catch Lani before she rushed inside. "Wait. Let's do this the smart way."

Frantic, she tried to pull her arm free. "I have to help Charming."

Milo grabbed her head and forcibly turned her so she could see into the kitchen.

She gasped and immediately froze as she tried to fully

understand what she saw.

Hell. Liev studied the nightmare in front of him, and even he didn't get it.

Then it hit him.

He'd forgotten to cancel Charming's order. That had likely been what had triggered this guy to find their house as a potential target in the first place. Large orders were often trouble. As they'd found out.

But he doubted this asshole would try this stunt again.

He shook his head, took another look, and started laughing.

Chapter 13

LANI STARED AROUND the kitchen, her mind still grasping the reality before her.

The kidnapper was on the floor, wrapped up in packing tape. He was so crazily bound that he was in a half-sitting, half-lying position, with one knee up to his chest and his arms crossed over his massive chest.

"What the …?"

The kitchen was overwhelmed with cans, as if the large crate had burst open, and the cans had sprung free and had spread far and wide.

"Serves you right. I hope they put you away for ten years," snapped Charming, sitting on top of the crate with one side blown open. "You're a thief, and no one steals from me."

"Charming, did you do that?"

He sniffed, his nose going high into the air. "Of course. Someone had to protect the house. After all, you took off."

"What? That's not fair." She ran and scooped him up and scolded him. "You be nice. I didn't take off. He kidnapped me."

She scratched Charming under the chin and grinned when his eyes crossed with pleasure.

"If you keep doing that," Charming said with a purr in his voice, "I'll believe you."

"Something attacked me. Help. Help!" cried Buck.

She rounded on him. "Why should I help you? You kidnapped me, stuck poor Charming here in the recycler, and was prepared to clean out the house. You're nothing but a low-down nasty thief."

"Yeah," Charming said. And damn if he didn't hawk up a hairball onto the thief's head. She quickly put Charming down. "That's just gross."

"He deserved it." Her cat hopped back up on top of the crate and proceeded to clean his butt.

She shook her head and watched as Liev and Milo bent over the robber. They removed something, ran it through the computer, then grinned at each other.

"What are you doing?"

"He's an escapee. Wanted for a long list of crimes. And there's a bounty on his head."

"A bounty?"

"That's mine," Charming crowed. "I caught him."

"Like that can happen. You don't have an identity number," she said. "Or a bank account."

He glared at her. "First you steal my salmon, and now you want to take my prize money." He sniffed, turned around, and curled up in a ball. "You guys work it out. After all that hard work, I'm tired."

And he went off to sleep.

Lani turned her attention back to the men and realized that the robber was unconscious. "What did you guys do to him?"

"We're implanting the suggestion that Charming is a new robopet."

She laughed. "That's a great cover actually. He's very *unpetlike*, but, hey, to each his own."

Then they did something else that caused a series of bells and chimes to happen. She stepped closer to Liev as the house almost shook with the vibration. "What's happening?"

"Calling in the ComBots to collect this guy. And, Charming, please don't talk while they are here."

Only snores could be heard from the orange fluff ball.

A flash of bright light filled the house.

Charming woke up, howled, and dashed into the bedroom. Lani wrapped her arms around Liev, trembling with the memories of the last time the ComBots had arrived. This time, however, they were polite and official. They quickly scanned Buck's ID, then scanned Liev's and Milo's, followed by Lani's. She waited nervously, desperately trying not to show it. Liev kept her tucked up close, while the formalities were done. The ComBots grabbed the unconscious Buck, and they were gone. Just like that.

"Wow. I'm glad this process was over quickly because those guys are still scary."

"Not when you are on the right side of the law." Liev turned to his brother. "Milo, do you want to check out the mess that Buck left behind and see if anything is of interest? I'll deal with this crate."

She didn't have a chance to ask what it was, before he had it whisked off to storage. Since they had movable space, they never ran out of room anymore, as the walls could shift to accommodate anything. Even this rental house had that capacity. And to make it even better, according to Liev, by modelling the kitchen here after the one at home, the products would move automatically into the same space at home. So no packing up this haul to take home. She loved that. Need a bigger closet? No problem. Just program it to make it bigger. Or keep stuffing it, and it grew intuitively.

She turned when she realized that she and Liev were alone again. Finally.

She ran into his arms and hugged him close.

"I'm sure glad you know how this world works," she said against his lips before she gave him a blazing kiss.

He laughed and said, "Me too. But I wish I knew how *your* world worked."

LATER THAT NIGHT, with Lani tucked up close to him, he realized he understood very little of how Lani's world had worked. What mattered back then? What did her society believe to be worth fighting for?

He slipped out of bed and walked out to the living room computer. And found Milo already on the unit. His kid brother looked up, a guilty look on his face.

Liev walked over, took a closer look at what he was doing, and laughed and laughed. "That's what I came out to do."

The two bent their heads together and got to work.

CHAPTER 14

SEVERAL DAYS LATER, Lani rolled over in bed and stretched. The last few days had been good. Peaceful and loving. In the aftermath of the kidnapping, she'd gone back to being exhausted from all the stress. Still, it was over, and life had slipped back to a normal pattern.

Half dozing, she lay here until finally something odd penetrated her senses. Music. Not that music was odd, but this kind was.

Christmas music. What the …?

She got up and wrapped herself in a warm robe lying on the edge of the bed and then stopped. Gone was the Pacific island cottage. She glanced out the window and gasped. Snow. On the ground, on the trees, and no palm trees were in sight. She ran out to the living room to find Charming skittering in ahead of her. She stared. Was that tinsel clinging to his butt?

She hit the brakes at the living room in shock. The living room was gone. Instead, they were in a huge log cabin with a rock fireplace blazing in front of her. Her stunned gaze traveled from the fire up the fireplace to something that had her hand slapping over her mouth. Tears crept into her eyes. She dragged her gaze away from full stockings hanging on the mantel to sweeping across the room. A huge tree to the left stood between a large bay window with a window seat and the fireplace. She zipped around to look at the other side to find Milo and Liev, both sporting bright red-and-white Santa caps. She burst into tears, frozen in place. Both men lost their huge grins. Through her tears, she watched Liev take several faltering steps toward her.

"Lani?"

She shook her head, scrubbing her face with the sleeves of her robe.

Charming rubbed down the side of her legs. "Is this for real?" he asked. "Do we get presents?"

She giggled, the sound huskier than usual. "I don't know. Have you been a good boy?"

"I'm the best." He puffed out his chest and strutted. Then he stopped and shot her a worried look. "They contacted Santa, didn't they?"

"Did you write him and tell him what you wanted?" she managed to get out between her giggles.

Charming stopped, his stare frozen on her face. "That was your job. You know that, right? You had one job to do. Did you do it?"

She couldn't hold it in and burst out in big guffaws, her tears gone now. She snagged him up, twirled him around and around, gave him a huge noisy kiss—much to his disgust—dropped him on the window seat, and raced toward Liev.

He laughed and twirled her around, like she had with Charming. When he was done, she still clung to him. "Thank you. Thank you!"

His laughter rumbled up, making her laugh again.

"You're welcome. Besides, we figured that, before you got carried away with ordering stuff, we'd better step in and do it so no one would know."

She turned to look at the tree decorated with tiny lights that twinkled, as if laughing in the dim light. There were tiny miniature carvings, little boxes tied up in bright ribbons. Snowflakes. "Oh my," she whispered. "Where did you find all this? I couldn't get anywhere with my searches."

"Just enough to trigger the bots," Liev teased.

She flushed. "I thought I was being so smart."

"You were. But it might take a little bit before you get the system down pat."

"That's all right. When I want something now, I'll ask for your help." She walked toward the tree. "You did this for me?"

"*We* did this for you."

She glanced at Milo, who looked mildly uncomfortable. She grinned. Then she ran over and hugged him—hard—before racing back to the tree.

"And not for me?" Charming asked in an injured tone.

"Absolutely for you too," she said with a special smile.

"*Humph.*"

And then she caught sight of the presents under the tree. Two of them. For her. One from Milo and one from Liev.

She laughed and raced back to the bedroom, calling behind her, "Wait. I have something to put under the tree too."

She dug through her closet, found the two gifts she'd managed to order with Charming's help, and ran back out to the living room. She was going to put them under the tree but couldn't wait. She headed toward the men and handed them their gifts. "You can open them now."

The looks on their faces were hilarious. They didn't know what to do with the odd packages.

"I had Charming's help," she said, then added with a

sheepish grin, "I ran into a little trouble."

Liev opened his first. His look of shock had her rushing into an explanation. "It's a cookbook. Of Christmas recipes. From my time. Or as close as I could come."

His surprise turned to interest. He went to sit down, stopped, and kissed her passionately. "Thank you. It's wonderful!"

She beamed. "You're welcome. I was trying to figure out what to get the guy who can buy everything."

"I think that's one reason they did away with the holidays," Liev said. "It became frustrating once everyone could make everything for themselves."

He spun around as if just remembering and looked at Milo. "What did you get?"

Milo was turning the package around in his hand. He looked up at Lani and shrugged. "I have no idea."

Yeah, she hadn't been too sure about his gift. "It's a hair paint set."

For the blank look on his face, she walked over, grateful she'd read the instructions on the package, and opened it. Then she took out a large circle, which she held up against his wild red-and-purple swirled pants. She clicked the unit. Then she held the circle up to his mohawk and clicked a second time. There were a few seconds of delay while he stared at her.

Then—*poof!*—his huge mohawk matched the color of his pants.

Liev gasped. He got up and walked around Milo, as Lani repeated her actions on the other side.

"Oh my." Liev howled with laughter.

Milo shot him a dirty look, then walked over to the window. He let out a scream, stared at his reflection in amazement, then turned to stare at her. "Holy yowsers," he whispered, turning once again to stare at his image. "This is the best thing ever."

"I'm glad," she said. "You're a little hard to buy for."

"Well, you found something that he'll drive us nuts with for a long time." Liev came up behind her, his arms sliding around her ribs. "It's so cool though. He'll set a trend with all his other geek friends."

She turned in the circle of his arms. "That's okay too."

He dropped a kiss on her nose. "Now it's your turn."

He led her over to the chair and sat her down. "Milo, yours or my gift first?"

Milo bounded forward. "Mine," he crowed. He ran to the tree and picked up the smaller of the two gifts and came back with it in his outstretched hands. "For you." After giving her the small packet, he stepped back, bouncing in place.

She turned it over, wondering what kind of tech gadget he'd gotten her. She ripped open the wrapping paper and stared. It was a small black box. She opened it and was no wiser. She raised a questioning look to Milo. "What is it?"

He grinned. "It's enhancements for you."

Her gaze widened, then she squealed, "Really?"

He nodded. "So you can have the tech savvy stuff." He moved an arm to the Christmas tree. "You obviously need them earlier rather than later."

She laughed. "Thank you." She meant it. It had been so frustrating knowing that Charming had gotten the en-hancements with their time-travel event that had been meant for her.

Liev stepped up and handed her a larger box. She stared at it. She was so happy to know he'd bought her something that she didn't really care what it was. Then she opened it.

And stared.

"Is it a clothing thing?"

"I realized that I was basically making your clothes, and you had very little input." He sat down beside her and tapped the box. "We'll have to show you how to work this, but now you can make any type of clothing you'd like. Including designing your own styles."

As gifts went, it was pretty special.

"I love it," she whispered.

"Hey, what about me?"

Everyone turned toward Charming. He sat on the window seat, staring at them. There was hope in his eyes but also a sense of disgust. "You guys forgot about me, didn't you?"

"No." Lani grinned. She went back to the bedroom and pulled out the one gift she'd made with needle and thread and an old outfit of hers. She came out holding it in her hands. A tiny vest.

"Oh no. No way I'm wearing that."

She was ready for his resistance. Before he could figure out what she was planning to do, she caught him and wrestled him into the vest.

While the two men looked on, she plunked him back on the window seat. "You look adorable," she said in admiration.

"Ha. I look stupid." But he was sniffing it and admiring himself in the reflective window pane. "At least it's my color."

She laughed. The vest was as orange as Charming was.

"We have something for you as well." Milo went to the far cupboard and pressed a series of codes.

And damn if that huge pallet that the kidnapper had

been trying to steal didn't pop out of the wall.

She stood up. "What *is* that?"

"Mine! Mine. Mine!" Charming bolted for the top of those cans. "It's all mine." He did a flip in the air and landed perfectly.

"But what is it?" she exclaimed.

Liev laughed. "It's something you apparently stole from him."

Confused, she stared at the box and shook her head. "I've never stolen anything from Charming." At his snort, she glared at him. "Ever."

"You stole one can." He sat back on his haunches. "I snuck one back and then placed an order all on my own." He cast a wary eye at Liev. "On Liev's account, to replace it."

And dimly she remembered the salmon incident from their attempt at dinner not long ago. "You ordered a *pallet* of salmon because I took one can from the cupboard?"

Not possible. But from the look on his flat face, apparently it was.

And then it clicked. "And that's the order that let the kidnapper realize we must have something worth stealing?"

Liev laughed.

Milo grinned.

Charming snorted. "Like I would let him get away with stealing this. I told you. *No more stealing.*" He gave her a huge fat grin. "And now they've given the whole thing to me for Christmas!"

"Oh, Lord," she said in fascination, walking closer. "You can't possibly eat all that yourself."

He reared back on his legs. "Get back. It's mine. All mine." But he misjudged the edge and tumbled backward.

They broke out laughing. Lani walked over and picked

him up. "You're so round now that soon you won't be able to climb on top of your stash. If you eat all of this salmon, you'll get fat."

He eyed her, eyed his own healthy-size rump, then dropped his glance back to the pallet. And said, "Okay, you can have one can."

With a snort, he pinned her with his huge orange eyes and added, "But only one!"

He flopped onto his back, threw his arms wide open, and yelled, "Best Christmas ever!"

The End

This concludes Book 1–4 of Broken Protocols.

Arsenic in the Azaleas

A new cozy mystery series from USA Today best-selling author Dale Mayer. Follow gardener and amateur sleuth Doreen Montgomery—and her amusing and mostly lovable cat, dog, and parrot—as they catch murderers and solve crimes in lovely Kelowna, British Columbia.

Riches to rags. … Controlling to chaos. … But murder … seriously?

After her ex-husband leaves her high and dry, former socialite Doreen Montgomery's chance at a new life comes in the form of her grandmother, Nan's, dilapidated old house in picturesque Kelowna … and the added job of caring for the animals Nan couldn't take into assisted living with her: Thaddeus, the loquacious African gray parrot with a ripe vocabulary, and his buddy, Goliath, a monster-size cat with an equally monstrous attitude.

It's the new start Doreen and her beloved basset hound, Mugs, desperately need. But, just as things start to look up for Doreen, Goliath the cat and Mugs the dog find a human finger in Nan's overrun garden.

And not just a finger. Once the police start digging, the rest of the body turns up and turns out to be connected to an old unsolved crime.

With her grandmother as the prime suspect, Doreen soon finds herself stumbling over clues and getting on Corporal Mack Moreau's last nerve, as she does her best to prove her beloved Nan innocent of murder.

Arsenic in the Azaleas is available now!

To find out more visit Dale Mayer's website.

https://geni.us/DMArsenicUniversal

Author's Note

Thank you for reading Broken Protocols 1–4! If you enjoyed the book, please take a moment and leave a short review.

Dear reader,

I love to hear from readers, and you can contact me at my website: www.dalemayer.com or at my Facebook author page. To be informed of new releases and special offers, sign up for my newsletter or follow me on BookBub. And if you are interested in joining Dale Mayer's Reader Group, here is the Facebook sign up page.
http://geni.us/DaleMayerFBGroup

Cheers,
Dale Mayer

About the Author

Dale Mayer is a *USA Today* best-selling author, best known for her SEALs military romances, her Psychic Visions series, and her Lovely Lethal Garden cozy series. Her contemporary romances are raw and full of passion and emotion (Broken But ... Mending, Hathaway House series). Her thrillers will keep you guessing (Kate Morgan, By Death series), and her romantic comedies will keep you giggling (*It's a Dog's Life*, a stand-alone novella; and the Broken Protocols series, starring Charming Marvin, the cat).

Dale honors the stories that come to her—and some of them are crazy, break all the rules and cross multiple genres!

To go with her fiction, she also writes nonfiction in many different fields, with books available on résumé writing, companion gardening, and the US mortgage system. All her books are available in print and ebook format.

Connect with Dale Mayer Online

Dale's Website – www.dalemayer.com
Twitter – @DaleMayer
Facebook Page – geni.us/DaleMayerFBFanPage
Facebook Group – geni.us/DaleMayerFBGroup
BookBub – geni.us/DaleMayerBookbub
Instagram – geni.us/DaleMayerInstagram
Goodreads – geni.us/DaleMayerGoodreads
Newsletter – geni.us/DaleNews

Also by Dale Mayer

Published Adult Books:

Hathaway House

Aaron, Book 1

Brock, Book 2

Cole, Book 3

Denton, Book 4

Elliot, Book 5

Finn, Book 6

Gregory, Book 7

Heath, Book 8

Iain, Book 9

Jaden, Book 10

Keith, Book 11

The K9 Files

Ethan, Book 1

Pierce, Book 2

Zane, Book 3

Blaze, Book 4

Lucas, Book 5

Parker, Book 6

Carter, Book 7

Weston, Book 8

Lovely Lethal Gardens
Arsenic in the Azaleas, Book 1
Bones in the Begonias, Book 2
Corpse in the Carnations, Book 3
Daggers in the Dahlias, Book 4
Evidence in the Echinacea, Book 5
Footprints in the Ferns, Book 6
Gun in the Gardenias, Book 7
Handcuffs in the Heather, Book 8
Ice Pick in the Ivy, Book 9

Psychic Vision Series
Tuesday's Child
Hide 'n Go Seek
Maddy's Floor
Garden of Sorrow
Knock Knock…
Rare Find
Eyes to the Soul
Now You See Her
Shattered
Into the Abyss
Seeds of Malice
Eye of the Falcon
Itsy-Bitsy Spider
Unmasked
Deep Beneath

From the Ashes

Stroke of Death

Psychic Visions Books 1–3

Psychic Visions Books 4–6

Psychic Visions Books 7–9

By Death Series

Touched by Death

Haunted by Death

Chilled by Death

By Death Books 1–3

Broken Protocols – Romantic Comedy Series

Cat's Meow

Cat's Pajamas

Cat's Cradle

Cat's Claus

Broken Protocols 1-4

Broken and... Mending

Skin

Scars

Scales (of Justice)

Broken but... Mending 1-3

Glory

Genesis

Tori

Celeste

Glory Trilogy

Biker Blues

Morgan: Biker Blues, Volume 1

Cash: Biker Blues, Volume 2

SEALs of Honor

Mason: SEALs of Honor, Book 1

Hawk: SEALs of Honor, Book 2

Dane: SEALs of Honor, Book 3

Swede: SEALs of Honor, Book 4

Shadow: SEALs of Honor, Book 5

Cooper: SEALs of Honor, Book 6

Markus: SEALs of Honor, Book 7

Evan: SEALs of Honor, Book 8

Mason's Wish: SEALs of Honor, Book 9

Chase: SEALs of Honor, Book 10

Brett: SEALs of Honor, Book 11

Devlin: SEALs of Honor, Book 12

Easton: SEALs of Honor, Book 13

Ryder: SEALs of Honor, Book 14

Macklin: SEALs of Honor, Book 15

Corey: SEALs of Honor, Book 16

Warrick: SEALs of Honor, Book 17

Tanner: SEALs of Honor, Book 18

Jackson: SEALs of Honor, Book 19

Kanen: SEALs of Honor, Book 20

Nelson: SEALs of Honor, Book 21

Taylor: SEALs of Honor, Book 22

Colton: SEALs of Honor, Book 23

Troy: SEALs of Honor, Book 24

Heroes for Hire

Johan's Joy: Heroes for Hire, Book 21

Heroes for Hire, Books 1–3

Heroes for Hire, Books 4–6

Heroes for Hire, Books 7–9

Heroes for Hire, Books 10–12

Heroes for Hire, Books 13–15

SEALs of Steel

Badger: SEALs of Steel, Book 1

Erick: SEALs of Steel, Book 2

Cade: SEALs of Steel, Book 3

Talon: SEALs of Steel, Book 4

Laszlo: SEALs of Steel, Book 5

Geir: SEALs of Steel, Book 6

Jager: SEALs of Steel, Book 7

The Final Reveal: SEALs of Steel, Book 8

SEALs of Steel, Books 1–4

SEALs of Steel, Books 5–8

SEALs of Steel, Books 1–8

The Mavericks

Kerrick, Book 1

Griffin, Book 2

Jax, Book 3

Beau, Book 4

Asher, Book 5

Ryker, Book 6

Miles, Book 7

Nico, Book 8

Keane, Book 9

Lennox, Book 10

Gavin, Book 11

Shane, Book 12

Bullard's Battle Series

Ryland's Reach, Book 1

Cain's Cross, Book 2

Eton's Escape, Book 3

Garret's Gambit, Book 4

Kano's Keep, Book 5

Fallon's Flaw, Book 6

Quinn's Quest, Book 7

Bullard's Beauty, Book 8

Collections

Dare to Be You...

Dare to Love...

Dare to be Strong...

RomanceX3

Standalone Novellas

It's a Dog's Life

Riana's Revenge

Second Chances

Published Young Adult Books:

Family Blood Ties Series

Vampire in Denial

Vampire in Distress

Vampire in Design

Vampire in Deceit

Vampire in Defiance

Vampire in Conflict

Vampire in Chaos

Vampire in Crisis

Vampire in Control

Vampire in Charge

Family Blood Ties Set 1–3

Family Blood Ties Set 1–5

Family Blood Ties Set 4–6

Family Blood Ties Set 7–9

Sian's Solution, A Family Blood Ties Series Prequel
Novelette

Design series

Dangerous Designs

Deadly Designs

Darkest Designs

Design Series Trilogy

Standalone

In Cassie's Corner

Gem Stone (a Gemma Stone Mystery)

Time Thieves

Published Non-Fiction Books:

Career Essentials

Career Essentials: The Résumé

Career Essentials: The Cover Letter

Career Essentials: The Interview

Career Essentials: 3 in 1

www.ingramcontent.com/pod-product-compliance
Lightning Source LLC
Chambersburg PA
CBHW070925100726
47908CB00001B/99